# SULTANA KOSEM

## *THE BLACK QUEEN*

**Part Two – of the Magnificent Century
TV Series**

DEMET ALTINYELEKLIOĞLU

Paperback ISBN: 978-1-945544-00-2
ePub ISBN: 978-1-947228-53-5

Written by Demet Altınyeleklioğlu

Published by Royal Hawaiian Press
Cover art by Aziz Hicham
Translated by Wieslawa Mentzen
Edited by Glenys Dreyer
Publishing Assistance by Cheeky Kea Printworks

Originally published in Turkish by Artemis Publications as Czarna
Królowa (Sułtanka Kösem, #2)
Translated and published in English with permission.

First Edition

# CHAPTER ONE

*Forty-two days since moving to the Haseki Hall.*

*Has it really been so long?* She counted again. Everything was right. Two days ago, it had been forty days since the death of Sultana Safiye.

She no longer had any doubts. *He forgot about me! So, what Eftalya once said, has indeed happened to me – 'and some of the concubines... Rejected, they wither in oblivion.'*

And now she was one of them. Rejected, forgotten, she'd even began to wither.

Her fairy-tale prince had abandoned her. She even no longer dreamed about him, so she couldn't even kiss him and inhale his scent again in them.

Something must have happened.

Mahfiruz did not show up. She never even went to the prayer for the dead Sultana that marked the end of the forty days of mourning. *How could she come, after the last time...* she thought?

*And I went. And this time no one told me: 'You are not a Muslim, so you have no business being here!'*

*But who knows what this witch is up to now,* Mahpeyker wondered.

The girls learned that the Ice Queen and Handan Sultan did not see each other unless it was necessary.

"They feel resentment to each other," Nevcihan told them when they once met at the rose garden. "When they meet in a larger group, they always tease each other..."

It could not be said that Valide Sultan was behaving much better toward her, either. There was something strange about her behavior, something Mahpeyker didn't understand and couldn't even describe. She was clearly subdued. Earlier, she liked to sit in the gazebo in the rose garden a lot. But now she only appeared there once in a blue moon. There, they sometimes exchanged a few sentences with each other, and that was it.

But she didn't really care. They tried to hide it from her, but she knew that the harem was seething with gossip.

"Sultan got himself a Haseki, but he allegedly said he would not see her at all."

"Did he? In that case, why did he bring her here?"

There was no doubt that Mahfiruz was spreading the gossip with the help of her court ladies.

"Why would His Majesty need such a favorite maid-servant, if he has a wife, the mother of his only son? That other one was just a passing whim."

Şarazad and Mürüvvet swore, however, that since the time of his disappearance, the sultan had not appeared even once to Mahfiruz, either.

*What is happening to him?* Mahpeyker wondered. Dark thoughts kept bothering her. *Could he get impotent at such a young age already?*

She tried to learn something from Daye many times: 'Oh please, Mother, Mom...' but she remained silent about the sultan, as if her lips were buttoned up. Each time she just looked at her with a smile, and repeated, stroking her hair: 'Daughter... Daughteeer!'

Meanwhile, she needed caresses from the Sultan, not from a nanny. She wanted to hear Ahmed whispering passionately: 'My Mahpeyker.'

She suddenly stood up. She got tired of waiting for his appearance every night.

"I'm going to bed!"

Nanny, who'd just come back from the Sultan Gallery, was very surprised.

"You are going to sleep? Daughter, but you haven't eaten supper yet."

"I'm tired. And besides, I'm not hungry."

Semiha exchanged glances with Daye. Mahpeyker was in such a bad mood that she didn't even notice that.

"Have a quiet night," she said and headed for the bedroom.

Semiha wanted to follow her to help her change.

"No need," she stopped her. "I can handle it myself."

She opened the bedroom door, went inside, and closed the door behind her.

She was still asleep when the door opened.

"Wake up," said a whisper.

"What? Who's there?"

"It's me."

"Semiha? What's going on?"

"Get up immediately. Sultan..."

As soon as she heard this word, her mind momentarily woke up from sleep. "Sultan?"

"He's in the harem. He called urgently for the Daye. Before she went there, she ordered to wake you up as soon as possible. Get up, something is up."

But what? She didn't ask her anything, though. She knew perfectly well that in the palace, this kind of question always remains unanswered. It could be anything.

She got up. The other girls were already bustling like bees. The turmoil in the room also awakened Sofia. Alarmed, she threw herself at her feet.

"Something happened, sister?"

Without a word, she stroked the girl's hair.

Semiha ran to the back of the apartment. Mahpeyker heard the sound of water. The woman was back with her a moment later.

"Water is what it is," she said. "We don't have time to warm it up. Wash yourself, even if it is freezing. Then wipe and leave, but fast, for God's sake!"

She rushed to the clothes chest.

"Semiha?"

Former Safiye Sultan's servant, busy looking for the right clothes, answered almost from inside the chest already. "Yes?"

"Will Ahmed come here?" Saying these words, she was afraid that together with them, her heart would also pop out of her mouth. Semiha stuck her head out of the trunk.

"Of course not! Haseki has to go to him."

She didn't expect such an answer, so the meaning of these words did not immediately reach her.

"Haseki has to go? To whom? To the Sultan?"

"Yes."

Suddenly she got it.

"I?!" she asked, screaming at the top of her lungs. "I? I'm going? Haseki is going? The king called his queen to him?"

"Shhh!" Semiha dropped everything in panic and ran to her. She took her in her arms to calm her down.

Mahpeyker trembled all over her body. "We don't know that," she whispered into her ear. "Nobody knows. But it's possible. In a moment, someone from him may come and say that the Padishah is expecting you. That's why we should be prepared, just in case..."

"I'm ready," Mahpeyker said, trying to free herself from the woman's shoulders. "The queen is ready. She can go to her king immediately!"

"Nastya!"

This time, Semiha's voice was sharp as a knife. She froze for a moment, startled by both such a reaction and the fact that the woman used her old name.

"Calm down!"

For a moment it seemed to her that Safiye Sultan was talking to her.

"This might be the night you have been looking forward to. If you say you're a sultana, then behave as befits a sultana!" She came close to her so that the woman's lips now touched her ears. "If he indeed calls you today, do not go there to give yourself away; go to conquer him!"

"But, but..." she was nervous.

Semiha didn't listen to her. She held out her hand vigorously and pointed to the room where a cold bath already waited for her.

She went hastily in the direction indicated, without saying anything else. She went in with all the baggage of various feelings before she was overtaken by delight, by joy; her heart filled with hope only to lose it completely a moment later – and her emotions fluctuated like this over and over again... She didn't even feel the coldness of the water when she rinsed her head with it. Flowing along her body, it also washed away her past, the hardships and sorrows she experienced, finally splashing down onto the marble floor.

"Go away!" she cried, pushing it away with her foot. "Go away. Leave me alone!"

What she'd been waiting for, had to happen that night. *That night or never!* If she really came out of the door today, it was not to submit to Ahmed, but to conquer him – just as Semiha said. She will go to him to become not a haseki but a sultana. Not a slave, but a queen!

"Semiha..."

The woman immediately jumped to her with a bundle of clothes. She was shocked to see her completely naked before her. However, she didn't have to say anything.

"Leave it," Mahpeyker said. "Better bring me that black tulle that I showed you yesterday." She understood that Semiha was going to protest. "Please... Give me free rein today... Let me trust my heart, my dreams! Come on, bring it, please..."

"All right, but at least you've got to wipe yourself dry in the meantime, you're all wet!"

She didn't even do that. She just waited impatiently for a moment when the fabric would get on her wet body. When, finally, her skin, cool with moisture, touched the silk fibers of tulle, shivers ran down her body, and her breasts hardened immediately. She imagined that the fabric that was striking her hips was really the caress of the Padishah. A fire burned in her when she felt tickling in her groin. Two ends of tulle fell to the ground, wrapping around her ankles.

"Mirror."

Şarazad immediately put it in front of her.

She looked at her reflection surrounded by a silver frame.

*Oh my God*... Bright red light from the oil lamps danced across the mirror's surface. She stood exactly in the middle. Her damp hair stuck to her bare arms. Her white cleavage looked as if it was alight with fire. From the valley between the breasts – where the tulle embroidered with silver first met her body – this fire spread downward, enveloping her all over. Under a thin fabric, the pearly gloss of her body, as well as her skin – pink like a flower bud – became scarlet. The light perfectly highlighted any protuberances, bringing out their outlines from the shadows.

Semiha and Şarazad stood enchanted in the door.

"Why are you looking at me that way? Have I charmed you?"

Yes, they were charmed. It took their breath away.

She bit her lips, again and again, to give them a more expressive color. For the same reason, she pinched herself on her cheeks.

"God protect you from the evil eye!" whispered Şarazad, once she awakened from the first enchantment. "Now let me dry your hair quickly..."

"It's not necessary," Mahpeyker stopped her. A mysterious smile wandered over her face. "On the contrary, if he calls for me before I leave, I will ask you to sprinkle me with water. With fingers, like this..."

Before they knew it, she demonstrated it on them. The women scattered, screaming at the top of their lungs.

"You're crazy!" Semiha shouted.

Yes, she was crazy.

"Do you want to appear all wet before the Sultan?"

Yes, she was going to appear all wet in front of him.

Forty-two days and forty-two nights she'd been ready, waiting for him. She endured hours of dressing up and changing whenever one of them didn't like something, without a single complaint. During all those preparations, she constantly stared at the door, hoping that in a moment the Sultan would come in and greet her with an exclamation: 'Mahpeyker, my beautiful Sultana!' She wanted to show herself to him in her most beautiful condition when the moment would come, with the most captivating smile on her lips. But when he didn't appear, she equally humbly submitted to the ritual of undressing. She still tried to continue smiling as she'd prepare to sleep. Forty-two nights. She spent them lying curled up in her bed, feeling abandoned, offended, and humiliated.

What woman would withstand the affront and rejection, the hidden mockery of the girls serving her? Which man would stay away from his chosen woman for so long? The answers to these questions were identical: None! None!

How many nights had she spent torturing herself with such grim thoughts? *So, all this was one big fraud. An inexplicable game all for sham...*

And now, in the middle of the night, he would finally call for her. Send his envoy for her, who would probably tell her: 'Hurry up. Let's not let the Sultan wait!' Yes, she should not forget that Ahmed is a Padishah, and she is one of many slaves. At any moment, he could call for another odalisque with one gesture of his hand. That's why it was necessary to be on standby all the time. She had to wait for him, all groomed, dressed, and adorned. At his request, she was supposed to immediately appear before him and fall to his feet.

*But it is all wrong!* she thought suddenly. *If he is a Sultan, then I am a Sultana. If he is Ahmed, I am Mahpeyker.* And so, she should rather go to him like a woman awakened in the middle of the night, who, after she had jumped out of bed, only hurriedly splashed herself with water... Without applying any fragrance. She was to stand in front of him just as she was.

Of course, if he calls her at all. If, as usual, after many hours of waiting, she won't have to undress and curl up sadly in her bed again.

He called – just before dawn. The messenger opened the door to Mahpeyker's apartment.

"His Majesty calls. Tell the girl to hurry up."

And now Mahpeyker was going to her king.

Her hair was damp. Droplets of water glistened on her face. The tulle, which she put on her moist body, clung to it so much in places that she looked as if she wasn't wearing anything. Her breasts also showed through the fabric, to the smallest details. Her legs, enveloped in a haze of damp tulle like in a mystery, emerged from it, only to plunge back into it again.

She was barefoot.

The only dry thing was a black hooded cloak that she'd thrown on her shoulders before leaving, following Semiha's advice. She tightened the edges of the cloak closely against her breast. Its hem almost swept the ground. Only her bare feet appeared from under them. She was supposed to throw it off only before the Padishah.

*Beware, Sultan Ahmed! Mahpeyker Sultan is coming to conquer you.*

One of the wings of the magnificent door slowly opened.

Mahpeyker looked over her shoulder at Daye who stood a step behind her. She crossed the doorway and plunged into the darkness on the other side.

She froze in her place. She was close to panic.

*What are you looking for here?* A voice bothered her.

*I'm here to become Padishah's woman,* a mocking laughter resounded in her head. *A Padishah's woman? I wonder how you will do it?*

Oh God! How was she going to do it? She had no idea.

From that night in Karayelzade's residence, images suggested by Satan sometimes got into her dreams: scenes full of lust and passion, that made her mad and incredibly embarrassed. But these were only dreams. How did it look in real life? She was ashamed to ask, so nobody taught her anything.

Suddenly she felt someone grabbing her arm.

"Come, child," a voice whispered in the darkness. She recognized it.

"Daye? I didn't notice you in this darkness."

"All the walls are covered with thick velvet curtains. After walking through the door, you found yourself among them, that's why you are in the dark. Now we need to open them..."

"Nanny..." worried and scared, she took her hands, as if she wanted to ask for something. However, she was unable to finish and say what she wanted, *I don't know how...*

From the glow in her eyes, she realized that nanny smiled in the dark.

"Don't be afraid," whispered the woman. "Listen to the voice of your heart and what your desires tell you. You will see! One day you will give the birth to another Padishah for the Ottomans!"

She felt a heavy touch of thick fabric. God is parting the curtain before her... parting... parting. The darkness was cut by a narrow sheaf of orange light.

Mahpeyker reflexively closed her suddenly blinded eyes. Daye pushed her lightly forward. She heard the rustle of the closing curtain.

*Blessed Miss. I am in front of my King! And I'm afraid to even open my eyes now...*

"My slender Mahpeyker!"

Hearing the Sultan's voice, she twitched. How much she had looked forward to it; how many times she'd imagined this moment when he would address her with the name he'd personally given her.

She still did not open her eyes. Only orange and red light seeped through her slightly raised eyelashes, but she couldn't see him. She didn't want to. It was as if she was afraid to wake up from a beautiful dream. She heard the crackling of logs, and her face and body were brushed by pleasant warmth. She had to be standing opposite the fireplace.

She suddenly got scared – the tulle will dry!

She was surprised that she could think of something like that at this moment. But she couldn't get rid of the thought that it would be good if someone from behind the curtain would now pour water over her.

*You are standing in front of your King already,* said her reason. *And you're still wearing this cape that covers your face and body. Well done!*

*Right! What am I doing?* she realized. She still had the hood on her head, she still held the cloak's edges pressed close to her chest.

"Lord..." she paused to take in some air. *Damn it,* she thought. *How can I say something if my heart is hammering?* Her throat got dry, her lips were dry, too. She moistened them with her tongue.

Padishah was looking at her surprised. A hooded figure in black was standing in front of him. He couldn't even see her face.

Suddenly he saw something move slightly on the carpet, exactly where the cloak's skirts touched the ground.

Her feet! Bare!

Ahmed felt a good mood overcoming him. *Just look at them*, he told himself. *How tiny.* A wave of warmth flooded him instantaneously. The suspicion that formed in his mind made him shiver. *Could she be wearing only this cape? Ah!* he groaned in his mind. His mouth also felt dry.

"Your Highness," she whispered. She hoped that this time the tone of her voice expressed what was happening in her soul, all her longings and desires, all her femininity. "You wanted to see your Mahpeyker... Here I am..."

*I think I'm going to faint any moment,* she thought at the same time. *I hope to at least see him before that.*

Her long, curled eyelashes twitched. She slowly lifted them. At first, she narrowed her eyes under the influence of the light and heat, coming exactly from the opposite direction. After a moment... she saw him. *Ahmed! My King.*

If it weren't for the flames of the fire playing in the fireplace, the room would be completely dark.

The Padishah lay on his side on a bearskin spread in front of the fireplace. He supported his head with an arm, and he was without a turban. He wore a long-sleeved white shirt, unbuttoned almost to his waist and red galligaskins. His torso was bathed in deep shadow.

She felt strange. Because he was out of the light falling from the fireplace, his face was invisible in the dark. She already knew, however, that he was handsome.

She realized that Ahmed, like her, had a hard time choosing the right words.

*Say something first,* her mind hinted. *Since he is quiet – you speak. If he does not do anything – you do something. If he doesn't caress you – you shower him with caresses. Conquer him even before the sunrise. And take that damned cloak off already, throw it off!*

She obeyed it.

"Out of longing for you..." she began, sliding the hood off her head and exposing her face to the light, "your slave woman felt as if she had been thrown into the fire, sir."

Ahmed remained laying in his place all the time, without making the slightest move.

He stared at the fire that suddenly burned in the black eyes of Mahpeyker.

*Interesting...* he thought. *Is there really such heat in her eyes, or is it just the fire that is reflecting in them? Is this really one of Eve's daughters? Or maybe God put a fairy made of fire in front of us?*

Whichever was true... She was beautiful... Amongst the play of light and shadow, her face bathed in scarlet, yellow, and red, was unbelievably beautiful. And this pair of burning eyes... When they looked at him, he was catching fire from them.

Without taking her eyes off the Padishah, Mahpeyker moved her head from left to right and from right to left, adjusting her hair, freed from the captivity of the hood. For a moment, her black hair spread in the air like a fan, tinted with a fiery red, then fell, cascading from her shoulders all the way to her waist.

The Sultan felt his body surge and twitch. *I never felt anything like that,* he thought. Neither with Mahfiruz nor with any of the concubines he took after her. He was overcome by an irresistible urge to suddenly jump to his feet, take her in his arms and possess her, at this moment, and in this place. His nostrils widened, he breathed faster and faster, and his breath became hot like fire. He experienced lust for the first time in his life. *Not so fast!* his inner voice mitigated him. *Enjoy this moment. You have plenty of time to kiss and smell her!*

His eyes rested on the girl's lips. He realized that he was just thinking crazily about sucking this woman's lips. And even to take them between teeth and... He was quickly embarrassed by his thoughts. When he tried to take his eyes off her lips, he noticed that the cape was slowly starting to slide off her shoulders. He held his breath.

First, he saw her swan neck. Then the naked, round arms. And finally, a fire-drenched chest.

In one moment, the cape was at Mahpeyker's feet.

*My God!* The Sultan felt this silent scream shake his entire soul.

After dropping this mysterious black cloak, a girl of unearthly beauty stood before him. She wore nothing but a black tulle wrapping her shivering body. The yellow spots on the fabric now shone in the firelight. One arm was completely exposed.

The swollen nipples of her rebelliously raised breasts drove him crazy. So did the narrowness of her waist, the roundness of her hips, the outline of her groin showing under the tulle and her legs... *Ah... Especially those legs...* he thought. Under that fabric, they looked like ivory columns.

Mahpeyker waited idly, aware of what had to be happening now with the Sultan.

His face still remained in the shadows, but she noticed his chest rising and falling – it was like a blacksmith's bellows. *I impressed him!* she triumphed in her thoughts. *I've charmed him!*

With a slight kick, she pushed aside the cape at her feet, then she took a step forward.

She knew he could not take his eyes off her naked legs.

It was difficult for Ahmed to breathe. *Say something finally!* an angry voice in his head reminded him. *I will, as soon as I can catch my breath, and when something comes to my mind!*

But it was Mahpeyker who first broke the silence again.

"Your invitation has brought your Mahpeyker back to life, Sir. We've already been melting like a candle from the longing for you..."

*Ah, this voice, this voice!* thought Ahmed. *Have you ever heard such a beautiful, so sweet and coquettish, so stunning voice?* Mahfiruz's voice rang in his ears. Dear God, next to Mahpeyker's chirping, it seemed to him like a stork's clatter.

"Yes..." he finally managed to say something. He took a deep breath. "I have been waiting... for the end of mourning... after my grandmother."

Suddenly he straightened in his place and sat cross-legged. Now the light gently fell on his face.

Mahpeyker looked at him closely through her eyelashes. First, she noticed a light shadow under the nose of the Sultan. Then, the quivering of his lips. Sultan had already begun to grow a mustache. *It wasn't probably there yet when I saw Ahmed the last time*, she thought. Or maybe it was, but she didn't notice anything from the excitement?

*The king fell in love with his queen,* she continued to think to herself. *The sultana has enchanted her sultan.*

He still had a clear difficulty breathing.

"It wasn't appropriate for us to meet earlier," Ahmed whispered. He took a few breaths. "Forgive us if we made you sad, making you wait for so long, Mahpeyker..." he was surprised by the seductive tone in his own voice.

Mahpeyker smiled gratefully.

"Lord," she whispered flirtatiously. "If because of the longing for you I take too much liberty and say words that are not appropriate to say to the ruler, then you should be asked to forgive your slave."

Ahmed didn't hear any of it. While she spoke, he couldn't help but admire her. *Ah, ah, ah... Look at this smile. God be my witness that I have never seen a more beautiful one. A smile probably doesn't fit any other face so well!* It took all the fatigue and tension out of him, it gave wings to his heart.

Mahpeyker was already completely at ease now. She looked around the room discreetly.

On the right, she saw a small table full of platters with various kinds of fruit, carafes, and bottles.

*What I need is there,* she thought and headed nonchalantly for the table. She was aware that Ahmed's gaze followed her. Every step she took, every move of her hips made the Sultan crazy.

"Joy and excitement because of meeting you, My Lord, has made my mouth really dry. With the permission of Your Majesty, I would like to quench my thirst..." Each of these words contained a hidden allusion. Their meaning clearly impressed the Padishah.

"We are also thirsty, my dear Mahpeyker," he stammered. "Don't you see? We are also burning..."

She pretended she did not understand the allusion.

"I'll pour you some wine."

"We do not drink alcohol..."

She didn't expect that – but she didn't let her confusion show though.

"Maybe some sorbet then? Or water? I will drink water."

Without waiting for an answer, she poured water into a glass and drank two sips from it. Then, with a whisper, "I'm burning," she turned slightly to one side as if to hide it from Ahmed. She moistened her fingertips in the water and sprinkled her face, arms, and breasts, then took the carafe and, not seeing the need to ask what was inside, poured a little into a glass in a golden basket. Holding it in her hand, she moved toward the Padishah.

She was sure – she'd charmed him. *Just wait, Ottoman,* she turned to him in her mind. *You will see what the queen will do for you in a minute!*

Passing the glass to him, she thought that in fact, the queen herself didn't know what she was going to do. She smiled at the thought. Ahmed took this smile as directed to himself. He took the girl's hand holding the glass between his hands.

"From the hand of a beloved one –

'I will drink even poison from my beloved's hand.

Of sadness, of death, I will not think for a moment.

My chest has caught fire, in silence I bear it;

let the death come and carry away my happy soul."

"Lord..." whispered delighted Mahpeyker. "What beautiful words. So sophisticated..."

Padishah pulled her toward him. Mahpeyker sank to her knees. They could now both better see the fire that burned in their eyes. The Sultan leaned toward her.

Mahpeyker felt his lips on the tips of her fingers. When his hot breath wandered over her hand, she thought that his chest must indeed have caught fire.

Padishah drank two sips of the sorbet from her hands.

"In vain –

Even the flood waters will not extinguish the fire in my heart,

this kiss of beloved lips will bring you relief, perhaps.

Hey, Bahti! Not in the sun, not in the moon is the incentive of love;

happiness will only smile on you at the tryst with the moon."

This time Mahpeyker laid a small kiss on the hands of the Sultan.

"Your Highness..." she whispered. She didn't quite understand everything, but she was impressed by the harmony in his voice. "You are spoiling your slave with these beautiful words."

Their faces were so close together that they almost touched. Their breaths mixed, almost burning the places they were falling on. The Sultan smiled and shrugged slightly.

"Just a few lines inspired by the light of your moonlike face. They came to my mind right now..."

Mahpeyker felt her cheeks grow red. *You're stupid, stupid, stupid,* she scolded herself in her head. *How could you not understand the poem!*

"Those verses were charming, Sir," she said aloud. "You should keep writing..."

"Sometimes I write something as Bahti. But... but..." he couldn't finish it. He held his breath.

Only now did she understand what the exclamation, 'Hey Bahti,' which appeared in the poem, meant. Nothing mattered anymore, however. Their lips almost met.

"Lord?" she breathed straight into his face, catching the air with difficulty.

"For the first time, I composed a poem for a woman, beloved Mahpeyker. I usually compose ghazals, you know, lyrical poems, about love for God... From the love of Him. But now... now..." he held his breath again.

"And now, Sir? Now..."

They didn't realize whose lips first touched the other. Padishah's or hers? It didn't matter anymore, anyway. A small, delicate, tender, and shy brush.

After it, Mahpeyker's moan resounded, which worked on Ahmed like a whip, as if to say, 'Now... now... Sir, now...'

Now the hurricane raged. Their lips met. Mahpeyker thought her mouth would melt in Ahmed's mouth at any moment. She didn't think that one could get lost in kissing so much.

At first, Sultan tried to be gentle so as not to hurt the girl's lips. However, the growing lust was stronger. Carefully he took them between his teeth, then began to bite and suck them.

Mahpeyker accepted the caress, not staying behind him. Her groans did not sound like a complaint, but rather encouraged him to continue. For the first time, Ahmed felt the kiss on his lips, in which the woman put in so much from herself. Their tongues tangled together.

When the Sultan slipped his hands from her shoulders to her breast, Mahpeyker shivered with pleasure.

"Lord... My Padishah..."

Her lips circled over his lips and face. Every place where they rested immediately caught fire. She kissed his lips, ears, then went down to his neck, and then lower.

Without hesitation, she reciprocated all the Sultan's caresses. She did as Daye told her – she succumbed to the promptings of her heart and desires. She kissed, bit, sucked, drew circles on the skin with her tongue.

She didn't even notice when they fell onto the bearskin. She saw that the Sultan was clumsily trying to take the spotted tulle off her. With one quick move, she tore it and threw it aside. A moan escaped from Ahmed's lips, resembling more of a passionate cry. Like a greedy child, he sucked on to the breasts sticking out to him. A cry escaped from Mahpeyker's throat.

The breath of the Padishah transformed into a murmur. He slid his hands from her breasts to her waist, and from there to her hips and legs. He lost control of himself.

"Ahmed," Mahpeyker panted in his ear. "My wonderful."

For the next three days, the door to the apartment of Sultan Ahmed remained closed. Padishah didn't even appear at his council known as the Divan, which acted as a part of the government.

Immediately after the first night, Daye did what she believed she should do. Regardless of what had happened between them in the bedroom, she couldn't let the palace begin to gossip about the Sultan, who was, after all, like a son to her, and the girl who was the only one who called her 'her mother.' Even if nothing happened there, both Valide Sultan and Mahfiruz, as well as all the residents of the harem, and the people should have no doubts that it was otherwise.

While the Sultan and Mahpeyker slept embraced, tired after the night of passion, Daye pretended to leave the bedroom carrying the sheet that she had previously stained with blood. She personally brought it to Valide.

It was a confirmation of both the masculinity of the Sultan and the virginity of the Haseki, but it was not a custom to show this proof to the Mother Sultana. When Handan got the word, that Daye came straight from the Sultan's bedroom, she told to let her in, even though she didn't feel well in recent days. The old woman unfolded the bundle she held under her arm before Handan. The Sultana only gave it a glance.

"So, it's over, Nanny," she said thoughtfully. "The girl has achieved her goal."

Nanny, as if very embarrassed, covered the smile that appeared on her face with her hand. "Sultan, too," she said. "Sultan too..."

In the afternoon, when the lovers finally left the bed, Daye sneaked into the bedroom and cleaned the original sheet.

For three days, the Sultan didn't accept visitations from anyone, not even the marshal of the court or the Chamberlain. Meals were left for them in the next room.

Mahpeyker fed her king herself and gave him refreshing sorbets.

She dragged the Sultan, tired from thousands of passions, to a small bathhouse adjoining the bedroom. She seated him at the marble water trough and sat in front of him, leaning her naked body against his chest.

She felt as if she could break free of his arms and fly out of the window, frrrrr! She wanted the whole world to see her happiness: mountains, stones, rivers, and the sea. She wanted to scream at the top of her lungs: 'I became a Sultana! I became a Sultana! Fly!' she would say to the seagulls. 'Run, foam, roll!' she would say to the waves. 'Let my mother on Milos know... Tell her, that her daughter Nastya has become the Sultana of the Ottomans!'

Her mind tried to restrain her. *Wait, you have not become one yet!* Mahpeyker, however, did not listen to it. *What should I wait for? I am sitting in the arms of the Padishah. I am his woman. I drove him crazy. I enslaved him. Those happiness tears that flow from my eyes, my King dries with his lips.*

After the third night, neither Sultan Ahmed nor Mahpeyker had the strength to move even a finger.

Padishah was lying on his back with his eyes closed. Mahpeyker turned to him sideways and leaned on her shoulder, watching her man. Her fingers ran along his cheek, where the first traces of facial hair were already beginning to appear.

*And I took Ahmed for a boy!* she thought, amused. Meanwhile, the Sultan was like a violent storm, like a hurricane. *If this is a boy, what can you expect from a man?*

She remembered the shameless scenes she'd seen in her sleep every now and then. Now she just smiled at their memory. She'd spent the last three days at the side of the Padishah, going from one pleasure to another. Compared with reality, these dreams were just an innocent play.

She moved slowly toward the Sultan and rested her head on his chest. His eyes were closed, but she knew he was awake. He wrapped his arm around her neck, ran one hand over her naked back and the other hand touched her breasts.

"Lord..." Mahpeyker groaned. "I'm thirsty. Won't you quench your slave's thirst?"

Even though he was exhausted, Padishah tried to get up on his knees.

He thought of that moment when he made Mahpeyker his haseki. He remembered perfectly well what he had answered to his mother: 'We've been frozen to the bone, mother. We need a fire that will warm us from within.'

This fire had already overtaken him completely.

However, he didn't complain about it. For three days, he'd felt fluid lava circulating in his veins instead of blood. He'd never experienced anything like it. He shook at the memory of the nightmare of the first night with Mahfiruz. Later, it wasn't any better, either. Not once did he experience with her such a crazy gallop to the top, and an equally crazy descent, completely releasing the reins. He even wondered then if Mahfiruz was with him at all. No reaction, no cry or moan on her part, no pleading or crying, nothing to make him feel that he held a real woman in his arms.

Mahfiruz was completely colorless as if she wasn't there at all. Also, sleeping with other concubines, he couldn't get rid of the impression that something was missing in them. At that time, he didn't know what, and it as only now that he understood – they all lacked passion.

Naturalness. Losing oneself completely in love. The exciting moans of pleasure of the woman he held in his arms. Climbing to the top together and roaring on it with one voice, like lions. And all these deficiencies were compensated by Mahpeyker.

But today...

"I have to appear at the Divan today, my beautiful," he said, stroking her hair.

She took it with a grimace.

"Whaaat? Is it possible for my Sultan to be so cruel to his concubine? That he would pour oil onto her fire?"

She rested one foot between his legs and pressed. She already knew that Ahmed couldn't resist it. In an instant, he reacted as she expected. A groan of pleasure escaped his lips.

"He will not pour oil," he whispered in her ear. "He won't..."

He pushed her on the pillow with a lascivious gesture. Her hair spilled like a waterfall. He took it between his fingers and began to smell it.

"My flame," he whispered. "My fire, water, rain..."

Mahpeyker, of course, could not know what was going on outside, but everything was going her way.

The entire grand palace talked about nothing else but the fact that Sultan had not left his bedroom for three days. Of course, no one could know exactly what was going on there, but Daye, with the help of the trio of Semiha, Şarazad, and Mürüvvet, whispered bits and pieces to the curious ears at every opportunity.

There was no such need anyway. Inhabitants of the harem had achieved the mastery of making an elephant out of a fly.

"Did you hear?" people whispered in quiet corners. "The girl wrapped herself around him so tightly that His Majesty can't get out of her embrace."

"Oh no way, I've heard something completely different. The half-naked girl tried to escape from the bedroom, so that the Padishah had to drag her back to bed: 'Come, I have not finished yet!'"

Slightly older women talked about it in a different way: "Do you remember the wedding night of Mahfiruz Sultan?"

The women gathered around shrugged.

"No, we don't know anything about it."

"I was on duty then, at the Sultan Gallery. I saw everything with my own eyes... I tell you, Mahfiruz Sultan stayed there literally for only a moment. I didn't even know when it started and ended. And look at this one..."

"At whom? A former maid, nothing more. Not like Sultana Mahfiruz. Born in the palace, noble blood... No wonder she is not like this harlot..."

"Look at her, crazy woman, what's your problem? Who cares if she is from a palace or not. A woman should be flirtatious, she must know how to kindle a man! And haseki, brave girl, she is like fire. At least our Lord warmed up a little by her, after your noblewoman."

On the second day, Şarazad crossed the corridors, spreading new rumors. "You'll see for yourself, sister. The Sultan gave her a ruby, as big as my fist, I tell you. And a necklace, too, you haven't seen a more beautiful one. As soon as the light falls on these diamonds, one can think that the sun shines on her neck."

"And exactly how do you know that, huh? One could think you were holding the oil lamp over the bed for them..."

The woman didn't care about the burst of laughter that followed those words.

"And who do you think was on watch behind the curtain in the bedroom all night? You can't even imagine what else these eyes have seen through the crack in that curtain... Anyway, soon you'll see for yourselves, at least that necklace."

Conversations made by Viziers and Pashas were much more staid:

"It has reached our ears that the Sultan is very happy. Let good God, never skimp on such joy for him.

"Amen, noble Pasha, Amen! I'm afraid, however, that the rebels don't care... We must finally take some steps!"

"We will, we will. They say that tomorrow, Üveysoğlu Mehmed Pasha is going to present his plan at the Divan."

They looked at each other, smiling under their mustaches. This confidential smile could be translated as, 'Of course, if after leaving the bedroom, he will still have enough strength to appear at the Divan...'

Mahfiruz was kept updated about everything.

"Sultan did not show up today at the Divan meeting." In the language of the palace, that meant 'the Sultan is still with her all the time.'

She expected him to appear to her on the afternoon of the second day, but he didn't come. When Taciser appeared before her, she didn't even have to open her mouth – her eyes already spoke for themselves.

"So, that's how it is..." murmured Mahfiruz. She bent close to her courtier with a threatening look on her face. "And all because of you! And because of him..."

Taciser twitched, scared. "My La..."

"Quiet! Don't say anything. You should be grateful that you haven't shared his fate..."

"But I am, My Lady, every day, every hour, and minute. May God..."

"Enough of this chatter! Do you realize what awaits you, if you make one more mistake?"

She bowed her head. She knew. She was to share the fate of that Eftalya, whose body was packed into a sack and thrown into the sea by the Palace Promontory.

Mahfiruz was almost certain that on the third day the Sultan would finally send Mahpeyker away and go to the Divan. And in the evening, he'd come to her, if only to see his son.

But again, he did not come.

Mahfiruz Sultan was as somber as a hailstorm. *I am the daughter of the snowy mountains, I come from the land of Adjarians,* she thought haughtily. *A sword, spear, bow and arrow, had been placed into my cradle already. I was not dressed in cotton and silks, just because I was a woman. I was raised on a horse.*

She nodded as if confirming everything she was thinking about. *So, it was...* she continued her memories – she raced with the wind, the reins clenched between her teeth. She stretched her bow and released an arrow that hit an escaping rabbit, a deer, a bear, or a man, it didn't matter. She never missed, even when hanging over the horse. She effortlessly lifted sheep's skin from the ground in a full gallop, inspiring the admiration of the audience on the playing field, which would almost shake from applause and cheers.

None of the Adjarian men could match her at a dagger throw. She would not let anyone trample on her pride, not even the powerful Ottoman dynasty with the Padishah in the lead.

*Damn it!* she thought as she remembered her father's words, still ringing in her ears: *'This country needs an Adjarian sultan, Hatice. Otherwise, our future looks bleak, between the Cossacks and the Safavids. And this Moscow bear in the North, slowly growing fat... Ottomans don't care what will happen to us. Well, unless they would be led by a Padishah of our blood...'*

It was her sacred duty that constrained her hands: to give the empire the Padishah with the blood of her people flowing in his veins. If not for this, she wouldn't resort to using executioners but would deal with her enemies with her own hands. She would enter this maid's room, and before she knew what was going on, she would be finished. She would see then what it means to take her man away! Take away the future of Adjarians!

But she couldn't do it. She'd already given the Adjarian Prince to the Ottomans. It was him – Osman – who was to take the throne after Ahmed in the future. Her son. And she was going to be Valide Sultan – a great Sultana Mother.

The country was rotting. She'd already spent enough time in the capital to notice it. It crumbled from the inside, covered with rust like a sword that hadn't been taken from the sheath for a long time. But if its rudders would pass into her and Osman's hands... Oh! They would show everyone how to rule the empire! How to face enemies on the battlefield. How to deal with rebels. Or maybe even if the Ottomans joined forces with Adjarians, they would build a completely new one – the Adjarian Empire?

But even with all this in mind, she could not let any servant humiliate her, and make her an object of mockery. She had to do something about it.

*This time she should disappear forever*, her mind told her.

She should have, but it didn't succeed. And the next attempt would be too dangerous – the devil was now in the public eye. But sooner or later her turn would come, and death will knock at the right door then.

Well... but what was she supposed to do until then? Sit back and watch as the other one glides higher and higher in the sky?

Hatice Mahfiruz Sultan spent a tough night but ultimately decided what to do.

Either way, she had to do it.


In the morning she went to visit Valide, without any invitation or announcement. She just arrived and went into her room. The chief lady of the court, Nevcihan, instantly jumped to her feet.

"Valide Sultan is sick," she tried to stop her.

"Well, then, we want to wish her a quick recovery!" she said as she pushed the girl away with her elbow.

As soon as she was in the reception room of the Mother Sultana, she was overwhelmed with astonishment. *So, it's true*, she thought. *She really is sick. When did she get so weak?*

"Mother..." she spoke to the woman, who was looking out the window thoughtfully.

"Yes?" Handan turned her head away as if she'd suddenly woken up from a deep sleep. "Who's there? Ah... It's you, Mahfiruz... You scared me... Without..."

"Are you sick, Mother?" she interrupted her.

Handan Valide Sultan looked at her with vacant, expressionless eyes.

*Sick?* she repeated her question in mind. *Am I really sick?*

"Nooo..." she tried to protest. "Just a common cold. Our bones hurt. The medic recommended a syrup... and a patch on the back. It should pass. Do you have something to tell us, child? If so, it will be better if you come at a more appropriate time..."

"I won't take much of your time, Mother."

Handan shuddered at the look and sound of her daughter's voice. *Our son is right,* she must have thought about it for the hundredth time. *This woman literally freezes people...*

"So, tell me."

"Your son..."

Handan became upset at these words.

"I guess you wanted to say, 'His Majesty...'

Mahfiruz ignored it.

"You've probably heard what's going on with him?"

"Well, there are various rumors around the palace..."

"What rumors, My Lady? The harem is roaring with gossip! They say, for example, that this woman does not allow the Sultan to visit his son... And this is just one of the more innocent things being told in the corners!"

Handan spread her hands helplessly as if to ask her, 'What can I do?'

"If such things are told in the palace, it's scary to think what's going on outside its walls. What kind of foulness do simple people pass from mouth to mouth? And Mother Sultana will tolerate it?"

"But what can I do? It's Padi..."

Mahfiruz waved her hand.

"I understand. However, I'm not going to leave it like this!"

"Oh yes?" There was an open mockery in the Valide's voice. "Tell us, if you please, what are you going to do about it then, Mahfiruz?"

"I'll leave, and immediately."

"But where? Don't tell me you will go to the Old Palace?"

"No, My Lady," she replied in an icy voice. "We are the daughter of Adjarians. The nature of our people is well known. You know very well that something like this is alien to us. Besides, we are also the legitimate wife of Sultan Ahmed. The mother of the heir to the throne. Our place is, and will always be, by the Sultan. But that does not mean that we must stay in the harem at any price. Tomorrow, along with Prince Osman, his nanny, nurses, and with all my retinue, we will move to the Sea Pavilion. I do not want my Prince to breathe the air contaminated by the sin of adultery any longer."

"Hatice!" Handan raised her voice despite her condition. "Isn't it you by any case, who tried to throw this girl out of the mosque, just because she is not a Muslim? Or maybe I'm wrong? She is not a Muslim, right? In that case, the fact that she spent a few nights with our son can not be considered a sin! Well, unless Sunullah Efendi gave you a special fatwa for that too?"

Mahfiruz turned back and headed for the door.

"For me, it's a sin!" she growled. "That's why I'm leaving here tomorrow."

She was on her way out when Valide Sultan asked, "Does the Sultan know that? I want to say it very clearly, my child: do not do it without his permission. You can be sure that exile – God forbid! – will offend your pride much more than tolerating what you call adultery..."

Mahfiruz left her apartment without a word.

*Idiot*, Handan thought. *Compare the cunning of Mahpeyker to Mahfiruz's stupidity... She leaves her alone on the battlefield. 'Adultery,' what an idea... If out of seven nights he spends one with you, and six with other concubines, it is fine. And with Mahpeyker – it's suddenly adultery?*

She turned back to the window. Without thinking about anything, she watched the sea for a while. *She might do something silly now*, she thought suddenly. *She will stand up to Ahmed, thinking that he will try to stop her...*

Suddenly, a sharp, stabbing pain pierced her. Slowly and inevitably, another attack was approaching. It was as if she had a cat inside her, tearing her intestines with its claws.

What Handan anticipated, did happen.

As soon as Mahfiruz learned that the Sultan finally left the bedroom, she stood in his path and began to wait for him. In the evening, Ahmed stumbled across her, while returning to the harem.

*Try to look happy,* she ordered herself in her mind. *Damn it, but how? I don't know how to do it...* Nevertheless, she tried.

"My Lord, what a wonderful coincidence!"

The Sultan almost burst out laughing, seeing how much effort his wife put in to bring a smile to her dull face. At the same time, Mahpeyker's smile appeared before his eyes. He got hot at this memory. He didn't stop, so Mahfiruz began to walk behind him.

"You're going to visit our Prince, sir, aren't you? If you could see how your son has already grown."

By saying this, she wanted to imply, 'You have not been to see your son for many days!'

The Padishah suddenly stopped.

"Mahfiruz!"

She almost bumped into him.

"I haven't seen the Prince for just three days."

"That's true," Mahfiruz said relentlessly. "Do you know, sir, what it means for such a small child to not to see his father for three days? It's an eternity for him..."

"He'll get used to it. Princes sometimes don't see their fathers for many months or even years."

*Now is the right time,* Mahfiruz decided.

"What about the Princes' mothers? Will they also have to get used to not seeing their husband for months and years?"

"Yes," Ahmed said shortly. "If necessary, they will also have to."

She felt something break inside her. It was time to make use of the last advantage.

"In that case..." she began, trying to give her voice an air of pain and sadness as much as she could, "I am leaving, My Lord. I should get used to it as soon as possible. I would like to take the Prince with me and move to the Sea Pavilion."

Ahmed moved forward again. *Thank God!* he thought.

"It's a very good idea. The proximity of the sea will have a good effect on Osman. From time to time, we will also stop by there to see him. Every now and then we will also order to bring him here, to his proper and worthy place."

Mahfiruz Sultan didn't know what to say. She stood in her place, frozen. "Go, Ahmed," she hissed after him. "Go to the embrace of this viper. With God's help, you'll never leave this lair of vipers again."

He never heard her, however, as Sultan Ahmed had long since walked away.

# CHAPTER TWO

## The New Palace, Mahpeyker Haseki Dairesi
## February 1605

The news of the sudden move of Mahfiruz Sultana to the Sea Pavilion fell upon the palace like a bolt from the blue.

Mahpeyker's apartments were filled with joyful laughter. Courtiers, servants, whoever was there, clapped cheerfully. Some of the girls even went so far as to start banging onto the bottoms of the trays, pretending to play the tambourine.

Everyone thought that hearing this noise, Mahpeyker Haseki would come out of her bedroom and join them. However, it didn't happen. Mahpeyker opened the door and faced the overjoyed crowd.

"What's going on here?" she asked, even though Ahmed had already told her all about it, last night. "What does this noise mean?"

Sofia was dancing to the beat played by Şarazad on the tray, but they all went quiet as soon as Mahpeyker appeared in the door. Their eyes narrowed, watching her closely. Everyone can say what they want, but the last trysts with the Sultan had apparently served her well. She had been beautiful before, but now her beauty had blossomed a thousand-fold.

"Congratulations!" Semiha cheered. "She left here this morning!"

"Who? Mahfiruz? Where to?"

"Is it important?" Mürüvvet interjected. "Our Sultan chased her away. Let her go wherever she wants, so long as it's far away from here!"

"One farmhand said something about the Sea Pavilion," added Şarazad. "She allegedly told the Sultan that she couldn't stay here anymore."

"Rubbish!" Mürüvvet became upset. "'Could not stay,' like hell! Sultan banished her, and that's it. He chased her to the four winds. Otherwise, no power would have moved her out of here!"

A chorus of voices joined her, chanting a song invented on the spot:

"He chased away, chased away, Padishah chased the ice-cold wife away!" Şarazad began to bang on the tray again. Sophia's arms rose into the air.

"Stop it, immediately!"

The room got silent instantly.

"You can't," said an upset Mahpeyker, "enjoy another's misfortune! At least I think so... Even if she is my mortal enemy... As one who experienced it, I know the bitterness of exile," she looked at the former courtier of Safiye Sultana. "Right, Semiha?"

The embarrassed woman lowered her head. "True..." she said quietly. "It's terrible, it slowly eats away from the inside like a woodworm... Even my powerful Lady couldn't stand it..."

Mahpeyker nodded at her words. She looked thoughtfully ahead. The time had come to say the last word in this scene, which she'd already precisely devised when the Sultan told her about his wife's departure.

"We should rather," she began, "try to help the Sultana now, and not to celebrate such misfortune behind her back. When I found out about it yesterday, I begged the Sultan to change his mind, unfortunately to no avail. I will fall to his feet again today, asking him to forgive her."

Daye watched all this through the half-open door.

"Right, too bad I'm not buying it..." she said under her breath.

Meanwhile, that night Mahpeyker really wanted to ask the Sultan to bring Mahfiruz back to the New Palace.

The news of how she scolded her servants, and with what compassion she stood up for Mahfiruz, had already spread around the harem. And tomorrow morning, people would also tell each other how she once again fell to the feet of the Sultan attempting to intervene in this matter – but he once again had his way.

However, she gave up on playing this scene when she saw that the Padishah was not in a good mood. Ahmed didn't need sorrow now, but joy. She did her best, but she couldn't cheer him up in any way. Suddenly she remembered Sofia's dance. Immediately, she jumped up from her place.

"Your slave girl has prepared a surprise for you, sir."

Ahmed forced himself to show joy and interest.

"Really? What is this surprise?"

"Close your eyes, sir."

"Mahpeyker..."

She was insistent, like an unruly little girl. "Pleeeease..."

The Sultan really laughed this time. He sighed. "All right, I've closed already."

Maypeyker immediately threw off her clothes. She covered her nakedness with carmine chiffon dangling from her head. There was just enough of it to wrap around her waist and hips. One breast remained uncovered. She took the silver tray in her hand.

She approached the Sultan, slowly placing her bare feet on the carpet. She stood on tiptoes, bending one leg in the knee, and stretching the other slightly to the side. The hand which held the tray was suspended in the air, while the other supported her waist.

"Ready," she giggled. "Your Majesty may open your eyes already."

When the Sultan saw Mahpeyker standing in front of him – completely naked under the carmine material – he completely lost his head. He blushed. The smile on his face gave way to lust, showing more and more clearly.

Mahpeyker raised her hand that she had held on her hips, and struck the tray raised above her head.

Tap, tap, patah, tap!

At the second blow, she moved her hips from right to left.

Tap, tap... Tap, patah, patah, patah, tap, tap!

After this introduction, she sang a lively song from Milos:

"If I were the wind, I would blow, ai, ah, oh!

If I were a wave, I would run, ai, ah, oh!

But I am a mermaid, in love with you

and I will not share you, I will keep you with me!"

She moved her legs and ankles, gracefully stepping back and forth; she curved her waist to one side and her hips in the other direction. Her breasts began a separate dance to the rhythm of the song.

Ahmed's throat went dry. He reached out to her.

"Come here, my moon," he moaned. "Come to me, my Mahpeyker. My Aegean girl. My mermaid, keep me with you, don't let me go!"

He didn't even wait for her to approach him. He embraced her waist and took her in his arms.

Mahpeyker kicked her legs in the air, clenching her lips tightly. Padishah completely forgot about the Divan that day, and she didn't think anymore, about exiled Mahfiruz.

She was already a sultana! Mahpeyker Sultana.


When the storm of passion subsided, they went for a walk to the sultan's garden, as usual. The evening began to slowly sink to the surface of the sea like a tulle curtain. On the horizon, behind the Princes' Islands, one could see a red strip in the sky – the last remnant of the passing day.

Mahpeyker tried to cheer up Ahmed. She jumped around him like crazy and faked running away from him, laughing to tears at the same time.

Padishah let himself be drawn into this game once or twice and pretended to catch her. However, he soon gave it up. He was thoughtful. He walked slowly toward the gazebo, dragging himself along the stone-paved path. Hundreds of torches burned along it.

Mahpeyker calmed down for a moment. She stopped.

*What's going on?* she worried. *Where does this bad mood come from?* She felt panic coming over her. *Did something happen? Maybe he doesn't have the courage to tell me something? Oh, God, has he got bored with me? Will he chase me away again, and bring his son's mother in my place?*

Sultan Ahmed also paused, waiting for Mahpeyker to catch up with him. When she approached him, he reached out to her and embraced her waist.

"My rose," he whispered.

"Lord..." *Don't worry about it in vain,*" she finally told herself. *Ahmed is the Sultan. He can't just take care of you all the time. What else do you want? After all, you live like in a dream. Enjoy it!*

But she couldn't. After all, they were in the palace, a place where life without fear was impossible, where even luck was seasoned with fear.

She recalled those days when she scoffed at herself that, under the influence of a prediction from a lying beggar, she began to dream of becoming a queen, a sultana – and he turned out to be right. How could one have believed in a similar nonsense about a slave who would become a queen? She, however, believed it, because it was the only bright spot on the horizon, so she clung to this lie with all her might.

*And what?* she thought. *You are now by the side of the Ottoman Sultan. He's holding his hand on your waist right now. You are now Sultana Mahpeyker, Sultan Ahmed's woman!*

She expected that as usual in her moments of happiness, her mind would speak out, raising some doubts. This time, however, it was silent. She laughed in her heart. Even it finally accepted that the queen's fate was written for her, it had no other choice – the fairy tale became true. The king from her dreams really appeared and made a maidservant a queen... *Mahpeyker has achieved her goal, and they lived happily ever after...*

*A goal? Mahpeyker took the throne, and they lived happily ever after.* Yes, it seemed to her a more appropriate ending to this story.

True, no one else besides herself called her Sultana, but it was already very close to that. Soon, not only an army of odalisques, servants, and courtiers but also the entire state of the Ottomans, the whole world, was going to worship her as Mahpeyker Sultan. In the fishermen's tavern on the island of Milos, the old men would tell each other: 'Have you heard? The daughter of our father Kostas became the sultana of the Ottomans!'

Everyone will probably open their mouths with astonishment...

"Is the joy of my heart cold?"

Ahmed's voice told her to put those thoughts aside. She immediately returned to earth.

"The fire of your love does not allow Mahpeyker to freeze, Sir. When you are with her, she will not get cold even during the most freezing weather."

Sultan smiled happily at her words.

"But the evening chill is something else..."

"Your Majesty will be able to warm your slave in any situation..."

The seductive tone in her voice made him excited. "Come on, we'll sit in the gazebo. Let them bring you something to cover."

Ahmed sat comfortably on the bench. The maidservants immediately rushed to adjust the pillows, but Mahpeyker interrupted them: "Today I will serve His Majesty."

When the servants left, she put the pillows under his back. She tried to do it to be as close as possible to him so that he could see her breasts spilling out from under the petticoat and smell the scent of her skin. In the end, she also sat down. Padishah embraced her and pulled her toward him.

She leaned her head on his shoulder.

For a time, they sat in silence, absorbed by the darkness of the night. They watched the lanterns light up and go out on the opposite bank. Mahpeyker watched the galley glide through the dark blue waters, leaving behind the red light of the stern. She felt a pang in her heart. *I wonder if it will get all the way there, to our...*

*There, to 'our'?* It was the voice of reason. It let itself be known for the first time in a long time. *You don't understand it yet? That place does not exist for you anymore!*

It was right. There was no 'there' anymore. Now it was only 'here' that counted. 'There' belonged to Nastya. 'Here' - to Mahpeyker.

She repaid him for his care, running her wet lips along his neck. First stubble appeared on it, gently tickling her lips now. She raised her head a bit higher and let her burning breath brush the Sultan's ear, leading him to the verge of madness.

"I see that Your Highness is, as if absent today, lost in thought... Has Mahpeyker committed any offense? If so, I will never forgive myself. I swear I will not be able to live with it any longer..."

Sultan Ahmed put a finger to her lips.

"What are you talking about?" he protested. "Today's Divan meeting depressed us a bit, that's all. State matters..."

*So, it's because of 'state matters'? We'll see what it's all about*, she thought. She moved away slightly and looked at him with her usual smile. She ran her finger across the hairs on his cheek.

"Perhaps the Sultan would like to share with his maidservant what is bothering him?"

"Public affairs, my love," said Ahmed. It was time to deal with Mahpeyker's body rather than with those. He wanted to pull her back toward him.

Mahpeyker sighed. She pursed her lips, taking on the pose of an unruly girl.

"His Majesty is right," she murmured. "What would a girl like Mahpeyker understand from this..." She moved away even more. "Will you have some sorbet, Sir?"

Sulky, she started to get up from the bench when she suddenly heard the Sultan's voice:

"Maybe you've already heard..." he began quietly. "For a long time, part of the country has been dealing with treason and conflict..."

*Ha!* she was happy. *So, he showed a glimpse of the secret for me.* From now on Ahmed was to talk with her not only about love but also about the Sublime Porte situation.

"Really?" she nodded worriedly. Looking at Mahpeyker, one could swear she'd just heard about it for the first time. Meanwhile, even back in the residence of Karayelzade, there were rumors of revolts tormenting the Ottoman state. "Who dared to come against you, Sir?"

"It began during the reign of my late father. Such a small inheritance from him..." the Sultan complained. "Dozens of pashas and viziers were thrown at them already, then whole armies. However, the fire was not put out. We are struggling with celali and we..."

"With celali?"

"With folk revolts... They call it like that themselves. A medley of ragamuffins and vagabonds, who incite the people to rebel against our reign. Their hands even reach the capital. Today…" The Padishah suddenly broke off. He sighed heavily. He tried to smile at her.

"But, for God's sake, we also torture you with it. Let's give it a rest and enjoy life in each other's arms…" he leaned towards Mahpeyker. "Open your arms, my moon. Balsam on my heart, come to your Sultan. Come on, smile…"

Mahpeyker, not hiding her dislike, protested weakly:

"But, My Lord… When Your Majesty is overwhelmed with sadness, how can the face of Mahpeyker laugh?" She turned her head aside as if she didn't want him to see the tears in her eyes. With the back of her hand, she struck the palm of the other one.

"Ah," she sighed worriedly. "I cannot stand it when you're so sad, Sir. It is worse for your Mahpeyker than death. What can I do to free you from sorrows and worries?" She fell silent for a while as if she was looking for an answer to her question.

"So much for a woman's reason. Nothing comes to my mind…"

She was soundlessly slapping her hand all the time as if she didn't notice that Ahmed was watching her with a smile. She bit her lip sadly. She was sure she looked helpless now, like someone who was thinking intensely about something but couldn't come up with anything. At the same time, she kept talking to herself:

"What can I do, what to do about it? Or maybe the Sultan will feel better if he confides his worries to a faithful friend, who will listen to him with full attention? As the saying goes, even the rock that holds back everything inside softens, and the ocean dries up…"

Mahpeyker was not aware that out of the dozens of words she had said, only two caused a real storm in the

Sultan's heart. He listened to her with a gentle smile on his face, but his eyes were stern. He kept repeating these two words to himself: 'Faithful friend.'

Those two words made him realize his loneliness very painfully. *That's true*, he thought. *I am lonely. Among hundreds of thousands of servants, I'm as lonely as it gets. That's what I was looking for: a faithful friend who would listen to me with attention. With whom I'll be able to share what is in my heart. Who, when listening to me, will not calculate what he can gain for himself. Someone with whom I'll be able to talk without worrying that my word will be used against me later.*

He looked at Mahpeyker, who was still sighing, tapping one hand against the other.

How honest was her helplessness? *Could there be anything that could harm me in this beautiful head?* He thought about it. *No*, he replied to himself after a moment. *Can a person, so generously gifted by God, be able to stain her heart, mind, and soul with any bad thought? How sad she became when I told her about Mahfiruz, how she kept asking me...*

"Listen then," he said aloud and settled back in his seat. He felt his soul lighten already. "The rebels have invaded our Divan today..."

He paused for a moment, waiting for her reaction. *Strange... Shouldn't she be scared, hearing these words?* Instead, she waited with bated breath for continuation.

So, he picked up again. Keeping his eyes on Mahpeyker, he told her how the rebels headed by Gödöslü Ali, Mad Derviş, Hamza The Stripling, Mehmed The Red Head, Hüseyin The Albanian, Little Halil, Tepesi Tüylü and Kumkapulu, without shying away from any audacity, carried out an assault on the Sultan's Divan today. They all came from the cavalry at the service of the palace. After they had done enough evil in the capital, they fled to Anatolia, and there they began to incite the people against the legitimate authority. He told her how the guardsmen couldn't stop them, how they were asked to let go, how they were warned that the Padishah himself was present at the Divan. They didn't care about anything, and finally, they forced the gate and broke in to face him.

"And..." he went on, "even though they were in our presence, they didn't hesitate to shout and curse. They attacked Üveysoğlu Mehmed Pasha, with whom we were discussing his plan to suppress the rebellion, as well as the Kaymakan, Sofu Sinan Pasha, and all the viziers who stood there with their arms folded. This is where our bad mood comes from. The impudence of the rebels has already reached this point..."

The Sultan paused for a moment to breathe. Mahpeyker remained quiet the entire time. When he talked, she didn't even blink an eye, only her face became a little red. Or maybe it just looked so in the light of the torches. *In any case*, Ahmed thought proudly, *there isn't a more beautiful woman in the world than my haseki.*

When, under the sudden surge of passion, he pulled her closer with a quick movement, something he'd not expected at all, happened.

"What do they want?" Mahpeyker said suddenly. Her voice was hard. Cold. Almost sharp.

"Hmm..." Ahmed muttered. "They shouted non-stop that they were facing injustice and that it was a betrayal on our part. Their insolence went so far as to rough up the poor Mehmed Pasha. They knocked him down to the ground – a powerful man! – and kicked at him. They shouted: 'If we experience such harm and oppression again, it won't stop at a kick or a slap on the face, you will pay for it with your head!' Then they dragged him before our face and threw him on the ground, addressing us: 'This is the man you wanted to hear, Sultan!'"

Mahpeyker felt fire pour over her cheeks. Her throat went dry. She couldn't swallow her saliva. *And what did you do? Tell me about it!* she thought feverishly.

"That's what it looks like, my beautiful," Ahmed said after a long break. He sighed. The expression of reflection immediately disappeared from his face, giving way to the passion. "Now let's focus on pleasant..."

He put his arms around her waist and tried to pull her toward him. He refrained, however, when he saw the state she was in: the shawl fell from her head to her shoulders, and her hair flew in the wind. Her bangs fell over her face, and her eyes...

*Ah!* Padishah got scared. *What's going on with her?* Her eyes glowed with an incredible glow. His hand went back to her breasts.

"Dear..." he whispered passionately. "My soul, my rosebud..."

But whatever he would say, didn't matter to her now. She didn't even feel his hand tighten on her breast.

"So, what did the Sultan do?"

Mahpeyker was sure that he would answer something like, 'Of course, we ordered all the rebels to be beheaded.'

Meanwhile, Sultan Ahmed was as surprised as if someone poured a bucket of cold water on him. *What?* he repeated her question in his mind. *What did the Sultan do?*

What could he do? *How could I behave in a situation where the Divan was taken over by a band of bloodthirsty robbers, and my viziers were insulted?* he thought. Suddenly he realized that the fire he saw in Mahpeyker's eyes terrified him. At first, he thought it was a reaction to his caress. He knew perfectly well that under the influence of his touch Mahpeyker squints her eyes and flexes like a petted cat. And as soon as she starts to reach the top, she looks at him with a look of fire, which seems to scream to him: 'Take me! Take me whole, my lion. Tear your haseki to shreds!'

This time, however, it was clearly visible that this fire was caused by something completely different. Mahpeyker waited for his reply without even moving her eyelashes.

*What did the Sultan do, right?* "Nothing," he finally said, trying to smile. "We resorted to the means used by our father. We pardoned them the penalty for all the faults they committed..."

A curse almost escaped Mahpeyker's mouth.

"We made them agas of the company. We gave them permission to go with their men to Anatolia to join the army of the commander-in-chief there. Our decisions have brought immediate effect. They pleased them so much that they kissed the skirts of our cloak and withdrew quietly, praying for our health. Their shouts, 'Long live the Sultan!' could still be heard even from afar."

He hoped that Mahpeyker would reward him with an admiring glance, that he would hear praise from her. The girl, however, was silent like a grave. So, he had to give himself the prize he was waiting for: "Thank God, we kept cool. Otherwise, God as my witness, things could've taken a very bad turn..."

That night, she did not dare yet.

She wanted to say maybe a hundred times to the Sultan, 'For now, they have contented themselves with a finger, but I'm afraid they'll soon demand the whole hand!' But she couldn't bring herself to do it.

Sultan Ahmed was aware that Mahpeyker didn't like his expedient. However, he couldn't manage to ask her openly: 'So what was I supposed to do?' All the time he kept saying to himself: *We kept cool. Otherwise, things could have taken a very bad turn*, as if to convince himself of it, too.

Despite everything, things did take a bad turn.

Not even a week passed, when the Janissaries, encouraged by the effects of the last cavalry raid on the Divan, also rebelled: 'Why didn't we get our uniforms and pay on time?' And even though a Divan gathered, during which they should have received their pay, they refused to eat the soup and threw stones towards the officers. Later, this refusal to eat the soup, followed by the overturning of the pot, marked the beginning of a rebellion by the Janissaries against the Ottoman Empire.

In every barracks, there was someone who encouraged rebellion.

"What are you waiting for?!" the ringleaders shouted. "Time to visit Ahmed and ask about our salary. Let's demand the head of anyone who is responsible for this delay. Go on, to the palace!"

No janissary commander, no aga or officer dared to upset the crowd of soldiers and defend the Padishah: 'How dare you speak of His Majesty by His name!'

As the rebel soldiers marched to the New Palace, Ahmed was just reciting to Mahpeyker the last quatrain he wrote for her:

"Last night I was picking flowers in the garden of my heart.

Longing eyes constantly looked for the beloved one everywhere.

Then the sky shone, the fairy stood before me;
what name should I give her: Mahpeyker or rose?"

"Ah, my dear Lord," Mahpeyker chirped. "Really, you are pampering your handmaiden..."

Suddenly, a voice came up from behind the curtain:
"Lord, sir!"

A breathless chamberlain stood before them. Ahmed jumped to his feet, angry at his impudence – he'd appeared unannounced, knowing that haseki was with him.

"What does it mean, damned... How dare you! Get out of here while you still have your head on your neck!"

But the man did not get scared of the threat. Instead of getting away as quickly as he could, he whispered something into the Sultan's ear. Ahmed's face first flushed red like on fire, and after a while, it became white as a sheet.

"Lord..." Mahpeyker worried. "Did something bad happen?"

There could be no doubt about it. Otherwise, would the chamberlain expose himself to certain death, by disturbing the Sultan's peace?

"Nothing's happened..." he stammered in reply. However, the tremble in his voice denied his words. "Something's happened..." he corrected himself after a moment, but he couldn't say anything more. "Something's happened..."

"Your Highness... You're pale..."

"The Janissaries turned the boiler over," he finally said. "They set out for the palace." He stood up and ran to the window. "I have to do something..." he said under his breath. "I have to do something right away!"

Mahpeyker knew that Padishah had no idea of what to do. He knew only one solution – to fulfill all the demands of the rebels, then continue to sit on the throne in complacency, still considering himself a ruler...

*Doesn't he understand that yielding to the mob is like giving all power to the street?* she thought, upset. At the same time, her mind said: *Come on. This is the moment you've been waiting for. He's helpless, he is afraid. It's the best time. Tell him what he should do, Mahpeyker. Show him the way out of this situation!*

She told him – with confidence, just as she'd said it to herself.

"This time the heads must roll. Your Majesty should appear in front of them in a scarlet jacket, as a sign that you will not hesitate to shed blood. No matter how many leaders of this rebellion, everyone should be beheaded. Because if they get what they want once, their demands will never end!"

That day, Sultan Ahmed appeared in the Bayezid Pavilion dressed in a red caftan. He called the viziers, agas, and pashas to appear before him. He also ordered to bring in the commanders of the soldiers that were yelling and churning at the gates of the palace. Everyone expected that it would end like last time, and the sultan would give them everything they demanded. They appeared in front of him, throwing threats: "God is our witness, either we'll get what is owed to us, or heads will roll!" They didn't know that there was already an executioner with helpers lurking nearby.

While the rebels were making their demands, the executioners left their hiding place and cracked down on the unsuspecting ringleaders on the spot: the guardsman Şahbaz, One-eyed Mahmud, and Kargazad – the cavalry writers – as well as one of the Janissaries' officers. Their heads were stuck on spears and shown to the Janissaries waiting outside the walls for good news. Guardsmen ran out of the gate and attacked the rebels. After some time, a deathly silence fell.

Not even an hour passed before the Janissaries returned to their Divan and grabbed the spoons to obediently eat the soup that had been set before them.

Mahpeyker went mad with happiness when she learned that the rebellion was quelled. Her joy, however, didn't last long. Padishah did not call her to him, although he should have done so long ago.

Panic grew slowly in her.

The sultan had done as she'd advised him: he dealt with the rebels bloodily. Apparently, though, he wasn't happy that this idea came from her. Perhaps he was afraid of rumors that he was following the promptings of a woman?

She waited for an hour, but neither the marshal nor the chamberlain showed up at her door.

*Eh... I offended the Sultan's pride,* she thought, trying to hide her growing worries from the girls.

She sat on the sofa by the window. There was darkness outside. In the glass, apart from the torch burning behind her, she could only see her own reflection. She stared at a trembling flame.

*It's over*, she thought grimly. *The dream is over.* Her reason and soul left her; they were somewhere far away from the New Palace. She saw in the reflection of the window how Semiha poked the embers on the hearth and put a pot with coffee on it, but her brain, however, didn't register this image – she was now watching her home on Milos. From downstairs came the calls of fishermen to her. 'Run, pass the message!' said one of them. They ran... Someone was running... She could hear him running. She saw in the window how Semiha jumped up from her place by the hearth, but again, her brain didn't notice it.

She just thought for a second: *O, coffee's now going to boil over*, and that was all. The runners arrived at their destination. With the message. But to whom? To her father? What is this message? Could the fishermen see the corsair ship in the distance? The steps of screaming people were getting closer to her. She thought she heard a woman's voice: 'Hurry! Fast, fast, for God's sake!' This voice seemed familiar to her. It wasn't, however, her mother's voice. Who in that case urged her to hurry?

A reflection of an older, beautiful woman suddenly appeared in the glass. 'Fast!' she said, waving her hands. 'Fast. He's coming!'

She wasn't her mother either... In that case, who? Who was to come?

She felt the stench of burnt coffee. *So, it has boiled over*, she thought. It had to happen. Coffee boiled over... Suddenly everything screamed in her: *Daye!*

She returned to reality in an instant.

"Mother, Nanny," she turned to her anxiously.

"Hurry up, Mahpeyker," she said breathlessly. "He's almost here!"

"But who?"

"Eh... Sultan is coming here!"

Mahpeyker didn't immediately understand what was happening. She froze dumbfounded.

"The Sultan's coming here," she repeated, while the nanny ran here and there. "Sultan... coming... here...."

"Oh my God!"

Suddenly, they heard the loud voice of one of the girls watching outside:

"It's a real honor for us, Your Highness!"

Mahpeyker ran to the door in a panic, and after a moment she retracted back again. Like every evening, she'd prepared to go to the sultan's bedroom. When the invitation didn't come, she sat down and then even fell asleep for some time. *What must my face look like now?* she thought worriedly. She wanted to adjust her hair.

Only then did she notice that Semiha was smoothing the dress on her, and Şarazad was hurriedly putting a hat on her head.

The door suddenly opened.

Everyone bowed to the ground.

Mahpeyker greeted Ahmed like a queen. She bent slightly in the waist and leaned forward. She made a loop from the top down with her right hand and extended it in front of herself. She had not seen anyone bow to the Sultan so deeply. *They should learn how to do it already,* she thought.

"Your Highness... Lord... Your handmaiden..."

When all the servants were leaving the room, Ahmed took a few steps toward her.

"Straighten up, I want to see your face, little rose," he asked her quietly.

She did as he wanted. The Sultan looked into her eyes with a smile. When he was sure that they were alone, he took her in his arms. Their lips joined in a kiss.

Breathless, they finally broke apart from each other. The Padishah looked at her for a while, then he put his hand behind his belt. When he pulled it out, she saw that he held something like a glimmer between his fingers.

"Do not think that this ruby," the Sultan began, "owes its luster to the blood we shed today. It is rather the aurora, the fire, the work of Ahmed's heart, which bleeds out of love for his beloved moon."

"But, sir..." Mahpeyker couldn't take her eyes off the big tear-shaped ruby. The light coming from the oil lamps made it shine with millions of sparks in Ahmed's fingers.

Padishah attached the jewel to the front of her cap. Its lower part fell on her forehead.

Mahpeyker felt it taking fire.

"Lord," she whispered, raising her knee to the Sultan's groin. "You made your handmaid happy..."

"It's you," he replied, covering her mouth with his hand. "Rather, it's you that have made the Sultan and the whole Sublime Porte happy today..."

Mahpeyker felt that she would soon rise in the air from happiness. She knew that if her heart wouldn't break free from her breast and survive this joy of today, it would probably remain there forever. Slowly, she moved her head and felt the touch of the ruby on her forehead. She was happy. She had never seen an equally large jewel, even on Mahfiruz's head.

When she indulged in Ahmed's caresses, she couldn't stop thinking about one thing: *It's already close. Almost there. Soon I will become a sultana. Mahpeyker Sultan.*

From that day on, the ruby of Sultan Ahmed was to shimmer on Mahpeyker Sultan's head.

She wallowed in her happiness all days long.

The news that the sultan had visited haseki in her chamber ran around the palace like a storm.

Mahpeyker's happiness reached its zenith when she learned what the word was in the palace corridors.

"Really? No way! Who'd ever seen a sultan visiting haseki in her chamber?"

"Well, he has just visited, I'm telling you that he did. And not particularly secretly... in front of everyone! Sultan left his apartments and went straight to Haseki Hall..."

"But was it for sure this girl's chamber?"

"I told you that already... After all, amazing things sometimes do happen! This Mahpeyker... You know what she did?"

"What did she do? Tell me!"

"When she saw him in front of herself, she threw herself on his neck."

"You're kidding! What kind of manners is that? This girl has no shame or what?"

"Just think what Sultana Mahfiruz will do when she finds out about all this."

"And what can she do? She shouldn't have let the Sultan out of her hand in the first place. Look, the female stranger has lit a fire in his heart in such a short time..."

When Mahpeyker was told about it, her heart also caught fire. From joy.

*Mahfiruz will probably go crazy with rage when she finds out!* she thought happily.

That happiness can disappear as quickly as it appeared, as she found out one day with the news that came to the palace from the Sea Pavilion. No one could bring themselves to tell her this message. Finally, Mürüvvet did it.

"Mahpeyker... She's pregnant again!"

She froze for a moment. *She? What she?* She knew from the very beginning who it was about. Her mind and heart, however, did not want to accept it.

"Who is pregnant, Abla?"

"Well, her... Mahfiruz."

To Mahpeyker it seemed that darkness fell on the world. *And me?* she thought with regret. She'd not thought about it at all before – this in itself, was amazing.

She wanted to count how much time had passed since she began to sleep with the Padishah but soon abandoned this intention. Many months had passed, and her womb was still as dry as a desert.

That night, for the first time, she ran her hands along her stomach this way. Her entire attention was focused on feeling some movement inside. But there was nothing there. Nothing.

The words of Safiye Sultan and Daye echoed in her head: 'You will give the Sublime Porte a Padishah, Mahpeyker!'

Her face darkened. *God hasn't heard your prayers. Just look... My womb, as it was, so it remains empty. And the other one expects a child again!*

At first, while still in shock, she didn't even think what Mahfiruz's pregnancy meant. But as soon as it reached her, a wave of suspicions flooded her – Ahmed, while visiting his son at the Sea Pavilion, also visited this devil's bed!

It hurt her. She was already used to the role of the only woman in his life.

Of course, she knew it was temporary, and sooner or later Ahmed would also take other concubines. But Mahfiruz was something different... The Ice Queen was her greatest enemy. And Ahmed shared his bed with this ice! Who knows, maybe he called her to him right after leaving it, still wearing her sweat? He kissed her with lips that had just kissed the other one, drove her crazy with his hands, which a moment ago were squeezing her hands? And she couldn't do anything about it. Only to bear it in silence.

So, she made a difficult and painful decision: that's exactly what she will do. She will bear it until she finds some other solution.

She suffered.

She thought that making this hard but necessary decision would make her heart a little bit lighter. Unfortunately, she immediately fell into the hands of a much more dangerous suspicion. She was terrified at the very thought of it.

*Or maybe I am barren?*

In an instant, she was in tears. Now she understood why Mahfiruz had retreated, supposedly giving her way. She didn't give her anything. Everything belonged completely to her. She was fertile. She'd already given Ahmed a son. When the prince grows up, she will be Valide Sultan.

*And you, mule?* she asked herself cruelly. *What will happen to you then?*

Nothing! On the day the son of Mahfiruz ascends the throne, he will immediately banish her from the palace.

Of course, if he doesn't decide to kill her.

It all came down to this.

More important than sharing a bed with a Padishah, even more important than success in this field, was to give him a son. As the mother of the prince, she wouldn't have to be afraid that someone would take his heart from her. He might sleep with whomever he wants. The most important thing was to give him a son, lead him to the throne and become a Sultana Mother. Meanwhile, she didn't have a son for whom she could have such hopes, and for whom she could fight. And Mahfiruz came closer and closer to the future power with each passing day. She understood that she was wrong, calling her a viper, devil, witch, or even the Ice Queen. Because Mahfiruz was a spider. An ugly, disgusting spider, constantly working with its black, hairy legs. She was weaving her web cunningly.

*When Ahmed dies – thank God, he is so young – I'll stay here alone like a finger,* she thought sadly. *Ahmed is my shield. If he's not here, who will defend me? No one!*

Then she will fall into the web set by her. The hairy spider will come out of hiding, and while it will slowly approach her, she won't be able to break free from the sticky cobweb holding her... And the spider, finally...

As she thought about it, fear grew new tentacles. One night, her mind whispered to her about another terrifying possibility: *And what if Ahmed is killed?*

All Saints! She was overcome by horror. Maybe someone... *Oh God, a droplet of poison...*

When she imagined Ahmed dying, curling up in pain, she panicked. She hadn't thought about it at all. Padishah was not as sure a shield as she'd considered him. *One droplet...* she raved for hours. Everything depended on one droplet! Both the life of the Padishah and hers.

In the palace, death was part of everyday life. Both for rank-and-file service and for those holding reins of power in their hands. The latter — viziers, pashas, agas, beys, sultanas, princes and above all, the sultan himself — were much closer to death than the rest. They were constantly walking along its edge.

This thought depressed Mahpeyker even more.

*Like Safiye Sultan...* she told herself one night. *She left, convinced that she was poisoned.*

The ring that Safiye gave to Sultana Handan through her stood before her eyes. Now, it was probably her turn. The woman seemed to be weaker and weaker every day. She remembered the mysterious words of Safiye: 'This time she was the first one to take his hand.' So, she too wanted to get rid of her daughter-in-law. Maybe with this ring? The ring was the revenge of the great Mother Sultana. She was taking revenge on her daughter-in-law from the place where Handan had sent her.

No one could be sure of his life. And especially women in a situation like hers. The only salvation for her was to give birth to a prince. *Damn it! And I can't do that. I am barren!*

How many nights had she spent thinking only of this: *And I can't do that. I am barren!*

Soon the Sultan will probably realize it too. And then the whole palace will know about it...

Maybe the spider was already asking everyone who came to her with the news from the New Palace: 'So this concubine has not become pregnant yet? Of course not. She is barren after all!'

Days passed. She had less and less time. The moment everyone considers her as barren would be her end. They will say: 'She's beautiful, it's true, but so what? She can't have children...' Then she'll definitely lose respect in everyone's eyes.

She should find some remedy for it. Or a baby!

She now passed sleepless nights dreaming of the craziest, fantastic plans. It occurred to her to pretend before everybody that she was pregnant. Maybe she could fool the whole palace with this lie. It wasn't that difficult to make her belly larger. But what about the baby? Where would she get the baby from?

*Is there anything money can't get you these days?* her inner voice whispered.

*Mürüvvet will buy a newborn baby from some pauper. Or steal it. You'll bribe a few midwives, and that's it!*

When the time to give birth comes, Mürüvvet will secretly give her the baby. And when Ahmed appears by her side, she will give it into his arms with the words: 'Lord, here is your son...'

*Are you out of your mind?* her reason spoke. *Do you really believe that you can make this absurd plan work?*

She didn't. How could the powerful house of the Ottomans believe this lie, if even she didn't believe it herself?


Another night, full of nightmarish dreams, brought another fear to her heart.

'Even if you give birth to a son, it will be of no use anymore!'

'Why?'

'According to the law, in the Ottoman's empire, the throne passes into the hands of the oldest male descendant. Even if you give birth to a boy now, the son of the spider will be the next Padishah. And you and your son... Understood?'

She understood, of course... This time Mahfiruz would kill not only her but her son as well. Whatever she could do, the spider had everything on her side. Both God and luck. She was too late. Very much so... Well, and besides, she was barren.

She pondered deeply. *If a miracle happened, and I could give birth... and if a boy was born... Even that wouldn't be enough. I should find a way to block the way to the throne for Mahfiruz's son.*

But it was impossible. No force could threaten the future power of Mahfiruz and her son.

Her mind chuckled quietly. *Except for death.*

*Oh God*, she sighed. Yes, it could be a solution. Death didn't just have to be a nightmare that haunted her – it could also be a salvation. If Prince Osman dies, and her son would be next in the queue to his throne, he would become a new Padishah. And she would then be Mahpeyker Valide Sultan.

*So, die, Osman!* she thought, tossing, and turning in her bed.

*Let your death be a salvation for my son and me.*

It surprised her that such a decision was born in her head so quickly. *Die, Osman?* It frightened her when she noticed that the devil living in Mahfiruz also existed in her, lurking in the darkest recesses of her soul. It seems that she, too, was able to decide on someone's death, without blinking an eye. Even a child... *If so, it means that I'm no different from this spider,* she thought. *There is a murderer also lurking inside me – ruthless to such an extent, that she would take the life of a small child.*

She shuddered. She held her breath.

*But I have to do it*, she thought with regret. *I have no other choice. It's either him or me. I can't let this woman's son take the throne. If fate led me to the palace, where in order to survive, sometimes you have to resort to murder... I will do that, too, and my hand will not even shake!*

*Yes!* Her reason applauded. *You found a solution. But there is one more way to prevent Prince Osman from taking the throne in the future.*

*What's that?* she asked, even though she didn't think anything was as sure and as effective as death.

*You don't have a son, yet. But one day you can have one, right?*

Of course. Probably, one day she will finally give birth. She must give birth.

*Until then, that is, until the boy you give birth to is declared the official successor of Ahmed, you must stop Prince Osman from taking the throne.*

*Well, yes, and I just found a way to do it, didn't I?*

*You did. But it is too bloody and dangerous. Listen to me carefully: if, for example, there was such a law, according to which the throne is granted not to the oldest son of the Padishah, but to the oldest man in the family... You know what I mean?*

She didn't understand. What kind of thoughts were going through her mind? However, she decided to continue following this voice in the hope that it would show her the best path.

*Just think about it,* it continued. *The throne wouldn't then come to the son, but to the oldest man in the family, for example, the sultan's brother...*

*And what's in it for me? In any case, someone else will get the throne.*

*It will give you more time. Until your prince grows up, there will be Sultan on the throne, with whom you will be able to communicate. Better him than your fierce enemy!*

During the sleepless nights, she considered this idea from all sides. *If you can't take power yourself, let someone, who won't use it against you, do it*, she thought. It was better than passive expectation. At least it gave some hope for the future. It was easy to think about it, but it was much harder to look at making this idea a reality. The Ottomans, after all, had their rights and customs. How was she supposed to change them?

*You can do it!* she tried to encourage herself. *If you only want, you will succeed. Think about it well, without hurry. Your fate and that of your unborn son depends on this. You should persuade Ahmed somehow to put an end to these fraternal disputes over power!*

She greeted the sunrise with the decision. She still didn't know how, but she had no doubt that she would do it. She would convince Sultan Ahmed about the necessity to make changes in the law.

She didn't start a quarrel with the Padishah. She didn't even mention Mahfiruz's pregnancy with a single word. There was no scene of jealousy, nor did she sulk or give reproaches like: 'You're sleeping with her!' On the contrary – she made love with him like crazy. She hugged him with more passion than usual. She responded to his caresses with even more passionate ones. The Sultan was very much surprised by the sudden growth of lust on her part, but he never complained about it.

Each time they made love, Mahpeyker longed for his cry meaning the end. When she heard it, she began to pray at the same time: *Blessed lady, I am begging you... Let a son be conceived from this seed!*

After each night she stroked her stomach, expecting some sound or movement inside.

In vain... There was nothing there.

Even when she was shouting a cry of pleasure, her mind wandered around her fears and the recent decision. She was condemned to live in fear, sowed by this terrible assumption. There was no one in the palace able to live without fear or suspicion.

She was very curious – how did he manage that? Ahmed behaved as if he didn't know anything, which was inconceivable to her. It was obvious that he must have already heard that Mahfiruz was carrying his next child – which also meant she knew he was still sleeping with her. How could a man, even if he was a Sultan, not understand how painful it must be for a woman?

*He's perfectly aware of this!* Mahpeyker grumbled every time she thought about it. This awareness wounded her even more. Because it meant that he didn't care about her feelings. He didn't care about anyone, not only her. He was a Padishah. The world was created for him. Nothing else mattered.

One day, for no good reason, Mahpeyker came to the conclusion that she was basically no different from him. When she was angry with Ahmed, her mind asked her a tricky question: *What about you? Don't you behave as if nothing happened?*

*Right...* she thought. It made her feel better right away. Everyone had a role to play in the palace life. For her and Ahmed, life has written the role of lovers, madly in love, burning in the fire of passion. *God knows,* she told herself, *that I play my role very well!*

She threw the next pregnancy of Mahfiruz, and what would be born of it, completely out of her mind.

There was only one thing on her mind now – to get pregnant and give Ahmed a son. Nothing, no silly feeling, could be more important than that. There was nothing that she would not do to achieve this goal.

One day she turned to Daye with a scowling face. "I still can't get pregnant, mother."

The woman wasn't surprised at all. She smiled as if she'd been expecting this confession earlier.

"It means your time has not come yet, my dear."

"There must be something wrong with me. Judging by that other one..."

Daye said something unintelligible under her breath.

"You know someone, Mother?" she asked, lowering her head shyly. "A healer who can make a potion, some ointment for my ailment?"

"One should not interfere with divine plans."

"But... in that case... I'll never become a mother!"

The woman grabbed her chin and lifted her head. "You will become one!"

This short answer shook Mahpeyker deeply. Again, these words that have already caused such confusion in her life: 'You will become one!'

'Can a maid become a queen?'

'You will become one!'

'Had anyone seen an ordinary servant become a Sultana before?'

'You will become one!'

And now Daye whispered the same prophecy again in her ear: 'You will become one!'

"But so much time has passed, Mother. And it doesn't look like anything is going to change. I'm so sorry that I haven't given Sultan a son yet. I'm afraid..."

Daye looked deeply into her eyes. Mahpeyker held this look. She knew that the woman now read her soul, line by line. She saw everything in her: her hopes... jealousy... fear... lust, everything. The old woman's face took on an expression now that she'd never seen before. More than a reprimand, it expressed something else... As if there was mysterious, joyous news hiding in a smile that appeared in the corners of the nanny's mouth.

"Maybe," said after a long moment, "God doesn't want to reward your sin with a child, Mahpeyker. If it were born now, it would be a fruit of adultery..."

*A fruit of adultery!*

She froze. It hadn't occurred to her at all. She was a great sinner. In the pursuit of her mad dream, she'd committed one of the greatest sins. She had lived with the Sultan without God's blessing. *You are not any favorite*, she scolded herself harshly, *but simply the most ordinary harlot. Not a queen, not a sultana – you're a harlot. A whore of the Sultan.*

She felt terrible. *How did I get to this state?* Tears stood in her eyes.

*Did you hear? The only daughter of father Kostas Vasilidis... She became a whore of the Ottomans!* This is what would be said about her on Milos.

There was no point in fooling herself anymore. Daye was right. God didn't want to give her a child conceived in sin. The womb of Mahfiruz was fertile and fruitful because she wasn't an adulteress but a legitimate wife. The spider was the Padishah's wife. First, she obtained a blessing from God, and only later she started sharing a bed with him. And now she could enjoy what God had sent her. Not one child, but almost two already!

She tried her best to hold back her sobs but to no avail. She didn't know how she found herself in the arms of the nanny. She buried her head in her neck and let herself cry.

"You're right, Mother," she complained through her tears. "I am a sinner, a harlot. I will go straight to hellfire. Every night I receive the seeds of sin inside me. And here is the punishment for my sin: I can't breathe life into them. They fall on barren soil."

The old woman stroked her hair.

"Cry, my child," she said tenderly. "Let these tears wash away your sins!"

If she knew it could really save her, she would cry all days long. There was no use for crying, however. She shook her head to show her resignation.

Daye patted her on the back.

"Pray with all your heart and ask for divine protection, daughter. God is merciful. He sees and hears everything."

Mahpeyker sighed. *What else is left for me? What else can I do, other than pray for the forgiveness of my sins?*

She was far from awaiting a miracle that a new life would be born from death.

# CHAPTER THREE

### The New Palace
### November 12th, 1605

That night did not stand out from any others.

The long corridors of the harem were under the rule of the mysterious darkness of the night.

In the dim light coming from the torches, their recesses were shrouded in frightening shadows. The incredible silence in the harem, rather than being calming, made people shiver. It was as if the twilight and haunting silence were a harbinger of something that was about to happen soon.

Mahpeyker was lying on her back and staring at the ceiling. The storm of passion calmed down only a moment ago. The Sultan fell asleep as soon as he buried his head between her breasts. But she, also, couldn't sleep that night. She counted the joining of boards on the ceiling, trying not to think about anything. She even gave up her earlier thoughts: *Maybe this time I'll be able to breathe life into Ahmed's seed?*

Her prayers still hadn't brought any results yet. No matter how much she prayed, the miracle did not happen – Death did not want to give life.

She heard footsteps outside. People running.

Suddenly there was a shout: "Disaster! Misfortune!"

*What's going on?* Mahpeyker wanted to get out of bed immediately, but Ahmed didn't hear anything. So, she didn't move right then, to not wake him up.

"Get up!" someone shouted.

"Run! Fast!"

Only then did the Sultan wake up. He lifted his head from Mahpeyker's bosom and looked ahead with unconscious eyes.

"Your Highness! Lord!"

As soon as he heard the noise of running outside the door and the voice that spoke to him, fear immediately appeared in his gaze.

"What happened?" He jumped to his feet, alarmed. "Did the soldiers turn the boiler over again?"

Mahpeyker felt strange. She also jumped out of bed. *So, this is what he's worried about most,* she thought, putting some clothes on. *Just as for me the mortal threat is infertility, so it is the rebellion of Janissaries for Ahmed.*

When the Padishah ran outside, she was still half-naked. She heard Ahmed's voice coming from the living room behind the door.

"What's going on, Nanny?"

"Your Highness. Pa..." It was Daye's voice, and she choked with a sob. "God bless you with a long life, Lord!"

Mahpeyker's mind lit up as if struck by lightning. *Did someone die? Is it Mahfiruz? Probably. Perhaps the child in her womb contaminated her blood? It is possible...*

The screams in the corridors turned to crying. Daye tried to control herself.

"Forgive me... Lord... My sincere con..."

"Don't drive me crazy, Nanny! Tell me, who died?"

Mahpeyker stood in the doorway. The answer the old woman whispered to him almost drowned out the noise of the wind howling outside.

"Valide Sultan... Handan Sultan left..."

*Mother of God! What?!*

Ahmed rushed out of the living room. Mahpeyker could not move from her place. Suddenly she felt very cold. She put her arms around herself, trying to warm up her body.

For some time, she couldn't think about anything – as if her brain instantly went empty.

*But how is that possible? So suddenly?* she began to wonder after a longer moment.

*Suddenly?* her mind sneered. *Stop pretending, at least before me... So, you didn't expect it, right?*

Not so fast. Not much time had passed since the death of Safiye Sultan.

*I... I... I thought it would happen later... Because... after all... she... wasn't sick at all!*

True, Sultana Handan had been pale and gloomy for some time – she had been apathetic, and her face seemed to be expressionless. But that was all. Otherwise, she was doing pretty well. She would go to the lobby and sit by the fire and take part in conversations over coffee, and she reprimanded the courtiers whenever she felt like it. Mahpeyker didn't hear anything about her losing her appetite, either.

*Only yesterday she told me I didn't have any talent for making lace*, Mahpeyker remembered. *She didn't look like someone who was about to die.*

But – nevertheless, Sultana Handan had left.

When Mahpeyker was going to the apartments of Valide Sultan, another flash of insight cut through her thoughts.

*The ring! Safiye Sultan has done her revenge. Did you forget how I told you that she made you the tool of her revenge?* hissed her mind. *There you go, this tool proved useful for her. You were the one who planted the seed of death in her, Mahpeyker!*

The following days reminded her of a storm. She couldn't compare what was happening to anything else – it was a real storm – and Mahpeyker couldn't stop wondering as she thought about all this. How many things happened just this year, one after the other.

Safiye Sultan died.

She returned to the New Palace, and this as a haseki of the Padishah.

She had enchanted the Sultan and spent all nights long with him.

The Ice Queen became pregnant again; while everything indicated that she personally, could not have children.

While she was inventing the most unlikely ways to give the Sultan a son, Handan Valide Sultan suddenly died.

She still couldn't forget what had happened that night in the dead woman's suite. As soon as she got inside, her gaze spontaneously traveled to the woman's right hand.

The ring!

It was there, on her finger.

There was no reason to look for any signs of suffering on Handan's face. She appeared calm as if she were sleeping – enjoying a dream from which she will never wake up again.

Ahmed gave the impression as if his mother's unexpected death did not quite surprise him. Was he sad? One could think so, looking at his face. However, his eyes said something entirely different. It was as if he breathed a sigh of relief – as if someone had just taken a weight off his back.

Mahfiruz didn't come to the palace until the morning. She entered the room, where her mother-in-law's body lay, and proudly walked past Mahpeyker. To present her belly in all its splendor, she leaned back so much that it seemed she would fall on her back at any moment.

Their eyes met only for a moment. The spider's hands immediately began to stroke its big belly. Writhing in pain, Mahpeyker guessed what she wanted to express with that sneering, icy look: 'Look, this is Ahmed's work! Have you seen? Take a good look. See what I can do – the Sultan has impregnated me again. And I hear your womb is still empty? Of course, it will be so. It is barren like desert sand. You are barren, do you understand this, mule? Ahmed can spend whole nights with you, but it's me who gives birth to his descendants. Tomorrow, my son will take his place on the throne. And then I will return here from the Sea Pavilion as Valide Sultan!'

Mahpeyker could have sworn that was what Mahfiruz was thinking about, as she watched her.

As Mahfiruz retreated, Mahpeyker mingled with the women gathered at the head of the dead Mother Sultana. They were preparing her for burial. Suddenly she looked at the hand of the deceased, dangling from the bed.

The ring! It was gone.

"Mahfiruz took it," one of the ladies of the court whispered. "She removed it from the Mother Sultana's finger, saying that after her mother-in-law's death, it now belongs to her."

Mahpeyker was overtaken by an unspecified joy. Is the ring already on the finger of its next victim?

She returned feverishly to her apartment.

*God... If this ring can indeed cause death, let it take the spider's life as soon as possible!*

It didn't take it – on the contrary, it added another one to her life.

When Mahpeyker saw her that night, she didn't look at all like she was about to give birth at any moment – and yet she did. It was immediately reported to her. On hearing this, her soul seemed to catch flames.

"What was born?"

"A son!"

*Oh, God, another boy!*

"Padishah named him Mehmed."

She was almost crazy with jealousy. So, what if Ahmed spent every night with her, when it was the spider who was getting pregnant, the spider gave birth to his sons?

And she couldn't give him a son – she was barren. Unlike Mahfiruz!

Mahpeyker hadn't seen Ahmed since Handan's death. Padishah disappeared somewhere again. She didn't ask anyone about him because she knew that even if she did, she'd probably not be told anything.

*Well, you can start the countdown now. Forty days. That's how strong your patience must be, Mahpeyker.* After the death of Safiye Sultan, Ahmed didn't show himself until the end of mourning, either. Now he'll probably do the same. She had no choice but to wait patiently for this fortieth night.

There was one issue on her mind that made her furious: *Did Ahmed, by any chance, run to his spider while neglecting me?*

Her mind told her that it was possible. *Why wouldn't he visit her? In the end, she gave him another son.*

*But he loves me, not her*, she tried to argue, but her reasoning was merciless:

*He loves you, but he impregnates the other one!*

Mahpeyker was losing her mind, imagining how Ahmed hurries to Mahfiruz's chamber, how he kisses her and showers her with presents. The thoughts of Padishah taking his newborn son in his hands, kissing and smelling him, were poisoning her. But was it really like that? Was it possible that without visiting her, he went to Mahfiruz, then he got completely lost somewhere?

So, that's what she was worth to him? A small pink body wrapped in diapers was enough for Ahmed to forget all the beautiful words he spoke about her, all the oaths he had made, the poems he had written for her?

She had to find out. She put everybody she could into action: 'Go there and ask if His Majesty has visited the Sea Pavilion in the last days.'

She always received the same answer: 'His Majesty Padishah, after the funeral of his mother went straight to the harbor, without going back to the palace. He was so depressed that despite the weather and the season, despite the raging storm, he left the capital on the same night on the deck of one of the galleys. However, we have not been able to find out where he went...'

But for Mahpeyker, the most important thing was that she'd found out where he had not gone.

"But are you sure? He didn't go to her? He didn't visit his son?"

"That's certain," Semiha replied. "Apparently Mahfiruz is mad at the world, and it boggles her mind that the Padishah could behave like that..."

*Very well!* She was happy. *So, he didn't see her, either!*

On Friday evening, on the twenty-second day after Handan's death, the silence of the palace was unexpectedly disturbed. The sound of hooves was heard in the outer courtyard and reached all the way to the Haseki Hall. Mahpeyker didn't even have time to ask what was happening when Semiha and Daye hurried into the room. Sofia stood behind them. It seemed to her that the girl was slightly paler than usual.

"What's happening?" she asked, surprised. "What's this confusion? Sofia, my love! What's with you? You are so pale. Are you okay?"

Instead of answering, the girl lowered her head and smiled. Since the return to the New Palace, Sofia had been quite subdued all the time. It wasn't difficult to guess that her thoughts remained at the Old Palace, with the groom Ahmed. *Oh, I forgot all about it because of my own worries,* Mahpeyker thought suddenly. *I should find a way to get him here as soon as possible.*

After a moment, however, she abandoned this idea. *No way,* she thought. *Sofia is no longer an ordinary servant. It's not appropriate for Mahpeyker Haseki's maid to hang out with a groom!* Nevertheless, she stroked her cheek and looked at her meaningfully, trying to comfort her.

The other two women, however, clearly had no intention of wasting time on Sofia's love affairs.

"Come on!" Semiha said, walking toward her. "We have to hurry. You should be ready as soon as possible."

"Ready? For what?"

Semiha didn't answer. Mahpeyker's eyes searched out the nanny, but the woman was already diving in the clothes chest.

"Mother Daye!" Mahpeyker cried as Semiha was taking her clothes off. "Can you tell me what's going on here? Has the Sultan returned a little earlier? Please, tell me..."

Instead of answering, the woman stood in front of her with a handful of clothes. She was surprised when she saw a red caftan decorated with pearls. *Red?*

"Should I wear this?"

Semiha hurriedly took the scarlet satin petticoat from Daye and put it on her over her head.

"What's that supposed to mean, for God's sake? Take it off immediately, Semiha. Don't you know I wear only black?"

At that time, no less embarrassed, Şarazad and Mürüvvet appeared. The first one took care of her hair, and the other began to put on her shoes. They did everything in silence and didn't answer any questions as if they had made a deal with each other.

Ten minutes later she was ready.

"Let's go," Semiha said, turning toward the door. Mahpeyker broke free from the women's hands.

"I'm not going anywhere!" she repeated stubbornly. "If you don't tell me what's going on, I'm not going to make a single step out of here!"

During this struggle, she heard Şarazad whisper: "The carriage has been waiting for a long time."

Mahpeyker panicked.

"Did you say 'carriage'? What carriage?!"

Seeing this strange haste, she thought that the Padishah was back and now he was calling for her. Apparently, he didn't want to come to her personally. He realized that this would give rise to rumors – 'the mourning has not ended yet, and he has already rushed to bed with haseki.' So, she thought that maybe he'd asked to bring her to him secretly. But now... when the word 'carriage' was spoken... Until now, she'd left the New Palace in a carriage only twice. The first time, the carriage took her to exile to the Old Palace. The second time she escaped in it from the executioners sent by Mahfiruz to get her. And now? Where would it take her this time? Why was it kept secret? Her closest friends were silent as if enchanted. Or maybe... Maybe even they had betrayed her?

The suspicion itself was terrifying.

"Leave me alone!" she protested. "I don't want to go anywhere. And I won't!"

"Come on! There is no time to lose. We're leaving, come!" They took her elbows and almost dragged her to the door.

When they were about to drag her out into the corridor, Mahpeyker noticed that Daye stayed back. She stopped at the door and looked at her. Streams of tears flowed from the eyes of the old woman. Why was she crying? Did she know they were taking her to a place, from which she would never come back here?

This time, another suspicion stabbed her brain like a drill. Maybe the spider has made her move, and after she gave birth to her second son, she's managed to persuade

Ahmed to throw her out of the palace? Right, why would he need a barren beauty, if she was the mother of his two sons? Beauty is here today, gone tomorrow. And the princes... One day he would leave the throne to them. He didn't want to hurt the mother of his children because of some concubine. Maybe he's already given the order: 'Throw her out of the palace. Put her in a carriage and take her out!'

Something in the depth of her heart told her, however, that it was impossible. *Ahmed would never do that!* she kept telling herself.

There was another possibility. Maybe Mahfiruz decided to take matters into her own hands?

*Finish what you did not finish last time!* and she's re-ordered the murderer. *But this time: no mistakes! Put the trollop in the carriage, take her somewhere far from here and kill her. And leave her scum in the mountains for vultures and eagles. We'll see what will remain of her beauty...* Mahpeyker shuddered, imagining the sharp beaks of the birds tearing her body apart.

"Nanny, Mother?" Her voice expressed everything – fear, love, anger, and disappointment. "Aren't you going with me?"

"Şarazad will go with you," she replied. "I can't."

*But where? With Şarazad... Why with her?*

"I won't leave Sofia here."

"You can't take her with you, daughter."

"No way! I promised her that. I promised I'd never leave her. For good and for bad, always toge..." she was unable to finish. She suddenly realized that something was missing. Strange...

"Sofia?"

She looked around. The girl was standing aside, watching her. It surprised her. Shouldn't she now cry and shout: 'Sister, beloved sister... My beautiful sister; don't leave me here alone!?'

But she didn't cry. Not only that, she saw a mysterious, almost playful expression on her face. Semiha and Mürüvet pulled her hands.

"Faster, time is running out!"

In an instant, Mahpeyker decided to give in to them. Let them take her wherever they want.

If all these suspicions that Satan had whispered to her were to be true - if indeed those, whom she thought were friends, had betrayed her; if Ahmed has chased her away, or the Ice Queen has sentenced her to death - what would it matter where the carriage would take her? So, she will get inside, even if it will take her to her death.

She freed herself from the grips of the women dragging her and approached the Nanny. She looked in her eyes. She saw the old woman trying to hold back her tears. She kept swallowing as if something was stuck in her throat. They hugged each other.

"Go," Daye whispered to her.

"But where, Mother? I'm afraid..."

She felt the tiny body of the old woman tremble in her arms. She sensed she was thinking about something.

"They are waiting for you."

She said it so quietly that Mahpeyker was not sure she had really heard it.

"Who? Who is waiting for me, Mother?"

Instead of answering her, Daye slowly pushed her away. It seemed to Mahpeyker that beside the sadness, she also saw the gleam of happiness in her eyes.

They moved through the corridors almost running. When they reached the door behind which was the corridor that led from the harem to the outer courtyard of the palace, the others were still following behind. Semiha waved goodbye to her and hurried back. Mürüvvet stood as still as a statue. And Sofia? She made a move as if she wanted to throw herself into her arms. However, she changed her mind immediately. Mahpeyker read from her mouth that she was saying to her: "Sister, my beautiful sister! Goodbye."

It was only when they were in the carriage that she noticed that Şarazad was holding a tiny bundle in her arms.

"What is it, Abla?"

"I don't know. Daye asked me to give it to you when we get there."

"Where are we going?"

"I don't know, Nastya. I swear to you, I have no idea."

"Why is it you accompanying me? Why couldn't I bring Sofia with me? Why did Semiha and Mürüvvet stay in the palace?"

The woman shrugged and turned her head away.

"Look at me!" Mahpeyker said in a dramatic tone. "Look at me, Şarazad. Are they taking me to my death?"

The woman covered her mouth with her hand in horror.

"God forbid! What kind of idea is this?"

"Why the secrets then? Why doesn't anyone know anything or don't want to say? Where are we going?"

Suddenly, a long unheard, but well-known sound came to her ears. The sea! She immediately recognized the sound of waves breaking on the shore.

She already knew where they were going. To the sea...
*Oh God, they'll throw me into the sea!* She shuddered in fear. So, this was how her fairy tale would end...

*Let it be this way*, said her inner voice quietly. *You came from the sea, you will return to the sea.*

It took her a lot of effort not to let her panic show. It was possible that Şarazad accompanied her as a witness – and when it's all over, she will swear under oath that she was indeed killed, and her body thrown into the sea.

And if so, she should show how Anastasia, daughter of father Kostas Vasilidis of Milos, goes to her death with dignity! Let her later tell the spider witch about the courage with which she faced death!

When the carriage stopped with a jerk, she did not wait for a moment. She opened the door and jumped outside. *Here I am*, she said in her heart to the sea. *Our paths have met again. Now we will be together forever!*

The dry coldness of winter and the damp chill of the sea hit her face. It was as if she was woken up from a deep sleep. Huge galleys were moored at the pier. A lot of people were getting on board over the gangplank or coming on land from it. In the light of the torches on deck, she saw sailors climbing the mast on the rope ladder.

They wanted to kill her in such a crowd? All right, but where is the executioner? Let him come already, and do what he needs to do, as soon as possible!

One man, who'd just left the ship ran up to them.

"Hurry up!" he said without looking her in the face. "The captain wants to leave immediately."

*What is going on here?* Mahpeyker wondered, now completely confused. How many times had she asked this question tonight? And she still couldn't get the answer.

"Where are we sailing to?"

The sailor, who'd already taken a few steps toward the ship, turned back to her as if surprised that she asked such a question.

"To Mudanya," he said in response.

*So, they will not kill me* she thought. *They decided to have me deported after all. To Mudanya, wherever that is.*

"If we want to be in place before noon, we should leave immediately. Otherwise, you'll be forced to spend the night there."

*What? So, I won't stay there?*

"Wait!" she stopped him once again. "So, we will go somewhere else from there?"

This time the sailor was no longer hiding his surprise.

"You haven't been told anything? From Mudanya you will go to Bursa. His Majesty is already waiting for you there, My Lady."

Maypeyker leaned on Şarazad's shoulder so as not to faint.

# CHAPTER FOUR

## The Palace in Bursa
## December 1605

Mahpeyker felt as if she was swimming in the clouds. Place, time, names, fears, and dreams - all this lost its importance for her. She did not remember when they got to this Mudanya. She wasn't even aware of the big ship submerging and emerging from the waves in a raging storm like a nutshell, snatched by the sea. At one point, she realized that she was sitting in a carriage surrounded by a cavalry escort. Şarazad was dozing in front of her. How did they find themselves in this carriage? She didn't know that either.

Since the time of the boarding, the words, 'His Majesty is already waiting for you there, Lady,' constantly rang in her mind.

In Bursa.

Mahpeyker could still only hear the same voice saying those few words: 'His Majesty is already waiting for you there, Lady.'

Padishah! Sultan Ahmed. He called not for the spider, the mother of his two sons, but for her! And now they were leading her to him.

Apparently, the Sultan couldn't stand the separation from her. He didn't think of Mahfiruz even for a moment.

He didn't even visit his newborn son. Instead, he ordered, 'I want to see Mahpeyker. Bring my darling here, right away!'

*I'm coming, sir,* she replied to him in her mind. *Your Mahpeyker is on her way to throw herself into your arms. She's coming to you all on fire!*

The journey, however, was dragging on forever.

The day advanced, and the afternoon changed into the evening – and still the journey did not end. Eventually, the darkness of the night finally fell on them. The cavalry escorting the carriage lit torches, and they kept riding in their light.

At last, the carriage stopped in a courtyard. She knew that from the clatter of the wheels. She hoped that when the door open, she would see Sultan Ahmed outside – but instead she saw the grinning black face of the stewardess Şetaret.

She felt disappointed but didn't let it show.

"Hello, beautiful Lady," Şetaret welcomed her enthusiastically. "Great to see you here!"

Mahpeyker wasn't used to something like that. She'd never seen the face of the stewardess shine with such a smile before, nor hear such pleasant words coming out of her mouth.

"What is this place?"

"The palace in Bursa, my beautiful one. Palace in Bursa."

Mahpeyker looked at the windows lit by torches.

"Come, my child, quickly," said Şetaret, pointing the way to her.

*Let's not make them wait for us...* she repeated to herself. *Let's not make my King wait!*

As she followed in the footsteps of Şetaret, her mind constantly urged her on: *Come on, faster, faster! You really can't go faster?*

Damn it! The corridors here also seemed to have no end. They kept walking, weaving, and turning. She noticed that the servants passing them watched her closely.

*Look, look... Take a good look at Mahpeyker Haseki, the beautiful favorite of Sultan Ahmed, who could not stand his longing for her!*

In the end, they turned into a corridor that ended with a door with a big guardsman in front.

*Finally!* she was glad. *We're here. My Padishah is waiting for me behind this door.*

The door opened, but before they entered inside, Mahpeyker probably said all the prayers she knew. At one point, she stopped, preparing for the moment when she would throw herself into the Sultan's arms. However, something she did not expect at all, happened.

Şarazad suddenly pulled out a red tulle from the bundle that she'd held under her arm all this time and put it over Mahpeyker's head. Her entire face was now hidden behind a red curtain.

"Ah!" she shouted, surprised. "What are you doing, Abla?"

She saw through the fabric that Şarazad was laughing.

"Daye wanted me to do it right now," she said in a whisper.

So that's how she was supposed to stand before Ahmed? But there was no time to think about it now, she shouldn't let the Sultan wait too long for her. As she already stood before the doorway, she took a deep breath and brought one of her most beautiful smiles on her face – so that Ahmed, when he lifts the tulle, would fall in love with her once again.

She took a step forward. She crossed the threshold. Through the red of the tulle, she saw something completely different than she had expected.

*What's going on here? Where is the Padishah?*

She had a chamber full of women in front of her, and all their eyes were fixed on her. Behind these jealous glances, she also saw hidden admiration.

When she wondered what it was all about, her reason warned her: *Be prepared. I don't know what is going on, either, but it looks like it's something important!*

Alright, but what could it be?

Mahpeyker abandoned the attitude of a woman who was going to meet her lover and instead, she straightened her shoulders and raised her head. She took on a queen's pose and went inside. She gave the women in the room a proud look. She thought about smiling at them, but she quickly changed her mind. *Because of this damned tulle, they won't see me anyway*, she complained to herself. *Neither my smile nor my beauty. The only thing they see is a figure dressed in red, hiding her face behind a scarlet tulle. No one knows whether I'm beautiful or ugly -- just a woman.*

She was already going to enjoy listening to the whispers when she heard a man's voice to her right, so she elegantly turned her head in that direction. The chamber was partitioned all the way to the ceiling with a checked screen. The voice came from behind this barrier. She wondered if the Padishah was there too? Why, instead of immediately taking her in his arms, did he call her to a room full of people? Why the screen here? What were other men doing here?

Şetaret pointed to her a sofa by the barred screen. Mahpeyker approached it with such grace that all the whispers in the chamber went silent.

She slowly sat on the edge of it. She'd learned this 'royal' way of sitting from Sultana Safiye. She laid her hands freely on her knees. Şarazad immediately rushed to her and slowly adjusted the scarlet caftan on her, so that her beautiful, swanlike neck, would be more visible. Then she knelt and pulled the skirts of her dress to her ankles to reveal her shoes embroidered with gold thread. When she decided that everything was right, she hurriedly took her place among other women.

It was only then that Mahpeyker bowed her head slightly to the grated screen in front of her. She wanted to see what was behind it. Or rather – she wanted to see Ahmed. But she couldn't see anything through it.

"Welcome, Mahpeyker Hanım, daughter."

The bass voice pierced her to the marrow of her bones.

"We've gathered here," the bass continued, "in the face of God, for a blessed matter..."

These words did not tell her anything. She wanted to see Ahmed – right now.

"... but first, you must answer me."

Answer? But for what; he'd not ask her anything.

"Do you want to light up your soul with the light of Islam, daughter?"

She had the impression that someone poured boiling water on her. *Did I understand well? Does he want me to abandon...*

"I will ask you openly then," said the bass, as if guessing what was happening in her head now. "His Majesty Sultan Ahmed Khan announced to us that he wants to take you before God as his wife."

At that moment, her brain stopped working. Her heart stopped. All kind of feelings flooded her. She didn't understand anything. *Wait a moment*, she said in her thoughts to the man as if he could hear her. *Ahmed? You said he wants to do what? Take as his wife? Who, me? Padishah wants to take me as his legitimate wife? Does it mean that he wants to marry me? Oh my God! Blessed Lady, Lord Jesus, and all the saints take care of me!*

She felt that she was close to insanity. Everything inside her screamed with joy.

*Padishah wants to marry me. Sultan wants to marry me...* Here, right now, the prophecy of a blind beggar is being fulfilled. The maid becomes a Queen. Or rather, as Safiye said, the Sultana. Mahpeyker Sultan!

If no disaster happens at the last moment, if at this crucial moment fate doesn't play with her again, her dreams will become a reality. She will never wake up again as a servant from a dream in which she saw herself as a queen. She won't long for the night and hate mornings anymore. Just as she loves the moon and the stars, she will also fall in love with the sun. She will fall asleep as a Sultana in the evening and wake up as a Sultana in the morning. She will not dream anymore – she will now live her dream all the time. Sultan Ahmed wanted to take her for his wife!

*So, let him take me! Let the great Padishah make me his rightful wife!*

"But," resumed the bass, "so we may fulfill his Majesty's wish, a woman whom he would take as a wife should be a follower of the only true religion. In other words - she should be a Muslim. So, if you also share our master's desire and want to become his wife..."

"I do!" she said without waiting for the man to finish his speech. "I want to become the wife of His Majesty!"

Laughter could be heard on both sides of the screen, but she didn't care.

She didn't remember anything that happened next. Neither how she drove away from herself the thought that she was just making the biggest sin, nor how she repeated the Arab words uttered in bass without a single stumble. She focused all her attention only on this.

Mahpeyker was given the title of Hatun, the highest title awarded to women in high position, and everyone heard her say the Shahada, the Muslim profession of faith, one of the five pillars of Islam.

"Mahpeyker Hatun has said the Shahada," intoned the Hodja Efendi, "thus enjoying the honor of joining the believers of the true faith. Nothing prevents us now from completing this blessed work... Grandson of Sultan Murad Khan of blessed memory, son of the late Sultan Mehmed Khan of blessed memory.

"Ahmed Khan! Do you affirm that you are taking this here Mahpeyker Hatun as your wife, in the sight of the great God?"

"I affirm, Hodja Efendi."

*He affirmed, affirmed, affirmed!* Mahpeyker was overflowing with happiness. *Sultan Ahmed affirmed that he took me in the sight of God as his wife.*

"And you, daughter?" Now he was to ask her the same thing. "Did you understand my words, daughter?"

"Yes."

"Well then..." There was something in his voice that suggested he did not quite believe it. It didn't matter to her, though. *Come on*, she repeated in her mind. *Come on, ask me about it, ask me!*

"Our Lord, the ruler of the seven climates, Ahmed Khan, in the sight of God, confirmed that he is taking you as his rightful wife. We have been all witnesses of that. Now I'm asking you, daughter. Grandson of the Sultan..."

Mahpeyker couldn't sit still when the Hodja was listing all those blessed memories, names, and titles. *Hurry, I'm begging you, hurry*, she repeated silently to herself, over and over again. Even now she was still afraid – what if something happens in the last moment or someone unexpected appears and turns her dream into a nightmare.

Hodja finally asked this question:

"Do you affirm in the sight of the great God that you take His Majesty Sultan Ahmed as your husband?"

"I do, Hodja Efendi."

Hodja then mumbled something in a language she didn't understand.

"And I," he finally arrived at the last part of the ceremony, "before God give you to His Majesty as his rightful wife."

*Hurrraaay! I became a Queen!*

While the men behind the screen talked about something, she heard the voice of Sultana Safiye: 'The Ottomans called us a Great Sultana Mother, my child. Let them call you Kösem.'

That night they did not fall asleep until morning.

Mahpeyker had never been as passionate and uninhibited as this first night with her husband. For the first time, they loved each other so passionately.

When Ahmed let out a groan of pleasure, she felt like crying. It was the moment when she freed herself from the sense of sin after giving up her religion. *Ultimately, I still follow the same God's path*, she decided, to deal with remorse once and for all. Now she just cried, washing her soul with tears. It wasn't a sin but rather God's will — because isn't it him who determines the fate of man? For her, apparently, he wrote one like this. And now he was seeping into her the greatest gift that he offered to man. Life! She was sure, now that the heavy sin of adultery had been lifted off her shoulders, that life would surely sprout from the semen filling her womb this time. She should give the Ottoman's the next prince as soon as possible.

Dawn found her in Ahmed's arms. She played with his beard and pulled at his mustache, which had already begun to reach beyond the corners of his mouth. The Padishah, in turn, tried to grab her fingers with his teeth.

"What does "Kösem" mean, sir?" She didn't plan to ask him this question right now at all — it just slipped out of her mouth.

Ahmed supported himself with one elbow and watched her for a long time. For a moment, the seriousness on his face scared Mahpeyker. Slowly, however, his face relaxed, and after a while, a smile even appeared on it. He began to laugh, running his finger over her lips.

"So, she told you," he said cheerfully. "She did."

"Who?"

"My grandmother. Safiye Sultan."

Ahmed kept laughing with a silent, suppressed laughter. Seeing this, Mahpeyker calmed down.

"Yes, yes," she said with a grimace, like a little girl. "She said that, but she didn't explain what it meant."

Sultan became serious again in an instant.

"The last will of my grandmother was that we would give you that name. That night, when we met for the first time, I was supposed to call you Kösem. Grandmother kept saying that this name suits you very well. In order not to hurt her, I pretended to agree with her..."

Mahpeyker worried. *How come? You pretended? So, now I won't be able to have this name?*

"... but faced with your beauty, my tongue refused to obey me. I forgot about everything. The name that most fully describes your beauty came to my head: Mahpeyker. I actually admitted my grandmother was right only when the rebellious Janissaries set out for the palace. Your mind guided me then, it illuminated my path. True, you are my beautiful Mahpeyker with a shining face, even more beautiful than the moon. But your intelligence, mind, and courage make you Kösem."

She leaned close to him flirtatiously and clung to his chest with her breasts. She brushed against his body. The time had come to solve the mystery of Kösem.

"I still don't know what this name means... Is it at least something good?"

"That's how you call the guide of a herd. It means someone who leads, points the way, and inspires.

*Leads, ha! Wonderful, wonderful!* However, she didn't let her joy show and looked at the Sultan hesitatingly as if she were thinking about something. She scowled.

"Does it mean that you now want to give me the name that you have previously agreed to, only for the sake of your grandmother? What will my Master call me now? Mahpeyker Kösem?"

"Yes. But not only me. From now on, the entire Empire will know you by this name, as the Sultana Hatice Mahpeyker Kösem. And you, my Mahpeyker, be its guide, Kösem."

She covered the Padishah with kisses. Happy, she repeated these three words in her head: *Mahpeyker Kösem Sultan...*

All the prophecies have come true – the servant has turned into a Queen, a Sultana.

She was both Mahpeyker and Kösem. Mahpeyker Kösem Sultan.

"I will be," she whispered into his ear in reply. "I will be a guide for the Ottomans!"

When she was alone, she lay on the bed for a while, staring at the ceiling. She stroked her belly. *There is no sin anymore. I have purified myself from the sin of adultery. God, fill my womb with life! Give me a son. A little prince. Let Mahpeyker Kösem Sultan give birth to a prince!*

The news that the Sultan married Mahpeyker Haseki in Bursa struck the capital like a lightning bolt from the sky. For the Sea Pavilion, it meant a real catastrophe.

Sultana Mahfiruz didn't leave her chambers for many days. She didn't even let the ladies of the court in. The last straw was the information that the Sultan gave his newly married wife, the name Kösem.

This time she had to consider herself defeated. She'd lost to an ordinary maid! But they haven't heard the last from fate yet. *Let's wait for my Osman to take the throne*, she thought, basking in hate. *Then we will see what will happen to you, Hatice Mahpeyker Kösem, we will see!*

# CHAPTER FIVE

## The New Palace
## Harem

Her return from Bursa was simply wonderful. It turned out to be much more impressive than all her dreams and fantasies of being a queen.

The whole palace turned out to welcome her. Viziers, Pashas, Beys, and all other dignitaries that counted in the Sublime Porte, lined up in rows. There were also their wives and daughters as well as an innumerable army of court ladies, odalisques, harem agas, servants, farm workers, treasurers, and stewards. And finally, a lot of other officials, whose names she didn't even know. As the clothing of each of these groups stood out in color, this mixture of colors made the huge courtyard resemble a garden full of different kinds of flowers.

From the window of the Sultan's carriage, she already noticed in this crowd the Aga of the Gate of Bliss, Mestan, and his assistant, Dilşad. Just like the others, they stood bowing almost to the ground.

The carriage rode through the middle of the crowd and arrived at the inner court of the harem. Mahpeyker smiled and waved to the people greeting her. The carriage stopped. Two farmhands quickly brought carpeted stairs to the door of the carriage. The stewardess and her assistants moved forward, towards the carriage. She checked to see for any bumps on a long, narrow carpet, spread between the carriage and the big gate of the harem. The new Sultana could not afford to stumble over something or, God forbid, to fall!

Although only a moment ago, Mahpeyker couldn't wait to leave the carriage – she was taking her time now. The welcome retinue should wait. Those who knew her were probably impatient to see if the new role suited her. And those who didn't know her personally were probably curious about the concubine, who made the Sultan so crazy about her that it ended with their wedding. As soon as she appears, everyone will probably start exchanging comments about her.

Suddenly she noticed fairies, dressed in white, standing in rows on both sides of the carpet. If she hadn't recognized Semiha at their front, she would have probably wondered who they were. The army of Mahpeyker Kösem courtiers came out to greet their Lady. They were all beautiful, tall, with rosy cheeks. Some of them had black hair and some gold.

Mürüvvet and Şarazad were waiting for her at the door. They, in turn, were dressed in red with tall, conical caps on their heads. Mürüvvet was wrapped white tulle, which fell from the top to the back, over her shoulder, and towards her breasts – giving her a very dignified appearance.

Her eyes searched for three more persons in the crowd: Nanny... Sofia, and that one, ice-cold witch, from whom she'd snatched Ahmed – the spider. But she didn't see any of them there.

She never expected Mahfiruz to honor her with her presence, anyway. But she will have certainly sent her spies here, who now watched her closely from this crowd, to later tell their Lady everything.

And Daye? She was probably waiting for her inside. Of course, it wasn't right for an elderly woman to greet her with the regular service.

And what about Sofia? Where is she? Hopefully, she wasn't sick?

"Welcome, My Lady."

The voice of the stewardess snatched her out of her reverie. The woman opened the carriage door and offered her hand to help her out.

She didn't take it. As she had visualized it, she slowly straightened up and put her right leg on the step of the stairs. Then she leaned over to get off the carriage. She grabbed the flaps of her black satin dress, over which she had put on a caftan lined with an ermine fur, given to her by the Sultan. She poked her head out.

The silence reigning in the courtyard was interrupted immediately by a wave of sighs, carrying both admiration and jealousy.

She was beautiful! Dazzling. She was the queen of her dreams.

She had a round toque on her head. The black chiffon attached to it was wrapped in golden fringes. It was topped by Sultana Nurban's tiny crown, which she'd received as a gift from Daye. On her forehead swayed a ruby, which Ahmed gave her right after the wedding ceremony when he removed the red veil from her face.

From beneath the collar of the ermine fur, flowed a black taffeta train. The fabric cascaded over her arms to the ground, opening like a fan. It flickered gleefully with each step and with sun rays falling on it, dragging behind her on the ground.

The caftan she wore was, in turn, a real work of art. To offer better protection from the cold, it was made of morocco covered with black velvet. Its collar and skirts were lined with fur, which stretched down on both sides along the edges and joined again in the back.

As always, her entire wardrobe was black. The exception was the ruby which sparkled on her forehead, and a scarlet scarf, embroidered with gold, that was tied around her waist.

She walked through the carpet gracefully like a swan, and with great dignity, like a powerful queen. Passing by the simple servants, she happily lent her ear to catch what they whispered about her.

"There are simply no words..."

"God was generous with beauty for her, no two ways about it..."

"What a wonderful match to our Sultan!"

"May good God save her from an evil eye..."

She knew that everyone was thinking something else, too: *Who said a concubine could not get that far? Here's the best example...* but she didn't care about it at all.

Other words hurt her, however – the wishes she heard while passing an elderly woman.

"Give the Sublime Porte many sons, My Lady."

Should something like this be wished to a woman convinced of her infertility?

*What sons, woman?* she thought. *Ah, if I could give birth to at least one... At least one.*

As she neared the row of court ladies, she saw Sofia standing behind Semiha.

Mahpeyker felt warmth fill her heart. Semiha had dressed Sofia in blue. She really looked like a fairy in this color.

The girl was smiling enigmatically. It was evident that if she could, she would throw herself into her arms – but they must have already taught her that such behavior toward the wife of the Padishah was improper. *And even if she embraced me, so what?* she thought defiantly. *Would anything terrible happen? If I kissed her and hugged her? Of course not.*

And yet it was impossible. That was the price all the queens had to pay: resignation from freedom. She learned it very quickly when she was still in Bursa. Neither she nor her loved ones could freely do what they wanted. Now, even the way she sat and stood up, how she looked and talked, was regulated by etiquette. She couldn't, for example, eat as before, or just drink water whenever she felt like it. First, someone had to check if poison was added to the meal or drink. Her surroundings will also have to get used to complying with a whole host of rules. Mahpeyker, however, wasn't complaining about it at all. After all, she wanted to become a queen. So, now she has to adapt to everything and pay the price for it, whatever it would be.

Sofia hesitated for a moment. Mahpeyker could hardly keep from laughing as she caught the furtive gaze the girl had sent to Semiha. In the end, clearly embarrassed, she gave her a deep, exaggerated bow, which she must have practiced many times before.

*Enough of this ado,* her mind murmured. She reached out to Sofia. The girl, radiant with happiness, rushed to her in two strides and took her hand.

"Sister…" she whispered almost silently. "My beautiful sister, sister-Sultana, sister-Queen!"

As she caught up with the row of courtiers, Semiha looked at the girls on the left, letting them know that they could begin. White and red rose petals sprinkled the carpet in front of her. The girls on the right tossed grains of rice and wheat.

Mahpeyker did not miss that her chief court lady was somewhat gloomy. Yes, even though she greeted her cheerfully, she was clearly depressed. *She's tired,* she thought. *Who knows how many days she had been preparing this welcome ceremony for me.* She stopped in front of her to single out the old companion of Sultana Safiye in front of everyone. The girl immediately bowed to her.

"Welcome to your palace, My Lady. How great to see you again!"

She took her hand from Sofia's hand and directed it toward Semiha. She stroked her cheek so that everyone could see it.

"How are you?"

"I keep praying for My Lady's health."

"I can't see Daye anywhere…"

Quite unexpectedly, instead of answering her, the girl tossed before her the rose petals she held in her hands.

It surprised her. *What is going on here? Why does she look away from me?*

She took Sofia's hand again and began to continue walking slowly. Şarazad and Mürüvvet sprinkled her with rose and jasmine water as a welcome greeting. She looked at them with the kindest smile she could afford and walked through the big, wide-open door.

"Şarazad..." She almost said 'Abla,' just as she was used to. It was already improper, however, for the Sultana to address a maid with such familiarity. "What's going on? Is mother Daye waiting for me upstairs?"

Şarazad also looked away. Mürüvvet, to avoid being asked the same, stepped forward and showed her the way.

Nervous, Mahpeyker paused, and so did the courtiers following her.

"Sofia?"

"Tell me, my sister... Lady?"

"Daye... Where's Mother Daye?"

She was horrified when she saw the girl's eyes suddenly fill with tears. Panic began to build up in her. And suspicions. Did she share the fate of Eftalya? Oh my God...

"Sofia, I'm asking you. What happened? Tell me immediately!" she said, pulling her arm.

The fairy in blue shook her shoulders and started crying for good. Semiha, who suddenly appeared next to her, finally gave her an answer.

"Unfortunately, Daye is dead, madam."

Mahpeyker stood as if struck by lightning.

"How come?" she hissed at Semiha. "How did this happen? Could it be..." She didn't manage to finish, but the courtier understood what she meant.

She nodded, denying her guesses.

"In hamam..." she whispered in her ear. "One of the wooden clogs slipped off her foot. She fell and hit her head against the water trough. She died on the spot..."

Damned clogs! Ever since she saw them for the first time in the palace in Kumanovo, she hated those narrow pieces of high-heeled wood. She never put them on. She was used to running barefoot through the white foam of the waves hitting the coast. These logs had no business being on her feet. Whenever she heard girls tapping in them in the bathhouse, she wondered when one of them would fall and break something.

"So, she was alone there? Was there no one in the bathhouse who could help her? How can you let a woman of her age go to hamam alone?!"

They answered something to her, but she didn't hear it. It didn't matter anymore.

Tears filled her eyes, so she bit her lip so as not to cry. Who knows, maybe crying was now also forbidden for her, and Semiha would come running at any moment to whisper to her, 'It is improper, My Lady'? She couldn't get rid of the thought that God had once again taken someone she loved away from her...

"When did it happen?"

"That same night, when His Highness announced that he had married you, Lady." The girl thought for a moment. "She was very happy, it was obvious that she was happy. She kept saying: 'The Sultan has not disappointed me, well done, my son! Someone as God-fearing as he, saying Namaz five times a day, could not live in adultery anymore. He obeyed me. May God reward him both on earth and in heaven!' We couldn't understand what she meant, mighty Lady."

*I understand,* thought Mahpeyker Kösem. Her heart was bleeding. She still had the bright, smiling face of the nanny in front of her eyes, and her voice still rang in her ears: 'Daughter.' She shook her head. She no longer thought about the etiquette or about being admonished by someone. She was, after all, Sultana Kösem. She appeared here to forbid what was allowed and to allow what was forbidden. The Sultanas and the Padishahs also had the right to tears. Becoming a queen did not turn her into a stone. She let her tears flow.

*God, why did you do it?* she rebelled in her heart. *Do you want to take away all the people I love? If so, I will never love anyone again. Nobody!*

"What did you just say to me, Semiha?" she asked suddenly.

The woman got scared of this unexpected question. She blushed.

"I don't understand, Lady. If I unintentionally committed..."

"You said, 'Lady.' And even 'mighty Lady'!"

Semiha lowered her head. Yes, she'd said that. After all, she wasn't that Hatice from the Old Palace, who polished the handles of the Safiye Sultan carriage door anymore. She was the rightful wife of the powerful Sultan Ahmed. She was Mahpeyker, she was Kösem. She couldn't call her by her name, or 'you' anymore, like when they used to laugh at her dreams of becoming a queen!

"I am forbidding you to use those words," said the Sultana. "When we're in our group, you will never talk to me like that, do you understand?"

This time it was Semiha who struggled to keep herself from crying.

"I will have two requests for you, Semiha. Firstly, I would like you to teach me Muslim prayers and rituals. We will start with Namaz. And secondly... I completely abandoned the writing lessons that I started in the Old Palace. Find me a Hodja. I should really start working on my scrawl."

"As you command, la..." she fell silent and smiled at the memory of her recent order. "Of course, Mahpeyker."

"We can now go to the Haseki Hall."

Semiha led her to the Valide Sultan's apartments, though. The same, in which Sultana Handan was living until recently, and Safiye before her.

"It must be a mistake," she told Mürüvvet who was opening the door for her. "I'm not Sultana Mother..." she sighed sadly and unconsciously put her hands on her stomach. "I'm not any kind of mother at all..."

"His Highness..." Şarazad hurried with explanations. "We received such an order: 'Because our Mother has already ended her earthly life, Sublime Porte no longer has its Valide Sultan. In such circumstances, we see no reason why not to make these apartments available to our wife, Mahpeyker Kösem Sultan.' So, we immediately prepared them for you, My Lady..." She looked into Mahpeyker's eyes and smiled gently. "Don't worry, my beautiful Sultana," she said slowly. "We exchanged everything, even the curtains. There isn't even a trace left of the deceased."

"Call the clerics," she said. "Let them recite the noble Quran for seven days and nights for the peace of my mother, Daye!"

She'd come here for the first time as a maid, and now she crossed the doorway of this apartment as a real Sultana.

*Fate must be making a fool of me*, she thought. *Death takes all beloved people from me, one by one. And now it*

*has brought me here – me, a barren woman – to live in the*
*room of the Sultana Mother. Isn't that a mockery?*

At the same time, in her heart of hearts, she raged with joy. She was ashamed of it, but she couldn't control the feeling. *Mahfiruz will be furious when they tell her about it. Padishah offered the apartments of Valide Sultan to me!*

When the Quran recitation began, she threw away all the dirt from her mind and soul. Although she didn't understand the words, she felt her heart cleaning in their divine harmony. She didn't see the need to hide her tears from everyone.

Just as she ordered, for seven days and nights, the Sultana Mahpeyker Kösem apartments resounded with sounds of recitation and prayers. *Mother Daye,* Mahpeyker prayed from the bottom of her heart, *I know you are in heaven now. I have no doubt that you will support your daughter from there, as you did in this mendacious world. I am no longer an adulteress, Mother. My womb, however, remains empty. Please plead with God, Mother, ask him to give me a son...*

A miracle happened. God finally listened to her prayers. Four months after returning from Bursa, Mahpeyker Kösem Sultan realized that she was pregnant. First, she kept it secret. When she was sure, she told Semiha about it. In the end, she also gave the happy news to Ahmed.

Padishah jumped to his feet out of happiness.

"Finally, come here, mother of my prince. Let me kiss your forehead!"

*'Mother of my prince,' huh!* If it weren't for being afraid, Mahpeyker would have danced the crazy dance of happiness long ago. She was instructed, however, that

such sudden outbursts of joy could harm her. She was even afraid of experiencing the emotion that had come over her at the news that she was in a blessed state.

She waited impatiently for the nine long months to pass. She watched the movements of the child in her belly. She talked to it, calling it 'her prince.' She also wondered about a name for him. If it were only her choice, she would call her son Alexander. It might not, however, be the right name for a descendant of the Ottomans. *I wonder what name the Sultan will choose for him?*

She counted down the days, month after month. Nine months passed and the time for delivery arrived. And... Mahpeyker Kösem Sultan gave the Sublime Porte another sultana.

She saw this as another malice of fate. She was forced to give a daughter into the arms of the Sultan, who'd expected the birth of his third son. She could not make herself look Ahmed in the face.

"Your Majesty..." she choked through her tears. "Forgive me..."

Sultan took his daughter in his arms, kissed, and hugged her.

"The little Sultana will be called Ayşe," he said and whispered shahada in her ear. Then he kissed his wife on the forehead and pinned a brooch decorated with diamonds and emeralds to her collar. Criers with drums went around the capital the whole week, declaring to the people that Kösem Sultan gave birth to the Sultan's daughter, whom he named Ayşe. The girl was, of course, unaware of all the confusion that arose because of her. In the lands subordinate to the Ottomans, lanterns, torches, and oil lamps were burned for her throughout the nights, and throughout the capital and in all the barracks, food and baklava were distributed on trays, and the poor were given alms.

All this, however, did not cheer her up. She thought she heard Mahfiruz laughing her head off in the Sea Pavilion. She could easily imagine what the spider might have been thinking now: 'Well, not every woman is able to give birth to two plump, healthy boys. Others can only afford to give a little girl, and even that with difficulty...'

The news of the second pregnancy made Mahpeyker euphoric. It was as if her womb was now trying to make up for the lost time. This time she was almost sure that she would give birth to a boy.

She was wrong. She didn't even wait for the midwife to give the newborn the customary slap and show it to her with its head down.

"What?" she asked weakly. "What did I give birth to?"

"A girl!"

The same ceremonies and the same grim reflections were repeated. Sultan Ahmed, who clearly indicated at the first pregnancy already, that he hoped for a son, did not, however, look worried this time either. He lifted the baby up and said: "Your name is Fatma."

Then he disappeared from everyone's eyes, as he always did in times of worry and sadness. Mahpeyker already knew that she wouldn't see him for many days.

*Or maybe*, she tormented herself, lying in her bed, *he's seeking consolation from the one who has already given him two sons?*

She suffered. Feeding Fatma, she couldn't hold back her tears.

*Why? Why is fate playing with me like this? Hasn't it gotten bored with harassing me yet?*

When it seemed that she was so close to victory – she lost. And for Mahfiruz, it was the other way around – while at first, it seemed she was losing miserably, only to have the fates turn everything around and give the win to her. *She gave birth to two successors to the throne. And I, only two sultanas...*

The future was certain already now. If something happens to Ahmed, the eldest son of Mahfiruz – Osman – will take over the throne after him. And only God knows what will happen to her and her daughters then...

*You must be strong then*, said her reason. *Open your eyes wide, Mahpeyker. You are now at the crossroads. One road goes to a quiet harbor, while the other one leads straight into the abyss. Think carefully which path you will continue to follow.*

As usual, it was right. She'd reached the crossroads so now she must choose – darkness or brightness; death or life.

*Give up those complaints of a jealous, in love, and irritable woman already!* her mind went on angrily. *Don't you get bored sitting inside four walls all the time, and crying over your fate? What else can it do to please you? You wanted to become a queen, and there you go – you are! From a peasant woman and a maid, the fate made you an Ottoman Sultana! Don't be ungrateful and stop being rebellious. Begin to finally live like a queen. You should gather trustworthy and faithful people around you, as befits a queen.*

*Meanwhile, you haven't met any Vizier or Pasha yet; you don't know anyone of the Beys or Agas. Look around them, think about which one of them you may need in the future? Who among them is your friend and who is your enemy? Did you understand what I mean, Mahpeyker?*

She understood – she understood very well. She nodded.

*Your life and that of your princesses depend on Sultan Ahmed. Do not let anything stand between you. Neither wars nor rebellions. Until you're ready.*

*This I don't understand,* Mahpeyker replied to her mind. *Until I'm ready? For what?*

*To take over the reins of Sublime Porte yourself. To become its first woman-Padishah, Mahpeyker!*

She shuddered at such a thought. The first woman-Padishah? Her heart began to beat like crazy. *Okay, but when will I be ready for that?*

*When you give birth to the heir to the throne!*

The hope, which had already begun to release its stems, suddenly crumpled in an instant.

*But God doesn't want to give me a son...*

*He will!*

And again, the prophecy was not going to leave her in peace for a single moment. The first one was already fulfilled. And now, instead of living in happiness and peace, was she going to chase the next one? – to wonder constantly again: will it come true or not?

*Will it come true? When?*

*Quiet!* The mind had had enough. *If your name is Kösem, then live up to your name. Since you are a Sultana, behave like one!*

Mahpeyker decided to push all dark thoughts and worries away from herself.

*So, it is, I am Kösem, the guide of the herd. It's high time to see how I will lead it!*

# CHAPTER SIX

### The New Palace, Harem
### October 1609

She understood that she was too fast to think that Ahmed distanced himself away from her, because she couldn't give the Padishah a son. It was as if the ruler was even more attached to her. He shared not only a bed with her, but also his fears and hopes; what made him angry; what he had in his soul, and on his mind. She was not only his woman but also a friend, a confidante. Contrary to her fears, he did not visit Mahfiruz either. When she wanted to see him, she brought Osman to the New Palace. Once, Mahpeyker probed the Padishah to find out what he thought.

"My Lord," she said. "I'm sad to think that you could neglect our little prince because of your maid, Mahpeyker Kösem. Doesn't Osman want to see his father more often?"

Ahmed said nothing – he just looked at her for a very long time. Mahpeyker understood, however, what she was to understand. The Sultan properly appreciated the compassion that she showed for his son.

One night, at a late hour, the Padishah came to Mahpeyker's chambers. After a fiery hug, he leaned his head against her chest and sighed in exhaustion.

"Oh, sir," Mahpeyker spoke immediately. "Did something happen that saddened or enraged you again? I look into His Majesty's eyes, and I want you to be calm and happy, but there are those who want to make you sad. Is there anything you can share with your maid?"

"Oh, my Mahpeyker, what can I tell you about? About the bad news from the borderland, about an endless bandit ferment? Or perhaps about all these great, powerful sages around me, constantly plotting in anticipation that one of the others slips up? About what? Or maybe about the thievery, greed, ignorance, and debauchery?"

"Oh, my Sultan, my dear ruler," she said, throwing herself into Ahmed's arms. She kissed his bearded neck and giggled flirtatiously as if the hair stung her on the lips.

"What would I do without you, my bright angel?" Sultan Ahmed sighed. "These are not matters for me, Mahpeyker. I never wanted to take the throne. 'No thanks. Put my brother Mustafa on the throne.' I refused as much as I could, but I never managed to make my mother or grandmother listen. No one has ever seen them agree on anything, but on that day, they said in one voice: 'Is the Ottoman dynasty going to have a madman at the throne?' And even if so... so what? Did that mean that Ahmed was qualified to be the Padishah?"

Such were also the rumors. According to the news brought by the people he'd begun to organize recently, it was said among the Viziers and Pashas, among people from markets and bazaars, that the Osman family was missing something. No one was able to say what was missing, but he knew. There was no will in the state. Padishah did not behave like the Padishah.

"Do not be unjust to yourself," said Mahpeyker, embracing his neck. "Where would the Ottoman dynasty find a ruler like you?"

She realized how untrue this flattery was. The Ottomans have seen many a great ruler. Who was it that Daye told her about when she was still alive? For example, about Selim the Grim, like a sword with two blades. Suleiman appeared after him. 'Oh, yes, yes,' said the nanny. 'The infidels knelt at the very sound of his name.'

But Ahmed wasn't like that. How he issued the order to execute Kasım Pasha in his presence, was now forgotten. From the day he sat on the throne, until today, nothing had been repaired, on the contrary, the state of affairs only deteriorated. Because the Padishah couldn't make decisions – what he said one day, he withdrew the following day.

"I couldn't quell the celali uprisings in any way," Ahmed complained. "And if that were not enough, Ferhat Pasha brought misfortune on my head."

"Did you say, pasha, My Lord? Isn't this pasha mentioned by you a slave, in any case, owned by the Sultan? What right does he have to bring misfortune on the head of the ruler?"

"Actually, the Great Vizier Dervish Mehmed Pasha is to blame here. He made him a serdar. The man completely loots Aydin with Saruhan. According to complaints, there is no such insolence, or cruelty that he wouldn't resort to, so I am telling him to deal with this weasel, and he replies to me: 'He brought water to villages from forty springs, all these are slanders. Ferhat is such a loyal, brave man.'"

*If the pasha didn't do it, why didn't you stop him?* Mahpeyker reproached Ahmed in her mind, but in order not to seem too interested in these matters, she further comforted the Sultan.

"Those words reminded me of your blessed memory grandmother's advice."

"Really? My grandmother loved to advise. What was the advice of Safiye Sultan, who, in the last will, told me to call the girl she entrusted to me Kösem?"

Mahpeyker looked absently as if she were listening to Safiye Sultan. In fact, she tried to gain time to come up with some non-existent advice. She sighed heavily.

"'What is the secret of a long life?' my benefactress once asked. Although I gave her a lot of answers, she didn't like any of them. 'The secret of a long life is to not take one's word back. To not come back from the chosen path when you stumbled after one step. And choosing the right people for your companions.' Of course, she was right."

Mahpeyker paused for a moment to look at Ahmed and see the impact of her words. Padishah listened to her intently, seriously.

*Great,* she told herself, and continued...

"'And what is this secret?' I asked that day. 'How do I recognize the right man? How do I recognize one that is not right?' 'Good question. How can you recognize him?' said my patron. The whole secret is found in the eyes, my Sultan – 'Beware of people who do not look you straight in the eye,' said my noble Mother. Apparently, if you want to make judgments about someone, you must also look at his friends. A cruel man keeps with other cruel men, a thief with a robber."

Padishah was so impressed that he got up. *That's exactly what's going on*, he thought to himself excitement. *Safiye Sultan comes to me with her advice even from the other world. A cruel man is a friend of another cruel man, a thief – of a robber, right? Exactly! Take care of Ferhad Pasha, hit the Great Vizier Dervish Mehmed! Take care of Dervish Mehmed, hit Ferhad! Maybe they even steal and rob together, sharing profit. That is why Mehmed Pasha took Ferhad under his wing. Write it down, Ahmed, write it down somewhere in your head!*

"Come here." Padishah, smiling happily, pulled her close to him, embraced her waist, and started showering her with his kisses, repeating again and again: "My light, my rose, my nightingale, my red-lipped."

She cuddled up to him like a cat and began to reciprocate the ruler's caresses with the same passion.

"My Sultan, my King, my great Padishah. Your eyebrows are like a bow, your looks are like arrows. My mighty man."

Mahpeyker didn't give the impression of dwelling on these topics for too long, but she didn't stop thinking about them. As if she was jumping to another matter, she now raised the right question that she wanted to present to Ahmed from the very beginning.

"Do you know...?" she said suddenly, and then as if it had escaped her, hung her head sadly.

"I know, of course," said Ahmed happily, sitting cross-legged. "Apparently, my beautiful bird can already recite the whole range of suras from memory, without any help."

"My Sultan," she pretended flirtatiously to be embarrassed. "How come you found out right away?"

"Who should know what happens in every corner of the palace, what's whispered in the corridors, if not the Sultan?"

"I worked in secret to one day come to our Lord and please him with a surprise."

"You would make us very happy, Mahpeyker. May the Lord hear your prayers."

"Amen." She hesitated for a moment. "But that's not all." She looked as if she wondered whether to speak or not. She suddenly made her decision. "I can already write in Ottoman."

"Look at that, great! I knew you would succeed. My Mahpeyker Sultan will surely bring a matter to an end."

*Rather, I will trudge through,* she said in her mind.

"But I write a bit like a monkey," she giggled.

"Doesn't matter. Over time, your hand will be trained. And you know what, whether it is a vizier or some aga, the handwriting of many people simply can't be read. Some, for example, read but can't write." Padishah fell silent for a moment. It occurred to him that Mahpeyker's 'Do you know?' could mean something else. "Actually... is this what you wanted to tell me, my beautiful?"

And again, she frowned in an instant.

"No... but..." she stopped. She'd already learned that it was the best way to make Padishah interested in some thought – to talk in a way that would light his curiosity.

"Tell me, Mahpeyker. Has someone made you upset by some tactlessness?"

"No," she denied again, "it's not that. I'm afraid you'll laugh at me."

"I won't, go on, tell me."

"There you go, you're laughing already. And still, a dream... I never believed any..."

Ahmed did not let her finish. "A dream?"

"Ha, ha," Mahpeyker chuckled with embarrassment, "the previous night... I saw you, My Lord, in a dream."

"May Allah make your dream propitious. What was it like? Was it beautiful and good?"

"You were dressed all in green, on the back of a scarlet horse. It was dark all around, like in a dungeon. You could see only my powerful Sultan and the mount, whom he rode. At some point, the horse came out of the darkness. Such a dream. Your mount was winged."

She looked furtively at Sultan Ahmed to see his reaction. Padishah delved into his own dreams. He must have seen himself now in the green on a scarlet horse with wings. Green, scarlet, and a winged horse. These were good signs. *I must strike while the iron is hot*, she told herself.

"And what happened next?" asked the Sultan.

The rest was easy. She could freely tell the dream she'd created.

"The horse flew to this gate with conical towers; the one in front of the palace. It landed there."

"By the Hagia Sophia Mosque?"

She shook her head. "Your horse turned back, shaking its mane, looked at Hagia Sophia, and then quickly turned its head. It took my ruler with one movement of the wing, carried him on to other squares. There was no one around. It reared with a neigh. It was such a neigh that a clap of thunder would seem like a whisper next to it. Your horse stubbornly poked at some place with its right hoof. Then it bent its leg as if to help our Lord come down from its back."

"And?"

"Suddenly an object appeared in your hand."

"A sword?"

Mahpeyker shook her head slowly.

"No, no, no... A book. Book from which light shone."

"The Qur'an!" shouted the Padishah, suddenly standing up. "The book in my hand was Qur'an." He raised his hands and ran them across his face like in prayer. "Lord, Lord! Thousands of thanks for your every blessing! What do you expect from me, what does it mean what you showed to my beloved?" He closed Mahpeyker's hands in his.

"You lifted the book up," said the woman, "and you spoke words that I did not hear. Later you walked around the horse and suddenly stopped."

"I stopped?"

"Thousands of people have suddenly appeared in this empty square. In one moment, everyone surrounded my Sultan. Everyone fell to the feet of the Padishah. And you gave the order: 'Here, right here.' At that moment, the dark sky fell apart. A bolt of lightning reached the place where my Sultan stood, and in an instant, the darkness surrendered to the light. That's when I saw an object in your other hand."

"What, Mahpeyker? What was that?"

"A spear from which lightning flashed, My Lord. In one hand you had a book, and in the other, a spear of lightning!"

Sultan Ahmed fell to his knees. A heavenly sign!

"In the darkness, for a moment, something... something like a mosque..."

Mahpeyker murmured some more words, but the Padishah didn't listen anymore.

*Thanks be to God,* he praised God in his mind. *Yes, Mahpeyer's dream is a heavenly sign that will brighten up my mind, choked with indecision.*

Mahpeyker's dream was so understandable that it didn't even have to be commented on.

The scarlet horse was the Ottoman empire. And wasn't he the Padishah of this empire? He sat on the back of a crimson mount. He was all in green. A goal. He had many goals. To quell the celali rebellions, ensure the security of the borderland, lead the army of the empire to new victories, make the people rich, bring peace, and the rule of law to the state.

Ahmed shook his head. *I know what the divine command given to my wife must mean*: *'Oh my slave, do not leave the path shown to you by the book I have sent you. Light up the world with its help, and build such a mosque for me, that the ezan resounding out of his minarets, the verses of the Qur'an coming from under its dome, and the prayers of my servants will not cease until the last day. Do not hesitate, Ahmed! Do not be afraid! We put a spear of lightning in your right hand for you to strike the enemies of the Ottoman Empire!'*

The Sultan repeatedly bowed down under the stealthy gaze of Mahpeyker.

"May your will be done, My Lord. May your will be done."

Mahpeyker thought this was enough for now, and began to talk about the mischief of girls, and, stroking his head, he sailed into the world of dreams because of her dream. She sang the new song he'd taught her. She knew that Ahmed loved it when she sang Turkish chants.

"There is no day, my beloved,

That I would not look for you,

That I would not shed tears with bitter sobs.

I am burning from the longing for him.

Oh, snowy mountains, go away

Before Azrael takes the soul of this black-browed."

She was not even sure if Ahmed could hear her. Padishah was in a completely different world already.

The first thing that Sultan Ahmed did in the morning was to call the chief architect. When Sedefkar Mehmet Aga stood before him in a bow, the ruler said:

"Look, Aga. Build a mosque on that square so that neither its dome nor its splendor would be smaller than Hagia Sophia. Make a mosque such that its slender minarets would touch the blue sky. Have you heard me, Sedefkar Aga? For the glory of Allah, raise such a mosque that my Lord, and I, and the Muslims coming with their begging to The Mightiest, would be pleased. What I want from you is that my name will last forever when I turn to dust already, and my bones will become one with the earth. So that people who come to pray, would remember me, and give peace to my soul with intent, reciting the opening sura of the Qur'an, the Fatiha."

The echoes of the change that occurred in Sultan Ahmed spread from the palace to the streets of the capital, and from there throughout the whole Ottoman state.

The frail and gentle youth, who did not want to take power, and who after his enthronement feared even the shadow of his own mother and grandmother, was gone. In his place, now appeared a strong Padishah with a stern, hawk look.

He was saying the five daily prayers again. He found no more excuses for indolence. His religious practice was flawless, but most of all, to earn the satisfaction of Allah, he began building a mosque opposite Hagia Sophia. Thanks to him, the great mosque was completed on the shores of the Golden Horn – the one whose foundation was established by his great-great-grandmother, Nurbanu Sultan, and whose construction could not be ended in the days of Safiye Sultan, even though she'd allocated all her income to it. The people were glad that the Padishah had become such a zealous follower.

Those who saw the ruler carrying stones on the construction site together with the workers, shouted from a distance: "May Allah make your rule eternal!"

"Long live the Padishah!"

In cafes and wineries, people also talked about news from the palace and what was happening with the Sultan.

"It looks like Allah is happy," people said.

They didn't know if they were happy with the ruler's other behaviors, however, and apparently, they weren't. Every day there was a new rumor. At first, they did not believe them.

"Give me a break!" they said. But it didn't take long before the rumors turned out to be true.

"Did you hear what happened yesterday at the Divan meeting?" This is how conversations began in wine bars.

"How could we not hear? People from Aydın and Saruhan came to the meeting and filed a complaint against Serdar Ferhad Pasha. Apparently, they said, 'Is some crook entitled to our dignity and property? Why doesn't the ruler come to us with help? Or maybe we have failed in something, and he sends Ferhad to us as a punishment from His Majesty?'"

The patrons nodded their heads.

"How many years this goes on, there is no such villainy that he wouldn't commit!" someone murmured.

"Even we here have heard of the vileness of this chap! Just think what had to be going on with those people!"

Others disagreed: "All right, so they said it and what happened? Has the order changed because of this request? Did the ruler get angry and say, 'Bring this oppressor here, let them cut his head'?"

"The Padishah prepared an even worse punishment for him," another man said suddenly.

Everyone turned their heads towards the owner of the voice. They looked at his outfit and from his purple galligaskins recognized the student from the palace.

"What could be worse?"

"Take the life of the one who defended the cruel man."

The winery became suddenly so silent that you could hear a pin drop. It was certain that the man knew a lot of things. He moved from the back of the room to the center.

"Let somebody fill this cup for me, and after I wet my dry throat, I can tell you the rest, dear companions."

Someone grabbed a pitcher of wine and filled the man's goblet.

"OK, now tell us. What did our ruler do that was worse?"

"After hearing the messengers, he roared at the Great Vizier: 'Hey you, Dervish Pasha! Would someone's word be more important than mine? The scoundrel, whom we told you to get rid of, is still alive, and my subjects come, lament, and call us to account.'"

Everyone in the wine bar shook their heads.

"He said it well, very well," said the voices.

"Certainly!" a challenger shouted. "Does Sultan Ahmed need your confirmation that he said it well? Be quiet and let the man finish."

"And what happened next?" someone else put in.

"The rest is obvious. 'Have mercy, these are calumnies,' whimpered the Grand Vizier. He fell to the feet of the Sultan and began to cry, and the Padishah said, 'Take this dog from under my feet. Let this wretch he looked after come and protect him from my anger now,' and as he said it, three executioners appeared."

At that moment, cries of delight broke out all around.

"What an executioner is like, everyone knows. He won't listen to moans and pleas for pity. They put a rope around Dervish Mehmed Pasha's neck. One pulled one way, the other pulled the other. But those who have heard about it, know this. Dervish Pasha is a strong man – a big guy. I'm just telling you what I heard, but supposedly he fought with oxen in his youth. He put on a yoke and overthrew great animals to the ground. So, if you could see how he caught the rope that choked him, how he threw around the executioners! They all fell together and began to fight in front of the Sultan."

"Oooh!"

"In front of the Sultan?"

"Yep! In front of the Sultan."

"No way!"

"Well, and then?"

"The executioners didn't let go. They gradually tightened the loop. Eh, three giant executioners for one condemned man. Even the strength of such a beast is not enough! Especially with a rope that tightens on the neck. Finally, Mehmed Pasha was unable to resist anymore. He fell and stayed like that. The executioners thought he was gone, so they removed the ropes."

"Good heavens! So, he was still...?"

"Yes, yes. Exactly what you think. Mehmed Pasha, who lay motionless, suddenly started shaking!"

"It means he did not give up the ghost."

"Afraid, all the viziers and beys parted, and the executioners fell to the floor: 'He left and came back!' they shouted. Just at this point, our master yelled: 'You, unfaithful dog! You have so many sins on your conscience that they don't want you even in the other world!' and he sank his own dagger into the neck of the Grand Vizier."

"Wow!"

"Wow! Well, of course, wow!"


Everyone told the story of how the Sultan ordered to kill the Great Vizier Dervish Mehmed Pasha differently, but everyone finished with the words: 'That's how it was.'

"Our Lord, Padishah, didn't leave the poor people in the hands of a cruel man. He took his life with his bare hands."

"But that's not how it was," another grumbled. "The ruler supposedly ordered to kill Mehmed Pasha for a completely different reason!"

"Really? And what was that?"

"It was supposedly about a rebellion, some kind of a plot, gentlemen."

"Ooooh!"

"Oh, indeed! You know about the palace that the Vizier Pasha ordered to erect at Demirkapi."

Everyone nodded their heads in confirmation. Even the Sultan did not have such a palace yet.

"Everyone said that whether it is a praiseworthy thing or not, the guy has money. He can afford that. Except that the truth was somewhere else. As it turned out, the Grand Vizier extorted all this money from a certain Jew by threatening him. Before, the poor fellow had kept his mouth shut out of fear, but finally, he'd had enough and sent his woman to Mahpeyker Kösem Sultan. He said, 'let the ruler know that the Grand Vizier had dug a secret passage in the basement into the Sultan's harem. One night when you, Lady, Prince Osman, and the Sultan's daughters will be sleeping, he will strike at our master.'"

"For God's sake! Really?!"

"What a traitor!"

"Some people!"

"The things that happen without our knowledge!"

"Maybe he even thought that he would become a Padishah, this dissembler? A Dervish dynasty in place of the Ottomans?"

"Well, and thus he paid with his life for the treason."

"But are you sure that's true? The man refused to die, and the Sultan personally slew him?"

"I swear to God, that's what someone told me. He saw it with his own eyes. One of the executioners reportedly later came over and tore Mehmed's head from the neck. I only pass on here what I heard."

'Just look at the Khan Ahmed now, and we all called him a youngster,' it was said during days in all the wine bars and cafes. 'And what a brave man, how daring! This great Pasha, like a sheep... We need to take it all back!'

Whoever was talking, people listened and believed.

The name Mahpeyker Kösem Sultan was as frequent in these discussions as Sultan Ahmed's. Once, it was the beauty of the Padishah's favorite that was talked about, but now people began to praise her wisdom.

They would say things like:

"It's thanks to her that our master acts like that."

"'My Kösem,' – that's the only way the Sultan calls her, my companions."

"He's forgotten about the one who gave him the successor. In his head, there is only Kösem."

The rumor about how the Sultan condemned his Grand Vizier to death or actually killed him himself wasn't the only one that found itself on people's tongues. The gossip that sped through the city from mouth to mouth was that on that same day at the Divan meeting, the ruler had passed the seal of the highest office, from out of all the terrified viziers' control, to Murad Pasha.

Nobody cared how much truth there was to this, and it wasn't important who spread the rumors because neither did anyone ask how these stories reached the streets. If it was talked about, everything was in place.

What Padishah said, giving the seal of the office to the man who was to be the new Grand Vizier from now on, was also important. After all, his words contained hints as to what would happen to people in the future. How much will a dirham of silver cost? How many units will be used to mint akçe? Will new taxes will be imposed, or is a new campaign approaching? – Everything was in his words. For many days, people talked about what Sultan Ahmed said to Murad Pasha, a man already in his nineties when he entrusted him with the office at the bloody deliberations of the Divan.

"Our master," someone began, "was still kneeling beside the headless body of Mehmed Pasha when he roared: 'Where is Serdar Murad Pasha, who signed the agreement with Austrian giaur in Zittau??'"

"Oh, I bet the man's heart went to his throat, brother. 'It's my turn to lose my head,' right?"

Everyone chortled at these words.

"Sure, he was scared out of his mind, who wouldn't be?" someone said. "If they were to cut off my head, I'd soil my... "

"Enough," the man who brought the message cut the laughter short. "He wasn't supposed to lose his head, but to cut them off."

"Heads, heads! What would it be like in the country if the heads were not rolling?"

"Listen! Pasha came in front of the line with a pale face, and the Sultan raised his right hand up and asked: 'What's in my hand, Pasha?'"

"So, what was in his hand?"

"Nothing. All the viziers and agas, and Murad Pasha along with them, were shocked. Is it possible to say to the ruler: 'There is nothing there?' Nobody said so. Murad Pasha also stands quietly and just looks around. And our master said in a loud voice: 'The Qur'an. What I hold in my right hand is the word of Allah.' The man who told me this said that at that moment, the eyes of the Padishah filled with tears."

All the regulars, whispering, were still imagining this scene when the narrator went on:

"After a moment, our Lord lifted his left hand and said to Murad Pasha: 'And what do you see in this one?' This one was also empty. Everyone on the council shivered with a cold sweat, thinking how much fury can follow the question of the Padishah — because everyone has already learned that when Sultan Ahmed starts asking questions, it means that things are going in the wrong direction. Murad Pasha, like everyone else, lowered his head in a bow. And how do you think, what did our Lord say?"

The elaborate narrative exhausted the patience of the groggy patrons of the winery. Someone said: "How are we supposed to know that, sir? Who are you, Sultan Ahmed, that you're grilling us here like this? 'What did the Padishah say?' Come on, spit out what he said already!"

The room filled with laughter, which fell silent as soon as the man spoke with all his might.

"A lightning bolt!"

"A lightning bolt?"

"Exactly, a lightning bolt. Our ruler announced it just that way. 'Look, Pasha,' he said. 'You've seen a lot in life. Your life was passed serving the Sublime Porte. Maybe you're not young anymore, but no one has your experience. But remember well, in my right hand I hold the word of Allah, and the anger of heaven rests on my left one. This is the weapon of Sultan Ahmed. And now...' The ruler looked at all the ministers in turn and said: 'I make you a Great Vizier, Murad Pasha! I'm handing to you the weapon I'm holding. Starting today, you will hit the ruffians with the Qur'an in the right hand and with a lightning bolt in the left. Rule fairly, but for a traitor, a bandit, a thief, a villain, do not have mercy! Save no one. Put an end to this chaos. Chop up wicked people – you can leave behind stacks of heads, so long as you save the Ottoman state from this misfortune. If it fails, you will fill the dried wells with bandits as a warning for the world, and no one will rise up against our power anymore.'"

When the words of the Padishah were heard in the wine bar, the listeners shook with an unpleasant shudder.

"Damn it!" someone said.

The drunken story-teller was pleased with the impression his story caused. "Not 'damn it,' sir," he said quietly. "'Woe,' you should say, 'woe!'"

But the news that would really cause lament among people began to come only after the Great Vizier Mehmed Pasha set out on an expedition to defeat the rebels.

Murad Pasha completed the order to the letter, and when it wasn't enough, he surpassed even the Sultan's commands in severity. He beat without mercy. He struck like a thunderbolt, he burned like fire from heaven. Wherever he passed, heads fell from shoulders, and there was not a stone left unturned.

Even the capital shook with the fear he instilled. People in cafes and wine bars listened with bated breath to the provincial visitors.

"You will see, gentlemen, what Murad Pasha can do. It was as if he wasn't a ninety-year-old, but a brave man with the first shadow of a mustache. He beats these robbers mercilessly. What a battle cry he has, how he swings a sword and a mace, man! Oh, and the head of his mace? I swear, it's at least as big as my head. And the spikes on it, that long!"

As the narrator said these words, he made it a custom to point to his head while telling the story, and when it got to the mace's spikes, he'd use his index finger to give the listeners a sense of horror. When the storyteller decided that everyone already imagined the deadly weapon properly, he'd continue:

"Whenever this Murad Pasha takes a swing, no matter whether it's a head, a shoulder, they're shattered like a watermelon, my dear. And besides, when a brawler sees him, he gets weak in his knees at once. He immediately throws himself to the ground and begs for mercy. Only who would listen to him?"

"But if he doesn't listen to him, then what does he do? How can he raise the sword at a capitulator?"

"That's right, he does that. Murad Pasha makes the cut and heads fall. And when the commander mows the heads, the Janissaries aren't going to just stand there and look. God knows, I saw it with my own eyes! I will tell you, a thousand heads, but maybe even ten thousand. That's how it is. Horses can't even gallop because of the skulls rolling on the ground."

"Oh God! Dear God!"

"Wait, I'm not done yet. Shortly after the battle, the Pasha orders to collect the heads and heap piles of them. Oh, I swear, there is a place called Gökçesu. One man counted them, and he got two hundred and fifty mounds. And if there are two, three hundred heads in each... then add for yourself, and you will find out how many people were killed in this one field only."

Someone broke the silence that fell over the terrified crowd.

"What about headless bodies? What are they doing with them? Does Murad Pasha leave them to wolves and ravens to devour?"

"Oh no! He tells the people to collect them and throw them into a well. The people lament that blood flows from the well instead of water. Women cry, pull their hair out, and the Pasha Murad is now called 'The Well-digger.' People talk about our Pasha and talk, and believe me, these are not nice things."

# CHAPTER SEVEN

Beylerbeyi Palace
July 9th, 1611

With time, the specter of horror that Well-Digger Pasha caused was even reflected in the rumors of the girls from the sultan's harem. The odalisques' eyes were wide open when they listened to the stories. On the day Mahpeyker Kösem Sultan heard the mention of the book and the lightning, she understood that the Padishah had remembered well the dream she had told him. She was pleased that she'd managed to produce the effect she was expecting, but slowly anxiety began to sneak into her heart.

In fact, she knew a lot more than what reached the people, and when she was alone with her own conscience, she admitted to herself that Murad Pasha was out of control.

She didn't let it show, but as the news reached her, her fears began to grow. Knowing that the dream, which she had told to the Padishah, was involved in the whole affair, did not make things any better.

*Do not think about it,* a voice whispered in her head. *It's impossible to defend this throne any other way. Besides, you told him to be a thunderbolt – not to allow killing tens of thousands of people by someone who considers it a divine service. And didn't you want to protect the Majesty from the troublemakers by any means? Well, here you go, the man protects it. If it goes on like this, soon there will be no one left in the nation to rebel. Leave it alone, and let the Well-Digger kill them all.*

For the first time, she thought that her mind was wrong. In the past, her heart and mind often disagreed, and she always chose the path of reason. Except now, for the first time, the paths of prudence and heart have diverged so much. Mahpeyker didn't want to be known as the one who, always in black dresses, makes the Padishah ruthless and cruel. In the long run, it could turn everything upside down. The people should remember her name with love, and not with fear and disgust. *Alims, soldiers, merchants, villagers -- everybody alive should love his queen*, she said to herself – at least until she has enough power.

But she knew that it was necessary to take control of this crazy old man who, on the orders of the Sultan, now brought terror wherever he appeared. Rumors should be cut short immediately, because the evil words that were thrown today at the Well-Digger, would hit the Padishah tomorrow, and from him, they would pass on Kösem, and she will be left with nothing but the hatred of the people.

One day, she caught a couple of courtiers secretly exchanging gossip. She heard one of them whisper: "They say blood was flowing from his chin."

"No way," objected the other, but it was obvious she believed it.

"For God's sake, girl, they say that he likes human meat. They bring him a piece of the youngest person killed on a given day, on a plate. I mean, a heart or something."

"Stop this rubbish," Mahpeyker interjected suddenly, "and don't babble nonsense. Whoever heard of eating human flesh? Who saw it? No one dares to repeat here the lies invented by the bandits."

"But he's apparently terribly ruthless," one of the women said. "He has no mercy even for those who surrender."

Mahpeyker raised her voice even more.

"And did these robbers have pity, that now, frightened by our Lord's wrath, they expect forgiveness? So, it wasn't bestiality when they burned villages and leveled towns, and were wiping out everybody, no matter whether old, women or children? And now, when the Ottoman Empire raises a grudging hand over their mountain hiding places, this is bestiality? I do not want to hear this nonsense here anymore!"

The courtiers fell silent and retreated, but it didn't help, and the girl who told how Murad Pasha tears the hearts of fallen youths to devour them, disappeared two days later.

Everything was boiling in Sultan Ahmed, too. Actually, he didn't want to hear one word about Murad Pasha's penal expedition. Under the influence of Mahpeyker's dream, he devoted himself entirely to charity. On the one hand, he dealt with the mosque, whose construction was started on his command on the Hippodrome, while on the other hand, he sent various specialists from the capital to make necessary repairs in the holy places of Mecca and Medina.

He ordered people to prepare such upholstery and curtains the likes that have never seen before for their most sacred place of Islam – the temple in Mecca – the Al-Kaba. So, in total, eight hundred meters of cloth and forty-eight thousand dirhems of silk were given for sewing. The curtains, composed of hundreds of parts, eighteen thousand miskals of golden wire and four hundred and sixty miskals of silver ones, were smelted. He became so involved in these matters that he ordered to transformation the garden of the Beylerbeyi palace into an outdoor workshop, then he called the best blacksmiths and goldsmiths of the capital there. He entrusted the task of assessing the prepared curtains for Al-Kaba to Kösem – whom he believed was a sincere believer and had never been late for prayer even once since the day she'd converted to Islam.

Ahmed ordered to create a life-size model of the Al-Kaba in the gardens of Davud Pasha, and from then on, he went there each day to sit with the feeling of God's fear in the shadow cast by the model, say prayers, and to call Allah.

Except, as news of recent events settled in his head, fears began to slowly grow in him that Murad Pasha's deeds tarnish the good name of the faith. In the end, it had been him who sent the old man to the provinces and wanted the man to strike the bandits with a spear of lightning. *If what is told is true, do my prayers have any meaning?* he asked himself.

One night, when he went to Mahpeyker's rooms, he didn't even hide that something troubled him.

"Eh, eh," he sighed constantly.

Although Mahpeyker understood the reason for these groans right away, she was silent. When Padishah was eating, he began to speak – she knew he'd touch on the subject sooner or later. And that's what happened. The Sultan suddenly fired the question:

"Tell me, my beautiful Kösem, what do you think? In the face of Allah, is right on the side of the one who, in the name of order and unity, takes life, and commits cruelty? What do you say?"

Mahpeyker became serious.

"My Lord, you are putting your maid to such test that it is not possible to give the right answer. How much time has passed since the light of Islam has flowed into Mahpeyker? What can she tell our Sultan? It's best to ask the Hodja Efendi. He will know."

Ahmed sighed inwardly. *Right, he'll know, only that it is on my command that the Grand Vizier is raising mounds out of heads. Wells don't give water, but blood, while we spend time on philanthropy and prayers here. How can I ask if a prayer will erase the sin of cruelty?*

"Well," he murmured, "you are a neophyte, your faith is purer because it flows straight from the heart. Tell me, Mahpeyker, can a prayer erase the sin of cruelty?"

Mahpeyker understood at this moment that the fate of Murad Pasha the Well-Digger depended on two words. *If I say: 'It can't,' this will be the end of the big Pasha,* passed through her head. But cutting to the chase with a simple, *it can,* didn't look convincing. At first, she panicked. If Ahmed was so worried about the feats of the Grand Vizier, he might have thought that the dream she'd apparently seen started the whole thing. *Look and think what does it bring you to? I have a thunderbolt in one hand and a book in the other. Alright, but what's going on here? Where is justice, where is mercy here?* He could accuse her. She was trying to smile.

"If only I knew the reason for this question..."

"The reason is obvious. Murad Pasha," snarled the Padishah. "He needs pages to get on his horse already, and when he gets off it, it's in their arms. Only that this white-bearded, old man, despite his condition, suddenly comes to life in the saddle and sow's death among my people."

"Did you say, 'my people,' sir?"

"I did. What else could I say?"

"Your maid thought it was about robbers. Aren't these the bestial rebels? A cruel man deserves to be handled with cruelty."

Ahmed looked at Mahpeyker without a word. How was the ruler different from a criminal, if he responded to barbarity with barbarity? *Damn it*, he swore in his mind. *Why haven't I thought about it earlier? It was me who gave the order to kill. And Murad killed. This means that if a man in power says 'Hit,' it makes his servants, on the very bottom of the ladder, look like monsters.*

"Tell me, honestly," he whispered. "Shouldn't one act fairly? Ask questions, separate the guilty from innocent?"

"Forgive me, sir, does it mean that the mighty Pasha cuts heads without judgment?"

"What judgment?" Ahmed growled. His face was bitter. "He hits the bandits with the army because the rebel troops come out to face him. Except that among them there are both volunteers, and people taken by force. Poor people, who seem to be on the side of criminals out of fear. But when the two sides close in a fight, there is no place for justice or judgments. Pasha chops with his sword, and strikes with the mace."

Mahpeyker got scared, noting that the Sultan's face became suddenly pale.

"My lord... you're pale. Have some water. If you didn't worry so much..."

But it seemed that Ahmed did not hear her.

"I heard only today," he murmured to himself. "Pasha saw a spahis pacing the battlefield. A local kid was sitting behind his saddle. When Murad Pasha asked him, 'What were you doing among the rebels?' The boy replied that his father had no job and that he had joined the bandits because of lack of money. Then our Grand Vizier asked what the father of the kid was doing. 'He played music on his oud' the other replied. 'You say that by providing entertainment to the rebels, he gave them courage,' Murad Pasha had said angrily. Mahpeyker, I was terrified when I heard that the Pasha ordered the henchmen to kill the child. They were pitying him: 'Why should we murder an innocent?' They objected, so he called for soldiers, but they also got angry: 'Do we look like executioners? Even if there were an executioner here, he wouldn't stain his hands with the blood of the innocent child.' This time the Vizier Pasha turned to the pages who helped him dismount the horse, but they also scattered. 'In that case,' Murad Pasha raged, 'I will be the executioner of faith,' and he strangled this poor boy with his bare hands. Can you imagine that, Mahpeyker? With his hands. Bare hands. A child."

The pale Padishah fell silent after his story. Mahpeyker hurriedly brought him sorbet, and he was so dazed, that when he put the drink down from his lips, it dripped down his chin. His wife immediately jumped to wipe it, but the Sultan didn't seem to notice it at all.

"And then Murad Pasha shouted to my soldiers: 'You cowards! The bandits did not get out of their mothers with swords in their hands. Everyone had been like this kid. But they grew up in vice. They stayed on the side of evil. None of you have heard how apples make each other go bad? I will tell you then. By looking at each other. The innocent have become criminals. There is no other way to burn the root of evil. When the hunter climbs the high rocks, hunting a deer, he must take advantage of its wounded leg.' Nice words. Suggestive words. Except, it was about the child he killed. Stifled by him without one thought – guilty or not..." The tone of the Sultan's voice hardened. "And that's why I am asking you," he continued strongly, "will anything good come from this brutality?"

Mahpeyker was terrified, too. She couldn't even imagine a ninety-year-old man strangling a tiny boy's neck. If she said, 'Yes,' she would show that she'd sold her soul to the devil, and if she said, 'No,' she would give the death sentence on Murad Pasha. She had to get rid of the problem and close the topic immediately. Reason murmured in her head: *A cruel man, but he quelled the uprising. No one will dare to oppose the Ottoman state anymore.*

She looked into Ahmed's eyes, and her fear grew even more. The Padishah's gaze was burning. It was a matter of minutes to give orders to add Murad The Well-Digger's head to the rest on the top of one of the mounds.

"Let the servant punish the bestiality. Let's not forgive a cruel man."

"I think so too, Mahpeyker..."

"Except what should be done with the executioner of the nation? Can you forgive the cruelty of bandits on our subjects? God forbid, what if the flame of revolt would have grown even more and reached the Ottoman dynasty? What would happen to your people? It is certain that if the rebels came to power, the position of the subjects would be deplorable. Isn't consent to such a thing an even greater sin?"

A doubt arose in the Sultan. *Yes*, he said in spirit. *It's a sin, of course. And if tomorrow was the Last Judgment, and Osman Gazi, Orchan Gazi, Hüdavendigar, Mehmed the Conqueror, Selim The Grim, Suleiman the Legislator, my blessed memory grandfather, and father, and all the dead came out in front of me in a row and they asked: 'What have you done, Ahmed? How could you have let the Ottoman family be endangered?' What would I say?*

At first, he felt relief. Thanking Kösem in his mind for being there, he looked at her with affection. And gratitude.

"So, you say that brave men, should sharpen swords against the cruelty of robbers, right?"

Mahpeyker did not repeat his words.

"Ah, my mighty Sultan," Kösem sweet-talked, "my handsome poet, the ruler of the world! What is your maid to say with her feminine reason? May the reign of our master, and with it, the happiness and serenity of the Ottoman family, last forever. Maybe this is the way if your successor, Osman, is to receive the throne and a dominion worth remembering."

Both sank in their thoughts.

Sultan Ahmed tried to convince himself that the savagery that was allowed to ensure the happiness of the state would not be ascribed to him as a sin. He remembered what Mahpeyker had said about the heritage for Osman. Something fluttered inside him. *Kösem's heart is as big as her mind* he thought. *She hates Mahfiruz, but look, she is preparing the throne for her son. And Mahfiruz makes her a devil when she talks or writes to me.*

Padishah decided to put the matter out of his head for the time being. *Let Murad Pasha serve us a bit more at least*, he said in his mind. *And later we will see.*

And everyone saw, indeed. Murad Pasha, called The Well-Digger, cut off heads and filled wells with corpses for a few more months, and when most of the riots were stopped, he returned to the capital to celebrate the victory, and soon after died of old age.

In his place, the Sultan appointed Serpa Nasuh Pasha from Komotini, who had fought effectively in Austria, as the next Great Vizier. There were also those who claimed that Kösem had an influence on the Sultan's decision to name Nasuh Pasha, who was against the cruelty of The Well-Digger, for the highest position, and thus cool some of the anger that great slaughter had caused in people.

"Ha, the Greek Sultana, it's obvious she will stand behind the Komotinian. Greek here, and Bulgarian there," such words circulated in the state.

But neither the Padishah nor Mahpeyker paid any attention to that. Their thoughts were in a completely different place.

Summer 1611 bought a terrible heatwave and Mahpeyker, having gathered the retinue, withdrew to the Beylerbeyi Palace. She decided to devote herself some time to do some thinking, away from the curious eyes.

She was pregnant again. Who knows if it was finally fate that gave in to Mahpeyker's will, or whether her prayers were answered. Or maybe the muskas – the triangular amulets she wore with spells or prayers locked inside – or the blessed waters from the Hodjas and medicine men, found by Semiha, proved useful for something.

One day, as she wandered in the rose garden, enjoying the feeling of the gentle evening breeze on her cheeks, she thought to herself: *Counting the miscarriage, this will be the fourth already.* She wasn't even saddened by the loss of a child. *It was also probably a girl...*

This time, she didn't feel the excitement swirling inside, either. Presumably, again she won't give birth to a boy.

But that's not what happened. On one hellishly hot July night, a message came to the Padishah in the New Palace that contractions had started for Mahpeyker Kösem Sultan. Prepared for this, midwives and their supervisor gathered at the headboard of her bed.

The delivery room was hotter than hell. Mahpeyker didn't remember to have experienced such tortures even during her first delivery. For four days and four nights, she writhed in pain. Her hands were all covered in blood, from when she bit them to stop herself from screaming. She finally started thinking she would die in the arms of the midwives. The midwives were terrified. Sophia's tears were coming down in streams. Semiha, Müruvvet, and Şarazad didn't want to betray their feelings, but their panicked eyes spoke volumes for themselves.

The whole situation, properly worded, was described to the Sultan. The ruler, who was stumbling over his own feet from constantly walking in circles around his gallery, ordered the court medics to come as soon as possible, and they indeed appeared quickly, all sweaty.

"Run to the Beylerbeyi Palace immediately! I want my child, together with its mother, to be safe and sound. If the Lord allows it, save my Mahpeyker!" Ahmed ordered the doctors, who rubbed their hands from nervousness.

The doctor's supervisor looked desperately at his assistants, while everyone ran as fast as they could into the courtyard, where prepared carriages waited for them.

One of the young physicians said what went through his head: "Well... but what if God's will is to take the woman and leave the child? What will we do then? Shall we tell Azrael, 'Take the baby and leave his mother to us? Our Lord needs her alive and well in his bed!' Is that what we should say?"

"You'll think what to say later. Now, hitch up your robes and run to the Beylerbeyi Palace. Otherwise, we will not even have time to greet Azrael," panted the master doctor.

During these four days and four nights, all her life passed before Mahpeyker's eyes – only everything was strange in it. She still saw herself as little Nastya from Milos; her bare feet kicking in the foam of the blue waves on her family's island, and even when she remembered the night when the Padishah made her his wife.

Suddenly the blind man from Kumanovo appeared at her head. The man laughed like a hyena... He made no sound, but Mahpeyker read the words from the movement of his twisted lips.

'Don't be afraid,' said the beggar. 'You still have much to see, girl.'

*What can I possibly see?* her mind objected. *I'm dying.*

'No,' the mouth said soundlessly. 'You're giving birth.'

*What, what am I giving birth to? A girl again?*

The blind beggar disappeared as quickly as he had appeared.

Mahpeyker, cursing, burst out crying. *It means, a girl again... A girl again!*

"You can do it, girl," a woman whispered in her ear.

"Come on, come on, push!" another one kept saying.

Mahpeyker felt a terrible weight on her stomach. An overwhelming, crushing weight, leaving her breathless. There was a terrible cry inside her.

*Azrael! Azrael sat on me!*

She didn't even have the strength to blink her eyelashes. With difficulty, after many attempts, as if through a mist, she saw what was crushing her and breathed a sigh of relief. *Not Azrael, it's not Azrael*, she said in her mind. *Two giant women are leaning on my stomach.*

*Come on, Mahpeyker Kösem Sultan*, she said to herself. *Last effort! You were supposed to fight death. This is the moment. Keep your word! Hold on, fight! Go on!*

Suddenly, a respite came. She suddenly felt herself begin to roll straight into the dark abyss. From a distance, from far away, her ear caught the most beautiful voice she had ever heard. *It's an angel calling me,* she said to herself.

And when she thought she was about to die, her mind shouted, *Get a grip! I beg you, pull yourself together. At least find out what you gave birth to.*

"What?" She did not even know if she managed to whisper it.

Before she fell into the darkness, it seemed to her that she heard the voice of the midwives' superior:

"Run, go! Let someone bring the good news to our Lord. Sultana Mahpeyker..."

*Son! Did I give birth to a son? My prince?*

*Yes,* said the voice in her head. *You can die now!*

*No!* her mind shouted back. *Now I really must live!*

"Bring me, my son... My God..." she moaned when they brought him. "Can there be something more beautiful?"

She took a tiny pink creature in her arms and inhaled her child's scent for the first time. Her son looked at his mother for the first time. The mother's tear joined the droplets on his pink cheeks.

"Welcome, my Sultan," Mahpeyker said to her son. "Your mother will give her life for you."

This time, when she was floating away, she saw Safiye Sultan at the headboard. She had a serious face.

'Do not forget my last will, daughter,' she said quietly. 'Do not dare be late. Do not act too soon or too late. Mind the time.'

She will mind it. From today on. And she will not be late. She will not start acting too soon or too late.

"I kept my word," she whispered, laying her head on the pillow. "The ring has not come off the finger. Why do I say it? You know it already. Is she with you? Have you two made peace?" Mahpeyker felt her thoughts fly away like butterflies for a moment. She didn't know if she really spoke them or they were just in her head, but before she fainted, she was going to tell Safiye Sultan something else. She had to tell her. "Do you know, my noble Mother? I gave birth to the Padishah today. He is so strong, so powerful, he manages to do everything right away. Do you remember your last words? 'People in the empire called me a Great Sultana Mother, let them call you Mahpeyker Kösem Sultan.' They call me that, dear Mother. I am Mahpeyker Kösem of the Ottomans. My word to India, to China..."

She felt a cold touch on her forehead. She didn't even notice the efforts of Sofia, who tried to cool her forehead with wet gauze. She was sinking into darkness and peace.

"She's raving," someone whispered. "Raving from fever."

A veil rose before her eyes. Everything was dark, except a bright point at the front, far ahead of her. She dreamed of going straight to this light.

"Mahpeykeeeer!"

She was surprised. It was as if the voice came to her from stars, clouds, from the sun. *Who are you?* she thought. *I've never heard you before.*

'I,' said the voice, 'am the fate against which you rebelled, daughter.'

She got scared. *What do you want?* she said in her mind. *You came to settle things?*

'I came to warn you, Mahpeyker. Calm down now. Hole up somewhere and wait for your time to come. Your hour will come. From now on, you are on guard.'

*On guard? What guard?*

'Of the Padishah. Murad's. Bring up the Great Sultan for the Ottoman family.'

She felt she was flowing happily through the darkness to meet the light. *I promise, fate. I stand on guard starting today,* went through her head. *So, I will do it. I will give brave Murad Khan to Ottomans!*

The sound of the city's herald drums after the morning ezan brought the streets of Istanbul to their feet: dum, dum, de dum, dum...

"Hear, people! A son was born to our Padishah and Lord, Sultan Ahmed Khan! Our Lord granted the boy, born from Mahpeyker Kösem Sultan, the following names. The holy name of Shahid – and Ghazi. Then Murad Khan, the name of his grandfather, whose place is in heaven, Sultan Murad Khan. May Allah send our ruler and Prince Murad health, prosperity, and long life! We welcome our new Prince Shahid Ghazi Murad Khan."

In the morning, the Padishah appeared at the Divan, almost flying with joy.

"Let them write," he ordered, "here is my decree: from today on, without exception, the helm of power will be given to the first-born prince. Let them write it! Here is my decree: let them observe the rule that the eldest one in dynasty will take the throne. Here's my decree! Let them write: from now it is unacceptable that in order to seize the throne, a brother would take his brother's life, the son his father's, father his son's, and a proper punishment is ordered accordingly..."

All the Viziers opened their mouths in surprise. The Padishah, whom all of them regarded as a child at one time, had just trampled on and rejected the heritage of the Fatih, the Law of Right of State. This was an Ottoman 'World Order,' created by Mehmed II the Conqueror, according to which it was necessary to kill all rivals from the family to preserve the unity of the State and the security of power!

"Ahhh," the second Vizier, Mehmed Pasha, called Buffalo, blurted out, "who would have thought that surly Mahfiruz would bring to her knees the one chosen by the Sultan, Kösem Sultan, and her newly born son, eh?"

Instead of scolding him, the Great Vizier Nasuh Pasha just gave him a dirty look.

When they were leaving the council, Mehmed Pasha whispered, "After all, Mahfiruz Sultan must be behind this decree. The right of the eldest to the throne, ha, and yet the first two princes are the children of Mahfiruz. First Osman, then Mehmed. Mahfiruz closed the path to the throne for Kösem's son. It is a pity for Prince Murad – he will go to the sand without seeing the throne. And they say that our Lord is so very much in love, and look – he has erased the right of his favorite with one stroke of the pen.

And Kösem Sultan was so clever, huh? Apparently not smart enough for this game. What a helplessness!"

Nasuh Pasha glanced at the second Vizier without saying a word. Mehmed Pasha, seeing the secretive smile on the man's face, began to suspect something.

"What is this, mighty Pasha? Why are you laughing, is there something you know about?"

"What laughter? Who is laughing?"

"Eh, they don't call me Buffalo by accident. I don't understand anything. Could there be something wrong with this decree, Nasuh Pasha?"

The Grand Vizier caught the skirts of his robe with an expression that only heightened the suspicions of the Second Vizier.

"Do not be ridiculous, dear Pasha. What can be wrong here?" He looked into the other man's eyes with malicious joy. "It looks to me like Mahpeyker Kösem is very happy that her son will not become a Sultan."

Despite this allusion, Mehmed Pasha continued to look at Nasuh with a veal's look, and the great Vizier thought they didn't call him Buffalo for nothing. In the end, he couldn't stand it.

"Come on! Let's leave this talk and go. And maybe roll up your robe, because it'll get dirty and stinky."

Everyone was talking about the joy of Mahpeyker Kösem Sultan. She became even more beautiful and was outright crazy with happiness. She took Murad in her arms and, like a butterfly, flew with him through the rose garden of the Beylerbeyi Palace.

However, after some time she began to notice something strange. Sometimes Prince Murad was getting all red in his swaddling clothes. In one moment, his mouth would close, the child would freeze and his tiny head on a thin neck, would sway insanely, left and right.

When the first symptoms appeared, she told herself that it was impossible. Fate can not be so merciless, after all!

One day, when Murad reddened again, she cried to the nurse: "Take him away! Take my son out of the swaddling clothes, fast!"

They did. The infant, released from the restraining clothes, began to tremble horribly. From the corner of his mouth, foam poured straight onto his pink arm.

They watched helplessly, with tears in their eyes.

Eventually, the convulsions slowed. Prince Murad's face, stretched in pain, tensed, and his cheeks became even pinker. Kösem leaned over the baby.

"My Khan, my Prince, dear Murad, what happened to you?"

The son rewarded his mother with a beautiful, "goo, goo," and a smile that showed dimples in his cheeks.

"Doctor," whispered one of the nurses, overcoming panic. "Let's call the doctors, My Lady."

"I don't want to. There's no need." Mahpeyker made the diagnosis herself. *My son has epilepsy! What can the medic do?*

She remembered how one night in a dream she had seen Mahfiruz giving birth to the bloodied children. Oh, how happy she was!

*I wonder if she also dreamed that I would give birth to an epileptic*, the thought flashed across her mind. *Was she happy?*

Her heart was bleeding.

# CHAPTER EIGHT

### The New Palace, Sultan Gallery
### Spring 1615

After the morning prayers, the Viziers began to gather one after the other, in the courtyard of the Sultan Gallery. Nobody spoke to anyone, but both scientists and soldiers felt a little anxious.

Padishah went out completely changed. As soon as he learned the little prince was an epileptic, he did not appear outside for many days. He never left Mahpeyker's rooms.

Doctors came and went, but they all gave the same diagnosis. "Our Lord, Prince Murad suffers from epilepsy."

And when the question was asked if there was any medicine for this disease, they gave the same response.

There wasn't!

It was such a torment that it couldn't be concealed.

And so, within a week, the news of the epilepsy of the little prince first arrived from the palace to the Sea Pavilion, and from there it spread throughout the capital.

"Well, well," said Mahfiruz to the courtiers that brought her the message. "God, what a punishment for his mother, it would have been better if she had not given birth to him at all."

Sultan Ahmed sank into sorrow, but stifling his own despair, he tried to support the ever-crying Mahpeyker, who stopped eating and drinking.

"What can we do?" he said. "Our Lord has decided so, but Allah does not allow you to give up hope. God, who sends suffering, also gives a cure to it."

A cure? But there wasn't any!

Mahpeyker finally stopped crying. Rebellious against fate, she finally abandoned complaints, too. She stopped tormenting herself and asked herself, *who knows what Mahfiruz says?* She didn't even ask, *what did this devil say?*

She didn't let Murad out of her embrace and did not put the prince into diapers anymore. Mahpeyker's son moved and stretched freely in his cradle, and when an attack came, he had convulsions under her watchful gaze.

*If he is an epileptic, let him be*, Mahpeyker dismissed unpleasant thoughts. *He is my Prince. My Khan. My Murad. My Sultan.*

She hid her suffering in the deepest recesses of her soul.

Sultan Ahmed, in turn, devoted himself to the affairs of the state again, and the first thing he did was an introduction of a prohibition – a decision which caused panic in the capital.

Ahmed abolished the Alcohol Society and ordered the closure of all wine bars. According to the people, it was the worst thing he could do. Wineries were a place where accumulated anger was discharged, where people relaxed among jokes and gossip. Maybe while doing that they did make mountains out of molehills, but they also learned about everything that was happening in the Ottoman state. Words of complaint came from every throat, and the loudest came from janissaries and sahis, who often participated in boozing. Merchants and craftsmen lost not only satisfaction but also income.

"What was our fault, that the Padishah found it necessary to treat us this way?" The complaints were endless. "Doesn't the Sultan know that the winery is our eyes, ears, and tongue? Or maybe he prefers to be the ruler of the blind, deaf and mute? Let him say, we want to know!"

The rage against the ban spread so much that it gave rise to poems and songs. In particular, the two verses of an unknown author passed from mouth to mouth in every corner of the empire:

'They ruined the winery like the heart of a lover.

A wine glass is now a symbol of a wedding.'

And so, all the devotion of Sultan Ahmed, his charitable activity, and even gold and silver handed out to the people on the Night of Innocence and Destiny, were gone into oblivion.

Rumors and jokes whispered in the smoky, dark corners of wine cellars, loud laughter, and curses moved to the barracks and the cabins of warships. There was a rumor that Padishah, along with Mahpeyker Kösem Sultan, had gone to Edirne for the winter, where he was going to partake in deer hunting, only added fuel to the fire.

"Here we go, gentlemen," janissaries whispered in the corners, "the Safavids' Shah has thrown the messenger of our Padishah, Mustafa Chavush, to the dungeons, and this guy chases the deer? When will he finally remove the sword from the sheath? Is it appropriate that he sent slaves to the border for death, while himself playing with a woman in bed?"

But although the Sultan and Mahpeyker heard every rumor and every whisper, nothing was able to overshadow their happiness. The Sultan's boat was transferred by land from the capital to Edirne, and Sultan

Ahmed could soothe his nerves, floating on the Danube, with Mahpeyker softly singing at his side. He handed her ice sorbet with his own hands.

*Hold on, my heart*, Mahpeyker told herself as news from the capital and the things that were said about her kept reaching her. *Do not hear. Do not see. Let my tongue be silent. I promised my fate that I would guard the Padishah. I closed my heart, mind, and soul to everyone. I raise brave Murad Khan for the Ottoman dynasty so that his mind would be sharper than his sword, and the sword sharper than the mind. I will weave my web until the right time comes. And when the hour strikes, I will launch the attack."*

That's what she was going to do. Never be late, nor to act too early. All at the right time, she will strike while the iron will be hot. Neither too early nor too late.

But how was she to understand when the right time would come? When she said to herself: 'Now, go on!' she was afraid that Mahfiruz would understand, like Safiye Sultan, that she could act quickly. She'd seen many times, that death was the price of being late. But the opposite was also true: what would she do if she were too early, thinking that the right moment had come? She would pay the same price – with her own life!

Meanwhile, Sultan Ahmed thought that Mahpeyker rejoiced at Edirne like a lark. After she gave birth to his son, she became a completely different woman. Stately, calm, and much more mature. And although she'd given birth to three children at this stage, she'd become even more beautiful. He gazed lovingly at his wife's pretty face and whispered the last verses she had written for her. Padishah was completely absorbed by the woman's thoughtful smile, her sweet words, and the harmony of poems he composed.

"My Lady," said Ahmed, laying his head on Mahpeyker's chest, "you are more beautiful today than ever, but above all, more thoughtful and absent than ever."

Mahpeyker was arguing with her own mind at that moment. *The trick is this*, her mind told her. *To predict when what will happen.*

*But how will you predict that? How will you understand it?*

"Mahpeyker? My soaring cypress?"

"Does My Lord need something?" she heard the voice of the Sultan, but during her thought dissertation, his words did not reach her.

"I said that you are more beautiful and thoughtful today than ever before."

She pulled herself together immediately. This time her smile was accompanied by a wistful, apologetic look.

"May the mighty Padishah forgive his maid. I drifted. I was thinking about our prince and his sisters."

Suddenly, a strange feeling woke up in Mahpeyker. She felt something like a shadow of worry in the Sultan's voice and eyes. *He didn't believe it*, she thought. *He did not believe me this time.*


A few days after returning from Edirne, Semiha announced to Mahpeyker that a tearful woman was asking for an audience.

"Couldn't she just tell you what she has to say?"

"I insisted, My Lady, but she only lowered her head and sobbed. Apparently, she has such a thing to say that she will only be able to get it out once in her life. And only in front of you."

The woman they had brought to Mahpeyker's presence, made a good impression on her. She was a little older but beautiful. *Sweet as sugar*, she thought. But she immediately noticed that there was a deep shame, and terrible suffering lurking in the eyes of the newcomer.

"I'm listening, my good woman. Tell me what's bothering you, and we'll try to find a solution."

"My husband comes from the Prophet's race," she said quietly. "One day, the governor of one of the statesmen... his name is Jebrail... he broke into my house and... and..."

Even from the place where she was sitting, Mahpeyker could see the red spots appear on her pale cheeks.

"I... I..." The wife of Sayyid sobbed once or twice, but her voice caught in her throat and tears flowed down her cheeks. She could not say anything further.

*There is no need anyway,* thought Mahpeyker.

"Did this man..." she said. "Did he...?"

She didn't finish, not to embarrass the woman even more. The Sayyid's wife nodded in confirmation.

For a moment, she didn't know what to say or what to do. The one who really should be ashamed was not. Humiliation, disgrace, lowering head in shame, was for some reason, almost always left to the assailed woman. *This world is distorted*, she complained in her mind. *If you were born a woman, you are already finished.*

Immediately, the scenes from the day she'd been kidnapped appeared before her eyes; Cyprian's assault, and how she'd bit off his ear; how a man, at whom her friend threw herself, fell over her, and how, among the screams of the girls, black-browed Kemal came to rescue and killed both bastards. The anger, dormant inside her, burned again. She stood up and stroked the head of the woman who was kneeling in front of her.

"Tell me," she said gently. "What can I do for you?"

The woman straightened up and looked at her with timid gratitude. She brushed her tears from her cheeks with the back of her hand.

"Forgive me, My Lady," she moaned. "What comes to mind, tongue... it's so..." She couldn't finish again.

This time, Mahpeyker patted the woman on the back.

"Come here, sit down at least," she said, showing her a place to sit. She waved her hand. "Bring us water. And put jasmine in it. Are you hungry, my good woman?"

Instead of answering, the guest shook her head – she was drinking water with shaky hands from the glass brought in by the courtier in a golden basket.

"What's your name?"

"Şaheste."

"Well, and whose servant is the man who did it? You forgot to say."

"I did not... for... forget..." stammered the woman. "I was afraid to say."

"Some big Lord?"

The woman bent her neck.

"Very big, right?"

The wife of Sayyid confirmed just by rubbing her eyes. Mahpeyker suddenly lost the control over her anger.

"Who, woman?" She raised her voice. "Whose manager is the one who did this to you?"

Seeing the lady's rage, the woman panicked. She looked at her side in fear that someone might hear, and then leaning forward, she whispered the name.

As soon as she heard the word, Mahpeyker withdrew her head. She was stunned.

"What do you demand from me, Şaheste? Don't be afraid to say."

"You see, My Lady," said the woman with difficulty. "The disgrace of the tragedy that happened to me wasn't enough. I'm still in fear even now... What happened to me, what Jebrail did... I told my husband... I mean, I had to. Isn't that right, My Lady? I had to tell him..."

"Of course. Did he treat you badly, too?"

"Oh no, Lady... he is a very good man. He never hurt me. He didn't hit me, he didn't say a bad word." She looked ahead with remorse on her face. "We just thought together what to do, we cried together. This man has connections, oh, what is a woman to do? She will take the blow, she will sit quietly. But is a man like that too? The man's anger looks different. It can not be suppressed so easily."

*And why is that*, Mahpeyker boiled inside. *A woman is supposed to sit quietly, and the man rages at will... And what about the fury of a woman? The woman is raped, but it is the man that gets furious.* She made a big effort to stop herself from saying: 'The anger of a woman can also be terrible. It should be so. To curse and annihilate. It should burn everything in its path like a conflagration.'

"My man," continued Şaheste, "ran amok. He said, 'It would be better if the Padishah ordered to cut my head than to live with such shame This Friday I will approach the Sultan when he will be entering the mosque. I will undo my turban and throw it at his feet. I will also say what I have on my mind.' As soon as he said it, he left... disappeared somewhere. He has not come back since that day. Eh, Lady, My Lady with a beautiful face and beautiful inside. Tomorrow's Friday. Hussein... Did I say my husband's name is Hussein? I have no idea what to do. Please, forgive me. If tomorrow Hussein does something unworthy in front of the Sultan, they will surely kill him... Help us, please!"

Mahpeyker tried to comfort the woman with a few broken words. She knew that whatever she said, would be useless. Şaheste won't only burn in pain and anger after being attacked, but she will also blame herself for tarnishing her husband's honor.

"A man's honor, a man's anger, huh," she murmured all day. She decided that even if the ruler does not come to her rooms in the evening, she would send a message and go to Ahmed.

But it was Sultan Ahmed who came. After eating a meal, the Padishah holed up in the corner of the couch prepared for him and leaned his back against the stuffed pillows. As usual, he put one knee under his chin and began to move the beads of a pearl tespihu.

Ahmed, not giving anything away, watched Mahpeyker's moves. He thought the woman didn't realize it, but she knew she was being observed. That evening, instead of a calm, balanced pose, which she always used to probe whether the Padishah was angry with something, she took on a completely different one. Her movements were quick, uncertain, sharp. Also, she didn't say anything to Ahmed during the meal, she did not make him laugh about what had happened during the day. She didn't even sing a song, though she knew how much he liked it.

"Do you have something to tell me?"

Mahpeyker did not beat around the bush.

"I have a problem, my Great Sultan. What would it mean to throw a turban at the Friday meeting?"

"In my presence, right?" When Ahmed saw that Mahpeyker was silent, he continued further. "Big insolence. 'Ha, you can take this turban and put it on your head. Being your subjects is incompatible with religion.' The punishment for this insult is severe."

"Is it death, My Lord?"

This time Ahmed was silent. He looked away.

"What if the one who dropped the turban is right?"

"Right? Oh, my beauty, the one who insults the Sultan, can not be right."

"And if he is, Ahmed? What then, my Sultan?"

Mahpeyker rushed to the couch where the Sultan was sitting, knelt before him, and told him what had happened to Saheste.

"I ask again: is it fair to kill a man who threw a turban?"

Ahmed looked at her for a long time without saying a word.


The next morning at a Friday ceremony in the mosque, a man in a white turban stepped out from the crowd. Looking Sultan Ahmed in the eye, he removed his head covering and threw it in front of him.

"Who should I complain to Allah about?" he shouted. "About you? About the one to whom you entrusted your seal and property? Or about the servant who is not ashamed to bring disgrace to his Lord or to you?"

The guards immediately rushed at the man and, catching his hands and legs, knocked him to the ground.

"Leave him alone!" the Padishah yelled at that moment. "I will cut the hand of the one who raises his hand at the subject seeking justice before us in the presence of Allah! Stay away!"

After the Friday service, the Sultan called the man to himself but did not disgrace him by asking about his grief.

"Go, Sayyid Hussein," he said. "Take your family and go to Bursa. I entrust to you the protection of my ancestors' graves. Look after them well. Let them be well cared for. May God Almighty hear your complaints. The penalty for the villain is now near. Come on, go! Go, so that we could do what is necessary."

Ahmed waited a week to do what was necessary. That Friday morning, people just got out the door, and they already sensed something strange was in the air. The soldiers created a living wall outside the embankments. The people who poured out onto the streets, expecting the exit of the Padishah from the mosque, and the few coins that were to be thrown, were disappointed because Sultan Ahmed did not show up after the Friday prayers. The mob watched with interest as the Sultan's guards came out from the palace, with the fringes of their conical hats dangling as they marched, and the battalion of soldiers following them. The squad quickly reached Paşakapısı.

Nasuh Pasha, still not understanding what was happening, was strangled by the guards rushing inside. He still struggled and shouted before he died: "Mercy! What did I do to deserve the Sultan's sentence?"

"Silence, degenerate!" The voice of one of the guardsmen seemed to pierce the sky and earth. "Instead of saying, 'There is one God,' and be happy that at least you are coming to face the Creator, you are still asking favors from our Lord? Tighten the loop!"

When they heard about the execution of their superior, the Viziers paled out of fear.

*If even Nasuh Pasha who beat Safavid Shah Abbas on the battlefield, and returned triumphantly to the palace after having imposed tribute on him, fell so suddenly, who knows what can await me?* Everyone in the capital was terrified. They were told that the Padishah was in a rage when he found out that Nasuh Pasha had made a fortune reaching into the millions of gold ducats thanks to bribes, but so what? Was it news for the Sultan, that nothing would happen in the country without bribery?

Very few people in Istanbul could know the real reason for killing Nasuh Pasha, and those who managed to find it out screamed in disbelief in their heads. The Sultan's slave first became a favorite, and now she was clearly elevated to be the Padishah, as she began to take life. May God have mercy on us!

# CHAPTER NINE

The New Palace, Harem
Beginning of Autumn, 1617

Sultan Ahmed did not finish the storm.

In place of Nasuh Pasha, whom he'd condemned to death, he made Mehmed Pasha, the Buffalo, the Grand Vizier. The new Sadrazam immediately set out on a trip to punish Shah Abbas, who was holding captive the Sultan's envoy, İncili Mustafa. His rule didn't even last a year, however. When he suffered a defeat under the Erevan fortress, and Ahmed made Halil Pasha the Grand Vizier.

Shah Abbas, realizing that the new Ottoman Serdar would attack him with more soldiers, started delaying tactics and sent a messenger with countless gifts to the capital. However, the Padishah did not receive the messenger Kasım and instead ordered him captured and thrown into the dungeons of the Seven Towers Fortress.

Meanwhile, he greeted the Habsburg ambassador Czernin, who'd arrived in Istanbul on the same day because he was saying offensive words towards the Shah. Czernin, who appeared in the palace with a magnificent retinue and gifts worth fifty thousand gold coins, asked for an extension of the peace.

Ahmed's thoughts, however, were focused on the Hippodrome, where the construction of a new mosque continued. He behaved like in a fever. Every day he inquired masters and architects about the details and went to the construction site to encourage the workers to do their work. When the minarets began to grow over the construction site, he could stand at their side for many hours in a devious fear, immersed in another world.

It was during one of those days that the Padishah asked Mahpeyker an unexpected question.

"I've heard that there is an instrument in the Sinana Pasha Pavilion that captivates anyone who hears it. Did you know about it?"

She nodded before answering.

"I haven't heard it, but I heard rumors about its wondrousness. They say it is enchanted and it was given long ago to your father, peace be to his soul, Sultan Mehmed, by an English envoy. The ruler ordered to play it and often listened to it, and later he ordered it to be moved to the Sinan Pasha Pavilion."

Suddenly, she began to doubt whether she had done the right thing. Ahmed hated when someone knew something he didn't have any idea about. This was especially true for women, and it didn't matter that this woman happened to be Mahpeyker.

"Supposedly, some women from the harem used to go there to play, sing, and dance." She stole a glance at Ahmed out of the corner of her eye, and Mahpeyker noticed that he wasn't happy. "I don't know that much, sir. If you want, I'll immediately ask questions and find out," she whispered. Adding a few words every now and then, she managed to change the subject.

In fact, it turned out that she only thought she managed to change it.

The next day the furious Sultan went to the Sinan Pasha Pavilion.

The people sitting there were dumbfounded, seeing the Padishah in a completely unexpected moment. The arrival of the great ruler without previous announcement did not bode well.

"Where is the instrument?" Ahmed asked.

They immediately led him into a salon with a dome. Padishah stood for many minutes by the side of organs made by Master Dallam. Without touching anything, he looked around here and there and studied the structure for a very long time. His attention was most attracted by tiny bells and carvings on the surface, in the shape of birds and angels.

He shook his head one way and the other. "Shame! What a shame!" he murmured.

The organist tried to say something to the ruler, but Ahmed stopped him.

"I don't want to! Just show me how you play it!"

The man sat down to the keyboard in a hurry. As he pressed on the pedal and huge bellows filled with air, a rustling sound began to come from inside the organ.

"What's this sound, master?"

"Air, My Lord. The pipes of this instrument blow out the air, so before you can play it, you should fill bellows with it. And then, pressing on these white and black keys...

"What is the sound like?"

The man pressed one of the buttons, arranged in four rows in front of him, and the bellow blew air into one of the long and short metal pipes, leaning against the wall. For a moment a bass sound C hung under the dome of the pavilion, then the thinner H flat, followed by the F's.

Instead of saying, 'Enough!' Padishah raised his hand.

"It blows air, white and black give a sound. The one who built it, apparently, God forbid, put himself in place of Allah," he grumbled, and just as he'd arrived in anger, so he left.

The next day, the wonderful work of art, which the organs of Master Dallam were, was broken into pieces with axes and hammers, and then completely burned.

Mahpeyker suffered when one of the girls, all in tears, told her the story, but she couldn't do anything. Besides, she was pregnant again.

At the right time, she gave birth to a third daughter, whom Sultan Ahmed named Hanzade.

Hanzade had not even started to walk yet, when Mahpeyker, embarrassed, whispered to the Padishah, that she was carrying his child again. Nine months later she gave birth to her second son.

Heralds announced in the capital the birth of another prince, playing on their drums, and Ahmed arrived in a hurry. He took his son in his arms, hugged him tightly and attached a huge gold coin to his clothes.

"Your name is Ibrahim," he whispered in the child's ear. "May you follow the path of Allah like the prophet Abraham. Be fair like him, blessed like he is."

And then he murmured the first Ezan to Ibrahim's ear in a hoarse voice.

Mahpeyker noticed with surprise that the voice of the Padishah had never been so full of affection.

Looking at the Sultan with her little son, she spoke to herself in her mind.

*I started late, but look, Mahfiruz, I outran you. You swaggered that you gave the Padishah two princes. Ha, I gave my Lord four children. Now take the two sons from me. I still have two Sultan's daughters!*"

"Be praised in both worlds, my Mahpeyker."

When she heard the voice of the Padishah, she abandoned the feud with Mahfiruz. Sultan Ahmed leaned forward and kissed her forehead, and put a ring on her finger, the splendor of which exceeded everything she had seen before. As the sun's rays reflected from it, sparkling glimmers exploded from the stone, dazzling her eyes.

"My lord, you have honored again..."

"Tell me what your wish is, my light."

"What can I wish for except for health and happiness of Your Majesty?"

"Tell me, go ahead! You made me so happy that whatever I do won't be enough, but never mind, say what you want!"

And just at this moment, Mahpeyker whispered in the ear of Sultan Ahmed the wish that she'd hidden in the deepest recesses of her mind for years.

Padishah was surprised to hear what she asked for.

"Is that all?"

"Mhm." She nodded like a shy little girl. "That's all."

What else could she want? How many things did she ask for?

The Sultan smiled and placed a kiss on her forehead.

"In that case, my beautiful Kösem, your wish will soon be fulfilled."

Not one by one, but in a group of five the disasters fell upon her, and none of Mahpeyker's wishes were fulfilled.

One afternoon she received the message that the Padishah was waiting for her in the rose garden, so she went there right away. Sofia and the nanny of Prince Ibrahim followed her every step.

Ahmed, as usual, whispered to her that she was as beautiful as an angel and pinched Ibrahim's cheek caressingly – but there was no joy in him. It seemed like he was about to say something, but he couldn't find the words.

Unexpectedly, he looked at Sofia sadly.

"She's grown up. The time has come to find her a husband," he said quietly to Mahpeyker.

Mahpeyker nodded to show that she agreed with the Sultan. She also didn't forget to throw a furtive look at Sofia to probe if she'd heard it. She was afraid to broach the subject herself because the girl had confessed to her at the first opportunity that she was in love with the groom Ahmed.

"Sister, sister, my beautiful older sister, I'd like to marry him." She dreamed about cuddling up to him, and Kösem winced at those words. She was sure that eventually, she'd be forced to raise the issue, but she'd prayed that the moment would come as late as possible.

Now, however, she couldn't get her mind to think about it. The concentrated expression on the Sultan's face and his silence began to fill her with more and more panic. *What will this man tell me?* went through her head. In the end, Mahpeyker couldn't stand it.

"Did you want to say something to your maid, My Lord?"

Padishah struggled to get up from his place, and after he walked around the gazebo for a moment, he stopped in front of her, and grasping her hands, lifted them up.

"I'm sorry for your loss, My Lady."

What? Shocked Mahpeyker suddenly lost the ability to think logically as if her brain and all the cells suddenly froze. Ahmed drew her toward himself and embraced her.

"Your father died much earlier, your mother last year. Both moved to eternal glory. May the Lord give you a long life, my beautiful lady."

For a moment she looked at the Sultan thoughtlessly with empty eyes. Ahmed's voice was still ringing in her ears.

*Your father died much earlier, your mother last year. Both moved to eternal glory. May the Lord give you a long life, my beautiful lady.*

*He died.* A scream rose inside her, and her mouth began to twitch. *Both died! Father a long time ago, but my mom lasted all this time until last year. Have mercy, God! I'm late, I'm late, I'm late!*

Tears flowed from her eyes. Sultan Ahmed leaned her head against his chest and patted her back.

And she was late. *Ah, if only I had asked Ahmed to bring my mother and father to the capital earlier.*

*Under no circumstances be late, daughter*, she heard the words of Safiye Sultan in her head. *I did it, my noble benefactor*, she moaned inside. *I am late. I overslept the search for my parents, mother Safiye.*

The Sultan sat her on the sofa under the gazebo and put a pillow under her back. In front of two stupefied slaves, he poured water into a glass, brought it to his wife, and then sat down next to Kösem and helped her drink.

"How?" Mahpeyker whispered. "How did this happen?"

"After you disappeared, your father left the village to find you and bring you back. Your mother also wanted to go with him, but he wouldn't let her. 'Stay in our home. If Nastya comes back, she can't find it empty,' he said and left."

*If Nastya comes back... And you did not come back, Nastya,* she reproached herself. She did not come back! She let herself be drawn into some crazy prophecy, a terrible desire, and never returned!

It means, her poor mother had been waiting for her for years. Dreaming about the day she would reappear, counting days and months.

*But you did not come back,* a broken voice said in her. *You did not come back because there was no room in your head for anything other than playing being a queen.*

The pain was tearing her to pieces. Yes, she was already a queen! An orphan Queen! She had neither mother nor father.

There was neither her father, Kostas Vasilidis, nor her mother, Maria.

*There is no Nadia, either,* she heard in her head. *You forgot? She died a long time ago. Now it's you. The beautiful and powerful queen of the Ottoman Empire, Mahpeyker Kösem Sultan!*

For the first time, she didn't lift her head proudly, thinking about her fulfilled dreams.

*What did it get me?* she said to herself. *I am an orphan queen!*

The vision in which Mahpeyker brought her parents to Istanbul and threw herself in their arms, crying, *Look at me! Look at me!* was shattered completely that day.

In those black moments, the only consolation for her was the birth of another son, whom the Padishah named Suleiman.

The second wish of Mahpeyker did not come true either. A month later, instead of Mirna, a letter appeared.

'*You crazy islander,*' she wrote at the beginning. '*I was surprised to see the gentlemen come to Kumanovo Estate. We have not had any guests for a long time. Ha, when I found out that you sent them to me, my surprise increased even more. I can't describe how happy I was, how proud I am of you.*'

It was as if Mahpeyker could hear the woman's voice. She had her bright, smiling face right in front of her eyes. Tears stood in her eyes from longing for her.

'*Of course, after Slobodan returned, we couldn't get any news about you. I asked our Lord once or twice. "They took Nastya to the palace," he said. "She now serves in the harem." Ah, and besides, the Lord's wife has passed away. May you enjoy a long life. Bey Ibrahim does not go to war anymore and spends all his days here.*'

From the woman's words, she concluded that Mirna was very pleased with this. *It means you are alone with your beloved one, dear sister*, seeped into her mind.

'*I can't even start to describe how happy I was when the gentlemen who came to the estate, said that you are the only chosen one of our Lord. Oh, my beautiful mermaid! This means that you followed that prophecy you laughed so much at, and you fulfilled your dreams. In the end, you became the queen of the Ottoman Empire, you gave birth to princes and princesses for the Ottomans. May Allah turn whatever you touch into gold. I imagine you in Sultana dresses now. Oh, how they must fit you and how much more beautiful you must be. That's for sure, after all, everyone in the state says how great your beauty is, and how madly the Padishah is in love with you. I swear that the Ottoman Turks have not seen a more beautiful Sultana than you before this day. May Allah cover you with gold.'*

It was only when she saw that the paper sheet in her hand was wet, that Mahpeyker understood tears were streaming from her eyes.

*'The gentlemen told me that they came to Kumanovo at the command of the mighty Padishah and that Mahpeyker Kösem Sultan invites me to the capital, where she would like us to live together as in the old days. You did not forget about me, Nastya.*

*You love me.'*

*Of course, I love you,* Mahpeyker sobbed. *If only you knew how much.* She continued reading, wiping her nose.

*'But all that's impossible, my beautiful mermaid. Please, do not drive your sister, Mirna, away from the rivers she missed so much. I'm far away, but I can smell the Danube and Sava from the pine-covered mountains. I also have no idea how to sit down and get up in the huge capital, in the palace of our Lord (and now also yours, of course). In short, I don't really know anything. Forgive me, my Sultana daughter. Let it go, here I...'*

She didn't have enough strength in her heart and eyes to read the rest. Mirna's words blurred behind the tears.

"Dear sister." Sofia looked at her face worryingly, but Mahpeyker didn't say anything and just moved the letter away.

She felt as if she had lost her mother for the second time in one month. She didn't care what the courtiers would think and say. She was howling, with tears streaming down her face – Mahpeyker Kösem sometimes cried, too.

Mahpeyker could not reach Mirna – but her older sister could finally unite with the Danube and Sava. At the behest of Sultan Ahmed, a home was purchased for her at the confluence of the two rivers. One of the men of the Rumelia beylerbey came to the estate of Kumanovo and brought with him the order to free Mirna, and the documents of the building that was bought for her in Belgrade.

It didn't take long before another letter from Mirna came to Mahpeyker:

*'You connected me with my rivers, you crazy islander. Now I believe that there is no such thing that Mahpeyker Kösem can not do. We moved here with bey Ibrahim, and now he watches the Danube, and I watch the Sava. Ah, if you saw how they are intertwined in frothy hugs! Nastya... I don't know what to say. May Allah cover you with gold...'*

It wasn't Sofia, but the Padishah, who began the conversation she'd been dreading.

One evening, Sultan Ahmed asked Mahpeyker how old Sofia was.

"Fifteen," she answered quietly, not showing her surprise. Actually, Sofia was already almost sixteen.

"Perfect," said the Padishah. "It is as I thought. She's the right age."

"You said 'right,' My Lord. What is it right for?"

"To marry, Mahpeyker. I want to wed her with one of my pashas."

Mahpeyker didn't know what to answer. Should she be happy or sad?

Of course, she was aware that Sofia was at the right age to get married. It was equally clear that she couldn't allow the girl to marry the groom Ahmed who'd won her heart. A good marriage was planned for her, one that would ensure her a safe future – as much as it was possible for an Ottoman woman, of course, but at least she had some guarantee. Sofia's wedding also meant separation with her, and God knew, oh, God knew that she didn't want that. Life without Sofia seemed impossible to her.

"A pasha? Which one?"

"İstanköylü Ali Pasha. He is also Greek. They can be considered compatriots."

*Except that Sofia is not Greek,* thought Mahpeyker, but she didn't say anything.

"What's the matter? You got quiet. Do you think it's wrong?"

"No, no," she shied. "Whatever My Lord believes to be appropriate, of course, it is so. I didn't expect it, so I'm surprised... only... there is one thing..."

"Do you want to say he's too old? Let's not exaggerate, my beautiful lady. Ali Pasha is not forty yet. And he is handsome, this İstanköylü. They call him Smooth Ali. He is clever, cunning. He has a future ahead of him. I am thinking of taking him to the Divan as a wedding present and making him the fifth Vizier. In this way, Sofia will once again be with one foot in the palace, and you won't have to part."

*But Sofia is only fifteen years old*, Mahpeyker thought, but she didn't let it show.

"It looks very appropriate, My Lord."

She didn't sleep that night. The thought of how Sofia would respond to this news terrified her.

It happened exactly as she was afraid it would.

Sofia didn't react at all. She didn't cry or shout, nor did she even wail in lament, 'I don't want to, I love Ahmed!'

She just raised her head and having looked into Mahpeyker's eyes, left without a word.

Wedding preparations began immediately.

Kösem saw the groom from behind the kafes crate. He was tall and graceful. No wonder they call him Smooth. He was a handsome man. She was sure he could steal Sofia's heart, and make her forget about Ahmed.

Sofia didn't wear a red veil during the wedding.

"Ah, girl, I keep telling you, and you still don't understand. It is a custom, I'm telling you. Get it? Custom. Tradition. Not to be broken. You should cover your hair with a red veil," complained Kalfa Hayganoş.

But Sofia did not.

From the other side of the kafes she listened to her future husband's voice.

Hodja Efendi asked: "Do you agree to get married, my daughter?"

It seemed to Mahpeyker that a thousand years passed before the girl broke the silence.

"I do," she whispered finally.

When the wedding was concluded, people crowded on both sides of the kafes with congratulations. The courtiers, daughters, and wives of the beys lined up to congratulate Sofia. The bride paled when Mahpeyker stepped forward. Kösem knew that she'd hurt the girl deeply. The beautiful older sister gave beautiful Sofia, not to the one she loved, but to an elderly man. Suddenly, Mahpeyker realized that tears were coming to her eyes, so she bit her lips so that she wouldn't cry.

"Come here," she said gently. "Come to me, my violet, my little Sofia, my veiled sister," she pulled her to herself by the elbows and embraced her. "Forgive me," she whispered in the girl's ear. "It will be better for you."

She embraced the girl even tighter, drew in her scent, stroked her hair, kissed her on both cheeks. Her lips were wet. Sofia's salty tears were left on her tongue.

"Don't cry," she pleaded. "Be happy. You'll be happy."

But Sofia gently freed herself from her embrace, and for a moment gazed deeply into Mahpeyker's eyes.

"No, you be happy. Goodbye, sister," she whispered. And then she turned around, walked over to her husband's relatives, and left with them.

Mahpeyker never saw her again.

Shortly before the evening Ezan, she heard Semiha shouting.

"Lady! Lady! For God's sake! A tragedy!"

Panicked, Mahpeyker ran to the door.

"What is it? What's going on, Semiha?"

The girl's hair was in disarray, and her face was chalk-like white. She almost fainted in the arms of the two courtiers who came to her aid. She was all in tears.

"Semiha, what happened to you?"

"Sofia," the girl sobbed. "Sofia..."

"What about Sofia?"

God! She felt blood freeze in her veins.

"What about Sofia? What..."

"She's dead!" Semiha exclaimed. "Sofia is dead! Behind Ali Pasha's house, there is an empty well. She..."

Mahpeyker didn't hear the rest. She fainted, and while she was falling to the ground, a horrible voice echoed in her head.

*Welcome to the land of darkness, the queen of death!*

*No! No!* She heard someone call. But who was it that shouted like that? Was it herself?

She didn't go to see her. She couldn't. What right would I have to go there? she kept asking herself. What right would I have to look at her beautiful but lifeless face? I am the one who killed her. I, the Queen of Death!"

It meant that she had decided on the girl's death already, on the day she found out that they would marry Sofia to someone other than her beloved. That's why Sofia did not wear a red veil. Why would she do it? After all, she was not a bride of her beloved.

She was being married to death, and it didn't matter for death whether there was a veil or not.

For many days Mahpeyker did not eat, drink, or speak. She didn't know what it was going to be, but she sensed that a catastrophe greater than all the others was approaching her.

She could never allow herself to be late again. Never.

Black clouds covered the capital in the autumn. The unpleasant wind blew from the northeast. There were days when Mahpeyker thought that half of the world was devoured by flooding. The gray cloud falling on the sea covered the hills on the opposite shore, where autumn repainted the beeches standing among the pines; first from green to red, then from red to yellow.

She was the daughter of the sea, so knew well what fog was. As soon as the gray fume fell on Milos, the women went out to the coast and waited for their husbands and sons who went fishing to emerge from the fog. A terrible noise was made on the shore so that people at sea wouldn't lose their way - drums, horns, trumpets, whatever was at hand, was used.

But here it was different, and sometimes half of the capital disappeared in this ominous gray for days.

With her soul embraced by darkness, among the darkness besieging the city, Mahpeyker sought solace in her sons. Murad was six years old, and apart from his epileptic attacks, he was strong and as healthy as an ox. But when an attack came... oh, her heart would bleed then. She couldn't stand it, seeing him fall to the ground, shaken by convulsions.

She was furious when she saw the nannies try to tie down Murad, in an effort to protect him from hurting himself.

"Leave it," she rushed to the women. "Leave it, let my Prince overcome the disease, let him tear it from the inside and throw it away. How can he do it if you tie him down?"

But she knew as well as the others, that Murad could neither defeat nor throw away the illness that devastated him, nor could it leave him.

Ibrahim was almost two years old, and Suleiman had started crawling already. She sat Murad by her side and told him fairy tales for hours – stories about handsome princes and beautiful princesses. Except Murad liked the story about a lumberjack and a monster the best.

In the fairy tale, an old, benevolent king promised that whoever would kill a beast threatening the country, would receive the ruler's beautiful daughter. All the princes and kings of the world hurried to be able to marry the princess of legendary beauty and entered the cave where the seven-headed monster lived, but none of them managed to kill the monster. They either disappeared without a trace in the unfathomable abyss of the cave, became a meal for the beast, or upon seeing the seven-headed monster breathe fire, fled in terror. And when the king began to believe that he would never free himself from the beast, a young lumberjack, who lived in a forest, came, and stood before him, saying that he wanted to join the suitors fighting hopelessly. Of course, the king didn't even take it into account that a poor lumberjack might succeed in a mission, in which valiant princes failed. But he said so nevertheless, 'Go, move, lumberjack, kill this monster!'

And when the young man asked, 'Do you promise that if I kill the beast, I will marry the princess?'

The King, not believing, of course, that the daredevil would manage to come out safe and sound from the cavern, smiled to himself and said: 'I promise.'

The lumberjack entered the cave and, proving his incredible dexterity and cunning, he cut off the heads of the monster one by one. But despite his efforts, in the place of each cut head, another one grew. That's when the lumberjack understood the secret of the beast. There was no point getting rid of the side heads of the creature if the biggest one still held on to the body. New ones would grow anyway. Finally, instead of taking care of the small side heads, the wise and heroic lumberjack cut the enormous, supreme head shielded by them, and so he managed to fill the sack with seven severed heads, which he took to the king.

He said, 'Here is what you asked for, give me what I asked for.'

And Mahpeyker always finished the story in the same way:

'... and the king agreed to give his daughter to the lumberjack, and they lived happily ever after.'

What surprised her was the fact that Murad was interested only in the part of the fairy tale in which she talked about the lumberjack's fight with the monster. He didn't care about the king, nor his beautiful daughter, nor the princes who entered the cave to kill the monster and fall into his terrible trap. He was most delighted with the scene in which the lumberjack jumped on the monster's huge head and plunged his sword between his eyes.

"Again," he'd say, opening his eyes wide, "tell me again!"

And Mahpeyker retold the scene again.

Ibrahim didn't care about fairy tales at all. He was unrestrained as if he was struggling with some invisible forces. He would climb on the couch, turn the pillows over, jump on them and kick, then jump down and start running with his arms outstretched wide. Nobody could stop him. He started crawling even before his first birthday, and at fifteen months he walked with ease. From that time, he ran until he fell exhausted on his face. He couldn't sit still for more than a minute. Courtiers, slaves, servants, wet nurse – everyone fawned all over him. With his laughter and cries, Ibrahim destroyed the order of the palace – a place in which people were so careful to keep quiet that they communicated with almost nothing else but the movements of eyebrows and eyes. Ibrahim shouted and cavorted, and the army of servants trembled in fear of the

Sultan's anger caused by the violation of the peace, but they could do nothing. The little prince screamed, shouted, and ran with all his strength.

It was during these dark days that Mahpeyker became pregnant again, and this time the pregnancy was worse than all the previous ones.

She was in the darkness when they took her to the birthing room. Sometimes the pain faded somewhat, then she came out of the darkness into the light, but immediately afterward, she fell again into a black abyss with a new wave of suffering.

Finally, she gave birth. Her fourth son delighted the palace. Sultan Ahmed was at the Divan meeting when he received the message. He stood up, washed himself immediately, and said the thanksgiving prayer. With his hands raised, he thanked God.

"Come to us, Kasım Khan," he whispered, taking the baby from Mahpeyker's hands. "Your name is Kasım."

The days became weeks, and weeks became months, but Mahpeyker didn't even notice that. She felt as if the wind had taken her and she was flying together with it. The nannies, wet nurses, and slaves could look after the children, but she still kept watching them – they were her treasure. *Four princes, and two living princesses*, she would talk to herself happily. *You have sealed your future, Mahpeyker. You gave birth to almost half a dozen of the sultans for the dynasty*.

She sat among the pillows and giggled cheerfully. She seemed to have left all worries and fears behind, but inside, something kept moving her very deeply. Mahpeyker knew well what it was.

Danger.

Şarazad told Mahpeyker in precise detail about the guest over these days.

"I'm not in the mood to see anyone. Already the air chokes me, and I don't want to hear about their problems. Who is it this time?"

"Mother of Prince Mustafa."

"What? Mother of our Sultan's brother?"

Şarazad nodded, looking at her mysteriously. "Her."

Suddenly Mahpeyker felt a strange shiver inside. Prince Mustafa and his mother.

The world had forgotten about them. Or, the mother and son had managed to make themselves be forgotten. They were removed from view to a hidden corner of the palace, where they managed to live in peace. It's been about ten years since Mahpeyker came to Istanbul, and she'd never seen the woman even once, nor Prince Mustafa, either. They said he was crazy; that he talked with flowers and sang to birds.

The courtiers and servants repeated rumors about him. "Did you hear? An adult man, and apparently, he hasn't been with a woman yet," they'd giggle.

"Nooo... really?"

"I'm telling you. Apparently, he asked, looking at what was in front of him: 'What did Lord create this for? If it was for pouring 'water,' wouldn't a small hole be enough?' Ha, that's what he said."

"Come on, that's impossible. They must be lying."

"No, our Silver Girl heard it with her own ears. She swore it was true."

For some unknown reason, the girls nicknamed a tiny, completely black slave Silver Girl, even though there was no other color to be seen on her body but the color of the tar. Of course, apart from the rows of her even, pearl-like teeth, and the whites of her eyes, whose beauty would make even a doe jealous.

Instantly, Mahpeyker felt as if burning coal fell on her heart. Sofia's voice echoed in her ears:

'I almost bumped into the Silver Girl when I walked the corridor at night. Luckily, she just smiled so I could see her teeth. By God, otherwise, I wouldn't have seen her. I would have walked right into her, and drop a tray or plate to the floor.' Sofia kept giggling, remembering the incident.

*Eh, Sofia*, she moaned in her mind. *Oh, my dear, my beautiful, the only one, oh, my undine*. She pulled herself together hearing Şarazad's voice again.

"Bring her here, it's a shame not to let her in."

She stood up to greet the guest, although she didn't have to. Somehow, it happened this way. Meanwhile, her mind kept asking: *Where did this woman come from?*

The shivers that had been shaking her a moment ago were even stronger now.


She was a very beautiful woman, and her face emanated inner peace. When she saw that Mahpeyker was waiting for her standing, a gentle smile passed across her face.

"My Lady," she murmured, walking straight in her direction. "You are very kind. Forgive me... standing up to welcome me..."

"Please, if I told you to wait, My Lady, then it's me who should ask for forgiveness. But in fact, you do not need permission or ceremony. My door is always open to the honorable mother of my brother-in-law.

The woman stopped just in front of her and fixed her green eyes on Kösem.

"You are beautiful even in your words, my good Mahpeyker. I even wonder what comes first, your beauty or mind?"

*My good Mahpeyker?* She immediately singled out these words, squeezed in before flattery, from the others. What's that supposed to mean? So, the woman didn't recognize her as a Lady?

Immediately, all her sympathy evaporated, but her mind warned immediately: *Calm down. Be nice to her. This visit must have a reason.*

"Would you like to sit down?" Mahpeyker showed a place to the woman. "How is the honorable Prince? I hope his health is good."

For a moment the woman looked into her eyes as if she wanted to read the thoughts in her mind.

"You must have heard it," she murmured. "They say my son is crazy. Besides that, he's fine."

Mahpeyker didn't know what to say. *Under no circumstances...* said her reason. *Under no circumstances underestimate this woman.*

"Not at all," Kösem swiftly retorted.

"Oh, yes, yes, they call my son a madman. The merciful ones say that he has 'a character of a dervish.'" She paused for a moment. "Actually, the honorable Prince does little to stop rumors circulating among the people. For example, yesterday he started a contest with a nightingale to see who sings more beautifully – in front of the servants."

Mahpeyker once heard that Mustafa had cried, shouting to a magpie: 'Teach me to fly!'

The servants supposedly saw him once stand on the top of a wall, spread his arms, and raise the caftan's skirts like wings. They barely managed to get the Prince down.

'Leave me alone, I will fly!' His laments reached as far as the palatial kitchen. Even if he wasn't crazy, there was certainly something wrong with his head.

"The honorable Prince is surely joking, My Lady. Besides, you know how people are. They exaggerate, and then they believe in the lies they said."

Prince Mustafa's mother didn't see the need to hide that she was weighing the words she'd just heard. She nodded.

"Personally, I'm not going to complain, my good Mahpeyker, but people in the state also believe in rumors."

*There you go, she did it again*, Mahpeyker got angry. *She did not say Lady again.*

And when she at least tried to give her face a benign expression, the woman said something unexpected.

"Let it be. Let them remember my son as a madman. One day, Allah forbid, if something happens to our Padishah and Mahfiruz's child will take over the throne, perhaps then the belief in my son's madness will save his life. We both know that the kid won't leave any of us in good health."

*Wait a minute, wait!* her mind shouted in panic. *The woman gives you encrypted messages.*

*The first one: if something happens to our Padishah...*

*Second: she doesn't even say 'good' about this woman – the ice queen is only Mahfiruz for her, and that means she hates her.*

*Third: she doesn't call Osman a prince. He's just Mahfiruz's child.*

*Fourth: the belief in madness. It means that, according to her, Mustafa is not sick.*

*Fifth: she is afraid that when Osman takes the throne, her son will be killed.*

"God, forbid. May Allah give our Lord and your Prince a long life," she said, but she still had the guest's words in her head. *The woman is throwing you a bait,* she inferred.

"It's known that he lived in fear of death sent by his father of holy memory. You could never be sure when his anger would explode and when it would end. It wasn't even impossible that one day, due to slander, he would take Mustafa's life. If I'm to be honest, I was a little supportive of Mustafa's madness, my good Mahpeyker. What was I supposed to do? I even invented quite a lot of what he did and said – so that they would call him a madman so that no one would touch him. Ah, Mustafa's quirks have also helped me. For days, he locked himself in a dark room and sat there, and when a bird perched on a window, he shouted, 'Help! Do not kill me, father, I'm innocent!' His screams tore my heart to pieces, but in my soul, I begged: 'Scream, my son, my brave Prince, even louder.'"

The woman's face stiffened with fear as if she were reliving those days again.

"Even me," she went on. "I hid in the closet whenever I heard the sound of footsteps outside because I thought it was the executioners. You know, people ask: 'What is worse than death?' And I have a ready answer – fear – there is no worse thing than fear. It devours you, it finishes you. It drives you crazy, like with my Mustafa. When you die, it happens once, and that's the end. You may even not feel death. Is not it breathing? They look, and your breath does not blow out the candle. Its flame does not tremble. They say this is the moment when the soul is leaving. But is it the same with fear? It kills you not once, but a million times over. Fear..."

"I know," Mahpeyker interrupted. "I, too, know what fear is, My Lady."

The woman pretended not to hear her.

"My prince hadn't even entered maturity, and he'd already lost his desires because of fear. Later, he clung to the disease and stayed like this. He never saw a woman. Neither the hodjas, nor the summoners of the jinns, nor the muskas, or prayers helped. 'I'm in love with a hyacinth, Mother,' he said one day. 'Do you have a more beautiful odalisque than a hyacinth to bring to me?' Neither houris nor fortune-tellers became a cure for Mustafa's torment. One night he almost strangled one of the slaves. 'My father sent you to kill me,' he said and threw himself at her. The servants struggled to free the girl from his hands."

Mahpeyker couldn't decide whether to laugh or be sad. It looked that there was more to the gossip than a grain of truth.

"There is definitely a solution to this problem, My Lady. I think that if fear goes away, everything will work out."

"God willing. Our Padishah's childhood has passed with the same fears, except that his mind resisted. And of course, he had Handan behind him. Because this woman was the favorite of the late Mehmed Khan, Prince Ahmed could feel much more confident. Anyway, as soon as our Lord became a Padishah, the fear has grown quite a lot for us. The new Sultan meant new deaths. My son suffered greatly by fearing that Ahmed would not want to have a year younger rival behind himself. He didn't care about the throne or anything, but who would understand this, who would listen to him? At that time, Mustafa jumped out of bed at night with the words: 'I am His Highness, Suleiman. What am I doing here? You must take me to Jerusalem immediately. Let's not make Queen Saba wait.' Doctors appeared immediately, and in their courtesy, they said: 'Your prince suffers through a spiritual breakdown.' Later, we heard that Safiye Sultan of holy memory advised our master not to take his brother Mustafa's life.

"As you can see, my good Mahpeyker, his madness and grandmother's words allowed my Prince to stay healthy in his body until now. Only that I don't know what will happen later. I have no idea if Osman will leave my son alone, and even if he has such a plan, his mother won't sit quietly. Either she will keep badgering Osman until he takes care of it, or she'll send assassins to my Prince.

Mahpeyker was already sure – Prince Mustafa's mother had not come here without a reason. Her every sentence was a veiled message. *Safiye Sultan took care of Mustafa. Protect my prince, just like her.*

*Well, except who will take care of me,* crossed Mahpeyker's mind.

And the last message: *For us to live, Osman should not become a Padishah.*

*Of course, he should not,* Mahpeyker said in her mind. *He won't leave you or me alone.*

That was the real message of the woman – death!

*If Osman becomes a sultan, we will all die.*

She shivered involuntarily. *Well, thankfully, Ahmed is alive,* she told herself as she tried to stifle the fear growing inside her. *Where and why has this whole Osman threat come here right now?*

"Don't be afraid, My Lady. Allah helps the righteous."

"In this palace, a lot of righteous princes found themselves in the hands of executioners, my good Mahpeyker."

"Allah works in mysterious ways; our Padishah is alive."

Suddenly a lightning bolt flashed in her head. *How many years have already passed since you thought about this possibility?* her mind reprimanded her. *How long will the change in the law, that Ahmed introduced, last?*

*Oh, my dear Lady* Mahpeyker said in her mind. *If you throw me a bait, let it be. Now I will throw one at you, and we'll see what will happen.*

"Besides, as you know," she said gently and looked attentively into the woman's eyes, "my noble Padishah," in this way she kindly reminded the woman that she was the Sultan's wife and should be referred to as 'Lady,' "made very serious changes in law and customs."

The woman nodded intently.

"Thanks to you. I'm guessing that you suggested this project to our master, and now that I've seen you, I'm sure of it."

"It doesn't have to be this way – the eldest son doesn't necessarily have to take the throne. With alim's fatwa, the oldest man of the dynasty may be a Padishah. My sons are too little for now..." It was a warning: I'm in the queue, too. "... and the son of this woman can't be called mature, either... How old would he be now? Thirteen? Not more. In this situation, the eldest prince of the family... well, following the law, alims may decide to enthrone Mustafa. With this in mind... maybe it's someone else that should be afraid?"

Fires flashed in the eyes of Prince Mustafa's mother, but they went out immediately.

"Would alims leave the throne to a madman?"

*Yes*, Mahpeyker thought. *She swallowed the bait.*

"Didn't you say that the state of the dear Prince results from fear and that many rumors have spread with your help? A little bit of effort and generosity, some threats and charity, should make the temporary problem of your Prince completely dissipate in people's opinion, or at least put it on the right path to that."

She noticed that the woman was rubbing her hands and flexing her fingers with excitement.

"Of course, I'm saying all this to calm you down. In the end, with God's will, my husband's reign will continue for long, long years."

Prince Mustafa's mother smiled at Mahpeyker, who let her understand that she was ready to leave her son an open path to the throne.

"With God's will, My Lady," she said quietly.

*Well, well*, Mahpeyker grunted in her mind. *Look at me well. Look. I am the woman who will save you and your son. And you, me, and my princes.*

"Our Lord," the mother of Prince Mustafa went on, "didn't call you 'Kösem' accidentally. You fill the human spirit with light, guidance, and show paths served with advice. When I came here, I was full of fears, but I will leave, Mahpeyker Kösem Sultan, enlightened and sure of what is ahead of me.

*Oh, look now*. Words came immediately to Mahpeyker's head. *Right now, it just didn't work. Such accumulation of words and so much flattery is a sign of danger. I'll have to be careful with you, woman. Your hypocrisy can be as dangerous as your cleverness.*

The woman took a sip of sweet sorbet brought by the courtiers.

"You will not ask, My Lady, why have I come here after all these years?"

"Isn't it to talk about these matters?"

"Yes, but the reason is actually different."

"Really? Well, now you made me curious, My Lady. What reason might be more important than the issue we were talking about?"

"I saw you in a dream last night, Mahpeyker."

The woman tried every possible way of addressing her. First, she exalts herself, then after she realizes it will serve her well, she begins to swear allegiance. Now she talks to her like to a friend. But she couldn't do the same, because she didn't even know the woman's name. Şarazad had only said 'the mother of Prince Mustafa.'

"In a dream? I hope it was propitious."

"With God's grace," the woman answered quickly.

"What was it about? Tell me, My Lady."

"You were sitting on a platform. Something was on your head. At first, I thought it was a crown, and maybe it was, but you had the sun just above your hair. Its rays brightened every corner, warmed souls, brought joy and life to the world."

"Have you heard yourself, My Lady?" she delicately mocked the woman's dream.

"Please, don't say that. I'm saying the sun has risen over your head, My Lady. God put it on your head like a crown. There were people standing in the rows before you. You told them something. I didn't hear the words, but apparently, they were orders. People, one by one, knelt in front of you and walked away... and then, My Lady... later..."

Even if she didn't admit it, the woman's words and voice impressed her.

"Later?" she wanted her to go on.

"And then a child appeared there. It was all of light... no, of gold. It came straight to you. You stretched out your hands and sat it at your side. And... merciful God, even now, when I'm telling you this, my hair..." The woman lifted the sleeve of her dress and showed her arm. "Look how they bristle."

"The child," Mahpeyker panted, "what happened? Did something happen to it?"

"Sun," the woman said in a strange, throaty voice, "another sun appeared over the head of the golden child..."

Mahpeyker didn't know what to think or what to say. *This woman,* she told herself, *is an unparalleled actress. Apparently, she wants to tell me to wait for my turn, because my Prince will also become a Padishah. Well, unless a life full of fear really gave her the ability to receive news from what's invisible.*

"That's all? What happened next?"

Prince Mustafa's mother looked at Mahpeyker for a long time and finally said gently: "No. You disappeared with the child in the rays of this sun... and suddenly a man emerged from this golden glow... a blind beggar..."

*What? A blind beggar?*

Apart from her, no one in the palace knew about the blind beggar. Actually, the two people whom she'd ever told about the incident were already dead – Safiye Sultan and Sofia – and they could not have told Mustafa's mother about that!

"A blind beggar?"

"Yes, only... he had a long black scepter in one of his hands, and stretched the other one straight ahead and came to me with a smile. His lips did not move, but I heard in my head: 'Do not be sad, because, with this woman, they will bring the sun to your son. They will come with the sun and go away with the sun. Wait, because the time is getting near already.' Then the dream dissipated. I woke up."

This time, it was Mahpeyker's hair that stood on end. What the woman said later, went in one ear and came out the other, but she already believed – this woman was sent to her by a divine power.

"I trust you already, Mahpeyker Kösem Sultan," the woman whispered to her as she left.

Mahpeyker looked at her. *And me?* she sighed. *Can I trust you?*

She knew she had to.

She did a lot of thinking that night. She created and destroyed plans and then recreated them again.

*A new day is coming, and fate is preparing for a new game*, she thought.

*Let it be so, fate. Roll the dice. Play. I'm ready.*

# CHAPTER TEN

## The New Palace, Harem
## November 16th, 1617

Padishah went to Tekirdağı for hunting. In the absence of the Sultan, each corner was embraced by a deep silence – at least, there was no hustle and bustle. However, two days later, spahis, driving in a mad rush through the Greeting Gate, set the palace on its feet. As soon as the cavalryman appeared in the front yard, setting sparks flying from his horse's shoes, he shouted:

"Hey, do something! Whoever loves life, run. Let them prepare the carriage right away."

The guard commander left the guard house furiously. "Do not yell like that, man. What is it, what is going on?"

"The Sultan is coming back. He's on his way. A carriage is needed, quickly!"

Mahpeyker also heard the shouting, but she didn't know what it was about.

"What's going on?" she asked Mürüvvet, who ran in as she returned from the courtyard. "Why are they screaming?"

"E..." the woman stammered, "supposedly our Lord... he's coming back."

*Ahmed? Coming back? But why? They shouldn't have even reached the hunting ground yet.*

Under the fire of her own questions, Mahpeyker began to panic. *Something must have happened! There must have been something serious. Could it be the catastrophe that I've sensed knocking at the door?* she thought to herself. She rose in a hurry.

"Why would the Padishah come back? Did something happen?"

Only now did she realize that Mürüvvet's face was completely white.

"I don't know... but the spahis came in galloping. It seems that they need to bring the carriage immediately. They didn't even put the harness on the horses properly and pushed it out onto the road."

*Something's happened to Ahmed!* Mahpeyker shouted in her head. *Something's happened to the Sultan. For God's sake, and if he died? Is the Padishah dead?*

She felt her blood thunder in her veins, and she heard a terrifying noise roar in her ears.

If the Padishah has died, the Ottoman dynasty needs a new one!

It seemed that the time had come. Fate went to attack!

*You must start acting, too,* her mind warned Mahpeyker. *And immediately.*

She heard the voice of Safiye Sultan in her ears – '*Do not dare be late. Do not act too soon or too late.*'

The moment has come – she had to take the first step even before Mahfiruz would roll up her sleeves.

"Mürüvvet, let them call the wives of Kaymakam Sofu Mehmed Pasha, and Sheikh al-Islam Esad Efendi, immediately. They must run here, come hell or high water. No discussion or laments, immediately!"

Even Mürüvvet, used to her unexpected orders, was surprised, but she didn't hesitate even for a moment. If Mahpeyker stood up and began to walk around the room with her hands joined behind her back, it meant that the situation was very serious.

And ominous.


Mahpeyker waited anxiously for the women. Harvest time has come, she repeated to herself. We planted the seed a long time ago, and now we will harvest.

However, she had her fears. *Will we be able to harvest?* crossed her mind. *Is there any other being created by Allah, beside a man, that would be able to betray? No. Betrayal belongs only to man. Perhaps women will repay me with treachery, who knows?*

They appeared before her together, terrified.

"My Lady," they came to her quickly. The wife of Sofu Mehmed Pasha, Ikbal, was as stout, as Esad Hades Efendi's wife, Fitnat, was skinny. Mahpeyker loved them both, and they loved her. Ikbal knew that her husband owed Kösem the position of Vice-Sadrazam – while everyone had expected that after the death of Sheikh al-Islam Hocazade Mehmed Chelebi, the Sultan would choose Zekeriyazade Jahja Efendi in his place, it was Esad Efendi who immediately took this position. The people who knew that lady Fitnat did not leave the chambers of Kösem Sultan, understood of course who had a hand in the matter.

Fitnat folded her hands.

"Have you heard any news, madam? Why is the ruler coming back?"

Ikbal spoke, leaving her no time to answer.

"My Pasha Sofu was extremely feverish, but I wasn't able to ask him anything. Mahfiruz Sultan called, so he ran quickly."

Mahpeyker shook as if someone had hit her. *Devilish Mahfiruz*, she got angry. *It means that the spider has also launched an attack.*

She panicked for a moment. *Have I made a mistake? And if instead of their wives, I should call the Kaymakam and Sheikh al-Islam themselves, so that Mahfiruz would not outrun me by meeting people from the front line?* She immediately threw the fear out of her head. What was done, was done. There was no time for fear and doubts.

"I know as much as you do," she said openly. "But it's certain that something bad has happened. Why else would they call for a carriage for the ruler?"

"Oh, oh, I hope it doesn't turn out that our Lord fell off his horse."

Mahpeyker gave her a hostile look.

"The Sultan does not fall off his horse, Ikbal. Everyone knows how great a rider he is."

The woman regretted her words.

"Anyway, we'll find out soon enough, but now we have to take precautions. Let's be ready for the worst so that the Ottoman state will not be left alone in need."

"Are you telling us, My Lady, that something could have happened to our ruler?" Fitnat began to hit her knees again and again. "Woe, My Lord, the ruler of the world, woe, My Lady... Hodja Efendi saw him in a dream, and I thought it would bode well."

Mahpeyker almost laughed out loud. *Something is going on in the empire,* she thought. *People dreaming under every stone.*

She looked at the woman as if she was very surprised.

"A dream? What did Esad Efendi see?"

"Our Lord... running down some hill. The beginning of the road was certain, but its end wasn't visible. He came across my husband. 'God bless you, sir,' said Esaf Efendi. 'Why this rush?' Of course, one doesn't ask Padishah, but it was just a dream. My husband asked, and the Sultan laughed, still running: 'Don't you see, Hodja? The tomb is ready. Angels brought the news, so I'm running there.' I hoped that with Allah's will, something good would come out from the story of Esad Efendi..."

Mahpeyker reproached herself for her recent mockery. *This dream was also a prophecy. Everything can be seen in it as clearly as in daylight,* she said to herself. *Everything is a sign. The time has come. The spider woke up, too. She's begun to spin her web.*

"My ladies," Mahpeyker sat up straight. "With God's grace it will turn out that we have rushed unnecessarily, but if what we fear has happened, chaos cannot prevail in the Ottoman Empire. The throne cannot be empty even for a second."

Both women confirmed, nodding their heads.

"Whether it's for good or bad, it's all related to what all three of us do together."

The wives of two statesmen, who had put a lot of effort into making their lives in the palace long and happy, immediately got the allusion.

*Show right away that you think of the throne for your son, Mahpeyker,* reason instructed her.

"But, you know that my Prince Murad is still too small for a Sultan."

Searching for the slightest sign of hesitation, she gave both women a scrutinizing look. They nodded again.

"But the son..." she realized that Ikbal and Fitnat were waiting for her words with bated breath. "The son of this woman will soon be fourteen years old. If they were to ask me, he is also a child, but she will surely demand his rights, saying that our master was the same age as Prince Osman when he took the throne."

"God forbid," both women clasped hands in a pleading gesture.

"Don't be surprised if she tries to convince the alims with the words: 'Look at the wisdom of Allah, it is a divine sentence that he gave his son the throne at the same age as his father.'"

"Oh yes, she will," said Fitnat, striking her right hand against the left one. "Of course. This woman is capable of anything."

Mahpeyker looked at her with her eyes full of lightning.

"If it were true," she snarled, "the Devil would push her son into the throne, and then throw away turbans, and cut off heads would roll around the empire – together, with yours and mine."

"Tfu, tfu, tfu!" Ikbal and Fitnat chased off the possible worries, pretending to spit on their collars. "May the merciful God forbid, My Lady."

"If the faithful does not show caution, how is Allah supposed to defend him? We ourselves must take precautions."

Ikbal opened her eyes wide with fear.

"What precautions?" she gasped. "The order is certain and belongs to the son of Mahfiruz."

"Oh, my dear!" Mahpeyker jumped to her feet. "Spit these words out, Ibkal. What order? Who will recognize the order if there is the law? Hasn't my magnanimous Padishah changed law and order? The throne, after all, is not necessarily going from father to son. If a brother is older than the son, then what? Doesn't the brother have any rights?"

Fitnat was much smarter, and she immediately understood what was going on.

"It means, you say, My Lady, that the throne stays for Prince Mustafa..." As soon as she spoke his name, she looked at Kösem in surprise. "But... but..."

"But he is crazy, you wanted to say. I know."

The pain hidden in the corner of her heart rose to scream. *So, what! If her son is a madman, yours has epilepsy!*

Mahpeyker tried to smile so that the women wouldn't notice her suffering. She reached out and closed Fitnat's hands in hers.

"But if our master -- the Sultan among the alims, enlightened by God – the wise Sheikh al-Islam, will prepare a fatwa about Prince Mustafa's mental state: That it was subjected to a temporary disorder due to his long imprisonment in the palace, and his life filled with the fear of being killed. He will soon recover, as the source of the problem has disappeared, and that all of this is in accordance with the law, order, and sharia..." She fell silent and looked sweetly into the woman's eyes... "Won't the madman become a rational man then, my dear Fitnat?"

*She is a dangerous woman,* the wife of Al-Islam's Sheikh thought once again. *A rational man, really?* She giggled.

"Then he will become rational, My Lady."

"Will Hodja Efendi do it?"

"If he knows you want to, he'll do it."

"If so, let him know. We want a madman on the throne. Let him know that under the rule of a madman, prosperity can be better than when there is a wise man in power. Then we'll talk about the prize for Esad Efendi. An inn or a hamam, palace or sandjak, or maybe a banner? Or maybe the Croesus's treasures? He will demand, and a madman will give him."

This time all three laughed. Mahpeyker turned to Ikbal.

"Well, Ikbal. If Esad Efendi creates this fatwa, will our Kaymakam, the esteemed Sofu Mehmed Pasha, order to issue a decree at the Divan saying that, 'under these conditions it is considered appropriate that Prince Mustafa be enthroned, fastens his sword, and that everybody, the viziers, scholars, and all the people swear allegiance to him?'" Saying this, she'd discretely reminded them that she was personally responsible for handing the position over to the man.

"God, My Lady, of course, he will order," Ikbal said without hesitation.

"Great. Let them make Ferman for him. If anyone asked me, our Pasha Sofu would look good with the Sultan's seal in his hand and the hilat of the Great Vizier on his back."

The woman's heart beat like crazy. She would be the wife of a Grand Vizier. She wouldn't live in modest mansions but in big palaces. She was already preparing to throw herself at the neck of Mahpeyker out of happiness and gratitude when all joy suddenly disappeared from her eyes.

"What's up, my good Ikbal? Did something happen?"

"Well," said the woman hesitantly. "Something occurred to me. Let's say everything will go according to the plan. You have succeeded in setting mad Mustafa on the throne, My Lady. But it won't be of any use to you."

Mahpeyker looked at her with a sly smile.

"Time, Ikbal. The passage of time will be our reward."

This time Fitnat spoke:

"But if Mustafa becomes the Sultan, then his mother will kick you, My Lady, and your four sons out. And what if she does something evil...

"Leave that part of the job to me," she said forcefully. "When someone goes hunting, he keeps both an arrow and a rifle at his side." She smiled at two women like a naughty daughter. "Come on, go now, and see. Open your eyes and ears. Don't let your husbands walk off the path because of this woman's words. God be my witness, that later on, I won't interfere. Just remember that until the tray comes to you, you will not reveal the plan to them. This will be our secret."

"A tray?" the women asked in unison.

"Yes, a tray. One tray will arrive for each of you. Then you will explain the issue to your husbands and convince them to act according to the plan. But first, the tray will come – do not forget. Don't say anything before that.

Leaving the Sea Pavilion, where he'd met with Mahfiruz Sultan, Sheikh al-Islam Esad Efendi saw the Vice-Sadrazam, Sofu Mehmed Pasha, entering the building. It was clear that the woman would want the same thing from them. *What is happening in the Ottoman state*, he complained in his mind. *We still don't know if there will be a funeral, and she is already hunting for the inheritance.*

He didn't hurry to leave the courtyard and waited for Mehmed Pasha to leave.

The deputy Grand Vizier left the Sea Pavilion visibly confused.

"Will you do what she wants?" Esad Efendi asked quietly. "Will you do what this woman orders you, Pasha?"

The Vice-Sadrazam nodded in disgust.

"I will not do anything, Hodja Efendi. Isn't it a sin? Isn't it a pity? Is it appropriate? It's all up in the air, and our Padishah, if God so wants, is sound and healthy. Maybe this carriage was called for another reason. Who knows? Does it befit, when we still don't know anything, that this woman would tell us, 'Now it's Prince Osman's turn to take over the reign? Do not wait with the preparations?' And she taught the child, too. 'You will regret it if you do not fulfill your duty well enough!' Something was telling me, 'Throw this sword and seal away, to hell with that! Get away, get out!' And he would lead the great Sultanate of his ancestors to such a state? The son would pray for the death of his father to take the throne?"

They walked side by side in silence for a moment.

"And you?" asked Mehmed Pasha. "Will you issue the fatwa?"

"I won't do anything until I see our master." He paused and walked for a moment, without saying anything. He listened to the sound of gravel crunching under their feet. "You know what, Sofu Pasha?" he said suddenly. "There's no point in hiding, I don't mind the Prince, but every word of this woman stabs into my heart like a dagger. I'm cold next to her. I am freezing."

Sofu Mehmed Pasha limited himself to a thoughtful nod of his head as a response.

Mahpeyker changed her outfit and left the harem. She took only Mürüvvet with her and they both thoroughly covered their faces with a feradje.

The thought that the Prince and his mother were condemned to live in such a place made her cringe. It wasn't without a reason that Mustafa was crazy. Narrow, dark corridors, damp, ruined rooms without windows. It was not a princely apartment, but a dungeon. Even the place they described as a garden was surrounded by a wall taller than three people, and if you didn't lift your head well, there was no way to see the sky. In such a setting, a man would talk both with the walls and with the birds, and if he saw any tiny hole, thought of becoming a bird or a butterfly, and flying away, flapping his wings, would surely pass through his head.

Without warning, she stormed into the room of Prince Mustafa's mother. The woman jumped in fear.

"You..." she blurted out when Mahpeyker lifted her feradje. "My Lady, you..."

"Shhh..." Mahpeyker immediately silenced her and approached her. "The time has come, my good woman."

The woman was in terrible shock. She didn't know what to do or what to say, and she unknowingly moved her arms like bird's wings.

"Can I trust you?"

"Of course."

"When His Majesty the Prince takes the throne..."

Mustafa's mother grabbed her hands, then let go of one, and grabbed the other as if she wanted to kiss her in a gesture of respect, but Mahpeyker wrenched her hand out a bit brutally.

"Will my children and I be safe?"

"Of course."

"I demand an oath, woman."

"I promise you, My Lady. My Prince's palace is your palace, and his mother is a friend and confidant. I will cut and throw away any hand that would be raised at you, even if it is my hand."

"I demand an oath, woman." Mahpeyker's whisper turned into a hiss. "Do you swear to God?"

"I swear to God."

"In that case, if you have watched over your Prince with one eye, now watch over him with a thousand eyes. Do not leave him one step away from you. And he better not get any ideas of becoming a bird or anything like that. And when they ask him if he is ready, he will answer: 'I have been from the very beginning, my mother gave birth to me for this day, what were you thinking?' Is it clear?"

She didn't wait for the woman's answer, and she left just as she came, like a storm. On the way back to the harem, she gave Mürüvvet and order.

"Take the trays. Ladies Fitnat and Ikbal must get their trays right now!"

# CHAPTER ELEVEN

## The New Palace, Sultan Gallery
## November 18th, 1617

Mahpeyker watched the Sultan's return from behind the kafes crate. Ahmed's sorrel horse was dazed and anxious as if he sensed that something was wrong. He probably didn't understand why the rider, whom he always carried on his back, now travels on a wagon pulled by a loose horse. The hunters arrived at the central courtyard in silence. All heads were lowered, and the faces were bleak.

The chief armorer ran to open the coach's door.

Mahpeyker waited with her head spinning for her husband to come out of the carriage. But he didn't appear. The commander of the guard slipped inside, and ten guards lined up in front of the carriage. When the commander reappeared at the door, Kösem let out a sigh.

"God!"

Ahmed was lying in the arms of the guard commander with his arms dangling. He didn't move.

*God!* she lamented in her mind. *And if it is the end, if he died?*

At the same time, another feeling sucked on her. *What if I was late sending the trays?*

The enormous guardsman gently laid down the Padishah on the arms of the guards standing in front of the door, and Ahmed, with the help of ten pairs of hands, was moved on a wooden platform, on which he was carefully brought to his chambers.

Mahpeyker immediately ran to the Sultan's rooms, followed by Semiha. The commander of the guard seemed to have no intention of letting her in, but he got out of the way as soon as he saw the expression on Mahpeyker's face. She rushed past him like the wind. The interior instantly filled with doctors. The deputy of the Grand Vizier, Sofu Mehmed Pasha, joined his hands on his stomach so that the sleeves of his robe were one on top of the other, his head hanging sadly over his left shoulder.

A few doctors gave the women an ill look as if asking what they were doing among so many men, but she didn't pay heed to them, and instead just pushed forward.

"Out of the way! I want to see my dignified Sultan!" she snarled.

They stepped aside and then she saw Ahmed. He was pale, and his body was shaking with horrible convulsions. *He's alive*, was her first thought. *He hasn't died. It turns out that I wasn't late with sending the trays to Fitnat and Ikbal,* she continued in her head.

Her husband's mouth twitched continuously. His eyes were closed.

"God," she murmured. "Help my dear Padishah. Return him to his children and me."

"To the Ottoman Empire," the sullen chief doctor corrected her.

Mahpeyker did not pay attention to it and leaned straight over Ahmed's ear.

"My husband, my Sultan, look, I came. Open your beautiful eyes, the ruler of the world."

Sultan Ahmed was covered with sweat. When she touched the bed with her hand, she noticed that even the sheet was damp. Salty drops poured on the ruler's forehead.

"What is with our master?"

The head medic turned his head in a different direction as if the question had not been directed at him.

She grabbed the Sultan's wrist.

"Wise Musa," Mahpeyker raised her voice. "I asked you a question. What is His Majesty the Sultan's ailment?"

Mahpeyker's sword-cutting voice woke up the doctors' master Musa. *If the Padishah gets better, this woman will stay on top. Just in case, it's better not to make an enemy of her,* he told himself instantly.

"We can't make a diagnosis yet, My Lady. All our Lord's doctors are here, and everyone will examine him one by one; but for the time being, we have not yet discovered the reasons for the disease. He has an unusually high fever, and sweats too much – his body is constantly losing water."

"What's your opinion, scholarly man?"

"If you look at seizures, it seems to resemble a malaria attack, but..."

"But what? Do you suspect that this may be from something else?" she tugged at her ear and knocked on wood to drive away bad luck. "God forbid, is it something bad?"

The man forced himself not to show his irritation.

"God forbid, you have to think about every..."

"What can you do to reduce his fever? Any medicine, a mixture?"

"We're working on it at this very moment, My Lady. We are brewing the mixture."

"And I, what can I do?"

The scholar Musa was unable to stand it anymore and turned to look at Mahpeyker.

"Right now, apart from Allah, no one is able to help our Master. In fact, it is not entirely appropriate that you are here, My Lady. It can be contagious." He fell silent. *The woman certainly understood that I meant plague.* He nodded his head as if he were throwing this possibility out of it. "I'm not saying we have something like that here, My Lady, but we have to think about every eventuality, isn't it so? The health of Princes and dignified ladies is on the line. Please, go to your chambers and have some rest. If we need something, then be sure that I will pass the message immediately."

She really couldn't do anything for Ahmed, but there were a lot of things she should do to save herself and her children.

"So, it shall be," she said reluctantly, with a sad expression on her face, "I entrust to you my dear Padishah, the first doctor. If only I can do anything for you..."

The man bowed his head slightly. "The best thing you can do for our Master and us right now is prayer, noble Lady. Pray as much as you can."

She left the Padishah's room with a sense of unfinished business, and a soft voice spoke inside her: *You saw him for the last time, Mahpeyker.*

Behind her, a huge heavy door closed, and Semiha immediately rushed to her. She didn't have to ask what state the Sultan was in – her Lady's face said it all.

Mahpeyker walked with an expression of great sadness and exhaustion on her face. As she walked among the viziers and agas waiting in the salon, her eyes searched for the governor of the capital, Sofu Mehmed Pasha. He seemed to be in pain, but Mahpeyker noticed with a single glance that what the man really felt was fear. The deputy Grand Vizier was clearly worried as if he was swaying under the weight of black thoughts and didn't know what to do.

She slowed her pace, and as she was passing by him, she whispered to Semiha, walking in front of her.

"If I were in his place, I wouldn't act without listening to my wife first. Otherwise, the effects could be tragic."

Semiha was surprised to hear words she couldn't give meaning to, but Sofu Pasha understood immediately that he was the one who should listen to his wife.


## Midnight
### November 22nd, 1617

Sultan Ahmed's disease developed rapidly. Neither the doctors nor the hodjas or summoners of jinns could understand what it was. After four days of torment in a fever, on the night between the twenty-first and twenty-second of November, 1617, the Padishah died.

Immediately after receiving the news of the Sultan's death, Mahpeyker rushed to the ruler's chambers, crying and lamenting, but this time the door did not open. The guard commander standing in front of it didn't even look her in the face.

The Padishah had died, and she had neither power nor value. The fate of Kösem depended now on the madman's mother and whether the two men would listen to their wives' words.

Ikbal and Fitnat did not return the trays Mürüvvet had sent them. It was the code she'd agreed on with the women; it meant that the deputy of the Grand Vizier and the Sheikh Al-Islam, following her advice, had decided to listen to the words of their wives.

Still, she couldn't feel relaxed. *Humankind*, Mahpeyker said to herself, *can betray at any moment, and until I see Mustafa attach a sword at his belt, there is no peace for me, no trust.*

After the morning Ezan, the first sounds of Sela rang in the same moment from the four minarets of the magnificent, almost finished mosque, erected on Ahmed's order. But it was not yet certain whose death was being announced by the four muezzins with moving voices. The viziers still didn't know that the Padishah had left this world. Kaymakam forbade the doctors from announcing the death of the Sultan and instructed the servants to keep their mouth shut. He also did not forget to mention that whoever opens his mouth, would say goodbye to his life. Until the Divan, everyone should think that the Sultan's serious illness still lasts.

The viziers rushing straight to the Divan after the morning prayer looked overwhelmed with despair. None of them would agree that someone else looked unhappier than him, although, in reality, everyone knew that no one was sad. They were only nervous, that's all. Two questions were floating non-stop around everyone's heads: *Will Prince Osman, after his accession to the throne, keep me at this position?*

As the Sultan's illness extended, more and more of them began to regret that they had not kept closer to Prince Osman and his mother, Mahfiruz Sultan, but they defended themselves in the spirit. *How could I stay close? As soon as Mahpeyker would hear about it, she would immediately order to get rid of me.*

In the heads of almost everyone, the same decision was made – *As soon as the meeting ends, I will run to the Sea Pavilion and kiss the edge of Prince Osman's robes. I will be among the first people to pay him tribute. I will congratulate Mahfiruz Valide Sultan.*

The second question was much more secretive. If the Sultan does not release them from service, what will happen to them? That's what they wondered – who would Osman raise to which position?

*Will Sultan Osman make me a treasurer in place of this idiot, a thief, and the catcher, Nasuhuttin? They say that the damned Nizamettin Chelybee also has his sights set on this job, but...*

*Will the Padishah send away Sofu and make me the Kaymakam?*

Morning Ezan
November 22nd, 1617

The message immediately reached Mahfiruz Sultan, who'd lived through sleepless nights at the Sea Pavilion.

"Our Lord died. Sultan Ahmed died."

Taken by surprise, Mahfiruz fell to the ground.

"God!" She stood up. "Thank you, God!" *The end of captivity, the rule of my son Osman will be the end of that woman!* "You showed me this day! Be praised a thousand times!"

Only after a long moment did she notice that the servants were looking at her in horror and at that moment she understood her mistake. It wasn't often to see Sultanas fall to the floor and thank God at the news of the Padishah's death.

*Pull yourself together*, her mind warned her. *You are Valide Sultan from now on. Behave properly*. So, she did.

"Run," she told her courtiers. "Let's pass the message to the ruler."

Reading the eyes of her servant girls, she realized they were thinking, *the ruler is dead*.

"Let the Sultan Osman know that the time has come for his reign."

They ran. Prince Osman woke up at their shouts.

"What's happening?" he scolded his sentry. "What's that noise?"

He understood when the watchman threw himself to his feet: *My father has gone to eternity*.

*If so... if so...* He didn't have time to finish his thoughts. The door opened, and his mother burst inside like a hurricane.

"May your life and rule last a long time, my son. Blessed be your reign."

Prince Osman, pushing aside his robe, prevented his mother from kissing it. He felt his heart beating faster, and he could almost hear his blood pulsating through his veins.

"Allah... do not let me disgrace myself," he murmured. *It means I have accepted the reign, I have made peace with it*.

"Come on, get to work," Mahfiruz rushed to his wardrobe. "You have to prepare immediately." Then she suddenly remembered that the messengers would want their tip, the baksheesh, in exchange for their minor duty in bringing her the news. "The messengers of the good news can come here for their baksheesh any moment," she added.

"Mother, mother..."

"Now, now, put on your clothes, my son, Padishah."

# CHAPTER TWELVE

The New Palace, Divan
Morning, November 22nd, 1617

The Divan gathered in a grim mood on this dark November morning. As the Grand Vizier and Commander-in-Chief, Halil Pasha were campaigning against Persia, the Governor of the capital, Kaymakam Sofu Mehmed Pasha, was to lead the meeting again – but he was nowhere to be seen. All heads hung over left arms, hands clasped on the bellies. The Ottoman Empire was in mourning.

Sofu Mehmed Pasha finally came in with a sad, thoughtful face, shuffling his legs.

"Salam alejkum," he murmured, sitting down in his seat.

He adjusted his clothes and hair as if it was very necessary, and pulled out the sleeves of his caftan. After a long moment, he finally spoke.

"The Ottoman Empire suffered a great loss," he said in a muffled voice.

The meeting room filled at once with groans and sighs.

"Rest in peace."

"May the Lord forgive the sins of our Ruler."

"Do not talk like that, Pasha. What sins did our Master commit? Will Allah show some other place than Paradise to the faithful, who ordered to build this great mosque on a hippodrome from the stones carried in his own robe?"

Those who knew that too many lamentations would not do much good, gently steered the conversation to other tracks, to talk about the future.

"What can we say, a divine sentence."

"Exactly, exactly. Fate is not a giaur so that it could be chased away from our Lord with a sword."

"May God not allow the State and the nation to fall."

That was what the Vice-Sadrazam Sofu Mehmed Pasha was waiting for.

"Of course," he tried to give his voice a tone of firmness. "Let Allah defend the Ottoman Empire and the Muhammad community. It's time to take some measures, gentlemen."

"Yes, yes, exactly," the whispers resounded.

Instead, in their minds, the words really sounded like this: *Come on, let's decide to bring good news to Prince Osman. We are in a hurry.*

Sofu Mehmed Pasha addressed Esat Efendi: "What should be done in this situation, noble Hodja? Do you have any fatwa?"

What? All the Viziers lifted their heads from their left shoulders in astonishment and looked at the Kaymakam. Fatwa? What fatwa? Padishah has died. Prince Osman will take the throne. Why does this man need a fatwa?

Esad Efendi moved his lips for a moment. For as long as the Hodja prayed, there was dead silence in the hall. Finally, he said:

"The situation is as follows. Because His Majesty the Padishah has joined our merciful God, the throne of the Ottomans is deserted. We know that our Lord left three sons: Prince Osman, Prince Murad, and Prince Ibrahim, but the last two are very small. It is understood that the eldest son is Prince Osman."

The Hodja fell silent, and the viziers confirmed his words, nodding their heads. Obviously, Prince Osman was the eldest son.

Esad Efendi moved his lips again – they thought that this time it was only to pray for Prince Osman.

"Yet it is known," Al-Islam continued, "that while he was still healthy, our Lord did not appoint anyone as his successor. Now you can ask why he should do it? We know who the successor is. The eldest prince, that is, Osman."

The heads began to nod again, but this time there were impatient whispers among the crowd.

"It means, we can assume that our Master did not designate his eldest son for the future ruler, because, anyway, the identity of the successor is known, right?"

"Yes, yes," a couple of the viziers murmured.

"Is it really?" Esad Efendi said doubtfully. "If we assume so, then what was the significance of the changes that our Padishah made in the law? If the right to the throne belongs to the eldest son, what about the right of the eldest Prince of the dynasty? Why would our Lord announce that power should be passed on to the eldest man from the family?"

Deputy Sadrazam, Sofu Mehmed Pasha, decided it was time to support Sheikh al-Islam.

"It should be so by definition, Noble Hodja. 'If there is an older representative of the Ottoman dynasty than the oldest son of the deceased Padishah, for example, a brother or an uncle, the reign should be his.' The purpose is no different here than the change introduced by our Sultan in law."

The two men looked at each other stealthily. Following the path laid down by Mahpeyker, they'd just burned bridges behind them, and if their words don't manifest, and the son of Mahfiruz takes the throne, then the greatest grace will be if they'll be allowed to choose their kind of death.

The rows of the viziers were startled with astonishment, and one of those in a lower position expressed what others had in mind.

"It means that the right to the throne does not belong to Prince Osman, but..."

It was certain that the man would say, 'to the madman,' but Sheikh al-Islam immediately reacted.

"We're not talking about specific people here, sir," he grumbled, then he muttered something under his breath and breathed the air in two directions like for a spell. "The purpose of my words was to issue a judgment consistent with Sharia, justice, divine precepts, and order, and also with the law that our Lord left as his Will. What other reason could I have?"

Mehmed Pasha then intervened so as not to drag the discussion too long.

"Gentlemen," he said in a confident voice, his face austere. "It is not befitting that, while the blessed body of our Padishah has not cooled yet, his slaves are sitting here and looking for the owner for his inheritance. The law is clear," he turned around. "Do you have a fatwa, Noble Hodja? Announce it to us. Who will take the throne? The eldest son or the oldest one of the Dynasty?"

Esad Efendi swallowed and finally said powerfully:

"The latter, Sofu Pasha. That's what the law says – not the oldest of sons, but of the lineage."

There was an uproar among the ranks of the viziers, and the deputy Sadrazam, together with Sheikh Al-Islam, both thought in this moment of the same thing. It was certain that Sultana Mahfiruz talked to many other officials, not only to them.

Mehmed Pasha decided that it was necessary to control the situation now. He had to suppress the commotion and lead to the issuance of the fatwa before the supporters of Mahfiruz gathered strength.

"Gentlemen!"

Nobody listened to him. The viziers were arguing, gesticulating lively.

"Is it proper to do so, my dear?"

"Certainly not."

"What are they saying?"

"Who heard of a brother becoming a Sultan if the son is alive?"

"Nobody, but the Hodja is also right. The law is clear."

"Right, the law is in force, and we are going to determine it here? In that case, we will trample the Sultan's firman."

The deputy Grand Vizier rose with rage.

"Gentlemen!" he roared.

This time his voice made the right impression. Alarmingly, he rested his hand on the sash wrapped around his waist. Viziers were not allowed to enter the debate with weapons, but who was to check what was inside the belt? There have been arguments at the Divan many times: sometimes it happened that people struggled, they beat each other, and even drew daggers.

"It seems that what I just said has not been heard!" Mehmed Pasha yelled. "And you call yourselves subordinates? Our Lord's body has not cooled down yet, and you already want to trample the law and order he has introduced? If principles can be abused, what will happen to peace and order in the empire?"

He sat down in his seat angrily. The third vizier stepped forward.

"We are not against the law, Sofu Pasha, but there is a problem."

"What's this problem?"

"If we would look at the commandment of our Padishah of the holy memory, then the throne would..."

The man did not say the rest, but another one finished for him: "A madman, crazy... This man is mad. Will you push Mad Mustafa on the throne? The Empire has a Sultan brave like a lion at hand, and it should be ruled by a loon? He's not only unpredictable but he's also a dullard. He can't even read or write. Are we to give the state into the hands of a complete idiot and a crank?"

Mehmed Pasha got all purple, but he managed to keep his nerves in check.

He nodded as if he shared the opinion of the third vizier.

"It doesn't matter that he is illiterate, because what is the Divan for? Aren't the viziers and scholars enough? But the state of mind..." he nodded again. "What do you say, Noble Hodja? It is quite clear what the mind of Prince Mustafa is like."

The moment of truth had arrived. The lives of countless people now depended on a few sentences that Esad Efendi would say at this moment.

"I have been thinking about this issue since the day our Ruler got ill. What should we base our decision on? How to combine the Sharia and the Sultan's judgment in one sentence so that justice can be preserved, and the empire enjoy eternal peace and order?"

The murmurs sounded again, but Esad Efendi silenced them, raising his hand. He didn't care who would become a Padishah. At that moment he had to save his head.

"Listen," he continued. "The law is on the side of Prince Mustafa. Conversely, the custom is in favor of Prince Osman. You're right, it has not happened to this day that a son of the Padishah lived, and somebody else took the throne. That was both the tradition and the code from the time of the Sultan the Conqueror. However, a new law is in force now. The paths of rules and customs have parted ways. Which one will we follow? Will we follow the tradition or the new law established by our Lord?" he paused for a moment and looked in turn at the faces of all the viziers. "I will tell you to stick to the letter of the law."

Once again, the murmurs rose, but this time they seemed less angry.

"Listen, listen," he raised his hand again. "Doesn't what I say, speak in your mind? I asked the doctors about the situation of Prince Mustafa and prayed for a prophetic dream, and here is what I have decided, gentlemen. The Prince's mind, due to long-term imprisonment in the palace and a life spent in fear of being killed, has been temporarily derailed, but there is no doubt that with the removal of the reason for this state of affairs, His Majesty will shortly recover. This solution is consistent with the law, order, and Sharia law." He put his hand under the caftan. "Here, Mehmed Pasha is the fatwa I wrote at his head, the night after our Ruler fell asleep in the Lord."

The Divan was silent. The fatwa of Sheikh al-Islam was now getting in the middle of the issue as well. As dangerous it was to go against the decree, it was equally dangerous to oppose the fatwa.

The deputy Sadrazam took the parchment drawn by Esad Efendi, parted it, and read carefully as if he didn't know what was written on it.

"Personally," he said later, "I am also of the opinion that the state of Prince Mustafa is completely temporary. And so, when we go to inform him about enthronement, we will see whether there is order in his head or not. There is one more thing that we must consider. Prince Osman is older than the others, but in fact, he is still a child, and the Ottoman Empire is threatened from everywhere. The peace with the unfaithful in the West is in the air, and the noble Sadrazam Pasha fights the Safavid Shah. Putting a child on the Sultan's throne in such conditions can give the enemy a message that we do not actually exist.

He raised his hand holding the fatwa.

"This is the Sharia judgment." He put his other hand on his chest. "The splendid judgment of our Master is also in my heart. This is what the situation and circumstances dictate to us." He paused for a moment, pointing to his head, and looked meaningfully at the viziers, who still had not come out of shock. He stood up. "If so, let it be written." The scribes immediately grabbed their pens.

Kaymakam dictated the firmans in a raised voice, one by one:

"'In view of these conditions, it is considered appropriate to enthrone Prince Mustafa. It is ordered that there was no obstacle for the viziers, scholars, and all other subjects to pay homage to him at the sword-dressing ceremony.'"

He waited for the scribes to finish writing and pressed the first seal to the parchment stretched out before him.

"God bless the Ottoman Empire."

Hence, what happened, happened. At that moment there was no turning back.

Mahpeyker Sultana's orders were fulfilled to the letter, one by one. It was time to check what Prince Mustafa's state of mind really was.

Mustafa's mother, the new Mother Sultana, opened the door to them, and without losing time, invited them inside.

"Our Master will receive you."

The viziers were surprised, thinking that they would find the Prince talking to birds or in the process of tumbling on the ground, but Mustafa was sitting on the couch. His turban, which had been ill-fitting on his head all his life, was in the right place that morning. The man's gaze was sharp but calm. His hands, folded slightly in the elbows, rested on his knees.

He was sitting as the Padishah should sit.

"My Prince," Sofu Mehmed Pasha said gently, "your older brother has joined the Lord. May Allah give you a long life."

Kaymakam and Sheikh Al-Islam were afraid that he would do something crazy now, but the prince Mustafa responded in a sad but tough voice: "And you be healthy, too. Same for the Empire. People are mortal, the state is eternal. May the Sublime Porte last forever."

Mehmed Pasha and Esed Efendi breathed a sigh of relief, and the viziers standing behind them were astonished. These were not the words of a madman, but a sage, and that meant that the noble Hodja was right. Mustafa's madness was temporary. It could even be that he pretended to be mad, for fear of being killed.

"The Divan decided about your enthronement, my Prince. Are you ready?"

Prince Mustafa rose with lightness and went straight to Deputy Sadrazam. Taking his time, he looked at the faces of the people who came to give him the good news, one by one.

*And he doesn't look at us like a madman at all,* went through everybody's mind.

Kaymakam spoke softly again. "My Prince. Are you ready to take the throne?"

These were the keywords: 'Are you ready?' that his mother had prepared him for. As soon as he would hear this, he knew should answer with the words that his mother had been teaching him all for many days without respite, without fatigue. And that's what Mustafa did.

"I have been from the very beginning. My mother gave birth to me for this day. What were you thinking?"

He passed the exam. Mehmed Pasha fell to his feet with the words: "My Sultan," and the others followed.

## Before Noon
### November 22nd, 1617

Mahfiruz, who had been waiting for people to come and collect the throne baksheesh, went berserk when she learned that reign was to be passed on to Mustafa, and she jumped on the messengers who brought the news.

"Liars! Get out of my sight! What kind of idea is that to give the Ottoman empire to a madman?"

She needed time to accept the truth. She shook violently with rage.

"Enough," Prince Osman said quietly. "That's enough, Mother. Enough." He sank in thoughts, deeply disappointed.

"Nooo...!" Mahfiruz shouted. "It is not the end. This is just the beginning." She lunged out of her seat as if she had a rival opposite her. "Until I tear your heart out of your breast with these here fingernails, this issue is not over, Mahpeykeeer...!"

Osman raised his head for a moment. His heart was bleeding as he watched his mother beating the air with her fists.

"Mother," he said. "Stop it already. We lost. She is stronger than you. Clever enough to put a madman on the Empire's throne. Can't you see? This hostility will cost us dearly. Stop it, enough!"

The woman looked at her son with eyes full of flames.

"No, *you* stop it!" she screamed. "Until I put you on the throne and take the life of this witch, I have no right to silence and peace, don't you understand?"

The feeling that Mahpeyker must be laughing victoriously at the same moment made her even angrier.

"Laugh all you want, peasant Sultana!" she howled. "Laugh! When the executioners come to cut your head, I will laugh like this, too!"

Meanwhile, Mahpeyker waited anxiously in her chambers for the news. She trembled from anxiety because she knew the taste of betrayal all too well. One of the courtiers stormed into the room like a hurricane.

"Lady, they just brought the news. The Divan has decided. It was announced that Prince Mustafa would take the throne. They asked if he was ready, and he reportedly replied: 'From the very beginning.'

*You are finished, spider...* was her first thought. *I crushed you.*

She turned toward the window and stared at the heavy clouds.

"Thanks be to God," she whispered. "We're saved! I bought the time needed for Murad to be able to take the throne!"

# CHAPTER THIRTEEN

## The New Palace
## February 1618

It didn't take long before she realized that she'd been too quick to think that they were saved.

She'd thoroughly thought over and planned everything, but she'd not taken into account the head of the black eunuchs, Hasanbeyzade Mustafa Aga, or the fact that it was harder to rule one madman than the entire state.

For the first few days, it seemed that everything was on the right track. On the same day that the Divan made their decision about the enthronement, and even before Ahmed's body was given away to the earth, a public homage ceremony was arranged for Mustafa in front of the Gate of Greeting. And that same afternoon, Sultan Ahmed, in accordance with his Will, was put to rest in an unfinished tomb next to the mosque he'd ordered to be built. Two days later, the ceremony of fitting the sword for Mustafa took place, and the meat of the slaughtered sacrifices was distributed to the poor in a gesture of charity.

Already on the third day, the first sign of danger appeared. The mother of Sultan Mustafa decided to move to the Valide Sultan rooms, occupied for years by Mahpeyker. Since the woman was unable to come in person and say it to Kösem's face, she sent a message:

'Forgive me, Lady, you are our blessed defender. Whatever you order, will happen in the palace, but due to the tradition and customs it would not be appropriate for the rumors to spread.'

Although she didn't let it show, Mahpeyker admitted that the woman was right. Mahfiruz was certainly prepared for spreading slanders. *Who rules the Ottoman Empire? Here, let them say who the Padishah is, let's find out. A mad Sultan or a woman called Mahpeyker?* So, without a word of complaint, she changed her apartment and began secretly telling the Padishah's mother, what should, and what should not be done – except that Mustafa wasn't able to listen to anyone.

The administrator of the black eunuchs quickly pulled the Padishah into the world of entertainment. He invented many ordinary and extraordinary games, from tag with girls in the rose garden, to races on alabaster in the Sultan's hamam, and in the meantime, he didn't forget to whisper who should be assigned where, and whom to dismiss.

The Sultan's mother noticed in the blink of an eye that her son was under the authority of the chief eunuch. What's more, as soon as she was certain that the man had secretly contacted Mahfiruz, she took measures that would, to the best of her understanding, prevent his meetings with the Padishah. For example, if Mustafa Aga had something to say to the Sultan, he would have to first see the Valide Sultan and give his words to her.

This move, although intended to be salutary, turned out to be deadly.

Understanding that he would no longer be able to reach the Ruler and persuade him to fulfill his whims, Hasanbeyzade Mustafa Aga changed his tactics and began spreading rumors about the mental under-development of the new Padishah. It was clear that many of them had been invented by Mahfiruz, but many were true.

"Have you heard?" That's how every whisper started. "The great Padishah is a holy simpleton, and that's why he neglects the affairs of the state."

"And this is news? He plays with servants and slaves, and he showers whoever wins with gold and diamonds."

"Don't ask. I heard things, too. Apparently, he organized a belly dance contest with one of the odalisques. He undressed like a dancer, showed his stomach, and swung his hips. When the girl won, it's a shame to even talk about it, he put a ruby the size of a walnut in her belly button."

"What a shame..."

"Shame, indeed! Apparently, alims say that if he rules a little longer, then they won't be surprised if he distributes all the gold and silver of the treasury, and leave it completely empty."

"They have no right to complain. Aren't they the ones who put Mustafa on our head, while they could have chosen the bravest of the brave, young Osman?"

The hodjas arriving to infuse spells to restore the mental health of the Padishah, ran to Sultana Mahpeyker begging for mercy:

"The ruler's condition has not improved at all. It is necessary to make His Highness's indisposition a state secret, but the administrator of the black eunuchs spreads the secrets of the throne in all directions. Hasanbeyzade Mustafa Aga must be dismissed as soon as possible."

Valide Sultan, however, didn't feel like following Kösem's instructions anymore.

According to her, there was only one reason why the Padishah went crazy – the need for a woman! She believed that once they manage to bring one to the Ruler, everything would go back to normal.

To wake up lust in her son, she brought girls from everywhere, from China, from India, from Anatolia, and led them to Mustafa's bedroom – but to no avail. At night, the half-naked odalisques jumped out of bed and escaped, and the Padishah chased after them calling out: 'Don't run away, girl. I touched you, now I'll run, and you will chase.' After this event, instructors were hired from among the specialists hunting for customers in Galata wineries, for fishermen and sailors. At night they were secretly brought to the palace and let into Mustafa's rooms – but this way didn't work either, and moreover – women couldn't keep silent and began to spread gossip.

"God, you know what kind of man this is? You tell him, 'Take this bird and place it in the nest,' and he looks at you and asks: 'What bird?'", and then they laughed.

At the end of the first month, Sultan Mustafa was fully out of control. He began to put the palace on its feet in the middle of the night and give orders.

"Prepare the forces. My carriage is to be ready. I'm going on an expedition!"

And when, pleading with the Ruler for mercy, the servants did not obey the order, he screamed at the top of his lungs. Reluctantly, the units formed and together with the Padishah went out for a night ride through the streets of Istanbul. Who knows in how many districts people were woken up at night by screams: "Beware, unfaithful dogs!

Son of Khan Mehmed, Sultan Mustafa goes for an expedition! I'm going to wrap my sword around your heads, huh!"

At night he visited graves.

He went out to the beach and threw gold as the bait for fish.

Finally, he began to take an interest in the Divan gatherings. He would enter the room in the middle of the meeting, snatch the viziers' turbans, kick them one by one, and he would give jewels to the owner of the one that had sailed the highest.

This time it was Mahfiruz who invited Ikbal and Fitnat to her chambers.

"Tell your husbands," her voice swished like a whip, "that they must choose a side. Let them decide. How long will they close their eyes to the scandals of the madman whom they have brought on our head, beguiled by this woman? Huh, I've got everything ready! This case will end, and they will fix their mistakes, begging my son for forgiveness. Otherwise, they should be ready to bear the consequences."

The Deputy Grand Vizier, Sofu Mehmed Pasha, and Sheikh al-Islam Esad Efendi regretted it very much already. Due to Mahpeyker Sultan's persuasion, they had thrown the Ottoman Empire into the abyss. It was not the time to ask her for advice or to listen to her anymore. Soldiers in the barracks had even started shouting: 'We want Osman!'

The manager of the black eunuchs, Mustafa, who'd been hiding in the shadows for some time, came back onto the stage, and after one of the meetings that he'd secretly organized with Mahfiruz Sultan, he began to talk everywhere:

"It's much more than a weakness of mind. I will not interfere if Mustafa Khan orders to strangle the sons of our Padishah of the holy memory. It's not my sin, but of those who let him off the leash."

This rumor was the final straw that broke the camel's back.

In mid-February 1618, Mehmed Pasha and Esad Efendi invited state officials to the palace. Mahpeyker immediately learned about the commotion. Men running in all directions passed the news that even a few Beylerbeys had arrived. *This is the wrong moment*, she thought, and swallowing her pride, she visited the Mother Sultana.

"Do you know what's going on? Why are there so many people here?" she asked.

"There's no reason to be afraid," answered the mother of the Padishah. "Sofu Pasha swore that it was only a meeting about Lafa."

"Strange," she grumbled. "A Lafa Divan gathering ninety-six days after the sword has been given to your son?"

"That's what I said," said the woman. "Beylerbeys who live far away need time to arrive."

"What about the soldiers filling the courtyard? Are they waiting for the Lafa, too? They've already been given a coronation baksheesh."

Valide Sultan had a ready answer to everything.

"I asked Pasha," she said. This time her voice and attitude said, 'I am as smart as you.' "They are supposedly the warriors of the beys, viziers, and agas, arriving for the Divan. They have gathered for their baksheesh."

Mahpeyker wasn't convinced at all, but she couldn't do anything. *Stupid,* she said to herself.

## February 18th, 1618

What she feared, indeed happened.

At the sign of Sofu Mehmed Pasha, the soldiers – who according to his words came for the Sultana Mother's baksheesh – blocked the door to the Padishah's chambers. Mustafa screamed from behind the door for a long time: "Leave the birds alone! Don't lock them up! Leave them, let them go!"

The ninety-six-day of the reign of Sultan Mustafa was ended by a coup d'état.

Sofu Mehmed Pasha together with the two Beylerbeys left in the middle of the Divan gathering to go to the Sea Pavilion. They fell at the feet of Prince Osman and begged for mercy.

Osman, waving his hand as if he were chasing away flies, managed to say: "You can go, you have been forgiven."

Mehmed Pasha informed him about the Divan's ordinance: "They've dealt with your Uncle Mustafa. He's now locked up. The time has come for your enthronement."

They took Prince Osman with them, along with Mahfiruz who was drowning in tears of happiness, and after introducing him to the throne, which they'd ordered to be placed before the Gate of Greetings, they announced the new Padishah.

Sofu Mehmed Pasha was the first among all those viziers, beys, agas, beylerbeys, and all officials summoned to the carpet that could come to mind, to shout:

"Let your life and rule last forever. Long live the Padishah!" And he paid homage to the new Sultan, kissing his hand and robe.

Mahpeyker heard the turmoil from afar.

"What's happening?" she stood up. "Open the windows, I want to hear it."

The courtiers ran up, opened the windows, and let the shouts of joy reach inside, along with the freezing February air.

"Long live the Padishah!"

She was surprised. The courtiers, sick of Mustafa, showing him the signs of affection?

"Let your life and rule last as long as possible!"

"A thousand years for the Ruler!"

"May you be as great as your ancestor, Osman Ghazi, Young Osman!"

*Osman!* Mahpeyker shivered in terror. *The spider,* her brain hissed. *The spider got her way!*

"Do they say, Osman?"

Nobody dared to say yes.

"They have overthrown Mustafa?"

She knew the answer to this question anyway. The mad Sultan went down in the palace revolution. Maybe they even killed him – she didn't care. Even if he was alive, death was already knocking on hers and her children's door. The wheel had turned, and this time the fortune smiled at the Ice Queen. Now the strength was in the hand of the devil.

"Run," she whispered to Mürüvvet, to not show her panic. She couldn't know that her pale face expressed all the fear that had seized her. "Bring my sons and daughters here. And their nannies, too. Let everyone gather here. Nobody will leave or get in without my knowledge. Order to close the door. Put on a guard. Let him not dare to open without giving his life – let him know that otherwise, I will kill him myself. And you, Semiha, send one of the girls, let her probe the moods."

Suddenly, she saw how stupid all the orders she'd issued were.

*Which door is to be kept close? Against whom? With what force? And why probe the moods? Everything was clear as day. I am defeated because of the thoughtlessness of some idiot woman. The spider had spun her web and drove us into it.*

A noise of trumpets, cymbals, and drums of the military orchestra joined the shouts now. Crazy Mustafa was gone, and young Osman appeared. The capital celebrated the rule of Sultan Osman.

*And my end*, she thought. *And the end of Mahpeyker Kösem Sultan.*


Mürüvvet returned with Prince Murad and Ibrahim. The girls had been brought in earlier. Suddenly Mahpeyker made a crazy decision. She would not wait in a trap until they kill them. They will leave the New Palace secretly, go to the Old one, and from there they will find a way out of the city.

"Şarazad," she called the woman. "Make them prepare two or three carriages. We'll go down the stairs to the courtyard of the grooms, no one will see us. Let one of the people loyal to us come out and take the carriage outside. We can't draw attention to ourselves, have you understood?"

Sarasad nodded and ran, but it wasn't even one or two minutes before she came back. Now her face was chalk-white, too.

"What happened? You made it?"

"They didn't let me through," the woman said quietly. "Guardsmen and soldiers guard the door. They say they won't let anyone in or out."

She felt blood filling her head at once. They let themselves be trapped.

"Wiiiitch...!" she shouted. "A mountain witch... a spider, a scorpion, a caterpillar, a snake... a devil!"

Semiha and Şarazad silenced Mahpeyker by force, covering her mouth with their hands. Her entire body was shaking.


Sultan Mahfiruz, laughing with joy, eagerly awaited her son's return.

She walked around the room for a moment, then finally opened a trunk and took a bundle from it. She chose one of several pouches, untied the knot, and picked up what was inside.

A ring!

She looked for a long time at the ring Safiye Sultan had given to Handan, which she'd taken off her mother-in-law's finger the night of her death.

"Hey, ring, end of the slavery," she whispered. "I have kept you until today in your pouch because apparently you only come to help to the Sultan's Mother. The day has just come. The Adjarian girl Mahfiruz has become the Sultana Mother of the Ottomans.

She put the ring on her finger and, holding her hand by the candlelight, looked at the hand with the jewel. Next to the diamonds and emeralds on her other fingers, its dead, dullness made her shiver. It crossed her mind that had she not heard of its power with her own ears, she wouldn't wear the ugly thing, not even for a moment.

*Look carefully. Make a good memory of the new Valide Sultan. From today on, you will show your charm and power on my finger. Do what you have to do – bring my son, the Padishah, and me, a healthy and happy reign.*

She couldn't kill time and kept walking back and forth around the room. After she put the ring on, she felt more powerful in some strange way, sprightlier, as if her senses had sharpened.

"I'm coming, Mahpeyker," she hissed loudly. "Just wait, I'm coming."

Her first order as a Mother Sultana was to start the preparations for moving to the New Palace.

"We're leaving here, my ladies," she said to her courtiers. "We're going to where we should be. Hurry up."

While the girls were moving feverishly, she gestured Taciser to stay and whispered something into her ear. Taciser bowed to her with an ominous smile and left.

Mahfiruz Valide Sultan looked for a moment at the departing courtier. *Your Azrael is on his way, Mahpeyker,* she thought. *Can you hear? The sound that comes to you is Azrael's steps!*

Sultan Osman, tired after a busy day, came to his mother.

"Give me your hand," he said. The voice of the new Padishah was caressing and respectful. "I shouldn't begin to rule without kissing my mother's hand and without asking for her blessing."

Mahfiruz let him kiss her hand.

"I have," she said in a voice thrilled with emotion and greed, "only one wish, my son and Ruler. My courageous young Osman."

"Osman will do anything you want, Mother. Say it already."

"This woman," Mahfiruz hissed. "That woman and her children... everybody..."

Sultan Osman freed himself from his mother's embrace and turned to the door.

"Do not demand it from me, Mother," he said firmly. "Don't tell me to shed the blood of my siblings. I will not do it, no matter what happens." He was about to leave when a possibility occurred to him, and he turned back. "And I will not let you do it either, Mother. You say she is a snake, so do not step on her tail."

He left. Mahfiruz stood there for a long time, stunned. *Let it be so, son,* she finally thought. *I hope that this snake that you've saved, who you are afraid of stepping on the tail of, will not turn back and bite you. May the brothers, with whose blood you did not stain your hands, not drink your blood!*

She couldn't allow herself to fall asleep. Ibrahim's disobedience was like salt rubbed into the wound of her nightmare. It was as if the Prince was aware of the situation and the danger they faced. He didn't stop crying – not even for a moment.

She jumped to her feet because there was a commotion outside. *They're coming. They're coming to kill us.*

If so, she will show them how Mahpeyker Kösem Sultan dies.

When Semiha appeared in the doorway with her face red, she scolded her: "Let them in, let them come. They are coming for one life, aren't they? Let them come and take it. But my Princes and Princesses are still very small. They should save the children."

"Pa... pa..." Semiha stuttered. "Padi... shah is coming..."

*What? Osman will come? What for? To watch them kill me? What am I supposed to do now? Should I greet him solemnly, as befits Mahpeyker Sultan, or fall to his feet and beg for the lives of my children?*

She would never do it. She would not whine in front of him to save her offspring, she wouldn't let them live with that shame. *Better for them to die*, she thought to herself. She chose the first way.

She sat comfortably on the couch, adjusted her clothes, raised her head, and straightened her shoulders. She tried her best to put a confident smile on her face. She wasn't even going to get up.

As soon as she heard the buzz, she understood that Osman was approaching.

"Let him come in," she said in an icy voice so that there would be no doubt that she was heard outside. "Let him come in."

Sultan Osman appeared on the threshold. She was going to assess the look and attitude of the Sultan standing opposite her, and draw conclusions, but she couldn't do it. Out of turmoil and anxiety, she'd forgotten that Prince Ibrahim was in the room. As soon as the boy saw that a stranger in a large turban stood in the doorway, he paused his lament for a second, then began to wail with even greater force.

Hearing the noise, the nanny immediately ran up, and taking Prince Ibrahim in her arms, led him out of the room. Everyone still had the boy's cries in their ears.

"Quite small, but he has very strong lungs," Osman said, smiling slightly.

Suddenly, suspicions rose in Mahpeyker. What did it mean, 'has strong lungs?' It is a pity, he will need them soon. He should not strain them in vain, right?

"Exactly," she said coldly. "He's very naughty."

The new Padishah nodded.

"How does Murad feel?"

Mahpeyker's distrust increased even more. Why does he ask about him? Will he ask about all my children in turn?"

"Well. Very well."

*He's grown a lot,* she thought. *Since I last saw him, he became a big man. You can even call him handsome.*

Suddenly, her heart was torn by enormous pain. *Oh, what would it be like if my Murad was this age? There wouldn't be the son of the spider, but my Prince appearing in that door, the Padishah with a turban on his head and in an ermine caftan.*

Young Osman hadn't seen Mahpeyker for years, either, and he'd only heard bad words and curses about her from his mother. But, of course, he'd also heard that she was beautiful, so beautiful that his father forgot about his mother. *True*, he thought to himself. *She's still beautiful.*

"You have become a Padishah," Mahpeyker said, though these words had not come from her mind. *God damn it*, she thundered inside. *Why did I say that?*

Osman nodded, and there was still a strange, frail, ever so vague, almost imperceptible smirk on his face.

*Maybe he's even laughing at my situation?* she snarled in her mind. Her reason didn't listen to her again. "I wish you happiness and prosperity," she said quickly.

Osman nodded again.

"Look," he said suddenly. "We both know each other well. You are the woman who, to prevent my reign, cooperated with my crazy uncle. My mother was..."

"Have you come to tell me about your Mother? Has Mahfiruz, on the day of her son's coronation, designate him to take revenge? Will you be our executioner?"

Young Osman smiled.

*He looks nice with a smile*, crossed Mahpeyker's head. She scolded herself at once for that thought, too.

"No," said the Padishah, sitting lightly on the edge of the couch opposite her. "I just wanted to express the feelings that we have about each other. I can guess what you are feeling now. You are afraid for yourself and my siblings. There is no need. You have acted against me, but know that I am not your enemy. I do not want to stain my reign with blood, and especially with the blood of my brothers. Some will probably think I'm wrong, but that's what I want, that's what I think. And so, it will be."

*What is this kid saying?* Mahpeyker said to herself. *He would not be my enemy? He wouldn't want to stain himself with the blood of his brothers? He probably means his mother, speaking about 'some.'*

She felt as if a giant weight had been taken off her shoulders.

"Be exalted for these feelings," she whispered.

"However," said Osman, "it would no longer be appropriate for you to stay here. I think you will agree to it too. Later this night, along with my siblings, you will move to the Old Palace."

The scream, which sounded in her head, shook all Mahpeyker's cells. The Old Palace! The palace of exile!

"I promise you," said Osman, "I promise you that you will live there in peace and safety. Nobody will be allowed to hurt you. And you will stay there, as tradition dictates."

Without giving her the opportunity to say anything, Sultan Osman turned around and left, sweeping the floor with his robe's hems.

At that moment she didn't know what to think.


"Come on, it's time to go," they said, less than an hour later.

They entered the carriages in the light of torches held by rows of soldiers on two sides of the courtyard. Whips snapped. Horseshoes hit the stones. The wheels turned. On the road leading to the Gate of the Greetings, guardsmen lined up on one side, and soldiers on the other. Torches painted the dark courtyards of the palace with a mysterious red. Suddenly, Mahpeyker remembered the night when Sultan Ahmed came to the Old Palace to take her. She thought the torches were the fireflies. Ahmed greeted her with them. Now, among the fireflies, she was going to the place of exile.

*What am I going to do?* she asked herself. *God, what am I going to do?*

Listening to the sounds of wheels and horseshoes in the darkness of the carriage, she still hadn't decided what she should think or do.

Despite herself, she looked at the dark emptiness opposite her. When she was going to the Old Palace, Sofia was sitting there. Now she was going back without her.

She didn't even know the place where the girl was. Who knows where they buried her. Her interior covered with flames. The undine became the victim of her insatiable ambition. A tear ran down her cheek.

"Forgive me," she whispered. "I didn't want it to happen, Sofia. Forgive your sister. I'm begging you, I'm..."

She shook these thoughts off abruptly.

"Hang on, Mahpeyker," she murmured. "It's not the time for sentiments. You are going to the Old Palace. To exile..."

She looked outside, poking her head out the window. Far away, in front of them, clouds of fireflies were flying in the darkness.

The Old Palace!

*The nest of my service and exile,* came into her head. *They lit torches and are waiting for me.*

The cold air striking her face did her good. She drew in the freezing air. For a moment, she thought about letting her hair out through the window, but she couldn't get herself to do it.

"Inside!" shouted the rider who suddenly appeared by her side. "Inside!"

She withdrew and covered the window with a leather curtain. She wiped the tears rolling down her cheeks with the back of her hand. She forgot that she was now a prisoner.

Later that night, she moved to the chambers of Safiye Sultan and stretched out on the bed in which she gave her life. She put her head on the pillow.

"My Mother, the Sultana." She let her tears flow. "I come to you. Help me. Show me the way... how to save myself from this exile. You gave the throne to your son, and now show me the coronation of Murad.

She threw back her pillow, wet with tears.

All night long she was settling things with Mahfiruz, without a moment's respite. She tried everything, but she found no way out.

"Oh, I promise you, Osman's mother," she said to the rising sun, "I don't know how I'll do it, but I promise — I'll turn your reign into dust!"

# Chapter Fourteen

### The Old Palace
### February 1618

The first day of exile was a nightmare. As if on the brim of exploding with anger, Mahpeyker seemed to be a black, lightning-throwing storm cloud. One wouldn't know when she would throw down pouring rain or blow with the wind. She even shouted at her favorite courtiers.

"Semiha! Watch it, for God's sake!"

"Mürüvvet, look where you're going!"

"Şarazad, how many times do I have to repeat it for you to get it?"

They didn't say anything, nor did they get offended or breakdown.

She interfered with everything and cursed everyone.

When voices were heard calling in the front yard, she got angry.

"What's that noise? Run and see. Or are you waiting until I find out for myself?"

It did not take long before they found out what it was about, but they were afraid to tell it to Mahpeyker.

"How long do I have to wait? You didn't find out? What are these crackles of carriages and the clatter of horseshoes?"

"So." Şarazad swallowed. "Someone came from the New Palace."

"Who?"

"Valide… Sultan… Mustafa Khan's mother."

"Ha!" she laughed maliciously. "You better say, 'another exile.' Mahfiruz didn't waste time. She got rid of both of us."

"The woman wants to see you."

She didn't receive her.

"She forgot where our door was when I put her son on the throne, and now she remembered it, right? She doesn't need to bother. Let them give her an apartment somewhere far away. She may sit there and meditate."

She didn't care about the cold or rain. She didn't take to heart Semiha's laments that she would catch a cold and get sick, either. She had something important to take care of. A debt to repay.

She went to the back courtyard. Her eyes sought Sultana Safiye's carriage, the one she once cleaned every day. She turned her head one way and the other. From now on, the spider will enjoy the carriage.

The courtyard was empty, and only one door to the stable was opened. The groom on guard saw her as he led two horses for watering. He was surprised and performed a clumsy bow. She realized that the man was going to bring animals back inside.

"Take care of your work, don't pay attention to me."

*Anyway, from now on, no one will pay attention to me anymore*, she grumbled in her mind.

She caught the sound that the horses made, drinking the water from the trough. She realized that she missed it.

248 | DEMET ALTINYELEKLIOĞLU

She smiled. She would never have thought about it. How much time had passed since she last saw horses drinking? She couldn't stop watching the animal's muscles tremble with pleasure.

"The main stableman is coming in late now?"

Ashamed to look at her, the man replied without turning around: "The main stableman?"

"Yes. You remember, his one leg was so slightly..."

"He... does not come any more, mighty Lady."

"He doesn't? Why? Did he leave the palace?"

The stableman froze.

"He died."

"He died?" Mahpeyker shuddered as if she'd lost someone from her family.

"Yhm," the man stuttered. "Last month."

"Was he ill? What happened?"

"He aged... He used to sit down there at the end, where you are standing, My Lady, and watched the horses walk."

"I know. He loved it." And at the same time, he'd watched her, without letting it show. Seemingly to see if she cleaned the Sultan's carriage well, but Mahpeyker understood he was looking at her beauty.

"That's where he died. Where he sat. Watching horses."

"Oh dear, I'm very sad."

"Why? He died happy. Doing what he loved... He left in the blink of an eye... Isn't that better?"

The groom suddenly decided he was talking too much, so he gathered his stuff and pulling two horses away from the troughs, moved with them towards the stable.

"Wait a moment," Mahpeyker said. "Who is the main stableman now?"

"No one. There's no one to do it." It was clear that he was forcing himself not to look at her over his shoulder. "Since the dignified Lady left... the palace has no owner."

"It has now."

The harsh tone of Mahpeyker frightened the horseman.

"Forgive me, My Lady," he said quietly. "As a man gets old, he doesn't keep his tongue in check." He grabbed the reins and directed the horses toward the stable. "Well, also there is no need I guess. Everyone is doing their job here. Why would we need a commander?"

"What is your name?"

The horseman stopped.

"Goran," he said quietly as if he were telling a secret, "but the Ottoman Turks call me Orhan."

No one could understand the pain in his voice better than her.

"Okay, Goran," she said gently.

Against all custom and decency, the horseman turned toward her, and Mahpeyker, in spite of the anger and hatred that had accumulated in her, responded to the grateful expression of the man's eyes with a smile.

He must have missed his real name a lot.

"Goran, yes," the groom whispered. "I'm Goran, noble Lady. Goran... they also say, from Zagreb. If you have any order..."

"I have one last question, Goran. When I was here, I mean, years ago, there was a horseman among the young grooms working in the stable. He was thirteen or fourteen years old back then. Ahhh... his name was... I think Ahmed."

"Ahmed?" The joy in the man's voice surprised Mahpeyker. "This boy is now an adult man, Madam. A brave lad. There is nobody he couldn't turn over in wrestling. In recent years, he was called to Edirne wrestling. He lifted and knocked down countless strong men onto the meadow... And how he stretches his bow! I haven't heard of any other shooter that would outrank him."

She didn't even have to ask where he was. The barn door, tightly closed, opened noisily, and he stepped out of the shadows of the interior.

Ahmed! Sofia's beloved! The chosen one of the undines, unseen by her before her death. Her throat tightened, and she froze. When Ahmed saw her, he also froze.

*He hasn't changed at all*, she told herself. Yes, he's grown. His shoulders were wider, and he'd become a big man. But his face was still the same: the same thick hair fell over his forehead, his almost hazel eyes, and a very childlike look on his face, with which he stole Sofia's heart.

After a long moment, Ahmed remembered that he should greet her, but his greeting was awkward. He looked around with his eyes gleaming with joy as if he was looking for someone.

Muttering, Goran went toward the stables. Mahpeyker noticed that when he passed by Ahmed, he said a few words also to him.

The young man approached with a few uncertain steps and greeted her again.

"Ahh..." he stammered. "I don't think I heard... about your arrival... otherwise... I would wait." He fell silent at once and frowned. It occurred to him that the Sultana could understand that by 'your arrival,' he also meant Sofia. He reddened. "I mean... I mean, in case you had an order."

Mahpeyker hadn't decided what or how to say what she needed to say.

"You're all grown up," she whispered. It was the stupidest thing she could say, but that's what she just said. He was right in front of her, but she could sense that the boy was still looking for someone nearby. His eyes were searching. *He doesn't know,* said a voice in her head. *He hasn't heard.*

What she had to do was now even harder.

Her lips began to tremble.

Ahmed saw that the woman had completely paled, and her lips were shaking. That scared him.

"Lady... you..."

"She died!" she blurted out, without control. Like a fist blow, like a slap or a heart-piercing arrow. "She's dead, Ahmed!"

She covered her face with her hands to stop her sobs. She raised her head and looked at Ahmed with tearful eyes.

*Yarabbi!* She moaned inwardly.

A wreck of a man was standing opposite her. A man who just a minute before was towering like a mountain, collapsed in a single moment. His shoulders hung loose, his eyes were extinguished.

He tried to say something, but his tongue tied, and he couldn't. Then he bit his lip and clenched his fists. He turned his head away to hide his eyes.

Mahpeyker thought to say: *I killed her. I made her marry someone other than you. A rich, powerful man. And also, older than her. My undine didn't say a word. She bit her tongue. She married him, Ahmed... but she did not give herself away to him... before the wedding night, she threw herself into a well. She left intact, pure as the driven snow.*

But she didn't say anything.

Ahmed turned away slowly and shuffled to the stables.

"She loved you!" she called after him. "She just wanted to be with you, Ahmed."

She didn't know if he heard it.

Sobbing broke from her throat.

"Can you hear me?! To not be with another man, my undine gave herself to death!"

It was then that Ahmed stopped, turned back, and looked at her sharply. Ahmed, the bravest hero described by Goran, unparalleled in wrestling, the most accurate archer – Ahmed was crying.

"If so!" he howled. "I should go. I can't make my Sofia wait any longer."

It didn't matter what she told him from a distance. Ahmed didn't stop anymore. He didn't turn around and did not look. He disappeared into the darkness of the stable.

She heard a shout inside her. *God, I killed another person!*

She hated herself.

Her own ambitions, her dreams, prophecies, and the blind beggar. What she loved and didn't love. Her enemies. Even being a queen. She hated being Mahpeyker Kösem Sultan. She missed Anastasia. She'd arrived here as an unhappy but hopeful servant Nastya.

Thanks to a whole array of scolding and destruction, which she led, the day passed quickly. She couldn't wait for the darkness of night – it was her refuge. She would pull the quilt over her head and retreat into an imaginary world she created.

She decided she had to think through everything from the beginning. One thing seemed incomprehensible to her – very incomprehensible. Crafty and hidden, one thing kept bothering her.

It was strange that when they waited for the executioners, they were saved so easily and quickly. Very strange. She couldn't understand it in any way.

Would Mahfiruz leave her alone so easily? All her ambition and enmity, the attempt to kill her and the murder of Eftalya due to the killer's mistake – everything was to be forgotten as soon as Osman became a Padishah.

She was told: 'Go away, live as you please in the Old Palace.' Why? Was that supposed to be the end of the whole dispute? The jealousy and rivalry would reach only that far? Was she really content to send her son to Kösem to tell her: 'Now, get out of my palace!'

Sleep was slowly closing her eyes, but she knew that her mind was still awake.

*Where are you?* she cried out in her mind, summoning the vision of the blind beggar. *You keep getting into everyone's dreams. Come here, then. I'm waiting, too. Where are you? What will happen now, tell me?*

Suddenly, she remembered the dream she'd had a long time ago. Bloody infants born by Mahfiruz.

So, what? Was it just such a stupid nightmare, that's what it was? All these years, she'd been telling herself that it had to have some meaning, some explanation. Newborns covered in blood!

Then the dream came back to her, which the mother of crazy Mustafa told her on the day she came to visit her, and which actually showed her clearly that the woman was making things up.

'You were sitting on a platform. Something was on your head,' said the woman.

'Maybe it was a crown, but just above the hair you had the sun.'

The sun! It was a symbol of life and power.

She thought she heard the voice of Mustafa's mother: 'The Lord put the sun on your head like a crown... and then... then...'

Then a child entered the woman's dream. Mahpeyker replayed every word she had said in her head. The child was all made of light. No, it was a golden child. 'It came straight to you,' she'd said. 'You stretched out your hand and sat the child by your side, and... for the Creator's sake, the sun... and the sun poured over the head of the golden child...'

A lie or truth. The woman mentioned two suns. One was on Mahpeyker's head, the other – on the golden child's one. Later, she disappeared together with the child in the sunshine, and he emerged from the golden light... He – the blind beggar!

Mahpeyker jumped out from under the quilt and sat down. *Why didn't I remember this earlier?* She was angry at herself. *Sure. Why am I still waiting for him, after all, the blind beggar told me about the future months ago already?*

She stared into the darkness. She stared at it as if she were to capture inside the words spoken that day by Mustafa's mother. One by one she found and pulled them out of the places they were hiding.

*In one of his hands, he had a long black scepter, and he stretched the other one straight ahead and came toward me with a smile. His lips did not move, but I heard in my head: 'Do not be sad because this woman will bring the sun to your son. They will come with the sun and go away with the sun. Wait, because the time is near now.'*

That was the sign. *Stupid, stupid, stupid.* She was angry at herself. The woman didn't take this into account in her story at all – she explained to herself that it was about Mustafa, and yet everything was crystal clear there. The blind beggar did talk about the madman and his mother, but also about Kösem and her son.

"This woman and her son," she said into the darkness. *Me and my Prince, my Murad. That's us the prophecy told about.*

*With this woman, they will bring the sun to your son. They will come with the sun and go away with the sun. Wait, because the time is now near.*

Mahpeyker got goosebumps. The deep darkness, whirling inside her, dispelled all at once. It meant – it wasn't over yet, in fact, it hadn't even started. They didn't bring the sun... 'This woman and her son,' have not come yet, so it can't be the end, but the time when they bring the sun is close. She just had to wait.

She smiled to herself. She could already see what was in front of her. Fate pulled her out of a terrible storm and hid her in a safe place. She will weave her cocoon here, and when the time comes, they will bring her the sun. To her and her son. Then the cocoon will fall apart, and the mother and her son will emerge, for whom God made the crowns out of the suns. She will take her golden son and sit him by her side. On the throne!

Mürüvvet didn't sleep a wink and kept tossing over in her bed.

*Mahpeyker is in bad shape*, she told herself. *So much anger, so much suffering, and even worse, fear. It devours you, it finishes you.*

If something happens to her, everyone will be finished.

Mahpeyker was their benefactor.

They existed because she existed. If she weren't there... they would just cease to.

All her moods and snarling were resulting from fear. She was the great Mahpeyker Kösem Sultan. She couldn't say, 'I'm scared. They won't let me, and my children live.' She had to lock the sadness and worries inside. Nothing could repair her shattered pride.

*Is it simple?* she told herself. *After all this power and splendor, they immediately threw you out here. This is not a palace. This is Mahpeyker's dungeon. If she wants to leave, the guards standing by the gate won't let her out. Beautiful Kösem will live here, grow old, wither, and pass away. If something doesn't happen to her earlier, of course.*

She sighed heavily, nodding her head sadly.

"Oh, if only she'd remained Nastya," she said quietly. "She wouldn't have so many worries and troubles then."

She lay down on her right side, but it didn't help. She turned to the left, but she couldn't stay still – it was as if she were lying on spikes, not on a bed. She got up and started walking around the room. She will go crazy if she doesn't find someone to share her sorrows. She decided to go and wake Şarazad. She was sure she had the same worries.

She opened the door quietly and stuck her head out into the corridor. Nobody. It was almost completely dark.

The lamps placed along the walls were useless for anything other than illuminating the floor to the width of the hand

and playing with shadows so that one's heart pounded with fear. A dragon appeared on the wall, then a giant.

Mürüvvet listened. Complete silence, so she left the room and quietly shut the door behind her. She started to walk tiptoed.

The corridor in the front of her went in two directions. To the right at the far end, was Mahpeyker's apartment. Actually, Mürüvvet didn't want the girl to stay there. "It's full of ghosts," she'd lamented. She was so sure that the ghost of Sultana Safiye was still circling somewhere there, that she'd have her head cut off for this – except, that it was of course, appropriate for Mahpeyker to stay in those rooms. She had to live there at least for some time, to make this caterpillar, Mahfiruz, angry. She laughed inwardly at the thought that the woman would surely get mad, hearing that Mahpeyker had moved into the chambers of the Great Mother Sultana. She enjoyed imagining rancorous Mahfiruz scream at her son, tearing her hair out.

Down the left corridor were the rooms of the courtiers, children, and nannies. The first one there was Semiha's bedroom, and the one which belonged to Şarazad was at the end. Murad had a separate apartment next to Semiha's chamber. The eldest Prince lived with his nannies and two doctors. In this way, she placed the children between the two women she trusted implicitly, and in addition, her own room was at the end of a corridor that stretched straight at the entrance to the upper floor. Mahpeyker accepted this arrangement as soon as she arrived at the Old Palace. In this way, the entrance and exit of the three corridors were under the control of her three most trusted companions. Even though this kid had said that nobody would hurt them and that they'd be safe, how could they be sure?

She stopped in the corner where the three corridors intersected, and in an unconscious movement, carefully poked her head out around the corner, and looked at the hallway that ended with Mahpeyker's apartment. She'd had this habit ever since she lived in the Novice Court. In dark galleries patrolled by jealousy and competition, a person had to be paranoid to not get caught. Nobody moved from one place to another without checking the situation beforehand.

She went to the left corner and peered down that corridor. There was nobody there. She walked around the corner quietly, taking two silent steps.

Stop!

Mürüvvet froze in a place because something caught her attention. There was something there. She didn't know what, but this something bothered her. Something that should not be there.

All her senses stood at attention. She flattened her back against the wall and carefully, step by step, returned to her corridor. This time she looked more closely at Mahpeyker's hallway. At the end of the long, dark gallery, two lamps softly flicked a faint light on the green door of the Sultana's apartment.

She waited, holding her breath.

Her instinct picked up on an unexpected detail. A smell. *What is this?* she thought. *What is this smell?*

Suddenly she knew what the smell was. The smell of a human. Sweat!

*God!* said a voice inside her. *There is someone there. Lurking and sweating.*

Mürüvvet's hand moved like a lightning bolt towards the knife at her waist. *Old, good times*, a voice in her head said. After the incident in the Novice Courtyard, she'd put it on Mahpeyker's neck to cut her throat, and now she squeezed its hilt with all her strength to protect her.

She looked even more carefully. She noticed that there was a pile ahead at the end of the corridor, to the right, by the wall. A still, dark pile. At first glance, it resembled a clothes pile as if the servants threw them there to take away later.

*Shit!* This time the voice inside her shouted. *This is not a pile of fabrics. It's a big black cape. Hiding the one who is underneath, but not able to suppress the smell of sweat, an ominous cape!*

She pulled the dagger from under her belt. At first, she thought to shout and put everyone on their feet, but she gave that idea up immediately. She could scare him then – and given that he'd come all the way here, he must have an escape route and someone who helped him. *Wait*, she said to herself. *Sooner or later this dark heap will move, and that's when you...*

She would throw herself at him like a hungry wolf and tear him to pieces.

But the pile did not move.

*Could he have sensed my presence?* Mürüvvet wondered for a moment. *Right. Just as I discovered him, so he could have noticed me.*

She sniffed herself and wrinkled her nose. Agitation caused people to sweat. Did the sweat give her away, too?

Her eyes began to ache from constant looking, but she didn't blink, not for a moment.

At last, she heard a rustle. The black pile deep in the corridor moved slightly and then stopped again. She noticed that he turned left from where he was standing.

*He looks back*, she thought. *He's checking whether someone saw or heard him moving.*

Mürüvvet held her breath. She waited.

After a long moment, the pile moved again, and this time it grew... and grew... Finally, it transformed into a human shape leaning against the wall.

*You damned serpent*, thought Mürüvvet. *You think nobody can see you and you are going to attack, huh? But I am here. Come on, go to your destination.*

The destination was clear. The figure began sneaking inch by inch towards Mahpeyker's door.

She did the same. She leaned her back against the wall and began to walk soundlessly, and as soon as she approached the candles, just like the shady suspect, she fell to the ground. She waited motionlessly. She slowly crawled on the ground until she finally came out of the circle of faint light above her head, straightened up, and continued to follow.

The black shadow had to finally come out into the light because it was impossible to avoid the glow of the lamps on both sides of the Sultana's door.

Mürüvvet hoped that when the figure gets to the door, she would be able to who it was, but she couldn't. The hood of the huge cloak didn't allow it. The villain's face was hidden in its depths.

He was with his back turned toward her, but Mürüvvet noticed that he was moving only one hand toward the doorknob.

*Why only one?* she wondered for a moment. *What does he have in the other hand?*

He couldn't open the door. The shadow was unable to turn the knob with one hand. He rocked in front of the door.

He now had to use his other hand. Even from the place where she stood, she could see that the door opened.

When the figure turned around to check for the last time if anybody was nearby before slipping inside, the hood fell from their head.

Mürüvvet saw their face and struggled to hold back a shout – Taciser!

The light of lamps reflected from her and steel lightning flashed in the eyes of Mahfiruz's courtier.

*What is it? What does this snake have in its mouth?* The brain answered Mürüvvet immediately. A dagger! Taciser had to grit her teeth on it so that she could open the door quietly!

The woman sneaked inside, and Mürüvvet jumped ahead like an arrow and ran on her toes. She didn't have to worry about someone seeing her anymore.

It seemed to her that she covered hundreds of meters with every step she took, but as she lifted her head, the door still seemed as distant as the end of the world. She hadn't realized that such a long distance separated her from Taciser. *The serpent must have passed from the salon to the hall*, she thought. *From there, she'll slip into Mahpeyker's bedroom and... merciful God!*

She didn't notice the moment she entered the Sultana's apartment, or how she passed through the living room and hallway. When she stormed into Mahpeyker's chamber, Taciser was kneeling at the head of the bed, with her right hand hanging in the air, holding the dagger.

Exactly at that moment, when death was to knock on the Sultana's door, Mürüvvet, catching the woman by the hair, pulled her back and opened her neck up all the way to the back of the head.

"Die!"

The terrible sound of the cut trachea drowned out the scream coming from Taciser's mouth.

Mahpeyker jumped out of bed and stood for a moment in the fountain of blood gushing from the woman's throat. Through the bloodstained eyelashes, she saw the dagger, still stretched out towards her, and the head twisted aside.

"God! God! What is this! God, mercy!"

In the bloody horror — and the thought appeared momentarily in her mind that she'd already participated in such a scene before. On the day she was kidnapped, in a wagon, when Cyprian, whose ear she'd torn off, leaned over to kill her. Just like that day, she quickly jumped to the side, while the woman with her throat slashed and a dagger in her hand, fell to one side, quite like Cyprian.

First, she watched the woman writhe in the dark. She heard a horrible wheezing coming out of her throat, created by blood and air. Finally, she raised her head and, with amazed eyes, looked at her savior standing with a bloodstained stiletto.

"Mürüvvet?"

"I finished the snake," panted the woman. "I slaughtered the serpent who crawled to bite my mistress."

Mahpeyker jumped out, turned up the wick of the lamp on her dresser, and light spilled over the room.

The figure lying on the bed face down wasn't moving anymore. Her body was bent to the right, and the depression created on the bed by her head and shoulders filled with blood. There was a curved dagger in her right hand.

"Who is this?" Mahpeyker said as if she was raving in a dream. "Who is it, who? How did he get all the way here? Who among us is a traitor?"

Without giving her courtier an opportunity to answer, Mahpeyker grabbed the body by the hair and turned its face toward herself, making the last tissue holding the throat cut by Mürüvvet fall apart, and the head separated from the shoulders. Mahpeyker, giving a cry of terror, quickly pulled her hand back from the hair of the slain.

"Taciser!"

She stood up, vomiting, and almost fell over, but Mürüvvet threw away the bloody dagger and held her up.

"Lady. My gracious Lady. God took care of you. And what if I were sleeping, if I had not noticed..." the woman started to sob.

Mahpeyker led her to the door.

"Come, come," she straightened up. The only bright point on Taciser's face, all red from the blood, was the whites of her eyes. She felt that the blood that had spilled on her hair, eyebrows, and eyelashes began to dry up. She was covered with blood from head to toe.

"I knew it," she hissed. "I knew that the devil would not stop persecuting me. I knew that snakes and assassins would ambush me, sister Mürüvvet. I knew it."

She laughed terrifyingly.

"Get up!" she shouted. "Get up! Look how the serpent's head has been cut off. Run, run! See how my beautiful Eftalya got avenged."

Suddenly, the possibility that came to her mind made her run wildly into the corridor.

"My princes... my princesses... what about my children?! Murad? Ibrahim? Are all children safe? God, God, I'm begging you... I'm begging you, no... I'm begging you..."

She calmed down a bit, seeing that the children were safe and sound. She stopped shivering.

Semiha fainted when she saw the bloody scene, but once she recovered, Mahpeyker asked her to bring paper and a pen.

"Lady, wouldn't you like to clean yourself before..."

"I am clean, Semiha. I bathed in the serpent's blood. Let it stay this way. I was thirsty for it. Leave it, I want to feel that disgusting smell a little longer. Now, when the blood of the killer is still fresh, there is even more cause, to help me do what I must do.

She decided to send a letter to Osman.

She wrote without hesitation:

'My son...' In this way, she did not refer to him as the Padishah.

She laughed when the girls saw the words.

"What, is it a lie?" The smile on her bloody face looked terrifying. "After all, Osman is my husband's son, which makes him my stepson, doesn't it? It is obvious that I will call him my son."

She continued to write:

'... something strange happened tonight in the Old Palace. I prefer to call it strange because terrible events do not fit my son's properties. While I was in a deep sleep, an assassin with a dagger raised over me, was caught at my bedside. Before they struck, my courtier did her duty. Kindly, I did not even look in the face of the would-be killer, but the girls said her name was Taciser. Apparently, she was one of your mother's courtiers. I did not think it was possible, and I left the corpse in the courtyard so that someone who knew her would come and take it. If not, it will become food for the dogs on the city walls. If you would ask about us, I am in full health. I still trust the pity of the Creator and the word of the Ottoman dynasty.'

She silently read the words she wrote a few times. She liked it. *Short but substantial*, she thought to herself. *Very substantial.*

At the end she also wrote her name:

'Great Sultana Mother Mahpeyker Kösem.'

The next morning, Sultan Osman stormed into the harem and without looking around, went straight to the rooms of Valide Sultan. The servants jumped up from their places as soon as they saw him, to take the news of his arrival to his mother, but he gestured to them to sit in their places.

He opened the door, stepped through, and closed it. Finally, he entered his mother's room. When she tried to get up from the sofa on which she was sitting, seeing him in front of her in such an unexpected moment, he threw Mahpeyker's letter in front of her nose.

"Never," he said, his voice cutting like a knife. "It is to never happen again, Mother!"

Mahfiruz understood immediately the reason for her son's rage and what the letter he was throwing at her was about. *Shit,* she snarled in her mind. *Damned Taciser screwed everything up again.*

"I…" She tried to smile. "Just… This woman is your ene…"

"Stop it, Mother. I can deal with my enemies myself."

He turned back angrily and opened the door.

"I don't know if you can read what she wrote. In case it occurred to you to tear it up, I'll tell you. Your killer's corpse was thrown into the courtyard of the Old Palace stable. Send someone to collect it. Or, maybe you'll leave it there, to be thrown away to hungry dogs. And if you say 'no,' and you want me to take care of it, then know that I will do just that."

"Osman!" Mahfiruz yelled after her son. "Know that this woman will tear your Sultanate down. She will not save you... She will..."

The young Padishah did not listen to anything and left.

# Chapter Fifteen

### The Old Palace
### 1619

Mahpeyker didn't have to destroy Osman's Sultanate. With their forces joined, mother and son capsized not just the Sultanate, but the whole world.

The first thing Osman did, in agreement with his mother's will, was to dismiss from office, the one who had given him the throne, the deputy Grand Vizier Sofu Mehmed Pasha.

"He should be happy he's still alive," Mahfiruz said. "Appoint Mehmed Buffalo Pasha in Sofu's place.

He didn't touch Esad Efendi, but he passed the function of the Sheikh al-Islam to his teacher, Ömer, whose entire life had been spent washing the dead.

The mother and son then created an inner circle around the throne, made up of bribers, thieves, people who craved power, the ignorant, and simpletons.

The unworthy head of the black eunuchs of Sultan Mustafa, Hasanbeyzade, was exiled, and Hadım Suleiman Aga was brought in his place, who was soon called 'The Cursed.' It didn't take long before people began to miss his predecessor. Siyahi Sünbül Ali Efendi became a chief military judge of the Ottoman Empire, the Kazasker of Rumelia. One of Mahfiruz doctors, Musa-yı Naşi, at whom people laughed that he could make a diagnosis just by looking at a bottle with urine, was elevated to the rank of the chief medic.

Osman dismissed Sadrazam Halil Pasha, who suffered a disgraceful defeat on the Eastern front in the fight against the Safavid Shakh, and called Mehmed Pasha the Buffalo in his place, whom he had previously made the Kaymakam of Istanbul.

He tightened the prohibition that his father had introduced, which no one had taken very seriously before. At night he went out in disguise and arranged raids on Galata's wine bars and brothels. Janissaries and spahis, whom he caught boozing or in the embrace of whores, were punished on the spot with falaka until they began to bleed. Then, salt was rubbed into the wounds of the condemned, and they were led to stone-filled boats.

Mahpeyker giggled with every rumor she heard.

"Oh," she said. "What can you do if a mother tightens a rope around her son's neck? All I can do is just to sit down and watch."

And that's what she did - she sat and watched. She would wait for the sun to be brought to her.

Then the catastrophes began.

First, fires broke out in many parts of the capital. In the spring of 1619, there were terrible rains, and many districts were flooded. Hundreds of houses collapsed near the Old Palace and Kasımpaşa.

Then summer came along with the usual fevers, but also the plague epidemic raging in Europe entered the capital. Within two months the disease took thousands of lives.

The people associated all disasters with a curse.

"This is what happens when you take your uncle from the throne and imprison him because he is crazy," they said. "Who knows what curses he cast on Osman while talking to the birds?"

"And this woman? Mahpeyker Kösem? As if she didn't curse. Can a man chase off a wife, father, and his siblings? She certainly casts curses, too."

The audience nodded.

"She does, sure thing."

Meanwhile, Mahpeyker didn't curse anymore. She focused all her attention on the health and education of Prince Murad. It seemed to her that his epileptic seizures came less often when compared to the past. The doctors gave Mahpeyker hope — "If God allows, then he will be much healthier when he reaches maturity. Well, and it would be good to circumcise our Prince."

She was interested in every single teacher of Murad, and she was constantly gathering information about her son's progress. Although he just recently turned only twelve, his strength, energy, and intelligence drew the attention of all the teachers. Someone who didn't know Murad was an epileptic, would never have guessed it. His instructors of archery were Hüsamzade Abdurrahman Efendi and Yellow Lefty.

"Even we have difficulties to match his shooting," both men informed Mahpeyker.

One day, the great stableman Cundi Halil Pasha spoke to Mahpeyker.

"Do not worry, My Lady," he said. "Our Prince rides a horse so well that I won't lie if I say he's like a wind or a storm. He got so skillful with the javelin that you can see him on the horse for a moment, then he disappears. And how he gets off the horse! He holds a mane and slides from the back straight onto the stomach!"

"My son will make a powerful Padishah," she would say with pride to people around her. "Sometimes, when my Prince is angry, he even looks at me in such a way that I tremble with fear."

The nurses knew Murad's gaze well. He only looked at his mother, but with them, it didn't end with a gaze. As soon as he lost control over himself, his fists and legs went into motion — especially when an epilepsy attack was approaching. The Prince had fits of rage that terrified everyone, including Mahpeyker.

Kösem tried to keep the whole retinue together. She also brought Kalfa Hayganoş and her assistants to the Old Palace.

She often went out into the stable yard and looked at the horseman Ahmed. The man had become a walking corpse. She suffered but couldn't do anything. As soon as he saw her, he lowered his head and moved away.

One day he did something that Mahpeyker did not expect. He walked to her and whispered: "Where? I am begging you, My Lady, tell me. Where..."

He couldn't say anything more. His voice broke off. He leaned his head forward. Mahpeyker couldn't tell him, *I don't know. My heart did not let me. I did not ask. I didn't even go to her funeral. I couldn't watch them leave her in the black earth*.

She just couldn't. How could she tell the suffering man that she didn't even look at the deceased so that Sofia would remain forever in her mind as an undine in a blue dress?

"Be patient," she only said. "Patience. I'll take you to her when the time comes. I swear I'll take you. But hold on right now. Return to life. Be as Sofia would like to see you. Smile like you did when she was in love with you. She is looking at you, Ahmed... that smile would be for her..."

She couldn't speak anymore. Her voice failed her, too. Her mouth went dry. They looked straight into each other's eyes and maybe if it weren't for the fact that one of them was a Sultana and the other a groomsman, they would fall into each other's arms and wail together, longing for the deceased.

Mahpeyker went away in a hurry, and Ahmed returned to the stable with his pain, but from that day on, a glow began to appear in his eyes.

*At least I managed to do that.* Mahpeyker was madly happy – *I resurrected someone I had killed!*

In the spring, the messenger of Safavid Shah Abbas, Yadigar Ali, came to the capital with great fanfare. Watched by the astonished crowd, he rode along the streets of Istanbul to the New Palace with a hundred carts filled with silk, four elephants, and one rhinoceros.

After that day, crowds everywhere were full of gossip about the gifts brought for Sultan Osman by the messenger.

"For God's sake," people would say. "How can you receive this envoy of the Persian Shah of whom so many subjects lost their lives to?"

"Never mind, he is already received," the others would shake their heads. "But how can you take the gifts that he brought?"

"Oh yes, you can, you can. Haven't you heard how much Sultan Osman loves money?"

"How could we not have heard?" grumbled another as if he knew everything. "Isn't young Osman the same man who gave the office of Grand Vizier to Kapudan Pasha, Smooth Ali, when Pasha gave him two hundred slaves abducted from six galleons, with their arms filled with bags of gold and silver? A man who does something like this will also accept presents from the Persian Shah."

They nodded their heads, and complaints rose to the heavens.

"And what was the sin of Mehmed Pasha, whom he made Sadrazam a few months earlier? Did he do something stupid like a buffalo as would follow from his nickname?"

Everyone around shook with laughter.

"No," one of them said. "Buffalo took most of the stolen money not for the Ruler, but for himself. Osman is supposedly hoping that Ali Pasha will give him at least half.

When Smooth Ali Pasha died, before finding time to ransack everything that was within his reach, Osman made Hussein Pasha of Ohrid the Sadrazam, and as soon as he took the job, along with the manager of the black eunuchs, Suleiman Aga, Hussein doubled the efforts to brainwash the Padishah.

Suleiman Aga and Hussein Pasha whispered in turns:

"Lechistan is on the verge of rebellion. One by one, the Polish magnates' rebel, and if King Zygmunt joins them and attacks us, it will end badly."

"You should react sooner; organize an expedition, sir."

At nights, Mahfiruz also badgered her son.

"Padishah should set out on expeditions. Take the sword and go to war, and when you return with victory, you will become a Ghazi, my Osman, my son, my mighty Ruler. Just think, after your ancestor you will become the second Osman Ghazi."

Osman's eyes shone at this vision.

"We're going to war, gentlemen," he said at the morning Divan. "Start the preparations. Since I am Osman, I want to be remembered like the ancestor of my ancestors, Osman Ghazi. Doesn't heroism befit me?"

"Of course, it does!" exclaimed Hussein from Ohrid, and after him, so did all the gathered.

"However," the Grand Vizier gently approached the Padishah, "there is an obstacle to deal with before the expedition."

"What's the obstacle, Pasha?"

"What if, God forbid, when you are, My Lord, on the expedition, your brother, Prince Mehmed, will take the opportunity and seize the throne?"

"Are you aware of something, Efendi? Could the brother coming from the same womb be preparing something against me?"

"Never in my life, My Lord," retreated the Sadrazam with a satanic smile on his face. "I wouldn't dare cast slanders on the noble Prince, I just gave an example. Just a 'what would it be if...' example. It is known that he is after you, My Lord, in the queue to the throne, and the son of Mahpeyker Sultan, Murad, is still small."

Two nights later, thinking about the 'what if's,' Osman sent executioners to his own brother, Prince Mehmed. A year younger than the Padishah, the son of Sultana

Mahfiruz, Mehmed thrashed when the executioners tightened their ropes around his neck and shouted:

"Osman, I am begging Allah that you give your life on the rope of a hangman!"

Word of the death of Prince Mehmed exploded like a bomb in the capital, and a rumor spread that he was going to rebel and start a civil war.

Mahfiruz stopped eating and drinking, and bloody tears flowed from her eyes.

Mahpeyker was surprised that the Padishah killed his brother.

"Mehmed?" she said.

The dream came to her mind right away – the bloody babies of Mahfiruz. Here the dream coming true. One of the children who fell out of Mahfiruz's womb was covered in blood. She felt a cold shiver.

"For God's sake," she hissed. I did not take him into account at all. I can't believe it."

Exactly. Mahfiruz had two sons. One was a Padishah. Mehmed also waited in the queue to the throne. She'd forgotten about him completely. For some reason, it never occurred to her to put him in any of her plans. After Osman, Mehmed was the oldest in the dynasty. *If you don't count crazy Mustafa, of course,* she laughed. True, Osman was doing such things that people started to miss the madman, but the Ottoman Turks probably would not put Mustafa back on the throne. For this reason, it was obvious that if something happened to Osman, Mehmed would become the Padishah.

"I can't believe it," she rumbled all day long. *How could I not have thought about it? If Osman hadn't killed his brother, perhaps my Prince wouldn't even smell the throne. Or I would never see it. First Osman, then Mehmed... who knows how many years it will be before Murad's turn.*

*But now... now is my son's time. The son of Mahpeyker Kösem Sultan, Prince Murad, has now become the successor. God, God, it's a miracle! As if Osman killed his own brother to open the way for Murad.*

"My son," she whispered excitedly. "My Murad Chan. After Osman, the throne is only for you."

Whether a kid or an adult, when Osman leaves, Murad will come, that's all. She didn't take Mustafa into account at all.

Maybe setting Murad on the throne when he was still a child would be even better.

She shook at the thought. She jumped up and started dancing, and Semiha, Mürüvvet, and Şarazad looked at her in amazement.

"Get up!" she called to them. "Get up and dance."

"What is this dance?" murmured Mürüvvet.

"Dance of the Queen, sister Mürüvvet. A Queen's dance!"


Her joy didn't last long, however. At night, she suddenly got out of bed and ran straight to Murad's room. Then she went to Ibrahim, Suleiman, and Kasım.

Everyone was asleep. She ordered her daughters brought to her and ordered that a place for her four princes be prepared. From now on, all the children were to live in her apartment, right at hand.

*The threat is even bigger now, Mahpeyker*, her mind murmured. *Be vigilant. Get ready. Do not fall asleep if necessary. Put a guard on when they are asleep. Will Osman, who ordered to kill his brother from the same womb, thinking that he had an eye on his position, leave your Prince alive?*

She had terrible remorse for her dancing in the morning in a fit of joy. *What if...* she said to herself – *it was a dance of death?*

# CHAPTER SIXTEEN

## The Capital
## Winter 1621

In January, so much snow fell, and it was so cold, that even the sea froze. People reached Üsküdar on foot. It even happened that someone crossed the Bosphorus estuary from Rumelia to Anatolia in a carriage. But ships with goods and food could not reach either Galata or the Golden Horn. In the capital, hunger spread through the city like it had never experienced before. The price of bread, which had cost seventy-five dirhams before, grew to one akçe, and an okka of meat skyrocketed to fifteen – that is if you could get it at all.

People finally openly expressed their dissatisfaction.

"This Osman is another Osman. Not Osman Ghazi but a fatal Osman."

Fires, floods, plague, crimes, cut heads, and now the bitter cold and hunger. No one found any conviction to protest against the new nickname that clung to Osman. Even those who were most kind and devoted to the Sultan sought a justification at most, stating that, 'there is some curse on the young man.'

Ironically, while ships with supplies did not reach the capital, a head of some rebellious Polish prince was delivered to the court almost every day. The heads were impaled in front of the magnificent Gate of Greetings and then exposed to public view, while the heralds announced: "The head of the Prince, a heretic, on a spiiiiike...! Whoever has not seen it, run and see! Hey, hey, hey, hey!"

Osman's goal was to divert the attention of the people from defeats and hunger. But it didn't work.

Closer to spring, the news spread that a shooting competition took place in the palace garden. Someone from the palace guard shared this rumor in one of the cafes. Those present froze in amazement.

"Come on." They were in disbelief.

The guard frowned angrily.

"Is there anyone here who doesn't know Damat Kara Davud Pasha?"

"Are you talking about Davud from Rumelia, aga? And what about him? Or maybe you want to say that the ruler shot Davud from Rumelia, mistaking him for a deer?"

The listeners chortled. He felt offended that they were talking this way about his Master, who had said while giving him a pouch full of akçe: 'Go and spread this news everywhere,' so he pretended not to hear.

"His Majesty Pasha told me about that. He saw it with his own eyes."

"It's a slander."

"I don't know that. I swear to God that His Majesty said so."

Immediately a few people moved curiously.

"And? How did this happen? Come on, tell us, man, what did Pasha say."

"Henchmen were placed in a row on one side. The Sultan pulled a string of his bow a hundred paces away. At the command of the guard commander: 'Run,' the henchman in front of him started running. The Sultan sent the arrow. Ah, gentlemen, the arrow hit the poor wretch right into the neck and pierced through it."

"Oh!"

"Did the poor man die?"

"He did, obviously."

"What did they do?"

"I asked Davud Pasha the same. Nothing. He said they did nothing. Two people came over and took away the body... Sultan pulled the bowstring again. The commander of the guard ordered: 'Run!'... and another henchman jumped to run. But he remembered what had happened to the previous one. After two steps, he threw himself to the ground. The arrow released by the Sultan flew away, missing the target.

"Oh, brave boy, he saved himself."

"You think so? They finished off this henchman on the spot. Do you prefer whips or what? 'Let me go!' he yelled, 'let me go, I'll run!' Can you imagine it, companions? In order not to get under the whip, he chose an arrow... So, they put him in the line again. Osman pulled his bowstring, and the henchman ran as far as he could on his bloodied legs. He got an arrow in the back. The poor man fell face down like a log. I don't know if the arrow pierced him or not. Kara Davud didn't say that, and I had no heart to ask."

A rumor sowed by Kara Davud Pasha about Dilaver Pasha, the last one of the incoming and departing Viziers, whose position was likely to be taken over by Hussein Pasha of Ohrid – the deadly enemy of Kara Davud Pasha – spread from the cafe in Galata all over the capital. Before two days passed, there was no one left that hadn't heard about the 'people hunting,' arranged by the Sultan in the palace garden.

Osman announced through the shouters that the story was a lie, but nobody believed it. The henchmen no longer had permission to leave the palace to go to the market.

It was only the war expedition to Lechistan that allowed the Sultan to save himself from rumors. A war came, whose source no one was able to discern, and it ended in a stalemate. However, Osman returned from the campaign like a winner, arranging a great parade. The shouters paid by his mother stood on the roads in two rows and cheered: 'Osman Ghazi, Osman Ghazi!'

But there was no joy or excitement among the people. 'What kind of a victory is that? It cost the lives of thousands of brave men, but brought no advantage to the Sublime Porte,' the said among themselves.

Those who had run out into the streets celebrating the dethronement of Mad Mustafa now turned away from Osman.

The rule of the young Sultan continued to turn into a series of misfortunes.

One night the palace harem woke up to screaming and laments that seemed to fill the air.

"She died!" the servants wailed. "Merciful God! Mahfiruz Sultan died."

The woman passed away completely unexpectedly.

News of the death of Mahfiruz reached the Old Palace with the selas sung after the morning Ezan.

"Get up." Semiha woke up Mahpeyker. "She died. Mahfiruz died. They are singing sela."

"What!?" The thought pierced Mahpeyker like a thunderbolt. *The Ice Queen died? The devil has kicked the bucket! Huh, the spider was gone?*

At first, she didn't believe it.

"Why?" she hissed, grabbing Semiha. "Was she sick?"

"She was fine. In the last days, she was a little pale and apathetic; that's all."

*Huh, pale,* Mahpeyker thought to herself. *Pale and apathetic. Just like Safiye Sultan.*

Handan Sultan was like that too. Pale and apathetic. Then... death came... suddenly...

"She suddenly got worse during the night," Semiha said. "Mahfiruz wanted to get out of bed. 'Something is wrong with me,' she said... Then she took a few steps and fell down. There, on the spot..."

Mahpeyker didn't listen any longer.

"Let them prepare the carriage. We will go and say a prayer at her headboard."

Her words surprised Semiha, but the order was carried out immediately.

The population of the New Palace didn't know what to think when they saw Mahpeyker Kösem Sultan. They bowed down before her.

"This way, dear Lady." One of Mahfiruz's courtiers wanted to show her the way, but Mahpeyker pushed her away.

"We know the way."

The Valide Sultan room was full of people. Mahfiruz lay like a lump of ice, and her eyes were closed. Only her head was visible from under the quilt covering her. Her bound chin made her lips turn into a thin line. Mahpeyker immediately recognized the quilt – it was the same quilt that Safiye Sultan sent along with other gifts for the birth of Osman.

She sat at the headboard with sadness on her face. *So, Mahfiruz?* she thought. *It's over.*

People present in the room attributed the movement of her lips to praying. *A great woman*, they thought. *What kindness she shows to the woman who was her enemy and banished her from her land, from her homeland. She's come running as soon as she found out about her death.*

News of Mahpeyker's goodness went beyond the walls of the palace and spread widely throughout the capital.

Coming back in the carriage to the Old Palace, she laughed quietly. Swallowing her pride, she went to the New Palace just to be sure. Carefully lifting the end of the quilt, she saw what she wanted to see. It was there.

The ring!

The ring was on Mahfiruz's finger – almost melted into her body. She saw the blue swelling immediately. The finger of late Handan Sultan was just as blue, as if rotten. Everyone thought it was a postmortem blue. But it was the external reflection of the rotting interior.

One of the courtiers, noticing that Mahpeyker was looking at the ring, wanted to take it off the dead woman's finger, but she stopped her.

"I was going to give it to you, My Lady. This ring is now yours."

*God forbid*, she said in mind with fear. *The Safiye Sultan's ring had fulfilled its role. Twice! The time has come to get rid of it.*

She shook her head.

"I can't. It would be improper. It was Mahfiruz Sultan's memento of Handan Sultan of a holy memory. And it was given to her in turn by Safiye Sultan. Nobody should wear this ring anymore. I am also sure that Valide Sultan did not want to part with it. It will be best if the ring is buried together with its owner.

And that's what happened. Mahfiruz Valide Sultan was buried together with the ring. She rested next to her son, killed by his brother.

At the beginning of March, young Osman ordered that from now on, all the Sultans would be associated with women through marriage – so, the daughter of Sheikh al-Islam Esad Efendi, Akile got married.

Soon after, it became clear what was behind this decision – Osman announced that he was going on a pilgrimage to Mecca.

"Ho, ho,' it was said, "our ruler apparently heard the Prophet's voice."

"So, here's the reason for this wedding, gentlemen."

"Well, good. If he were to walk near the Kaba with the sin of adultery on his conscience, he could be paralyzed."

"We would be lucky if it would paralyze just him. I'm afraid to think what Allah would send to us. If the Padishah is like this, then who knows how sinful his subjects must be."

The actual secret plan of Osman came to light after some time, and it regarded the uprisings that had taken place during the reign of his father, the silent consent to the unlawful taking of the throne by crazy Mustafa, and the disorder that he saw during his expedition to Lechistan that caused Osman to turn away from the army.

Behind closed doors, he spoke to several trusted people:

"We will not get anywhere with this army, agas. We must eliminate the forces of Janissaries and Spahis. During our pilgrimage in Anatolia, in the Mamluk country, in Egypt, we will gather soldiers; we will organize them, we will dress, we will arm them, and then we will return to the capital. And we'll let those gadabouts go. That's what we will do," he said. "But no one dare say a word. It's a state secret. I will be forced to behead anyone who would reveal the secret. Let that be clear."

In his naiveté, the Sultan couldn't have foreseen that the secret plan that he revealed to the Viziers on the condition they would keep it secret, would spread within a few hours.

"Is it true?"

"That can't be. I don't believe it."

"Believe me, sir, the Sultan confessed his plan to just three or four people."

"The Ruler intends to destroy our holy forces."

"Listen, and what if this Osman is a heretic? We don't know, maybe he renounced his faith?"

"Good God, you can't be sure of anything. Who else but a heretic would undertake such a thing?"

On that day, the Sultan gained a new nickname in the place of 'Cursed'— 'Osman the Heretic.'


Mahpeyker learned about the plan from the Janissary Commander, Ali Aga, who secretly went to the Old Palace. Behind the screen, breathing with difficulty, he told her about what had happened and the conversations that took place in the military quarters.

"That's how things are," the aga ended the story.

"The real madman is not Mustafa, but this boy."

The commander of the Janissaries nodded behind the partition. "The soldiers have begun to say the same. We hear all the time now: 'We need Mustafa Khan.'

Mahpeyker said nothing, but thought, *Well, well, how will it end? Will Crazy Mustafa be a savior now? What will be the role of Khan Murad and his mother?*

"The capital is a boiling pot," Ali Aga continued, "and the smallest spark would be enough for it to catch fire like a furnace."

"God forbid," Mahpeyker said, but her mind clung to Mustafa. It seemed that the military didn't consider her and her son at all. Upon seeing Osman's antics, they intended to announce Mustafa as the ruler again. "Everyone's going crazy," she murmured.

"Yes, My Lady? Did you need something?"

Mahpeyker pulled herself together. "Everyone's going crazy. Unthinkable! Such things!"

"Eh, which things do you mean?"

"Why, is there anything else, aga?"

"There sure is! Sultan's stuck to the idea now that he will move the capital from Istanbul to Bursa. It's not enough for him to make enemies of the army and the clergy, he's also got into conflict with guilds and the people. What kind of idea is that? To abandon Fatih's trophy..."

"What do you expect from me, Ali Aga? You didn't come here to confide in me, did you?"

"Right," replied the commander. "If you, My Lady, could talk to our Ruler, advise him. Tell him that the solution he's chosen is no solution at all. One shouldn't play with fire. He will listen to you, My Lady. You are almost like a mother to him... He respects and loves you... Dethronement..."

The commander unexpectedly fell silent. *May my tongue be taken away,* he thought. But Mahpeyker understood what he was going to say.

*He kept you and your children alive, and he could have killed you!*

"We'll see," she said, getting up.

But there was nothing to look at. *You reap what you sow*, she said to herself, throwing the Janissary Commander out of her head. *If Mahfiruz's son wants to drown in blood, it's his choice. What can I do?*

Deep inside she knew that her heart wasn't of the same opinion. However, it wasn't a time to listen to the heart, but to reason. And in her head, she still heard the words of Ali Aga: 'The soldiers say we need Mustafa Khan.'

She thought all night long.

In the end, she concluded that it wasn't important at all. Was she supposed to interfere if fate entrusted extinguishing the fire to a madman? Let him go and quench it.

Dawn was approaching.

"They'll come to me eventually anyway," she murmured. "The new day will belong to Mustafa Khan and me."

The first thing she did in the morning, was to send Semiha to the mother of Mustafa.

"I'd like to see the Lady Mother."

The woman didn't object, and she came without saying: 'There was a time I wanted to come, but she did not receive me. Now, when the talk began about the enthronement of our son, it suddenly occurred to her to see me.'

"Listen to me well, My Lady," Mahpeyker said, drawing the mother of madman closer to herself.

The woman who enjoyed the title of Mother Sultana for only ninety-six days, listened to her, nodding her head.

"Do we understand each other?" Mahpeyker asked finally. "Agreed?"

"Yes. Nobody will touch him. If you say so; if you want so. You have my word. He will live."

"Fine. Now go. The time when your son will take the sword out of the sheath is coming."

# CHAPTER SEVENTEEN

### The Capital
### May 18th-19th, 1622

Finally, what was inevitable, happened.

On the eighteenth of May, when the preparations were being made for the Sultan's public show of his pilgrimage to Mecca, and his tent was being transferred from Istanbul to Üsküdar, the uprising broke out. A group of soldiers in the forces of Janissaries and Spahis turned over the cauldron of soup in a gesture of protest. They were immediately joined by some other people dissatisfied with the current state of affairs, as well as a group of onlookers wandering nearby.

Attempts taken by Dilaver Pasha to stifle the uprising were fruitless.

Sultan Osman sent away the alim, who came to present the demands of the rebels. The next day all hell broke loose. Upon the news of the Padishah's reaction, the angry guard troops turned the capital upside down.

Black smoke of fires rising ominously above the city was first noticed in the Old Palace by Mustafa's mother. With a cry: "Osman is burning the capital!" she rushed to Mahpeyker's room. The courtiers barely managed to calm the woman down.

Mahpeyker sent sentries to the roof. She also sent several servants to the New Palace to get the news of what was happening in the city. Hayganoş Kalfa, who'd set off for the New Palace in the afternoon with some job, returned breathless. Carrying her big body, she ran up the stairs, and when she stood in the doorway of Mahpeyker's room, she didn't even have the air to greet her. She fell silently on the sofa.

"Water," she rasped, pressing her hand to her chest. "Waaater... Hayganoş is dying..."

It took some time before she turned to the girls crowded at her bedside.

"They've broken into the palace," she finally said, breathing hard. "The guards broke into the palace. They went through the Greeting Gate to the courtyard."

This was amazing and unheard of. People who didn't belong to the palace services entered the inner courtyard.

"They stopped the pages and asked where Mustafa Khan was."

At these words, Mustafa's mother shouted, and began to beat on her knees in despair: "They will hurt my son! They'll kill my Mustafa!"

"Not Mustafa, but it's Hayganoş that dies, don't you see?" The chief dressmaker shrugged. Out of fear and fatigue, she didn't manage to empathize with the Padishah and his mother anymore. "You don't have an ounce of patience, after all, I'm telling you what happened. At first, nobody wanted to reveal where they were holding the Sultan, but when one of the men threatened: 'Speak, I say, and if not, I will tear your tongue out and toss it to the dogs; the eyes of one of the pages slid to the side. The guards rushed to the Sultan's chambers."

At this point, even Mahpeyker, who thought that nothing could surprise her anymore, covered her mouth with horror. The Sultan's chambers were the heart of the empire. If the robber's foot had stood even there, it meant that no one was safe in the Sublime Porte anymore. There was no offense or crime left that one could not expect. She gave Semiha a worried look. The girl immediately understood her Lady's order: *Gather the children*. She stood up reluctantly, curious to hear the continuation of Hayganoş's story. The chief dressmaker's story, amazing and terrifying at the same time, was breathtaking.

"Someone, seeing the crowd pressing straight at the pages and crowded in the courtyard in front of Sultan's chambers, ran away and while screaming, pointed to the place where the harem was located. For a moment, the soldiers were unsure what to do. It wasn't so easy to get inside the harem. Also, all entrances were closed. And behind them, who knows how many henchmen, guards, and servants waited with their swords bared. They had a high wall in front of them. 'We have no choice but to turn back,' murmurs rang through the crowd, but at that moment one of the leaders ran forward.

"'Hey, heroes, your breasts are bare, and the heat is burning in them!' he called. These words alone were enough to rekindle the fading fluster and anger in soldiers.

"'You, who turned the fortress into dust, you will bend your neck before a wall?'

"'We won't bend, we won't!' the soldiers shouted. 'Look for a pale. Bring a pale. A pale, a pale!'

"Several long pales were brought and leaned against the wall. Rebels began to climb up like ants. They climbed barefoot onto the domes of the harem roof. They pried the roof tiles with axes brought from the Divan. After having split three domes, they looked down. But what they were looking for still wasn't there. Only after splitting the fourth dome, one of them called to the companions waiting below:

"'Here! Mustafa Khan is here!'"

Recalling this scene, Hayganoş paused for a moment and looked at the listeners with satisfaction. Seeing how Mustafa's mother began to hit her knees again with her hands, and the rest, frozen and waiting with bated breath, she continued with even more excitement in her voice.

"And that's when all hell broke loose."

A few girls screamed.

"Right, and what else," murmured Mürüvvet.

The chief dressmaker gave her an angry look.

"As I say, it broke loose... I mean, all hell broke loose! You don't believe? Would Hayganoş lie?"

Only, it was very hard to believe Hayganoş's story. After demolishing the roof on the harem domes with axes, and seeing the chamber in which crazy Mustafa lived as a prisoner, the soldiers descended on ropes among calls and screams.

Mustafa was sitting cross-legged on a thin mattress thrown over the bed.

Two slaves fell to their knees before him.

"Sir, sir!" The girls shouted in horror, seeing a swarm of people falling into the room through the vault. Each clutched at the strange robe of Mustafa, revealing half of his chest.

The soldiers landed on the floor one after the other and ran up, prostrating before Mustafa. But while the roof was being demolished, and shards of roof tiles were falling on the floor, Mustafa didn't even raise his head, nor did he ask the slaves what was happening. He cast a long glance with his unseeing eyes at people who threw themselves at his feet to kiss the skirts of his robe.

"What the hell is that?" One of the rebels spoke. "Are we supposed to put such guy at the head of the state as a Sultan?"

Another got angry. "And you, who are you to fuss?! Shall we choose the Padishah according to your taste? What is wrong with him? A strong man, like an oak tree."

"We're out of here," someone else in the crowd whispered. "Can't you see, he is a madman. We wrecked the roof over his head. We burst inside screaming, and he didn't even notice. He's crazy, I tell you, crazy."

"If you, sir, were locked up between four walls for four years, it would shuffle the marbles in your head, too."

And then Mustafa did something that no one expected. He spoke.

"Did you bring food?"

The insurgents froze in astonishment.

"Food?" they repeated, looking at each other.

Meanwhile, Mustafa nudged one of the slaves who encircled him, with his leg. "Sanuber, ask the servants. Have they brought food for the birdie?"

Sanuber was the only maid who'd continuously accompanied Mustafa before his reign of ninety-six days, while he was in power, and for years of his lock up. She was Mustafa's arm, leg, and tongue.

She read and wrote letters for the illiterate Mustafa, and even prepared fermans during his reign. A frightening text arose from the combination of Mustafa's mumble and Sanuber's awkward scrawl, but Sanuber was making efforts to guess together with alims what Mustafa said and what he wanted.

"'A birdie? Bird,' he said?" the people began to ask among themselves, but then Sanuber cut in, saving the situation.

"Our Master is hungry. Nobody has come with food or water for three days."

"He will have plenty of food and drink where we are going," interrupted one of the officers. "We can't stay here anymore. We should go as soon as possible."

"But there's no way out," Sanuber said. "The door is bolted. The windows have iron bars."

The insurgents hesitated.

"Heh, heh, why would we need a door?" one of them jested. "We opened the cage from the top. Is he a bad bird? We'll say whirrr! and he will fly out."

A wave of croaking rolled through the room.

Mustafa resisted and thrashed around for a long time, not wanting to leave his room. "They'll kill the birdie, they'll kill the birdie."

"Lord," Sanuber pleaded, catching his hands, "they will give you a sword. You will sit on the throne again."

"I don't believe it!" Mustafa howled. "I don't want the throne! These are Osman's executioners. They will strangle the birdie."

Partly by force, partly insidiously, they tied a lariat to Mustafa's belt while trying to calm him. With the words 'come on, up,' men standing on the roof pulled the rope. Mustafa, suddenly feeling that he lost ground under his feet, waved his hands cheerfully.

"I knew it, I knew it. I knew that one day I would fly!"

"Long live the Padishah!" shouted the crowd of soldiers filling the courtyard, seeing Mustafa on the roof.

This time, dropping him to the ground turned out to the problem. Sanuber had to intervene again. Pulled up on a rope just like her master, she managed to convince him with some pleading, to slip down along a rope.

They planted him on Sheikh Al-Islam's horse. Among the shouts of the rebel army, armed with piles, axes, swords, flails, and shotguns, he was led to the Audience Hall, and from there to the Divan. A few alims present at the Divan were forced to pay homage to Mustafa under the threat of a sword. One of them, Faizi Efendi, had a heart attack out of fear and died at the feet of the mad Sultan.

The rebels, clapping their hands and shoving Mustafa in front of them, put him in a carriage and headed towards the Old Palace.

The sentries sent by Mahpeyker to keep watch on the Sultan's route – some of them on horseback, some on foot -- returned one by one through the large courtyard.

"They're coming!" they cried, crossing the threshold. "They're near!"

Mahpeyker was prepared. After she'd heard how things had got out of hand, she realized that further developments were inevitable. The rebels couldn't stay in the harem. *They will come here too,* she'd thought. She hid all her children in one of the endless corridors of the Old Palace, in a passage known to only one, at most two persons. She left them with Mürüvvet and Şarazad.

In the corridor, she also hid several servants with their tongues cut out. They would defend the children in case something happened. She herself wore the most magnificent dress left from the time when she was at the head of the state. She intended to greet the rebels not as a resident of the Old Palace, shoved to the shadow, but as the moon of Sultan Ahmed and the mother of future ruler Murad Khan, Mahpeyker Kösem Sultan.

If they demand blood, she will give them blood, if it's the Khan they demand, she will give them the Khan!

This was not the time to run away and hide. No time to avoid men. If they were holding fate in their hands, she had something to tell them. She entered one of the galleries of the grand courtyard.

"Open!" she cried. "They are not enemies to be met with a rifle and a sword in hand. Open the gate. Prepare to welcome your fellow men. Feed the hungry, give water to the thirsty."

It took a long time before the rebels, armed with shotguns and axes, all made their way into the courtyard. A voice came from each breast. She didn't know what was going on, noticing an enclosed carriage among the crowd. She suddenly understood. *They chose the best carriage to carry the madman,* she thought.

The rebels hesitated, seeing the woman looking down at them. A murmur ripped through the crowd. "It's her, it's her. It's Mahpeyker Kösem."

"You want to say: Serene Lady, man. Don't you know she is the moon of our Padishah of holy memory?"

"Mother of Prince Murad and Prince Ibrahim."

"She may be whoever she wants," said someone else. "It's not her we have business with, but the mother of the madman."

Mahpeyker noticed the crowd's hesitation when they saw her. She gave them a confident and proud look. She looked at them like a queen at her subjects. At one point she raised her hand in greeting.

"Welcome, gentlemen," she said in a calm voice. She was the queen receiving her guests. "If you are coming in such a crowd, you have something to tell us."

"We have," an unfriendly voice could be heard from below.

"What we are here to say, we will say, and we will go when we get what we want," someone else said.

Mahpeyker smiled.

"We thought so, too. But first, tell us what you are going to do, let the moon of Ahmed Khan, the mother of his successors, know what it is."

"Nothing much," one of the soldiers grinned. "We announced Mustafa the Sultan."

There was a giggle coming from the back of the crowd.

"A madman, madman..."

There was no surprise or anger on her face.

"May Allah keep him in his care. Blessed be his reign. But since you chose a Sultan, whom you are looking for here, gentlemen?"

"Lady Mother."

"Give her to us here, woman. We know she is here. Tell us where."

"Give her, give her. We demand! We demand Valide Sultan!"

"Without her, we'll never get out of he..."

"Gentlemen!" Mahpeyker called suddenly. There was silence in the courtyard. "You turned the cauldron over, you spilled blood. The empire had its Sultan, and in his lifetime, you proclaimed Sultan Mustafa Khan. Won't the men, who have done so much, be able to force the door to the rooms of concubines and servants and lead the mother of our ruler out?"

She suddenly fell silent. The crowd below listened to her with their heads up.

"You will say that no, we did not give her!" Mahpeyker cried out, throwing lightning bolts from her eyes. "You will come in and take her. Because you brought order by violence. We only hear your 'we want' and 'we don't want.' Who is the Sultan, who is your Master? Come on, answer, as befits men. Who is the Padishah? Mustafa or Osman? Or maybe you?"

She paused. There was not the slightest rustling from below.

"Ha, it won't pass through your lips, dear guests. Now you decide, you give orders. It means that now you are the Padishah, you are the Sultan. If so, you'll take your Lady Mother from here and go... But do not forget who you're talking to. Who is welcomed by the open door, whom the beys, viziers, even the Sultan's family, beg for forgiveness, falling at her feet, who is telling you this? Am I not the mother of the sons of our Sultan Ahmed Khan of holy memory, Mahpeyker Kösem Sultan, that you are trampling my dignity shouting, 'Woman!'?"

There was no answer from below again. Faces turned up to her a moment ago, now looked down at the ground. After a long moment, one of the journeymen in a torn turban stepped in front of the crowd.

"Forgive us, Lady," he said from below. "The will to forgive belongs to the great, Mahpeyker Sultan. We have committed insults."

Someone else also stepped forward: "Do not be angry, My Lady."

"Put it down to everything we've suffered for four years," another voice said from the crowd.

"The fear in which we have lived for months, My Lady, and the agitation," a soldier with an ax on his shoulder stepped out of the crowd.

Immediately after him came a janissary: "Osman raised his hand at our troops. The heretic became an enemy to us. It was against him that we rebelled."

*It's enough,* Mahpeyker decided in her mind. She raised her hand.

"I understand," she said firmly. "Now leave the courtyard."

She waited, but her order did not meet with opposition.

"I will tell the servants to put the vehicle at the gate for Her Majesty. We were expecting your arrival, so Lady Mother is ready. You will not wait long at the square. Go with God. Keep law and order. Haven't you said a moment ago: 'The will to forgive belongs to the great?' Now you are the great. Have mercy. Do not spill the Sultan's blood. Do not spill it, and let the order reign within our borders – let the empire breath peacefully again."

"Amen, amen," murmured across the crowd, but they were drowned out by a terrifying voice:

"Death to Osman! Death to the heretic!"

"Death to him!"

Mahpeyker didn't wait any longer. When the crowd filling the courtyard began to pour outside toward the square, she turned away haughtily and entered the building. Outside, one could still hear shouts, "Let the heretic die!"

So, Osman was alive. But given the shouts from the courtyard, it wouldn't stay like that for long. *Let's hope they will listen to my words*, she thought. *May Allah save him*, she said to herself.

Her own words surprised her again. She didn't know why, but she couldn't find hatred for Osman in herself. Perhaps it was the merit of the young man who protected her and her children from the madness of Mahfiruz. Either way, it was a real feeling. That's why she felt sadness earlier and why she now felt regret and fear for Osman. She was a mother, too. She saw his naivety. Everything he'd had to endure was caused by the venom seeped by the spider mother — that's what Mahpeyker's heart suggested. And even if reason didn't, her heart always remained a mirror of her true feelings. But reason was her only guide, the only adviser. For the sake of her children, she had to continue the path it had set for her.

Sultan Mustafa's mother awaited her in great excitement.

"Your son ascended the throne," Mahpeyker said coldly. "You're now the Sultana Mother again. Do not forget what I told you so that what falls today on Osman's head, won't fall on your son's and yours tomorrow. Don't get your hands dirty with Osman's blood."

The woman threw herself around her neck in tears. Mahpeyker stopped her, half-jokingly, half seriously. She slowly bowed her head.

"Let yours and your son's reign be blessed."

Lady Mother hesitated. *Since you are now Valide Sultan, behave as befits it*. She corrected herself and straightened up.

"Amen," she answered in a shaky voice. "This time I will remember your words, Mahpeyker."

Mahpeyker laughed.

"I hope so. Now, go," she said. "They put Sultan in the closed carriage. You get into the carriage prepared for you. Please bring your son to it. Keep yourself straight. And most importantly, do not let your fear show... Come on, go already, go. Your subjects are waiting for you."

When the woman left, she listened for applause, but she didn't hear anything like that. The turmoil in the crowd continued.

"Death for Osman, the heretic!"

"We will kill him!"

*Where can Osman be?* Mahpeyker thought. Reason immediately told her. *He must have escaped. Or he should run away.*

"Death to Osman!"

"Let him die!"

*The last hope remained for Osman*, she thought with a sigh. *Mustafa's mother. We'll see if she keeps her word. I can't do anything more.*

The screams slowly moved away.

"Death for Osman, heretic..."

"Death for Osman..."

"Death Osm..."

"Die... Osm...!"


That day, Osman escaped from the New Palace and hid in one of the janissaries' quarters. Once he learned that the rebels had brought Mustafa to the New Rooms, he sent his Janissary Commander, Ali Aga, under the pretense of negotiating. Ali, sneaking up to Mustafa, stabbed him with a dagger in his chest, but the assassination failed. The one who was killed, the one who was bound with a rope and thrown to the ground, was the Janissaries Commander, Ali Aga.

At the same time when the tragic events took place, a series of comic scenes also happened. The rebels were caught up in hard dilemmas. Several acts had to be issued in writing, but who was to fulfill this task? Finally, a solution was found.

One of the leaders with the nickname Black Lucky, who knew a little about writing, sat down in front of Mustafa and his mother, to create a ferman. The Padishah's skirt was still in the hands of Sanuber. They didn't understand why the woman stubbornly clung to his robe, but it didn't occur to them to ask.

The man who was proclaimed the Sultan gave the impression that he didn't realize what was going on anyway. He just stared blankly.

"Your Highness," one of the men said, bowing to Mustafa. "Two Sultans can not sit on one throne. Will it be right to take Osman the Heretic's life?"

Mustafa looked at his mother. She thought she heard Mahpeyker's voice. 'Do not get your hands dirty with Osman's blood.'

*Easier said than done*, she thought. *If Osman survives, we will die. If I say, 'spare Osman,' these bandits will cut off my head first and then Mustafa's.*

The Sultana shook her head as if in response to the accusation. *If it's so simple, stand in my place and we'll see, Mahpeyker,* she said in her heart. Sometimes to live, one must take life away from others. Otherwise, they will not hesitate to take your life.

She turned to her son. She nodded as if saying, 'Yes.'

Mustafa's gaze stopped for a moment at his mother. Then he leaned to her ear: "Is it Osman who killed the birdies, Mom?"

The woman nodded again.

Then Mustafa turned to the man waiting for the answer. His eyes flashed.

"It will be right," he ordered. "Whoever takes life from the birdie, his neck will be broken."

Black Lucky grabbed the pen immediately and wrote a ferman ordering to kill Sultan Osman.

Then Mustafa was asked: "Who will the Sultan's seal belong to?"

Padishah didn't even hear the question.

"Who is entitled to the seal, Your Majesty?"

Seeing that Mustafa was absent again, Lady Mother nudged her son with her elbow.

"Damad Kara Davud Pasha," she whispered, barely parting her lips. "He cared a lot for birdies."

Padishah leaned forward sharply.

"Kara Davud. Write!" the ruler immediately ordered Black Lucky. At that moment, he was absorbed in making a ferman appointing himself a Chamberlain. When he didn't hear, Padishah became angry.

"Write, I'm telling you! We nominate Kara Davud Pasha the Vizier of the Great Empire."

When these matters were settled successfully, Mustafa and his mother were taken to Orta Cami.

The prisoners in port docks and on ships were released. Immediately, the capital was flooded with thieves, outlaws, and criminals. There wasn't a single craft house that wouldn't be plundered and burnt to the ground. What was worse, simple people joined in the plunder.

In the evening, news reached Orta Cami.

"We killed Dilver Pasha and the headman of the black eunuchs, Suleiman Aga. Suleiman was unconscious from fear anyway. We hit him with a log in the head, the skull split in half like a pitcher."

The crowd in the courtyard of Orta Cami got excited.

"It's Osman's turn! Osman's turn!"

"Death to Osman!"

# CHAPTER EIGHTEEN

## The Capital
## May 20th, 1622

Everything that happened was relayed to Mahpeyker. She learned that Mustafa and his mother were in the mosque in Ortaköy, and that Sultan Osman escaped from the palace at night in disguise and hid in the Ağakapısı estate.

*He's made a mistake* she thought. It is a pity. He's fallen into a trap. It was the caftan he was wearing, and the turban with the decorative feather, that made him a Padishah. Now he's become one of the street crowd — who would listen to him now, who would show him respect now?

It happened just as Mahpeyker predicted. Before the sun rose, the insurgents broke into Ağakapısı. Osman, in a half-wrapped turban, in a long white shirt, was led out into the courtyard. The Vizier Hussein Pasha from Ohrid, who tried to save himself by escaping, was quartered.

Osman, who was no longer wearing Sultan robes, was sat on a worn-out mare. They set off towards Ortaköy among teasing and curses. Padishah wasn't spared the worst insults. Someone, reaching under the long, wind-blown shirt, smacked him.

"Mighty Lord Osman," he said mockingly. "He who arranges the raid on the winery, and sends Janissaries and Spahis to the galleys, parades just like that, with a naked ass.

A man named Altuncuoğlu approached the jade and, pinching the young Osman in his bare thigh, threw the most terrible curses.

"Dog's son!" Osman howled. "Am I not your Sultan? Have you forgotten that you were once young yourselves?"

Laughter, mockery, and curses resounded in response.

When Osman was brought to the Ortaköy mosque, Mustafa was sitting motionless in front of the mihrab, the niche which indicated the direction of Mecca.

For the first time, the Empire saw two Padishahs in the same moment — two Padishahs, one of which was crazy and the other overthrown!

On Mustafa's right hand sat his mother, and on his left, Damat Kara Davud Pasha, appointed as Vizier. Sanuber sat down this time a bit in the back, a step away. She watched carefully every move of her Lord, ready to catch the skirts of his robe.

Mustafa was dressed in a clumsy caftan that had been brought from who knows where, and a twisted turban had been put on his head. Despite the efforts of his mother, slaves, and even the Vizier, the turban did not want to stay straight on the Sultan's head. Attempts to straighten were to no effect. The turban stubbornly fell over Mustafa's right eyebrow. In this state, the Padishah reminded one of the young officials from the Galata district, chasing after beautiful girls.

Upon seeing Osman entering inside, Mustafa jumped up. It became then clear why Sanuber was not letting go of his robe. Mustafa reacted with such speed that despite all her attention, the girl did not manage to catch him by his caftan and sit him back down.

"Free the birdie, free the birdie!" Mustafa shouted, running from one window of the mosque to another.

"Calm down, sit down, my son," his mother pleaded, trying to catch him among dumbfounded glances, but Mustafa remained deaf to her prayers, fighting to free himself and running from window to window.

"Osman came, Osman came. He'll kill the bird! Free the birdie! Tell them to free the birdie!"

Even the chief provocateur of the insurgents, Damat Kara Davud Pasha, was horrified. The soldiers of the palace guard, Spahis, Janissaries – all who were now their support, could turn away at any moment. *This is the crazy Sultan you promised to us? The one who was supposed to be a bit feeble minded? But Pasha, he doesn't even have a mind to be called feeble.* He had no answer to words like those. Then it would be enough for Osman to renounce the idea of liquidating the troops, and everybody would go back to his side.

Osman, in turn, was not a lunatic. He could just say 'I renounce' and he'd get himself off the hook. 'Especially that I did not intend to liquidate the troops. It's all a slander, a rumor. Get back to your barracks. You will receive your pay on Friday.'

And Sultan Osman did not waste the opportunity.

"Look, my guests," he thundered. Of course, he didn't know that his stepmother Mahpeyker greeted people with the very same words. He thought that by addressing the rebels as 'guests,' he would suggest that he forgives them and shows his kindness. "Here is the man whom you have chosen as your ruler."

Nobody objected. Nobody stopped him. Nobody threw himself at him.

Mustafa's mother was aware that things were going in the wrong direction. She remembered neither Mahpeyker's face nor her words. Nor the oath she gave her. The next few seconds would decide about everything. She dragged her son, whom she took by the arm, back before the mihrab.

"Hey, soldiers!" She turned to the insurgents staring at her in a daze. "Defenders of the Empire, how much longer will you let this heretic speak? What are you waiting for? What is our Lord's fermans? If you were going to keep this snake alive, why did you demand our Sultan to issue fermans? Can peace and order prevail, if the orders of the Ruler are not obeyed?"

"Allah, Bismillah!" Damat Kara Davud Pasha exclaimed. Tearing the rope from the hands of one of the guards, he threw it on Osman's neck. A few other rebels threw the ropes, knocking the Sultan to the ground. Several officers rushed to help the struggling Osman.

"What are you doing?!" cried someone from the crowd.

"Will you take the life given by Allah in His sanctuary?" another said.

"Was the agreement like that?" one of the officers attacked Kara Davud Pasha. "Wasn't it said that Osman would not be hurt?"

Osman was released from the ropes thrown on him. Bloody traces were visible on his neck. He rubbed his neck with both fear and relief on his face.

In this situation, Mustafa's mother could no longer remember the words of Mahpeyker. The woman fiercely attacked the crowd.

"You do not realize, gentlemen," there was a threat in her voice, "what a snake he is. If he leaves freely from here, none of us, none of you will survive, just to let you know."

But no one listened to her.

The young Osman was taken to the mosque under guard, and Mustafa was put in a carriage. The carriage was sent to the New Palace, where Mustafa was seated on the throne. Since it was Friday, the Friday sermon in the mosque during which the reigning ruler was mentioned, the khutba, was read on his behalf and he was announced to the people as a Sultan. First, the new Vizier Damat Kara Davud Pasha, and then the guilds and the commander of the Janissaries, Dervish Aga, paid homage to him.

Vizier Davud Pasha understood that in the light of Mustafa's insanity, which was revealed to everyone, his position was not safe until Osman was removed. *Besides, who knows,* he wondered, rubbing his hands, *even if Osman is removed, there are still the sons of Mahpeyker. If I send Murad and Ibrahim to hell, the Ottoman lineage will end. Ha, what if it is written to be like that? The Ottomans will leave, and the Davuds will come.*

Dazed by dreams of the throne, he returned to Ortaköy, taking with him the leader of the Janissaries, Dervish. The young Osman was loaded onto a cart. Spitting, lashing, casting curses, and stones, the crowd escorted him to the Fortress of the Seven Towers.

The young Sultan was dragged on the ground through seven floors, and thrown into an underground dungeon. His limbs and head, battered at the slimy walls of the musty dungeon, were covered with blood. In the abyss, polluted with the soot from torches and a thousand different odors, the guards kicked and pushed him, and tossed a rope around his neck. Despite this, Osman managed to avoid blows. Then one of the guards lost his patience.

"Get out of the way! Can't you deal with such a colt?" He was one of the spahis-deserters called the Humble Thief.

The Thief, having thrown himself at Osman, seized him by his private parts and brought him to the ground. The others, throwing him on his back, put greased ropes around his neck and began to tighten them with ferocity.

"Die, heretic!" The Humble Thief howled. "You wanted to liquidate troops, huh?"

"Die," joined Vizier Damad Kara Davud Pasha. "Die!"

A wave of hate flowed from all lips:

"You want to throw me from the arms of my wife into the galley, eh? Die!"

"Who are you, you cub, to arrange a raid on the winery? Now we will deal with you."

Osman's soul-crushing screaming and crying didn't manage to soften the hearts, solidified in hatred. On the contrary, the more he struggled, the louder they laughed. They kicked. Pinched. Bit.

"Die!"

"Die, Heretic, die!"

Eventually, Osman's resistance weakened. Exhausted on one side by the burning pain of the organs, which the Thief still did not let go of, and on the other by air-hungry lungs, he jerked couple more times and froze motionless.

Davud Pasha was still tightening the rope on the Heretic's neck.

One of the people grabbed his hand.

"It's enough, Pasha."

The guard grinned.

"Heretic. Now he can settle his accounts with hell."

Vizier Davud Pasha, furious with the rage and his willingness to serve the Sultan, still panting heavily, pulled a knife from behind his belt and cut off the right ear of the young Padishah, lying lifeless. He straightened up with a terrible expression on his face. Holding the end of the blood dripping ear, he showed it to the rebels gathered around. He laughed horribly.

"Now only one Padishah remains on the throne. Let this ear be the proof that we have finished the heretic, eh?"

The rebels nodded.

"That's right. We need proof, a testimony."

He ripped apart the Sultan's long shirt, which during the struggle managed to turn into a rag. He wrapped the bloody ear in a piece of cloth he tore off and hid it on his bosom.

"We'll have good news for Lady Mother."

In joy and excitement, he ran up the narrow and steep stairs of the dungeon, jumping over the steps. *You did something today that nobody dared to undertake before, Davud,* he said to himself. *You gave such a blow that you managed to throw the Padishah off the throne. You took his life. The reward for this will be who knows how great. From now on, treasures will not satisfy you.*

An hour later he handed the ear of the young Osman to the Sultana Mother, who was busy with moving into the New Palace.

"A gift for His Majesty from his servant."

Seeing the terrible smile on the Vizier's face, she shuddered involuntarily. *One should be afraid of this man,* she thought. He'd opened the doors of the Sultan's palace wide in front of her and her son, but anything could be expected of him. Treason, too. *I must be careful with him. Or even at the first opportunity...*

Worried that the Vizier would read her thoughts, she immediately smiled. "If it was you who crushed the serpent's head, sir," she said in a whisper, "let your gift be our gift. I am sure his Majesty will reward you generously even tonight."

Davud Pasha bowed to the ground. *Reward*, he repeated in his mind. *He will reward generously, huh! Do you think that there may be a more generous reward for me than the throne of the Padishah, you, old bat?* Money, ornaments, houses, palaces, diamonds, rubies no longer had value for him.

How many opponents has he already defeated with one blow? He's deprived Osman of his throne and life and quartered his greatest enemies Dilaver Pasha and Hussein of Ohrid. And he's put a crazy man at the head of the state – *and he's here today, and he will be gone tomorrow.* In a few months, he will start a new uprising against the madman. Then... *Isn't it enough for you what you have suffered from the madman? After you freed yourselves from the madman, you will now hand the throne of the empire to the epileptic Murad? The state needs a healthy Padishah, brave like a lion.* Saying something like that would do the job.

*I just need to deal with this madman and his mother, this Rumelian simpleton Mahpeyker Kösem and her children, and then we will see*, he decided in a spirit.

A sly smile appeared on his face. *But the first thing I will do,* he decided, *I will change my name from Kara to Lion. Let people start getting used to the title Lion Davud Pasha.*

The death of young Osman shook Mahpeyker more than she expected, especially after hearing the phrase that came from Osman's lips while he was dragged to death to the fortress of the Seven Towers. Her heart squeezed painfully, and she whispered: "Ah, Osman."

Şarazad and Semiha were surprised that the death of their Lady's greatest enemy, moved her to tears.

"Tell me again, Semiha," Mahpeyker said quietly, "what words did my son say before he died?"

*My son!*

The term 'my son,' which fell from Mahpeyker's mouth in reference to Osman, also amazed the courtiers. However, neither her own voice nor the words sounded strange to Mahpeyker.

Semiha couldn't stand it and approaching her mistress took her hand. After kissing it, she brought it close to her forehead.

"Whoever says, My Lady, that you have a heart of stone, may his tongue dry out."

The girl kissed Mahpeyker's hand. When she lifted it to her forehead, she felt the moisture of the tears that fell from the Sultana's eyes.

"Tell me," Mahpeyker said. She looked thoughtfully. "Try to repeat, not omitting even one word," Semiha.

"'Rose garden,'" Semiha whispered. She stopped. She felt as if someone was squeezing her throat. She swallowed and started again:

"'There is no flower without thorns in a rose garden;
in this world, jealousy of others curses the loved.
I wanted to serve the state, not for my own boasting,
but jealousy and its servants wanted my destruction.'"

At the last verse, tears also flowed from Semiha's eyes.

"May God watch over his soul," murmured Mürüvvet. Sarasad nodded.

Hayganoş, who had not left the Old Palace since the outbreak of the uprising, interjected in a whisper: "May he be damned. Whoever raised his hand, be accursed."

Mahpeyker didn't eat dinner that night. She walked in circles in the children's room. She did everything in her power so that they wouldn't know what had happened, but they were all aware of everything. Prince Murad got two epileptic seizures in a row. When the seizures subsided, he got up from the ground and demanded firmly: "Sword. Give me a sword so that if the rebels come, I will take the lives of at least a few."

Only after a small-sized sword was strapped to his belt, could Mahpeyker's son be calmed down.

Ibrahim curled up in the corner. At the smallest rustle, he hid his head between the pillows. "They're coming!" he cried, and then he hid in the darkest corner of the wardrobe with his bedding.

The girls were calmer. Mahpeyker, having harshly reminded nannies and servants in the corridors, went to her room early. She extinguished the candles and lamps. Oh, she would willingly hide behind the clouds, being ashamed of the grave sin that she'd committed, the bloody crime.

She stared into the darkness outside the window for a long time.

"Children in the blood," she whispered. How cruel fate was. Everything that she saw in her dream, one after another, became the truth. She saw Mahfiruz giving birth to bloodied babies, and now both her sons have died a bloody death. She regretted once that the children of the

Ice Queen had survived, and now she was crying over their horrible end. The death of the younger son of Mahfiruz, Mehmet, at the behest of his older brother, also caused her pain. However, death finally reached Osman for the fratricide. The fate he met moved her considerably.

Thousands of conflicting feelings swirled in Mahpeyker's soul. She enjoyed the overthrow of Osman, which opened the way for her sons to rule. However, she ached over his death, especially after she learned everything that happened, and about the last words of Osman.

"That boy," she whispered into the darkness, "he didn't deserve that."

*He didn't deserve that?* objected her reason. *He killed his brother. He was a murderer.*

She nodded thoughtfully as if confirming her thoughts. She sighed heavily. *Who doesn't kill for the throne, for power, for reign, and for dominion! So why would Osman not kill?* she defended him in her mind. *That's the order of things. Either you kill, or they kill you. And that's all... Besides, Mehmet was plotting some intrigues behind Osman's back.*

Certainly she, too, wanted to overthrow Osman. But it wasn't supposed to happen this way.

*What way then?* objected her reason. *How did you imagine removing him? With a chain instead of an oiled rope? Or, after you removed Safiye Sultan's ring from the finger of his buried mother, you intended to put it on Osman's hand? Enough of this already. The boy died. Someone else has done it for you. What else do you want? The road is clear for Murad. You have not stained your hands with blood.*

Her reason was right. Life was like this. Ruthless! It didn't take pity on her at one point. Today, it buried Osman.

*How old was he?* she suddenly thought. As she tried to count on her fingers, a wave of memories flooded her. Her throat tightened.

*Nineteen.*

An involuntary scream escaped from Mahpeyker's chest: "God, he was only nineteen! He was only eight years older than my Murad."

Mahpeyker tried not to think about anything for a moment. She stared into the darkness.

"See, Mahfiruz?" she said quietly after a while. Her own voice seemed alien to her. "Do you see what happened? But know that I have no part in what happened to your son. None at all!" She fell silent and swallowed. "If it depended on me," she continued, "I would have sent, not the son of the Ice Queen, but Osman Khan, away somewhere. I would have told him: 'Go wherever you want, where you will live happily.' I even whispered it into the ear of the mother of this madman. 'Eh,' she'd said, and she didn't say anything more. But you know, Mahfiruz, just let the lust of power take over a man. Both you and I know it well, don't we? Your own words and oaths did not manage to stop you."

She was silent for a long time. She sighed deeply several times.

"Well," she finally said. "You can't deceive your destiny. Have you managed to escape your fate? And me? Did I save my neck? What can we do? It's fate's will. I was to become your enemy, and you mine. The game between our sons is over. Ours continues. We will see what role destiny will have for my sons and me.

She continued to stare into the darkness. *God, show me the light*, she pleaded in her thoughts. *Show me the light in this darkness*. It wasn't there. There was not the slightest flash in this darkness.

*Don't think I forgot. Osman defended my children and me, defying you. I couldn't help him. Forgive me. But I swear to you, Mahfiruz, I am not Mahpeyker Kösem Sultan if I don't avenge Osman. Let your son's revenge be my revenge from today on.*

These words made her feel a strange relief in her heart as if she'd been forgiven. She stared out the window for some time, and finally, she nodded her head.

"Osman," she whispered, "the son with a fate written in blood. I promise you. I will take revenge on those who have done this to you. Your death paved the way for the madman. The revenge will pave the way to the throne for your brother, Prince Murad. Your assassins will bring the sun for me and your brother, Osman, I swear they will! My Osman. My unfortunate son."

# CHAPTER NINETEEN

### The Old Palace
### January 1623

Things went just as Mahpeyker predicted. Mustafa was still a madman, and his mother a power-hungry woman.

Damad Kara Davud Pasha took over the helm of the state completely. Mustafa sat on the throne, the slave Sanuber held onto his lap, but the real Sultan was the Sadrazam, the murderer of young Osman.

Despite this, peace and order still couldn't be brought to the capital. Rowdy gangs prowled the streets, and there was no end to robberies and rapes. High prices, hunger, and poverty also continued.

Davud Pasha was just an observer. In his heart, he rejoiced in seeing all the misfortunes as the premises for the next uprising – premises for a rebellion that would bring down Mustafa and take him closer to the throne.

There was only one obstacle ahead of him: Mahpeyker Kösem Sultan and her children.

Sadrazam Davud Pasha did almost nothing to ensure peace in the state, but at the same time, he never missed the opportunity to pass sinister news to the Valide.

"They've plundered five houses again today, My Lady. One of our officers has sworn to God, that there were also Mahpeyker's servants among the bandits...

Whenever he said this, the Sultana Mother, listening to him with her eyelids closed as though napping, would open her eyes wide.

"Until I see it with my own eyes, I don't want to make accusations, but, My Lady, a lot of things comes to ones...

He didn't have to finish the sentence. He knew she would ask.

"What comes to one's mind, Sadrazam Pasha?"

"Hm... how to put it, My Lady... I don't want to accuse anyone... But is it possible, I am asking, that the Old Palace would keep this never-ending turmoil hot?"

He didn't have to ask if it was Mahpeyker's doing. Because to say, 'The Old Palace,' meant the same as saying, 'Mahpeyker Kösem Sultan.'

"Lady Mahpeyker is our friend, Pasha. She has helped us a lot. And she loves our Sultan." But Damad Kara Davud could swear that the woman's eyes flashed. "I don't think she could engage in intrigues against us, Your Eminence."

"Oh, of course," he said every time, with a suggestive look. "I do not expect that either. But at the thought of the four scions of this Lady, Satan plants such unwarranted suspicion in a man, My Lady.

The woman didn't let it show, but Satan also sowed the very same suspicion in her.

And in Mahpeyker, too.

Firstly, Osman was killed. A bottle was opened, and jinn was released. From now on, it was impossible to predict what he would do next. Would the murderer of a dynasty member hesitate before any other murder? Her children were in danger. Mustafa's mother, breaking the word given to Mahpeyker, gave a free hand to Osman's assassins, and even incited them to commit crimes. And now she certainly sees Mahpeyker's children as a threat to her power.

*And even if she doesn't see it herself, Kara Davud, the murderer, will help her see*, she gritted her teeth. *The damned bastard is trying to rename himself as Lion Pasha.*

In that case, the hour has come. If she doesn't make a move, the others won't remain in place.

The time has come to keep the word given to Safiye Sultan. She could not be late. 'Neither too early, nor too late' – weren't those the words of Safiye Sultan? Here comes the right time now. The time for action.

The time when they will bring them the sun! She will put a sunny crown on Murad's head with her own hands.

She hesitated for a moment. A never-ending pain squeezed her heart. She straightened up and stood up.

Even if my Murad is an epileptic, so what? At least he is not crazy!

She sent secret messengers in all directions. The trusted messengers delivered Mahpeyker Kösem Sultan's letters. In the event of their capture, they had the order to destroy them. For the price of their lives, they were to prevent the letters from getting into the hands of the Valide Sultan's spies and the Vizier's men.

She even wrote by hand to her old master from Kumanovo. Karayelzade Ibrahim Bey was already an elderly man, but he still had considerable influence in the army and the council of alims.

*'To venerable Karayelzade Ibrahim Bey,*

*The state of affairs leaves no doubt. As long as the killer remains unpunished, peace will not prevail in the empire. I believe that Osman was sent to the Fortress of the Seven Towers to be imprisoned. If they wanted to kill him, he would not be sent to the dungeon.'*

She didn't think anyone could think otherwise – especially Ibrahim Bey. Now came the turn for the news she wanted to spread among the army and the people.

*'Now we hear that Janissaries and Spahis are being hounded in their wilayahs. 'You have killed your Sultan' – they blame them. Here the situation looks the same. Neither the alims, nor the officials, nor the Janissaries, nor the soldiers, nor the Spahis, even the peace-keepers are ashamed to look in the face of the people. Everyone has their heads down.*

*Of course, the one who caused the murder is responsible, but whoever killed, should not avoid punishment. If the Padishah issued a ferman, it was his will. But let the murderer be put to death so that all subjects do not have to suffer because of this serious offense.'*

Mahpeyker put her pen down for a moment. Her thoughts returned to the past; to those days when she was listening in the Kumanovo palace to the conversations of Bey Ibrahim and Beylerbey Mehmet. If they had told her then how bloody the poisoned life of the capital palace would turn out to be, she would never have believed it.

She sighed and reached for the pen again.

*'You, after all, belong to those who consider justice and loyalty to be their duty. I have learned to be just and loyal both from you and my father and mother. You are like a second father to me, with whom I associate the most beautiful feelings of my heart. You are a hero, Karayelzade Ibrahim Bey. I do not doubt that you are of one mind with us. If we are not right, say: "In the Ottoman empire, there is no place for justice, law, code, religion, conscience, loyalty, faithfulness. It is fair for a state in which there is no*

justice, no law, no codex, no religion, no conscience, no loyalty, no faithfulness, to fall." *I swear, therefore, that I am also grieved for our fate. I will say: "If so, what else has been left to me when the empire is already gone; let the seas get rough, let the rivers flood, the mountains fall, let this whole world be gone together with it."'*

At the end she wrote her name:

*'The little girl you knew as Nastya. The lady of the Ottoman Empire, Mahpeyker Kösem Sultan, the Great Sultana Mother.'*

The secret letters sent to beys, viziers, beylerbeys, hodjas, leaders, whom she knew while her husband was alive, circulating from hand to hand, soon became a declaration of a new uprising.

The Spahis units, recruited by Karayelzade Ibrahim Bey, set off on horseback to the capital. From other places, from other lands, Janissaries followed them.

Valide Sultan, understanding that the current state of affairs did not bode well, called Sanuber one night and issued a ferman on behalf of her son, depriving Damad Davud Pasha of the title of Sadrazam.

Davud, seduced by the dream of a future reign, and accustomed to the shouts 'Lion' at military appeals, didn't expect such a turn of events but saw divine providence in it. Now it was better to lurk on the side than to be in plain view.

The new Vizier didn't rise to the occasion either. The Sultana Mother instructed her puppet to replace him with another one, too. First, Lefkeli Mustafa, then a Georgian Mehmed Pasha were appointed Great Viziers.

But things had already gone completely out of hand. Sultan Mustafa issued absurd orders right and left.

"Sanuber, I'm issuing a ferman, write it down. Let all the cages in the capital be destroyed. Let the birds be released!"

The poor girl wrote what she was told.

Another day, the Sultan summoned the Sadrazam Georgian Mehmed Pasha.

"Where are, dear sir... where are the birds? Aren't you the main bird breeder? We demand an answer. Where are the birds?" he burst out. "Why are there no birds flying in my palace?"

Then he jumped up from the pearl-lined chair and gathering his robes, escorted by the Vizier's stupefied gaze, rushed out into the corridor. Waving his arms like wings, he trotted away.

"Whirr, whirrrr! Whirrr!"

The appointment of the Georgian Mehmed Pasha for the Grand Vizier made the cauldron, already boiling in the branches of the Janissaries, finally explode. After breaking into the soldier's Divan, they attacked Mehmed Pasha.

"We will never allow a eunuch to be a Great Vizier. If you resist, we will take out a knife and cut you up."

The Vizier returned the seal to Sultan Mustafa in fear and withdrew to his palace. Padishah, on the advice of his mother, issued another ferman proclaiming that 'we will pass the seal to whoever the people want.' Under the pressure of the army, the Albanian, Mere Hussein Pasha, who didn't know the Turkish language, became a Vizier again.

Valide Sultan thought that from then on things would start to go well – but she was wrong. It didn't take long for the rebels to demand a removal of the main treasurer Hussein Pasha.

Mere Hussein Pasha, who believed that he'd gained the favor of the army, was one of those who said, 'fight fire with fire.' He punished with falaka the qadi, of whom he learned that had accepted a bribe at the Divan. All the qadis, when they assembled in the Fatih mosque, wrote a fatwa saying that 'Mere is a heretic and his blood should be spilled. Sultan Mustafa's mind is not healthy. It is improper for him to lead the state,' and they announced they would not recognize Mustafa's reign.

But no one could lift a hand against Mere Hussein. The Sultana Mother, knowing about the army's support for Mere, dared not order her son to dismiss the Vizier from his office.

*And what if we asked Mahpeyker?* she thought. *To hell with that!* she muttered angrily. *Where is my pride?*

She didn't look forward to going to Mahpeyker for advice, but the days had come that a man broke his sworn word and the oath. What was one's pride compared to that?

And so, it was during those days, a messenger from the New Palace appeared in the Old Palace.

"Her Majesty, Valide Sultan," the girl said haughtily to Semiha, "wants Lady Mahpeyker to visit the New Palace. I will pass the day and the hour convenient for Lady Mahpeyker to Her Majesty."

Semiha knew what Mahpeyker's answer would be, but raising her head, she looked at her. She was surprised to see a bright, joyful look instead of drawn eyebrows and angry face.

"The sun," Mahpeyker whispered. "You understand? The sunrise is approaching."

*And what was it supposed to mean? What sunrise? It was the middle of the day,* thought the courier. Mahpeyker could see that she couldn't make sense of her words. She smiled.

"They'll bring us the sun soon, Semiha. I feel it with every fiber of my body."

The girl didn't understand anything again. Mahpeyker smiled with a slight irony this time.

"You know, Semiha, I don't feel well. I feel a cold coming on. I'm staying in bed. Pass it on to the girl. As soon as I feel better, I will order to send the message."

The Sultana Mother understood that such a message would never come.

"I see, Mahpeyker," she murmured. "So, you burned bridges behind you."

She closed her eyes. *Do as you wish,* she thought. *My son is crazy, but he is on the throne. And I am the Valide. And you? You and your son, an epileptic - who are you?*

*Nobody. Your lives depend on my order.*

She glanced at the arriving servant from between half-closed eyelids.

In recent months, it has become her habit. Whoever didn't know it, could think that she was asleep, but in reality, the woman was watching her surroundings from between the eyelids with fox eyes.

"I'm afraid," she hissed, "that from now, on this woman will often have a headache. Let's finally deal with this problem."

Crazy Mustafa and his mother could not get rid of the trouble.

Sadrazam Mere Hussein Pasha became so bold that this time he punished one of the Beylerbeys with falaki at the Divan. The man gave up his life under whips in front of dozens of ministers. Then, when appearing at a meeting in the Fatih mosque, he issued successive death sentences for the qadis who prepared fatwas about his heresy. To strengthen his position, he also set up Spahis and Janissaries against himself.

First, the Spahis troops, flowing into the capital from provinces, rebelled. After them, the Janissaries. In January 1623, they attacked the Sultan's palace, demanding 'justice' and 'death for the Osman assassins.'

All the troops gathered together in front of the Greetings Gate, united in one shout:

"Osman was sent to the Seven Towers Fortress to be imprisoned. If they wanted to kill him, he would not have been sent to the dungeon. We are being hunted in wilayah. 'You killed your Sultan,' – they blame us. Of course, the one who caused the murder is responsible, and he should not avoid punishment. If the Padishah issued a ferman, it was his will. But let the murderer be put to death so that all subjects will not have to suffer for this serious offense."

These were the thoughts of Mahpeyker, written down and sent out in letters. They were memorized word-for-word and shouted in the streets of the capital as a harbinger of vengeance for the blood of Osman.

Spahis and Janissaries, supported by the people, began to look for Osman's assassins on the streets of Istanbul. First, Humble Thief was found, who had held the young Padishah's private parts by force, making him perish forever. Whatever was in hand – a shotgun, a spear, a sword – they used to quarter the perpetrator.

The initiator of the uprising, Kara Davud Pasha, after dreaming of becoming a Padishah, fled in fear for his own skin. Davud, to whom betrayal clung to him like a middle name, after a few days became a victim himself. He was found hiding in a barn in one of the villages and brought to the capital. Dragged like Osman to the hellish dungeon, seven floors underground in the Seven Towers Fortress, he heard the same shout:

"Die, die, heretic!" In the same place where he'd choked Osman and had cut off his ear while unable to control his rage, had exactly the same things he once considered necessary to do to Osman, done to him, before his head was cut off.

Eventually, all who threw the rope around Osman's neck in the Fortress of the Seven Towers were either hanged or beheaded, while Mustafa the Dunger, Blind Çökürcü, Hasan the Cook, Mustafa the Rafter, Handless Mehmed, Muslu the Goldsmith were quartered. The leaders of the uprising, such as the instigators Cerrahzade Mehmet Chelebi and Feridun Efendi, were each caught and killed. Mere Hussein Pasha, realizing that his turn was also coming, disappeared from the court one day. The Sultana Mother made the illiterate Kemankesh Ali Pasha the Vizier.

When Semiha ran into the room barely catching her breath, Mahpeyker had just fallen asleep. The daily tracking of news and the development of events tired her. The iron was ready. It was being forged. The time was coming.

"Get up, My Lady."

Mahpeyker jumped in fear. She panicked seeing Semiha over her.

"What? What's happening? Are they coming here? Children? Semiha, where are my children? Where's my Murad?"

"No, nothing like that," the girl grabbed her hands. To calm her down, she even laughed. "They announced that Sadrazam Pasha has arrived. He's waiting in the room with the partition."

In a dreamy daze, she didn't understand at first.

"Sadrazam? But Mere escaped, didn't he?"

"I'm talking about Kemankesh Ali Pasha. He took his place. The Padishah made him the Great Vizier this evening."

Only then did Mahpeyker wake up. "Sun," she whispered to herself. "He brought me the sun."

She immediately got out of bed.

"Didn't I say?" she asked Semiha happily. "Didn't I say that the sun would rise? Look, here it's risen. They brought me the sun. They brought me the sun. You understand me? They brought the sun to Murad and me! Understand me?"

She didn't understand.

Mahpeyker didn't try to explain. Having dressed quickly, she ran to the room where Ali Pasha was waiting.

"Pasha," she said from the doorway.

She noticed the shadow on the other side of the partition rising from its place with excitement.

"My Lady."

"Blessed be your rule."

The shadow approached the grating. "The time has come for service, My Lady."

To make sure, she pretended she didn't understand. "It's not easy to serve at Mustafa's court. May God…"

"It is clear," Kemankesh interrupted, "that from now on every subject of the great empire will serve Murad Khan."

*The sun!* resounded in Mahpeyker's head. *The sun has risen!* Despite the excitement filling her, she managed to hide her joy.

"However," she whispered to the Pasha listening to her on the other side of the partition, "the successor is still very young."

"That's true, but his mother, Mahpeyker Kösem Sultan, is experienced enough to guide our young Padishah."

In her head, the same scream sounded again...

*The sun! They brought me the sun.*

"Until the Ruler is ready to take the burden of governing a great empire on himself, if Valide Sultan agrees to take on the role of a Regent, there will be no problem."

"Have you consulted the alims council? Does the law accept a woman Padishah? Will they issue an appropriate fatwa?"

The shadow behind the grating cleared his throat.

"If Your Majesty deems it right, we will not say Lady Sultana. I think that such titles as an Older Mother, a Senior Mother, a Great Mother, a Magnificent Mother will be more appropriate phrases."

*God! I'm really becoming the Queen. Little Nastya from Milos becomes a real Ottoman Queen.*

She was silent for a moment as if she was considering.

"After all, our intentions are pure," she finally said in a calm voice. "We remember what happened when two Padishahs sat on the throne. Mustafa..."

"I don't think that we would have to face difficulties in dealing with this issue. We can plan it together," replied the shadow behind the divider.

As they conferred, they approached each other on two sides of the grating to such an extent that their lips almost touched the pearly decorations.

When Kemankesh Ali Pasha left, Mahpeyer returned to her room calmer than she expected.

"Let them wake up Murad Khan," she ordered.

"But it's still early," said the girl.

Mayhpeyker responded with an exalted cry: "Wake him up! The sun rose. The Padishahs don't sleep late!"

"Murad, my Padishah," Mahpeyker whispered affectionately after the girl left. "I'm just begging you don't get an attack from excitement. I am begging you, my God, don't let him be caught by epilepsy. Give him strength."

Kemankesh Ali Pasha, having left the Old Palace, went immediately to the palace of Sheikh al-Islam Yahya Efendi.

The Sheikh al-Islam was waiting at this late hour for his visit.

"How did it go?" he asked immediately as he came out to meet the Great Vizier. "Did she agree?"

"Yes, but she gave a condition."

"A condition?"

"Yes. And she is right. The holy memory Ahmed Khan did not call her Mahpeyker Kösem for nothing. The promises are not enough for the Sultana Mother. She demands a fatwa from the alims council and you, confirming her right to use the title of Regent Mother until Murad Khan reaches an appropriate age."

Yahya Efendi scratched his beard.

"A fatwa, eh?" For a moment his face took on a thoughtful expression. "Why wouldn't she have the right, Sadrazam Pasha. Murad Khan hasn't been circumcised yet. After all, it is the duty imposed on the mother by Allah, so that, until the ruler reaches maturity, she would be his guardian and adviser."

He sat down at the desk.

"We will write a fatwa. You do the rest. If this matter is not resolved by tomorrow, it will end badly."

"It will be resolved," Kemankesh Ali replied. "One way or another, it will be resolved. The empire no longer has patience for the madman. Otherwise, all this confusion and the murders will lead us, God forbid, to anarchy."

Ali Pasha rushed from the palace of Sheikh al-Islam to the New Palace. The Valide Sultan was awakened. The woman, seeing the Great Vizier arriving so early, understood everything. Ali Pasha did not prolong things unnecessarily, either.

"Things are getting worse every minute," he said firmly. "I'm afraid that it will be necessary to prove to a selected group of Spahis and Janissaries that the ruler is healthy in his mind. Otherwise, God forb..."

"What are you saying, Pasha – our son's state of mind will be tested?"

"The alims are of the same opinion, My Lady. They say, 'If he is not weak in his mind, we are at his orders. But if... just like the rumors are circulating, he pats the ministers at the Divan on their backs, so that their turbans fall off their heads, we do not want him.' In this situation, there is no other way."

"The condition of the Ruler is known. Our heart doesn't allow us to agree to such a humiliation of our son."

"There's no other way."

The woman was silent. She stared for a long time from under the half-closed eyelids. Ali Pasha thought for a moment that she was asleep. Suddenly the Sultana mother spoke.

"There is," she said. "There is another way out. If we are given the word that nothing will happen to our son and us, we will renounce the throne. I do not think the Ruler will even realize this."

Kemankesh Ali Pasha bowed with respect. He immediately remembered Mahpeyker's words: 'If you frighten her, suggesting that her son may be killed, and then you offer a bribe in the form of their life, the woman will agree to resign from the throne.' He didn't expect that the Sultana's tactics would bring the desired result in such a short time.

"Having taken the throne from my son, will you give it to the child of this woman? A successor who is still a little boy?"

"The Ruler," replied Pasha, "will return in peace to his old apartment in the New Palace. Although..."

The woman tried to straighten up in her chair.

"There is no need to say it, Pasha," she hissed. "We know where we will go."

On the tenth day of September 1623, at sunrise, the capital's streets echoed with the clatter of hoofs and the rattling of wheels. Three carriages rushed from the Old Palace to the New one, and one from the New to the Old. Fate wanted the carriages with tightly closed curtains to meet at some point. The people who rode inside didn't see each other, but they heard the wheels rattling, they sensed their presence.

Twelve-year-old Murad stepped out from one of the three carriages that reached the New Palace. Sadrazam Kemankesh Ali Pasha, Sheikh al-Islam Yahya Efendi, and several Viziers approached him to kiss the flap of his robe with the words: 'Long live my Padishah.' Murad, following what his mother taught him, ignored them.

Having been forced to get up earlier, he was now sleepy and irritated. Throwing the flap firmly back, he didn't allow anyone to kiss it. His first order consisted of two words: "Let's go."

The Older Mother, a Senior Mother, a Magnificent Mother, the Great Mother Mahpeyker Kösem Sultan, and her daughters got off from the second vehicle. Everyone was impressed with how beautiful and wonderful the Mother Sultana looked at such an early hour. The Sadrazam bowed to her.

"How bright the sun is today! Isn't it true?" Mahpeyker smiled at them.

Ali Pasha and Yahya Efendi looked at each other as if asking what this meant. The night sky was just beginning to gray. There wasn't even a presage of the sun. But they nodded their heads as if a secret meaning was hidden in her words. The sun was very bright, very much so!

Mahpeyker stopped, proudly erect. All the courtiers ran up to adjust her skirts and the gorgeous black gown, embroidered with silver. With the passage of time, the black color suited Mahpeyker even more. A long, black, and gold embroidered tulle of a flat cap rested on her shoulders. Without changing her pose, Valide Sultan slowly turned her head in the direction from which the sound of rattling wheels came. The courtiers, the nannies, and the odalisques ran toward the third carriage.

The other children of Mahpeyker got out of the vehicle: Suleiman, Kasım, Ayşe, and Fatma.

But the door was still open.

"Come," one of the women asked, peering inside. But someone who was inside, did not intend to get out.

Mahpeyker raised her voice: "Fitnat!" Despite the proud pose she kept, her voice showed her irritation. "Instead of calling, go inside and lead him out."

Frightened, Fitnat obeyed the order. She led Ibrahim out of the carriage, almost dragging him.

"No!" the boy shouted. "No, I'm not going to go! No. I don't agree. I command. Leave me alone!"

Ibrahim, who with the enthronement of his brother had now become the heir to the throne, was terrified. With his eyes wide open in fear, he hid his face in the folds of his nanny's tightly wrapped dress. On the way to the New Palace, he resisted desperately.

"Have mercy, have mercy. I'm still small!" he struggled, crying. The servants who had resorted to a series of tricks were able to calm Prince Ibrahim down somewhat.

Mahpeyker tried to divert attention from Ibrahim's hysteria, rewarding the palace dignitary who had come to meet her with one of her most beautiful smiles.

"I'm glad to see you again."

She went past the heads bowed before her without looking at them. Two young courtiers carried the magnificent end of her skirt that stretched from under the black dress.

"I just said the same to Sadrazam Pasha and Hodja Efendi. How bright the sun is today, isn't it?"

She knew that if she turned, she would see the palace people seeking the sun in wonder.

*Fools*, she thought. *The sun is walking before you. Look!*

Awakened by Sanuber, Mustafa asked while he was led to the old apartment: "Where are we going?"

"To the birdies," answered the girl. "Birdies are waiting for you, my Sultan."

Mustafa jumped for joy like a child.

"Oh, great, let's fly then. We got bored in this cage."

Waving his arms and running, he chirped: "Whirr, whirr!"

# Chapter Twenty

## The Capital, Hippodrome
## October 1623

Here is what it is like to be a Queen!

Mahpeyker triumphed. To be beautiful like an angel, majestic as snow-covered peaks, joyful as a butterfly!

She was beautiful. Very beautiful. Even though she had thirty-three summers behind her already, she was beautiful as a dream. In a beautifully dress sewn with golden thread and a conical cap with a red chiffon cascading down over her arms, she exceeded the mountains with her majesty.

But she couldn't fly! She wouldn't let it show, but she was deathly scared. *My God,* she prayed inwardly. *Please, help Murad. Save my son from the tremors of epilepsy during the ceremony!*

She tossed in her bed all night long. She still had that terrible scene in front of her eyes -- Murad throwing himself on the ground in front of the Viziers and Pashas, and rolling in convulsions with foam on his lips...

Her heart was dying in her chest at the thought. Who knows what they would say, seeing her son in this condition?

'We dismissed the madman, and now we've brought in an epileptic, gentlemen!'

*Look, Pasha, what's going on in this empire. One day we're at the mercy of a madman, another day at the epileptics!* Damn it, damn it! That's what Mahpeyker thought, guessing their reaction.

That day, when Murad was taken to the Eyüp Sultan Mosque, she said all the prayers she knew for him. For the first time, Murad was so far away from her, and he faced the most important test in his life – and she was forced to wait, surrounded by four walls. Her Majesty Mahpeyker prayed many times on that day to the Prophet Muhammad, God the Father, and the Virgin Mary, to help her son.

Finally, as she suffered through the terrible waiting, she said, *No,* to herself, trying to drown out her fear. *God will not do it to Murad. He will not let the illness sent by him discredit, shame, my son in front of his subjects.*

While the ceremony continued in Eyüp Sultan, she silently counted the minutes and hours. *Now they are giving Murad the sword of Osman Ghazi*, she guessed in her mind. *Now the Vizier and the council of viziers, the beys, the agas, will be approaching one after another to kiss the hem of his robe.*

At last her patience broke. She couldn't stand it anymore.

"Close the windows," she ordered the courtiers. "Close everything. Otherwise, your Sultan's Mother, the Great Mother, the Magnificent Mother, the Older Mother, or whatever, anyway, this mother will grow wings out of happiness and fly."

Not just her. Şarazad, Mürüvvet, Semiha, other courtiers, odalisques, servants – everyone without exception was happy.

She didn't see a single face that didn't have a smile on it. There was not a single head that would not bend down in front of her – so many people would not arrange a masquerade of this scale just to please her.

But on that day, the most difficult role fell to her. A cry of joy was rising in her breast. She wanted to grab a tambourine and play: "Tam, tam... Tam, tam, ta, tam, tam... Tam, ta, tam... Tam, tam, ta, tam, tam! Hey!"

Just as in her childhood when she danced barefoot on the grass on Milos, singing songs, she wanted to sing and dance now.

But, of course, she couldn't do anything like that. She was a Queen. Her majesty, pride, and honor could not suffer the slightest detriment. Her soul could dance and sing, but the Great Mother Mahpeyker Kösem Sultan had to stand with a raised head and proud face. She should look at her people the way she had practiced thousands of times, casting glances at window panes and silver mirrors, until the end of her life.

*My God*, she thought. *The prophecy has been fulfilled: A beautiful young maid became a queen. Dreams come true. From now on I am a queen. I have my subjects. Mine are the subjects, viziers, commanders, soldiers. I am the Queen in the Ottoman state, in a state of seven climates, three continents, and a great power!*

When the noise outside the window intensified, all the girls in the room, having even forgotten that they were in the presence of their mistress, ran to the window, shouting with joy.

The band of Janissaries made not only their seven drums shake, but the whole court, the entire capital.

"Dum... dum... dummmm...!"

Girls, servants, henchmen, all shouted over one another:

"He's coming!"

"Our Master is coming!"

"Our Ruler returns from Eyüp Sultan!"

"Our Master," Mahpeyker repeated. "Our Ruler. My son! My Murad. My Padishah!"

Everyone rushed to the windows from which the Greeting Gate was visible.

It could be seen how much they too, wanted to be by the window. They all looked at her with pleading eyes.

"Well," Mahpeyker said proudly. "What are you waiting for? We also want to witness the return of our Rul..."

She didn't have a chance to finish. Şarazad caught the long end of the red-yellow-blue silk underskirt that fell all the way to her ankles. Semiha took her hand. Mürüvvet stepped forward to clear the way. Hayganoş Kalfa, too, despite her huge breasts and impressive buttocks of the size of a kettle, ran behind them. At the same time, she shouted in a broken voice:

"Make way, I tell you! Maaaake...! Can't you hear? Can't you see? The Great Mother Kösem Sultan is comiiiing...!"

The crowd parted, giving her the way. All heads were lowered, everybody bowed at the waist. She had been used to bowing since she became the moon of Ahmed, but this was something else. It wasn't respect for the slave liked by her Padishah, tainted with envy. Now she felt sympathy, delight, and contentment with being in her subjection. They were greeting the Queen, not a concubine!

Both the Greeting Gate and the big square behind it could be seen from the window. It seemed that the end of the world had come. The capital city jumped to its feet, crowds poured out onto the streets. How quickly the people learned about the enthronement of her son and ran to meet him!

At the sight of the procession, the crowd waved.

The glass windows were buzzing from the shouts: "Long live the Padishah!"

A crowd outside the window echoed: "Long live Murad Khan!" There were also shouts, "Long live Great Mother Kösem!" mixed with applause. Hayganoş was praying just behind her.

"Well, well..." she said. "Maşallah... maşallah... keep my Sultan and Sultana from the evil eye, God, you hear me?"

Mahpeyker also recited in her heart all the prayers she knew. When the procession passed the arcade, she saw him. *There he is*, she exclaimed to herself. *My son!*

Sultan Murad was riding at the front, sitting upright and strong, on a chestnut horse, called Chestnut Aga. Padishah was magnificent in a turban with a huge feather and a collar thrown over his shoulders in a gold-embroidered caftan – a little bit too large. Brilliant emeralds and rubies shone in the midday sun with a blinding glare. Mahpeyker thought it was as if her son carried the sun over his head instead of the crown. He was majestic, not like a twelve-year-old, but like an adult man.

*It suits him,* Mahpeyker thought at once. *The Sultan's power fits him.*

On his left, slightly away from Chestnut Aga, rode a scary man on a huge gray horse – Aga the Armorer. He carried the Padishah's sword. It seemed that both the Aga and his horse understood the importance of their task.

The animal trod, swaying sideways, and Aga the Armorer aroused immense fear, casting glances from under his drawn eyebrows that apparently were capable of penetrating a shield.

Right behind Murad, seven giants followed on horses as black like night. They carried seven Sultan's feathers on their halberds.

In his right hand, the new Padishah of the Great Empire held the reins of Chestnut Aga, while he leaned his left hand, bent at the elbow, on his left thigh. He looked straight ahead, his face serious. There was no joy, no satisfaction, no childish stare on it. He displayed his unwavering will, hard as a rock, strong as a double-tempered sword, in front of his people – just as she had taught it, just as she had prepared him!

At once her eyes filled with tears.

*No, not now*, she told herself. *Not now. Queens do not cry. Neither from pain nor from joy.*

That day, Sultan Murad sat on the throne in the Audience Hall. He had not even been circumcised yet. Mahpeyker, as Valide Sultan, sat down a bit to the back to her son's right, on a small sofa. She sat upright, her hands on her knees. She wore a crown on top of her head – a souvenir passed by Sultana Nurbanu to Sultana Safiye, and then to her.

Her son, under the rays of the light falling through the windows decorated with colored panes, seemed bathed in the sun. The Alims interpreted this view as an auspicious sign.

"God willing, the Great Empire will shine again like the sun under the rule of our Sultan. That is our goal."

Mahpeyker never once moved during the few hours of the coronation ceremony. *I finally put a sunny crown on my son's head*, she thought proudly. She knew. The sun was also shining on her head.

Five days later Murad underwent the ceremony of circumcision.

When Sadrazam Kemankesh Ali Pasha appeared to inform her about the successful course of the ritual, and the well-being of the Padishah, Mahpeyker saw a strange flash in his eye.

"We ordered," he said firmly, "that the circumcision ceremonies would take place when His Majesty would fully recover. The first week of October. The capital city has not seen such glamor, such solemn celebrations yet."

Mahpeyker Kösem did not listen anymore. *He ordered,* she murmured in her mind. She felt a slight twinge of anxiety. *Watch out*, said her reason at once. *This is not a man you can trust, Sultana Mother. Do not let him out of your sight. Get rid of him as soon as possible.*

As Sadrazam left the room, Mahpeyker decided to listen to her voice of reason.

The Hippodrome was prepared for the ceremonies related to the circumcision. Sadrazam Kemankesh Ali Pasha ordered to set up a tent only for the Padishah. Special benches were placed in front of the Ruler's tent for representatives of foreign countries. But they too, like the ordinary people, would watch the festivities in the sun, under the open sky. Mahpeyker first thought that she would watch the ceremony from the Sultan's tent. But when she heard from the Pasha that he guessed that 'Her Majesty the Sultan's Mother will think that it is not fitting for matrons to be in the presence of men,' and he didn't issue 'commands regarding the harem,' she went mad with rage.

"Will the hippodrome be filled by men? Are we to send back home all those who take their wives and daughters with them to the ceremony in honor of our son? What an arrogance! Or maybe there are no women in the Ottoman Empire, and Allah creates men from stone?" she thundered.

The intent of the Pasha was clear – Sadrazam was trying to move her into the shadows. It meant as much as: 'Murad Khan is standing at the head of the empire, and I am behind him – you are not there.'

She called the harem manager.

"Announce it, let somebody take care of it, and hurry up!" she cried. "My tent will stand next to the tent of our son. And if it does not, there's no telling what I will do. I swear I do not know what I will do. The mother wouldn't get to see her son in glory, and Kemankesh will?!"

Ali Pasha found out about Kösem Sultan's anger. *I was too fast*, he thought anxiously. He ran quickly to beg for forgiveness.

But Mahpeyker said to turn him away, using the words: "We don't feel well today. We will call for you when we get better."

She wasn't going to share her power with anyone. Until her son would take responsibility for the state affairs, she was the head of the Great Empire. No one else. When the time comes, they both will manage the Empire. That's how she'd planned this game, she had fought for this for years, brushing aside death. That's why she'd been waiting for the sun to come down from heaven to rest on their heads.

The expression on Sadrazam's face as he was leaving the palace did not bode well, as Semiha hastened to let Mahpeyker know. Mahpeyker shrugged.

"You should see the expression on my face when I heard about this impertinence!"

For seven days and seven nights of the celebrations, the capital was boiling with excitement. Sultan Murad and Mahpeyker Kösem Sultan watched the performances from the common tent, together with the Princes Suleiman and Kasım, and the Sultanas Ayşe and Fatma. Despite pleading and begging, Ibrahim couldn't be tempted to come with anyone. He locked himself in his room, and nothing they did could get him out of there.

Mahpeyker was aware of the change that had taken place in her son. He'd been a capricious and restless child before, but from the moment he found out that Murad had become a Padishah, he became really strange.

"Leave him," she decided. "Don't press. If he wants it so, let it be. Let him stay with the nannies. Maybe he'll show up tomorrow."

But Prince Ibrahim didn't leave his room, neither tomorrow nor the next day.

Acrobats and jugglers showed all their mastery. Six exotic animals that the capital had never seen before brought in cages from six countries – a crocodile, a boa snake, a rhinoceros, a hippopotamus, an ostrich, and a sea lion – caused enormous excitement. The Janissaries organized parades, the guards and Spahis showed spectacles. Swords fights of the Janissaries and horse tricks of Spahis produced roaring applause. Wrestlers' fights, javelin throws, and climbing a greasy pole drew the greatest interest.

The festivities lasted well into the nights also. In the huge crowd filling the hippodrome, pots of pilaf, roasted chickens, meats, and saffron desserts prepared in palace kitchens were distributed on Mahpeyker's orders.

"If I hear from just one of my subjects that he has not eaten enough, I will order this kitchen to be leveled, and you with it too," she warned. The trays of baklava, böreks, and boilers filled with pistachio sorbets were served. The carriages filled with trays of baklava and boilers of soup were drawn one after the other to the lodges of Janissaries, Spahis, and sailors.

On the last day, sailors were going to arrange a spectacle. When the time came for the show, Sultan Murad and the Sultana Mother took their seats. People, after praying for the Padishah and his Mother, fell silent. Everyone was waiting, curious about the spectacle that the people of the sea would arrange.

"Well," one could hear among the rows, "what kind of things will people who walk on the water be doing on the land?"

They didn't have to wait long for the answer. There was a noise at one end of the Hippodrome. All heads turned in that direction. The rumor that set everyone on their feet was the rattle of twenty wooden wheels of a huge wagon, dragged by fifty oxen, swaying their heads. The wagon was so large that it looked like an island under a huge gallery that was loaded on it. The sailors running on both sides poured water over the wheels, which got hot from carrying the weight of the wagon and the ship. The galley sails were rolled up. The flag of the Ottoman Empire and the Empire's navy fluttered over the ship's mainmast and the aft.

Sailors, wearing red vests and short blue galligaskins, lined up along both sides of the ship. They had red bands tied on their heads, and their chests were bared. They stood with their legs wide, their arms folded behind their backs, and squeezing curved knives between their teeth. Ovations shook the Hippodrome.

A moment later, a noise came from the direction where Ibrahim Pasha's palace was located. Soon, a black galleon loaded onto an even larger wagon appeared. There was a white flag with a blue cross on its mast – it was a model of the Crusader fleet.

So, the sailors were going to fight the enemy in the Hippodrome in a naval battle!

The people turned in that direction with a cry of excitement. The enemy ship rolled into the square amidst teasing, derision, and curses. People rushed at the soldiers of the giaours who stood on deck with artificial shields. There were even those, who took the ajwa they were eating out of their mouth and threw it at the enemy.

Finally, there was silence. Mahpeyker also waited anxiously behind the tulle curtain. She felt a strange, incomprehensible excitement. She smiled at the girls.

"What emotions!"

Prince Kasım moved forward to see better. Suleiman, on the other hand, seemed absent.

Unexpectedly, there was a commotion on board the Crusader ship. A fire flashed and disappeared. Immediately afterward an explosion was heard. Smoke rose from an empty cannon loaded with just powder.

"Hurray, hurray!" screams were heard. The deck and rope ladders filled with enemy sailors armed with swords, spears, and curved sticks in their hands.

At the same time as if on command, the assembled crowd turned their heads towards the galley with the flag of the Empire.

"Hey!" someone shouted, raising his hand to his mouth. "Heretics are attacking, what are you waiting for, eh?"

Suddenly, a roar, "Ya Allah!" brought out a cry of surprise from the breasts gathered in the square.

The sailors, lined up along the rail, grabbed the knives they held in their mouths, and responded with one roar, "Bismillah!"

The Hippodrome was in an uproar. A cry escaped from thousands of throats, which was supposed to encourage the sailors rushing from the deck to the battlefield for the fight.

"Ya Allah, Bismillah!"

Mahpeyker felt shivers down her spine. Rolling up the sleeve of her dress, she showed goose bumps on her forearm to Semiha. Each of the girls was no less moved.

When she turned back with the intention of continuing to watch the show battle, she saw him.

She lost her breath for a moment. She stifled a scream in her chest.

Holy God! It's him!

She couldn't believe it. A sailor with a naked sword was standing near the helmsman on the galley. A black-bearded, black-browed sailor. His outfit was different from the rest. There was a white wrap on his head. He wore a blue vest, but his chest, covered with black hair, was exposed. He was dressed in wide red pants.

He had lightning in his eyes — that's how she recognized him.

She straightened up, involuntarily pressing her hands to her breasts as she usually did when she was preoccupied. She looked closer.

She was sure.

Oh God, God! It's him - Kemal!

"How many years have passed?" she thought. "Ten? Twenty? Or a thousand?"

Kemal, raising his sword, shouted something. The ovations and cries of the crowd drowned out his words. But at the same moment, several bullets were fired from the galley.

Semiha and Mürüvvet understood at once that Mahpeyker's excitement was not due to the battle scene being watched. They shot each other a quick look.

"Who is that?" Mahpeyker asked in a whisper.

Semiha leaned forward.

"Who are you asking about, My Lady?"

"About that one... The man who is standing next to the helmsman on our galley."

Mürüvvet and Semiha exchanged a brief glance again.

"I do not know, My Lady," she said in a whisper. "I'll find out if you wish."

The Sultan's Mother didn't answer. There was no need.

Semiha, bowing slightly, turned away and slipped out of the tent.

Mahpeyker didn't hear her. She didn't see the battle that unfolded in front of her eyes, either. Her eyes were fixed on the sailor with lightning in his eyes. She sank into a sea of memories. Just like a young maid once did in Kumanovo, in the home of Karayelzade Ibrahim Bey.

The news Semiha brought that evening didn't surprise her.

"I found out, My Lady. The sailor you pointed to on our galley is Captain Kemal. A great man, they say."

She nodded. *That's true*, she agreed in her mind. *A great man.*

That night she couldn't sleep for long. If she were that young maid, she would now run into Kemal's embrace. But she wasn't her anymore. She was a Great Mother, a Magnificent Mother, the kind of mother who knows Mahpeyker Kösem Sultan – that's who she was. A Queen; and Queens can not do anything they can think of.

*Can't they?* A voice asked inside her. It was her reason.

She closed her eyes. She tried not to hear what it was saying.

She saw, but Kemal didn't see. He didn't even know she existed. How could he know that the beautiful Nastya, sold to Bey Ibrahim, had become the Valide Sultan?

She felt a tear run down her cheek. *Kemal,* she whispered to herself. *Kemal with eyebrows like bows. If only we didn't have to part, you said... Look, here we found each other.*

Had they really found each other?

That night, for the first time in years, Satan played with her while she slept. The whole night she curled up with desire, lifted by a storm of pleasure greater than ever. He didn't have the face of a man, the one in whose arms she trembled, who drove her mad with his mouth, hands, caresses, but she knew – it was Kemal.

"Kemal!" she shouted. She sat bolt upright in bed from a pleasure she had never experienced awake. She was all wet.

She could not decide what to do. Was she supposed to go to him?

Should she send a message: 'Come, my dear. I am here. Nastya.'

Or, in agreement with the rule, that Queens do not do anything they feel like doing, should she sit with her head lowered?

She could go to him in disguise, but that would be very dangerous.

She could find a way to smuggle him into the palace – that was even more dangerous. The first way was worse for her, the second for Kemal.

She was ready to endure a wave of rumors, but if the matter came to light, there would be no help for Kemal.

The most reasonable thing was to forget. Live her love for Kemal in dreams and fantasies.

She kept to the decision she made for many days. She was already in a huge dilemma anyway.

Prince Ibrahim was doing crazy things. The news from the nannies was scary; her son didn't leave the room even to get a breath of fresh air.

"You don't know Murad," he whispered in one of the nannies' ear. "He won't leave me alive, he will kill me!"

At night he stacked boxes, baskets, everything at hand, against the door. He wouldn't let in any servant who brought food. He sat down to the meal two hours after one of the girls tried the food – by which time it was already completely cold.

Even his eyes changed. Mahpeyker knew that look well. Sultan Mustafa looked the same way; with nervous, wondering eyes.

He jumped unexpectedly from where he sat.

"Do not kill me, mister Murad," he'd cry.

Recently, he'd become fond of pearls. He threaded pearls for hours. Odalisques kept bringing the beads to him.

Even Mahpeyker couldn't call him strange anymore. Ibrahim was a madman.

*My God, my son is a madman*, she thought, her heart racing in her chest. *My Ibrahim is a madman! The fear of death has driven my son crazy.*

Did God punish her for the pride she succumbed to after becoming a Queen? Or maybe she unconsciously laughed at Mustafa's madness? She couldn't remember, but she was afraid it could be so. If that were the case, she'd certainly offended God. *Are you laughing at a madman? I'll give you a madman, and then we'll see how you will laugh*, he must have decided.

For many weeks she was overwhelmed by Ibrahim's tragedy on the one hand, and on the other hand, with her feelings towards Kemal. She now spent days with Ibrahim, asking him questions with which she tried to weigh the state of his mind.

"What day is it today?"

"Friday."

"How old are you?"

"Eight."

"Who is this?"

"My sister. Sultana Ayşe."

"And who am I, Ibrahim?"

Her son's eyes moved nervously.

"A guard."

*Oh my God!* Mahpeyker moaned inwardly, but outwardly, she laughed.

"My prince is very witty today again. He calls his mother a guard."

"Yeah, you're a guard. My mother is dead. Murad killed her!"

She reached out and covered Ibrahim's mouth with her hand, trying to silence him.

"Where do you live?"

"In the dungeon."

Her son was right. He lived in a dungeon. He'd created a dungeon for himself, and he imprisoned himself in it.

Mahpeyker tried to bring relief to her sore soul with dreams of Kemal.

In her dreams and fantasies, she made love to him. She sang songs for him, danced for him. Then Kemal grasped her in his embrace and kidnapped her to the ship. The wind filled the sails, the waves carried the ship. She didn't ask, because she knew where they were sailing – to Nastya's beautiful island – to Milos.

One morning after such a night, she couldn't stand it anymore. Be that as it may, she'd decided as she got out of bed.

"Go and find him," she said quietly to Semiha. "Either lead me to him or bring him to me."

The girl didn't even ask whom. She disappeared in an instant.

Mahpeyker Kösem Sultan eagerly awaited the return of the girl. She couldn't sit, she couldn't speak, she couldn't listen. Her heart pounded madly in her breast. When she finally heard the girl's steps, she was about to faint.

When she saw Semiha's face, she couldn't guess her own feelings at first. Was she devastated? Why, then, did her reason tell her, *Be happy?*

"Lady," said the girl quietly. "He's sailed away."

*Sailed away!*

"Captain Kemal sailed away with the fleet to the war last week."

*He sailed to war!*

*Kemal... sailed away. He rolled down a sail and sailed away.*

That night she waited a long time, she begged for a long time, she wanted very much, but Kemal did not come to her in her sleep.

She never saw him again. Neither in a dream nor in reality. She had to erase him from her dreams too. It was difficult, but she had to. It was better like this.

This time the fate rightly threw a curtain up and protected her.

# CHAPTER TWENTY-ONE

### The Beylerbeyi Palace
### Summer 1630

At the sight of the Great Mother Mahpeyker heading straight for the pond, the servants hid in the shade of the trees trying to stay as far as possible from her sight.

This friendly, peaceful, fair, smiling Mahpeyker Sultan, remembered from the first years of Murad Khan's rule, had gone and in her place was now a snappish, interfering with everything, angry Kösem Sultan.

That's why the servants and courtiers of the Beylerbeyi Palace didn't want the spring to come – because, at the end of April, the Sultana Mother took with her all the courtiers she had, and with them, their children, and nannies with grandchildren, and they all went to the garden.

Valide Sultan didn't mess around with the service. She no longer knew the concept of forbearance. She didn't forgive the slightest stumble. She administered the slightest punishment with the words: 'Put your hand out,' and she didn't entrust the punishment to anyone else – she personally inflicted the rod. The hand of the punished swelled even before the pain passed. There were even times the punishment was given with falaka.

But Kösem Sultan considered 'expulsion from service,' as the most severe punishment. She didn't realize that many servants were praying to receive it.

Her face was dark like a hail cloud again. Along with the eight courtiers following her, she went to the edge of the pool. The girls took care of setting up the ottoman. One of them put a pot with coffee on the glowing mangal, set in the distance. Another drew a low table closer, with glass pitchers filled with sorbet chilled in the snow on it.

Mahpeyker didn't seem to notice the bustle. She stared at the thin trickles of water spurting from the fountain. The courtiers believed that the Sultana Mother watched the water spouting from the fountain, which, falling on leaves of water lilies floating in the pool, reflected from them with a thousand tiny droplets. But it was not like that at all.

*I can't take it anymore*, thought Mahpeyker Kösem Sultan at that moment. *I can not take it anymore. What happened to this child? Who did he take after? Me? No. His father? What an idea. Someone from his ancestors?*

The son she'd once been so protective of, and because of whom she suffocated in tears when he was rolling in an epileptic attack, she was now afraid of. Beautiful, gentle, but at the same time strong Murad, with his attachment and respect for her, wasn't here anymore. Although he was alive and sat on the throne of the Great Empire, he forgot that he owed it to his mother.

Both her sons were crazy. Ibrahim's condition had left no doubt for a long time. Locked in his room, he threaded pearls or played hide and seek with his servants. It was a strange game. "Nanny," he'd whisper to them, "hide me so that Murad can't find me. If my brother finds me, he'll kill me."

Sultan Mustafa became attached to birds, her son to pearls – but both had been led to madness by the same thing: fear of being murdered!

The palace walls were steeped in the smell of death.

And Murad? What happened to him? Wasn't Murad, like his uncle and younger brother Ibrahim, living while constantly brushing against death? Wasn't his life in the mouth of one man, dependent on a single slander? He also grew up in fear. He'd listened to the approaching steps. He knew about the murders of princes that had happened in the past in the palace. The Padishahs killed their children, their brothers. And if the children were the Padishahs – their brothers and even the fathers.

But fear had left a different mark on him. Her son turned out to be a tyrant.

Hanging and cutting heads was the order of the day. Sadrazams didn't stay long by Murad. It even happened that a man who received a seal one day, lost his head the next.

Unexpectedly, Mahpeyker remembered the moments when as the Great Mother, the Senior Mother, Elder Mother, and the Magnificent Mother, she sat next to, but a little bit behind her son. What a kind child he was. Feeling that an epileptic attack was approaching, he'd run to her chamber: "Mother, hide me. Don't let the Viziers see me thrashing around like that."

So, she'd close the door, take her son in her arms, and with the advent of the attack she only looked on helplessly. All she could do was to wipe foaming saliva from his mouth.

She didn't have to repeat requests and orders twice, but that didn't last long; Murad quickly unlearned saying, 'Yes, mother.'

When she remembered the day when she noticed the change that had taken place in him, her heart squeezed painfully. It was when she'd suggested to him that Kemankesh Ali Pasha was not the right person for his position, and Murad had looked deep into her eyes.

"What should be done, Mother?"

"Remove him from the position of Sadrazam. Is it fitting for Murad Khan to have an illiterate for Sadrazam?"

Mahpeyker wiped the drops of water that fell on her face from the gushing fountain with her fingertip. *I should have understood on that day, that my son had given up his obedience to me already,* she sighed.

"We'll think about it, Mother," Murad had said in a smart tone.

What was there to think about?

Someone – not probably, but undoubtedly – had stuffed him with thoughts like: 'It is not fitting for the Padishah to behave as if he were listening to her every word."

Murad also probably became convinced that it shouldn't be as his mother says, but as he says himself. She agreed with him when he turned fifteen.

Indeed, at least it should look like this from the outside. Mahpeyker decided that day that if it were necessary to maintain her control over Murad, she would step into the shadow.

In fact, the illiteracy of Ali Pasha was not the major problem. Sadrazam was overwhelmed by the desire to rule the state on his own. Yes, she was a Regent, but it was also clear that the Pasha had his own opinion on the subject: 'Since when do women know about governing the state? This is our job.' She didn't forget the impudence he'd made during the preparations for the circumcision celebrations. Undoubtedly, if ruling the state becomes 'his job,' he will increase his millions of akçe by another one.

To try Sadrazam again, she summoned the exiled old harem administrator to the capital, black Mustafa Aga, and demanded that he returned to service.

While the Viziers warned him, 'Oh, Your Majesty, this black Mustafa is the most ordinary traitor and schemer,' the Pasha did what she demanded. But the spies reported to Mahpeyker what he'd replied to some of the Viziers: 'Let it be as the Valide Sultan wishes. But you will see that the air of the capital will not help Mustafa Efendi.'

Having learned about it, she spoke threateningly to the Pasha:

"We've already damaged your reputation for the second time so that you can not fix it anymore. Let's find out who will be hurt by the capital's air."

As soon as Mustafa Aga appeared back at the palace, he made sure, according to her order, that the river of gossip flowed in a fast current. Filling the harem of the then thirteen-year-old Murad with beautiful odalisques, organizing entertainment every evening, he tried to wake up the passion for an intimate atmosphere in the Padishah.

When Murad's mind was already quite drowsy under the influence of the wine given to him by the odalisques, the administrator of the black eunuchs did not neglect his obligation to Kösem, whispering to him everything she ordered. In fact, Aga didn't realize that he was getting Murad accustomed to a libation, but if it was supposed to be like this, then let it be so — each master has his own method. She had this one.

"My Lord," that's how Mustafa Aga addressed her son in accordance with her order. "Your humble servant is not concerned, but Sadrazam Kemankesh Ali Pasha has hidden from you that Baghdad passed into the hands of the Safavid Shah Abbas. The Safavid army is moving forward; he doesn't tell you that, either. The uprising of Abaz Pasha in the East is rolling like a snowball. The people join Abaz Pasha, who promised that he would avenge the young Osman – Ali Pasha does not mention it either. The country is in chaos, the treasury is emptying, and the soldiers do not obey orders. What does Kemankesh do in this situation?"

What Kemankesh was doing in such a moment, Mahpeyker had not forgotten to mention to the black harem manager, either.

"He is plotting intrigues to hand the office of Sheikh Al-Islam to his future father-in-law."

"What intrigues?" Murad asked, and then Mustafa Aga mumbled something indistinctly as if letting him understand that he did not want to answer.

Her son reacted as Mahpeyker predicted: "What is he plotting, aga? Speak openly."

"Hodja Yahya Efendi is to ask you to be removed from the office so that you could appoint Kemankesh's father-in-law in his place. Ali Pasha is spreading these rumors all over the city."

The next day Murad called for Yahya Efendi.

"They say such and such, Hodja. Did such a conversation with Kemankesh Pasha take place or not?"

Hodja lost his voice in surprise. *Look at that bald Ali*, he thought, offended. *How quickly he forgot that he had come to me asking for a fatwa to put this kid on the throne! Now he reserves my place for his wife's insane father*.

Just as Mahkeyker assumed, Yahya Efendi, unaware that everything was a game intricately planned by the Sultana Mother, threw himself on the ground in front of Murad.

"But My Lord, if we were to have such a plan, would we hide it from our Padishah while revealing it to his subject? We consider serving our Ruler a sacred thing. Would we violate sanctity?"

It was a sentence for Kemankesh Ali Pasha.

When, two days later, Mahpeyker learned that her son had called Ali Pasha to the palace and ordered him beheaded, she wasn't surprised one bit. *You thought well, son*, she thought back then. In that case, all I will tell you, I will tell through others, so that it will not be repeated that, 'the ruler does everything his mother orders.'

She finally understood how big a mistake it was. But it happened very late. Murad had already experienced the taste of making independent decisions, of not sharing the reign or authority – whether with his mother or with anyone else – and above all else, of cutting off heads.

Mahpeyker found through her people the treasure of Kemankesh Ali Pasha, worth seven million akçe, in the place where he'd hidden it. She covered the budget hole with this money. On the same day, one of the main culprits of the miseries, Mere Hussein Pasha, was captured and killed.

Mahpeyker basically didn't oppose her son's decisions, but she was already aware that he had taken the helm of power away from her. The question of, 'What should be done, Mother?' did not come from Murad's mouth anymore.

One day, when she went to him with a certain idea, he drew his eyebrows together and replied in a raised voice:

"Mother, the sword was put on us, making us a Padishah. We wear the sword of Osman Ghazi at the waist. Leave the matters of the sword to us. Go and take care of pious affairs, Mother."

Mahpeyker felt like she'd been wounded with an arrow. *Go and take care of pious affairs, huh! And you... what will you do?*

She learned about Murad's actions from Mustafa Aga:

"The ruler gave the office of Sadrazam to Cherkiez Ali Pasha." Without asking her.

He made Hafiz Ahmed Pasha from Plovdiv, Damat Halil Pasha, Ghazi Ekrem Hüsrev Pasha Sadrazams too, without even asking once, 'What do you think, Mother?'

Later, he ordered to hang or strangle most of them, too.

When she listened to Mustafa Aga, the blood hit her head. She couldn't believe her ears.

"Our Sultan," Mustafa Aga said quietly one day, "follows in the footsteps of his holy memory father and the heroic brother, young Osman. Do not worry."

"Really? And what are these footsteps?"

"He introduced prohibition. There will be no mercy for those organizing libations."

Murad was already seventeen. At nights he left the palace in disguise and walked around the capital. He took only Mustafa Aga with him because the black man merged with the darkness.

Old wine bars, cafes, fishermen shelters, marinas in the Galata district – he looked everywhere, and even, entering a conversation, he provoked the curses against the Sultan and asked for wine for himself.

"It's dry in our throat, gentlemen. Because of this youngster Murad, we'll carbonize in our own enthusiasm. Let the one, who while drinking a grape drink, would not share a sip, be judged by God. And the sharing person should have a reward; every girl should be loving him. And by saying 'loving him,' we do not mean the respectable youngster, huh!"

The audience burst out laughing.

Those who, trusting a young boy with a first shadow of a mustache, began to make speeches against the

Padishah or, in a gesture of compassion, poured him a few sips of wine from the hidden jugs, paid dearly for it the next day. Whoever hid wine for his own use, was punished by breaking jugs and spilling wine. The one who sold wine to others had the counter shattered on his head, and the poor man wouldn't even know where the misfortune came from. And if they let the reins loose too much, cursing the Padishah, they suffered the punishment of falaka.

"So, will you continue to drink, will you drink?"

"I won't, I won't drink, take pity, gentlemen!" the tavern's patron would beg in tears while the unfortunate's feet swelled under the whips.


And that was not all yet.

Murad was merciless on those who used wine and tobacco. He burned and destroyed wineries and even the houses that had smoke rising from their chimneys.

"Padishah, thinking that we smoke tobacco, destroys our home fires to the ground," people said and feared to kindle a fire in the oven, even when it was cold.

But Sultan Murad, who was responsible for all this, personally didn't give up his table full of liquors in the palace. In the winter by the fireplace, in the summer in the rose or tulip garden, or on the banks of the pond where red and goldfish swam, he downed pitchers of wine one after another.

"Do not be angry, My Lady," said Mustafa Aga. "He is young. Young blood. The blood is boiling, the soul desires. These are ordinary earthly pleasures."

"Earthly pleasures, aga? Is it fair to oppress and tyrannize your subjects, stigmatizing it as a sin, as an impurity, and then to enjoy wine in your own chambers? What is a sin for the people, is a boon for the Padishah?"

Mahpeyker was the most annoyed by a mocking expression on Mustafa Aga's face.

"Yes," Aga said one day. "What is forbidden for the subjects, is allowed to the Padishah. Besides, is it easy to turn away the beauties bringing wine, and the smooth pages?"

She knew about the fact that Mustafa was bringing girls to her son, one more beautiful than the other. In a sense, she even encouraged him. She had expected that Murad, having given himself to the harem pleasures in the arms of beautiful women, would leave her to deal with the affairs of the state. But where did the idea of feasting with pages come from?

She felt a wave of heat flood her.

"Sister," Mahpeyker said to Mürüvvet, who was standing nearby. The woman already had gray hair on her head. "Tell Ruhsar to prepare some sorbet for us. Let her add some lemon juice. I still feel pressure in my heart. Maybe it will ease the tension."

Mürüvvet headed straight for the courtiers seated on the other side of the pond and waiting for orders.

"Ruhsar," she said to one of the courtiers with pink cheeks and slender like a minaret. The girl immediately came forward. "Great Sultana Mother wants to drink sorbet. Add four drops of lemon juice. Just don't overdo it."

She gazed affectionately after Ruhsar retreating hastily towards the table hidden behind one of the trees. The girl reminded her of Sofia. *Maybe she does to Mahpeyker, too*, she thought. However, she never touched on this topic, but she knew the Sultana liked

Ruhsar. She had been with her for years. No one knew better than her how Mahpeyker looked at the enemy, and how she looked at someone she liked.

Mahpeyker froze again, staring at the small drops reflecting off the water lily leaves. Suddenly she thought her brain was in flames. She remembered the panic she'd experienced when she first noticed the word 'smooth,' when Mustafa Aga mentioned the pages. What was behind his words?

"Pages, aga? What do you mean by saying 'smooth?' Speak up, do not murmur, aga. You know I don't like beating around the bush."

"Nothing," said Aga, rubbing his hands. "Our Lord has a new courtier. They call him Unruly Chelebi."

"And?"

Aga pretended to swallow.

"Speak, aga!" Mahpeyker screamed, jumping to her feet. "Spit it out!"

"Hm... I mean... I don't know how to describe it. Am I to say, a man or a woman? This is just not entirely clear. That's how Allah created him. He is very close to our Ruler."

Understanding the suggestion contained in aga's tone, Mahpeyker felt her blood rise to her head. 'A man or a woman, it is not entirely clear... He is very close to our Ruler!'

Holy God! Could it be?!

Her son, who used to be red with shame like beetroot when he was looked at in the face, her son was supposed to be...

Neither her mind nor her heart would allow her to think more for now, but she raised the subject that same night.

"Who is this Unruly Chelebi, son?"

She received an answer right away.

"My sincere friend, Mother. A soulmate..."

The tongue clung to her palate. It didn't happen many times in her life that she would be speechless. What Mahpeyker experienced that night was just one of those times.

"Haven't you heard, Mother, about a famous man called Alexander the Great?" Murad asked, looking her in the eye. "One of your ancestors. He didn't come from the islands though, he was a Macedonian. According to one of our teachers, he was a great hero. He conquered the world. In each conquest, he was always accompanied by a friend – a friend in whom he confided about everything that was in his heart. We also want to be accompanied by Unruly Chelebi when we conquer Baghdad. Or do you think that it's too much to wish, to be accompanied by a friend like Alexander was? Why? What are we lacking? Heroism, strength, bravery?"

*My God*, Mahpeyker shuddered, hearing those words spoken by her son without the slightest shame. She wanted to say something in response, but she didn't know what. What could she say to her son, speaking so arrogantly to his mother? And what's more, the Padishah?

Seeing her silence, Murad laughed.

"Come on. We dealt with it a long time ago, do not worry... By the way, how are things with charity? If you need gold from the treasury, do not hesitate to say."

Every time she remembered her son's words, she felt as if her heart was pierced by an arrow. *Go and take care of pious affairs, Mother.*

She didn't even notice when Mürüvvet brought the sorbet prepared by Ruhsar. The woman spoke to her several times, but she didn't hear. It wasn't until the fourth time that she moved, leaving the world of her thoughts:

"Huh? What did you want, sister?"

"Sorbet is ready, My Lady. Ruhsar prepared it herself. It's nice and cool."

After hearing the name of the girl, she involuntarily turned to the side where Ruhsar stood.

"God bless you," she whispered, "who prepared it and who brought it."

She leaned over to smell the lemon. She took a sip.

"I can't stand it, sister," she whispered. "I'm burning inside."

Mürüvvet bowed her head. She didn't dare say anything, but she knew of the strange actions of Murad, to whom Mahpeyker gave her whole life. Was there still anyone in the empire who didn't know?

He drank until his senses were confused. In the winter, he ordered the slave women to immerse themselves naked in an ice-covered garden pond and, with laughter, he watched them tremble and shout. He married old servants to young girls of their grandchildren age, and seventy-year-old matrons to fifteen or twenty-year-old youths.

He made Kazasker drunk with wine under the threat of a sword. And when the poor man, staggering, tripped over a deliberately stuck out leg, he ordered to whip him, saying: "Why have you clutched to the Ruler's leg, dog! Or maybe you wanted to threaten our life?!"

The armorer Musa Pasha was built like a wrestler. His hands were the size of loaves of bread, and one person could sit easily on each of his shoulders. The armorer was so impressive. Murad caught the giant around the waist with one hand and after turning him around several times, threw him to the ground. "Well, well," said the Viziers. "Congratulations, what a strength, what a power."

Besides, it was impossible to read the slightest sign of fatigue from the Padishah's face.

At the Divan meetings, he harassed the old gray Viziers, either trying to grope the unfortunate man after he caught him by the neck, or grabbing them around the waist like the armorer, pretending to want to pick him up. The poor men didn't know how to behave in fear. Submission might result in broken ribs or other places, but resistance or escape – in calling the executioners.

One night, the Padishah, getting up from the table full of liquors, turned to the page with a bare chest sitting beside him.

"Look, Unruly Chelebi, what I will do now! Let's see how great my strength is!"

Odalisques heard the Unruly answer, "God, my Murad." Their whispers also reached the ear of Mahpeyker, eavesdropping outside the door.

"Did you hear what he answered to our Ruler?"

"What, what did he say?"

"'Doesn't your servant Unruly know your strength and power, my man?' he said and put his arms around his neck."

"Ah!" shouted another. "He's really lost his morals and shame."

What was implied made even the black odalisques get a blush on their dark cheeks.

"So, continue. What did Murad Khan do?"

What her son did, Mahpeyker heard from Mustafa Aga:

"Our Lord got up from the bed where he sat with Unruly Chelebi. 'Bring me my bow and arrow,' he said. Not giving me the time to say, 'There is no chance, he will not pull this bow,' he stretched the bull skin-wrapped bow as far as possible and released the arrow. No doubt Allah gave our master the strength of a lion. The arrow he shot... Do you remember, My Lady, the gate, through which you step out of the inner courtyard to the Sultan Gallery? Well, it pierced the gates almost halfway through. If I didn't see it with my own eyes, I would not have believed it. The gates are iron and covered with silver. For God's sake, the arrow of the Ruler pierces metal."

'Crazy rider.' That was the nickname Murad earned. But the lad really knew how to ride, especially when he rode Winged or Windmountain. He left a hail of stones spurting from the horse's hooves into the faces of the quickest Spahis.

Mürüvvet, lowering her head, fell silently to the ground. Mahpeyker couldn't take it. The heart of the devoted courtier was also squeezed by sorrow.

It seemed that the tales of Murad's exploits could go on being told forever. Each one had a continuation. Hundreds... thousands of continuations.

Mahpeyker even began to doubt. *Which one is crazier – Ibrahim or Murad?*

*Mustafa was crazy because of birds, Ibrahim – pearls, and Murad because of Baghdad*, she counted in spirit. Murad sent Viziers and organized war expeditions one after another, to take Baghdad from the hands of the Abasid Shah – but no one was able to cross the gates of Baghdad.

The pasha returning empty-handed was deprived of either his position or life. No one knew how many pashas lost their heads for Baghdad.

Hüsrev Pasha, whom her son made a Sadrazam, went to Erzurum and caught, and then brought back to the capital, Abaza Pasha, who for four years of 'avenging the death of young Osman,' had been a real nuisance for the state. Wonderful, great. Therefore, Hüsrev Pasha was greeted in Istanbul with a victorious parade.

But what was the role of Abaza in the parade? Did anyone hear that the hostage would ride proudly on the horse next to the commander-in-chief during the victory parade?

People, although surprised by what they saw, were convinced that the Padishah would order to behead Abaza. But Murad appointed the Pasha as a Beylerbey in Bosnia. "Since you have avenged the blood of our brother Osman, you are a noble man. Take your office and serve us faithfully," Murad had said and even patted him on the back.

Sometime later, he ordered Ghazi Hüsrev Pasha beheaded.

*Can the state that gives office to those who act against it, stay on its feet?* Mahpeyker asked herself, pondering her son's mistakes. *If you give an office to a rebel, what is the value of fidelity and the reward for it?*

*Well, let it be, you made him a Beylerbey.* But no. Two years later, Murad called Abaza to the capital. They sat down together for a libation, and before the Beylerbey even got up from the table, Murad ordered to strangle him on the spot.

However, there was one good thing Murad did.

At her request, he dismissed Şarazad and Semiha. Mürüvvet did not want to leave.

"Are you fed up with your servant, My Lady?" she said with tears streaming from her eyes. "Let Mürüvvet give out her soul by your knees."

Mahpeyker, having placed Şarazad on a ship heading for the Mediterranean Sea, sent her back to her homeland. The woman clutched at her hands, then fell to her feet, finally throwing her arms around her neck.

Mahpeyker didn't know if she reached the place she was going to. Well, what could she do? She still thought that Şarazad returned to her nest.

And she married Semiha.

Only that the woman chose the groom herself. A pupil of Enderun, he was tall and handsome. Semiha, who grew up by Safiye Sultan and served Mahpeyker for years, found a way to persuade her to accept the man her heart had chosen.

The girl was happy. So was Mahpeyker. At least she managed to make two people happy. She assigned one of the palace villas for her. Semiha lived there with her husband and continued to accompany her.

Mahpeyker also kept another word she had given.

"Bring the horseman Ahmed from the Old Palace," she ordered.

A little time later, a bitter man stood in front of her.

"Do not think that we forgot the promise. Today we will go to her."

Ahmed turned his tired eyes to her.

"You'll drive our carriage."

The man's eyes glistened.

Mahpeyker ordered to place the carriage in front of the harem gate, which at one time she was wiping and polishing for Safiye Sultan in the courtyard in front of the stables in the Old Palace.

"Describe the place to Ahmed," she said quietly to Mürüvvet. "From now on he is our main driver."

In addition to Semiha, she also took Ruhsar with her.

She didn't see, but she heard his voice. Ahmed shot with a whip so eagerly that the horses seemed to understand that he was in a hurry to Sofia's grave. They shot ahead and rushed, ringing their hooves on the streets of the capital.

As so it was, she saw Sofia's grave for the first time.

Flowers bloomed on the grave. Her beloved violets. Turning, she looked at Semiha. It was definitely her idea. She once told her that she would go with Ahmed to Sofia's grave. No one except Semiha could show such sensitivity.

Mahpeyker didn't even think for a moment about her golden embroidery, which could get dirty. She didn't care about the wet earth. She knelt over the grave in which Sofia rested.

"Look... whom I... brought to you."

Her lips spoke the words with difficulty.

"You know..." She couldn't go on. Her voice broke. "Him... Ahmed with myself..."

She couldn't continue. She felt crying burst in her throat. She sobbed, choking. She turned away and ran toward the carriage. The girls ran after her in her footsteps.

They left Ahmed alone with his unfortunate dove.

They couldn't stand the heart-rending view of the lovers meeting, the view of the man huge like a mountain, embracing the earth. Four women – one of them a Sultana, the other three the servants – sobbed uncontrollably.

Mahpeyker thought that tears washed away the sin of the crime. She'd killed Sofia. And she'd brought her beloved to her. She didn't give her to Ahmed alive, but she gave him the earth in which she rested.

None of them knew how long they stayed there. Maybe a few minutes, maybe a few hours.

When the man returned to the carriage, he sat in his seat without a word. There was neither light nor grief in Ahmed's eyes. There was no expression left on his darkened face.

He shot the whip. This time the horses, as if not wanting to move away from Sofia, pulled the carriage tired and resistant.

They returned to the palace. Ahmed didn't jump off the stool to open the door.

Mahpeyker got off with the help of the servants who ran out to meet them. Shielding her eyes with her hand from the sun shining in her face, she looked at Ahmed where he continued to sit in the carriage.

"We've prepared a place for you," she said slowly. "Two rooms in the horseman's barracks. From now on you will be living with us in the palace."

The boy said nothing again.

Mahpeyker could only see the figure of Ahmed through her squinting eyes. He didn't even take the whip in hand. He moved the reigns. The carriage slowly moved towards the stables.

No one ever saw Ahmed again.


Suddenly there was a scream.

"Help! Help!" One of the servants was shouting.

"Misfortune, My Lady, My Lady!"

This cry brought Mahpeyker out from her reverie in which she was immersed.

"What's happening?" she asked in a distracted voice. "What is this screaming about? Semiha, Mürüvet, Ruhsar." All the courtiers jumped to their feet.

"Hi!" she shouted in the direction of the girl running straight toward them. "Why are you screaming? What happened?"

The first thing that came to Mahpeyker's mind was fire. *God forbid*, she thought. There was no fire, no flood, no plague, that had not hurt the capital. The first thing she thought of when someone said 'misfortune,' were those disasters.

The girls were running, waving their arms, and shouting, "A nightmare! Nightmare!"

"For God's sake!"

Suddenly she felt as if a knife sank into her breast. A hunch had crept into her heart.

She shuddered in panic. *God,* she whispered to herself. She knew this state well. How many times she had already experienced it. This fever she felt in her chest was not unfounded. Whenever this feeling overwhelmed her, a disaster occurred soon afterward.

"Tell me, girl, what happened!" she cried, standing up. "Is there a fire?"

*God,* she prayed inwardly. *Please, don't let it be what I'm afraid of. I am no longer able to bear another catastrophe.*

"Children!"

At first, she did not understand the exclamation of the breathless girl.

*What did she say?* Mahpeyker thought, her brain falling to pieces. *Children? Oh no! Children?*

Mahpeyker was like in a fever; she wasn't even aware that she was running towards the girl.

"Children?" she shouted. "Children? What about my children, woman, talk to me!?"

The girl couldn't run anymore. She fell to her knees. Gathering gravel from the ground, she tossed it on her head and beat herself in the chest.

Mahpeyker and the courtiers ran to the girl. Mahpeyker threw herself at her and, grasping her shoulders, shook with all her strength.

"Tell me! Tell me! What happened to the children? Speak up!"

The girl's eyes were bloody from crying and horror. They weren't even sure if she had not lost her mind.

While the girl continued to drop pebbles on herself, a terrible moan escaped her breast.

"Killed! Killed! Children kiiiilled...!"

"Nooo...!" A howling cry escaped from Mahpeyker's breast. "Noooo...!"

Tearing hair from her head, she began to slap the girl.

"Not true! Not true! You lie, bitch! I will skin you and sprinkle the wounds with salt! Admit it, tell me you lied! Tell me that the children are alive and well. Immediately! I beg you. Tell me they are alive!"

The servants caught Mahpeyker's hands. Mürüvvet and the other girls tried to calm her down. But Mahpeyker couldn't be restrained and kept constantly slapping the girl.

"Speak, speak! Say, 'I lied!'"

"If only I could say that, Lady, Mother!" the girl howled. Bloody marks appeared on her face, down her cheeks, from Mahpeyker's nails. "If only it were a lie, and I was the one handed over to the executioner."

Mahpeyker froze unexpectedly.

"The executioner?"

The tangled hair, traces of tears left on her cheeks, gave her face a terrible expression.

"The executioners... executioners of our Lord... At night... Prince Suleiman and Prince Kasım..."

She could not say the rest. Again, she started to pour gravel on herself and pummel her knees.

Mahpeyker, who rose from the ground, looked as if she turned to stone. She gave no voice or breath. The servants expected that the Sultana Mother would roll on the ground faced with this terrible tragedy, tear her hair from her head, cry with bloody tears. But she didn't do anything like this. She just stood there.

"Oh." After a long moment, a barely audible moan escaped Mahpeyker's lips. "Suleiman, Kasım. My unfortunate sons."

They were still so little. One was ten, the other eight.

Her eyes shone strangely. No one, not even Mürüvvet, had seen such a terrible gleam before. Death! Their mistress looked into the eyes of death. Her gaze was the look of someone ready to give and take life.

*Right now, if he stood here...* she thought. *If my son Murad appeared in front of me at this moment, right here, I would tear him to pieces with my bare hands.*

"Ibrahim is alive, My Lady. That's what they said," mumbled the girl who had recovered a bit. "The executioners didn't come for him."

Mahpeyker didn't ask about anything else, she didn't say anything else. She guessed what had happened. Murad was setting out for Baghdad himself this time. They'd certainly fuddled his mind.

"When the Padishah goes to war, his eyes should not look back."

"Why? We will leave Kaymakam as the deputy, of course."

"But there are still two princes."

"Suleiman and Kasım? But they are still very little, Pasha."

"You're right, Sultan. They are little, but the Safavids' Shah, along with those whose eyes are blinded by the lust for power, is great. God forbid, but we fear that by using princes, they will bring a fight for the throne to the Empire. God, three pretenders to the throne, will lead the state to destruction."

Mahpeyker was sure of every word of this conversation.

"Bodies," she mumbled absent-minded, walking towards the palace. "We want to see the bodies of our sons."

The girls were following her, beating their knees.

"They were immediately brought to the mausoleum, where their father of holy memory rests, Lady Mother."

*Oh, Murad*, she moaned in her mind. *You didn't even give me the opportunity to see my sons for the last time. May God curse you, Murad.*

She locked herself in her room. Hiding her head in the pillows, she let out a long cry. Hours passed, and she beat herself in the chest, repeating: "Ah, my Suleiman," "Ah, my Kasım." She was crying. "How could you raise your hand on my children? How could you have sent an executioner to Kasım, who threw himself at your feet with the words: 'My brother, lion?' And Suleiman? How could you give his thin neck to greasy ropes, son?"

"The curse," she repeated, tearing her hair from her head. *Is it what being a queen was about? Reign, throne, power? The greed for power sending brother against brother? If so, may it be damned!*

She cried until her tears dried up and she could cry no more. She was petrified, but inside she still cried. Her soul, mind, heart cried.

With the advent of the day, she straightened up. She went to the window and looked at the sun rising from the opposite direction.

"The sun, huh!" she murmured. "The king, for whom you made a crown from the sun, ha! Let the sun go down, Murad! Oh, if only they had taken your life, Murad, not Osman's! If instead of the ear of my son Osman, they had cut off yours and brought it to me!"

She returned to the New Palace as if nothing happened.

Ibrahim, hearing about the murder of his brothers on the orders of his older brother, completely lost his mind. He sat in the window recess.

Murad didn't touch him because he was crazy.

*Crazy, yes*, Mahpeyker said in her mind. *Crazy Ibrahim... You think that he can not be a Padishah, but you forget that his mother is Mahpeyker Kösem.*

From that day on, she didn't interfere with any of her son's affairs. *I am not any queen*, she told herself. *I'm the slave of my son in this drama. If the door opens and there are Murad's executioners on the doorstep, I won't be surprised.*

But she had to live.

"I have a lot of work to do," she murmured. "I will make another madman a king."

# CHAPTER TWENTY-TWO

### The New Palace
### February 1640

She had to wait ten years to make the madman a king. When she thought what had happened over these ten long years, she was amazed. It was as if a whole life had passed.

*We'll hide the death of his brothers at Murad's hand from Ibrahim,* she decided, though she knew it would be impossible – the things you could learn about in the palace! So, it was impossible to keep a bloody crime secret from anyone. Even more so, from the always suspicious Ibrahim. Not even two days passed before he learned everything – how his brothers trembled, how they pleaded, how they cried... everything.

And, just as she had predicted, he went completely crazy.

"He will kill me. Murad will hand me to the executioners," he trembled all day long, every day. He threw himself at anyone who came into his room, shouting: "A hangman came, a hangman came!"

And he wasn't being completely unreasonable. Murad could feel remorse on one day and then kill on the next day. His suspicion or anger could turn against Ibrahim at any moment.

Also, as the disease progressed with each passing day, Ibrahim's craziness was discussed everywhere.

Mahpeyker's mourning hadn't lasted a week before she decided to hide Ibrahim. From that day on, she hid her son in dark, stuffy hiding places, niches, wardrobes hidden in the endless corridors of the harem. She wouldn't let him stay for long in one place. She even hid him in the palace cold room once.

Staying in the dark, stifling, and cramped rooms with low vaults caused Ibrahim's physical health to also begin to deteriorate. His eyesight got poor. His skin became so thin that it was almost transparent and almost all his veins were visible beneath it. It glowed like it was covered with mother-of-pearl. Because he couldn't stand straight upright, he developed a hump. He couldn't walk with his back straight. And to what extent it all could develop, Mahpeyker didn't know.

Then there was Mürüvvet – her dream came true. One day, sitting at Mahpeyker's knees, she unexpectedly collapsed and left this world.

She died with her eyes open. So, when dying, she was still longing for something. Mahpeyker closed the eyes of her companion herself. She didn't neglect the smallest duty.

Semiha had children. Mahpeyker's secretly gave the place of Suleiman and Kasım to the girl's sons. Nothing could compare to the love that a man has for his own blood, but she pressed both to her chest every day. One was named Cihan, the other Selim. It was only in the evening that they left Mahpeyker's rooms with their mother. The boys loved her too. "Mommy, mommy," – they'd babble, constantly playing at her feet.

Semiha also gave birth to a daughter. Both, without thinking, decided to call her Safiye. The name was similar to Sofia. Most often, Mahpeyker called the girl 'Sofia,' anyway.

Neither Şarazad nor Mürüvvet were with her anymore. Semiha came every day, but she also had her own life. When the girl was slipping out of her hands, she didn't press, didn't dash her to work. It was just enough for her that she was nearby.

Semih's responsibilities were taken over by Ruhsar. "My good Lady, my benefactress." Her red-haired Ruhsar was always busy nearby.

*I swear*, she said to herself, watching Ruhsar. *If one day she will say, 'This one is chosen by my heart,' he may be even a porter from Galata – I will not oppose it. I won't say, 'Marry that one.' I killed my Sofia – I will give Ruhsar life.*

The slaves of Sultan Murad gave birth to a whole lot of sons and daughters, but Valide Sultan never went to her son to bless the descendants. She sent a few gifts to the mothers, nothing more. What was the fault of these women? Murad's sons didn't make it. Ahmed, Suleiman, Mehmed, and Alaeddin died one after the other.

Each of the deaths barely moved Mahpeyker. But on each occasion, a voice inside her chuckled: *Good, good.*

If she was to make a king out of yet another madman, her son should not leave successors.

Murad didn't care about his mother's coldness.

*Whatever I do*, he said to himself, laying his head on the pillow at night, *and whatever I will do, I do for the good of the Great Empire. I even stained my hands with my own siblings' blood and, if need be, I would also stain them tomorrow.*

Mahpeyker sensed that he tried to calm his conscience. But she didn't care about any excuses he found for himself. She threw Murad out of her heart, and that was it. She didn't say of him 'mine,' anymore. *I have*

*two sultans and one son. God had to love the two of our
sons more than us because he took them to himself.*

She wasn't even happy to hear that Murad walked with
pomp into Baghdad, which he managed to conquer after
fourteen years of Safavid occupation. The servants who
came with the news said Murad was disappointed. For how
else, could anyone understand the words of Murad, when
he addressed the Pashas: "Would the conquer of Baghdad
turn out to be greater than Baghdad itself?"

"Was Smooth Unruly with him?" she asked Kethüda.

"He was, My Lady."

Murad entered Baghdad with Unruly but returned to
the capital without him.

She was told that Chelebi, unexpectedly, died in a
mysterious way.

"Oooh," she just said. Nothing else.

The people who couldn't withstand the oppression of
Murad any longer, incited by rival viziers and pashas,
rebelled again and again. They kept coming to the palace.
It even happened that they got into the inner courtyard.
But Mahpeyker was never scared by the thought: *Will my
son, end up like Osman? Will they kill him in a dungeon like
they did to Osman?*

*Why should I be afraid?* she asked herself. *Wasn't it me,
praying that fatal day at the Beylerbeyi Palace, saying: 'Let
the sun set, Murad! Let them take your life instead of
Osman's, Murad! Instead of the ear of my son, Osman, let
them cut yours off and bring it to me!?' It will be whatever
Allah will decide. If it is written for him, nothing can be done.*

The uprisings broke out one after another, and the
Padishah never came to her rooms. He didn't ask:
'Mother, it is so and so. What to do?'

He followed the strategy he knew. He stifled each of the uprisings, spilling lots of blood. He crushed with a flail the heads of the Janissaries caught in libation or smoking. He ordered Sadrazam Bayram Pasha beheaded because he'd judged him in a poem he wrote. The passion for flying of two good men – Hezarfen Ahmed and Legari Hasan – made him scared, so that when Hezarfen crossed from the Galata Tower to Üsküdar on wings, he ordered them both to be caught and brought before himself. "Men like you," he said, giving them a long look, "are very scary people. They achieve everything they will think about. That's why you do not deserve a life." But for some reason, he didn't call the hangman. He banished Hezarfen to Algeria, and Legari to Ukraine.

Four murderers, hired by a group of people who decided to kill him, managed to get through to his bedroom, but Murad woke up and smashed the skulls of all four with his famous flail.

Sultan Murad, who withstood the insurrections, murderers, curses of his siblings, and his mother's prayers, was eventually confined to bed by a disease. Some of the doctors diagnosed it as cirrhosis of the liver; others described it as gout.

Even the news that death stood at the head of her son did not soften Mahpeyker's, petrified heart. That night she locked herself in her room. *The hour is approaching*, she said to herself.

She'd managed to survive and protect Ibrahim. It was time to take Ibrahim out of the dark corridors and lay the sun on his head.

She was sure. They will bring her the sun again. She just had to wait a little longer and be vigilant. That's all.

Epileptic Murad had poisoned the Queen's life for her. But she was determined to get most of the power during Ibrahim's reign.

When Ruhsar informed her that Kemankesh Kara Mustafa Pasha wanted to see her, she smiled. *I have been waiting for him*.

Having noticed that the girls were in a hurry to clothe her, she said: "Take your time." She was completely calm. "Let one of you go to Ibrahim's rooms and check if there is anything missed or any oversight of steps taken by us. Are the guards in place?"

When everything was ready, she looked into the mirror that Ruhsar was holding. *Beautiful,* she thought. *If I weren't mourning my sons, I would be even more beautiful*.

No one could guess that Mahpeyker Kösem Valide Sultan had already left fifty springs behind her. But she knew.

She was beautiful outside, but she was starting to break inside. Her back hurt and getting up and sitting down had become exhausting.

"Let's move, Ruhsar. Let's see what His Highness Pasha brought to us?"

The girl was surprised.

"Was pasha supposed to bring something?"

Mahpeyker giggled.

"The sun."

"You wanted to see us, Sadrazam Pasha," Mahpeyker said, entering the room with a partition.

Kemankesh Kara Mustafa Pasha straightened behind the screen. He greeted her with a nod. They sat down on a bench on their sides of the screen.

Mustafa cleared his throat once and then again.

"I am disturbing you because of an important issue that I would like to raise."

"I'm listening."

"I have a message for you, Your Highness."

*Tell me what you have to say*, she thought to herself impatiently. *Whatever you have to say, just say it. Say, 'I brought you the sun of the Empire,' and then get out of here.*

"Has the hour of the Padishah come?"

Her voice was so cold that even the Sadrazam was surprised. Was that how a mother should ask about the condition of her son, who was on his deathbed?

"No," he replied. "Not yet. But I don't think there is much time left. Doctors do not give hope."

Mahpeyker sighed. She didn't say anything.

Kemankesh Kara Mustafa Pasha cleared his throat again. He was Hungarian by origin.

*They're all like that*, she thought. *Of the many Hungarians I've seen in the palace, every one of them was like that. Before they spit out two words out of themselves, they will make you die out of curiosity.*

"The Ruler..." he finally spoke. He spoke so quietly that Mahpeyker had to touch the crate with her ear to hear. "He called me to himself last night."

*Look at that,* she grumbled in her mind. *And supposedly, he was seriously ill.* To keep him on track, again, she remained silent.

"His Highness turned to me with a certain demand."

*With a demand? What demand?* The mysterious tone of the Pasha aroused suspicions in her.

"With what demand did the Padishah turn to you, Pasha?"

Pasha grunted and cleared his throat for a long time. Finally, he cleared his throat again. Suddenly, she felt the urge to jump to her feet, to turn the screen over and grabbing him by the collar, shake him well. *Tell me, man, what did Murad want from you?*

Sadrazam seemed to sense the impatience of the Mother Sultana.

"That," he said in a whisper, "that I would find the place where you hide Ibrahim and kill him."

Mahpeyker felt as if Murad's flail crushed her head.

"What!?" she jumped up from her seat.

"Yes," Sadrazam moaned on the other side. "Unfortunately, this is the order issued by the Ruler to his servant, but... if the Pa... Padishah... dies..." he stammered.

Kemankesh didn't manage to say anything more.

In one moment, Mahpeyker exploded.

"And you, now, with no regard to your old age, to your gray beard, you come to ask me where Ibrahim is?! After leaving from here, you will go to kill..." her voice broke off. She was shaking with anger. "If Murad dies, and Ibrahim is killed, what will happen next, did you think about it, Pasha?"

The man nodded behind the screen. He'd thought about it.

"If you had thought, didn't you tell him?"

"I did. I swear, I told him. Risking my head, I said, 'If the Prince is executed, the throne will be without a successor.'"

"And?"

"He grabbed me by the caftan and pulled me to himself. 'It will not!' he growled. 'You can not pass the state into the hands of a madman. Hasn't the reign of uncle Mustafa taught you anything? Carry out the order, Pasha. The throne has a successor. Don't worry.'"

Mahpeyker was close to madness. What kind of man was this? Being himself on his deathbed, he was trying to take away life from another – not only the only brother he had left – but an insane, innocent one! The only descendant of Osman!

"Listen," she growled. "Is there a hidden prince somewhere that we do not know about? Who is he, the heir to the throne of the Sublime Porte?"

"Mehmed Girej Chan. Crimean Khan."

"What?! He's crazy," Mahpeyker hissed. "The disease has made him crazy. He wants to demolish the Empire's nest? Destroy the line? The family of Osman will go away, and in his place, the Mehmed family will come? From now on they will say 'Girej's state' of us?"

The Pasha was silent.

"Listen, Pasha," Mahpeyker said, rising from her place. "If you came here to obey the orders of the madman, I have no son to give to you. Go and tell your Lord: 'As long as his mother is alive, no one will raise a hand to Prince Ibrahim. He will carry on the line and take over the throne.'"

And then the sun rose.

"That's what I came to tell you," the Pasha replied unexpectedly quickly. "Murad Khan could have given this order to other people as well. Ibrahim should be given good protection and be ready for the enthronement. We don't know what His Majesty decided in the matter of Mehmed Girej Khan. It would be good to act quickly and preventively."

Mahpeyker didn't hesitate.

"It will be preventive if the Padishah gives up his spirit as soon as possible," she replied. "Otherwise, the Empire will be in flames. This time he will stain his flail with Ottoman blood."

Fortunately, it didn't happen that way. On the eighteenth day of February 1640, at sunset, Sultan Murad gave his soul to the angels. Many were happy, and there were also many who self-beat their chests with tears.

Mustafa Pasha did on that day what they had decided to do with Mahpeyker Sultan. The red light of the last rays of the setting sun bounced off the inner courtyard onto the windows of the harem. While selas were being sung, Kara Mustafa Pasha, taking along with him the second Vizier and the chief of the black eunuchs, hurried to the Sultana Mother.

"My condolences."

"Thank you, Pasha."

"The time has come to pass the news to the new Padishah."

Mahpeyker looked into their eyes for a moment. She was afraid that all this could be a trap. Was it just a game Murad pulled her into, to find out where she was hiding Ibrahim? But there was no time to lose. She had to take the risk.

"Have you taken measures at sea that I talked about, Sadrazam Pasha?"

"The fleet has sailed from the Bay of Poyraz to the Black Sea, My Lady."

It was a precaution against a possible attack on the capital by the Crimean Khan in alliance with the Cossack pirates who were always abundant in the Black Sea.

"City gates closed?"

"Since this morning."

"The situation in the barracks, in the harbor, in the sailors' cabins?"

"Quiet."

It was evening, but with Ibrahim coming out from his hiding place, the sun would rise in her son's life.

"Come with me."

They walked down countless corridors. Neither the Sadrazam nor the Viziers knew the way. They didn't even think that the palace had such places in it. How could they have known, if they'd never gone through the Novice Courtyard in their lives? They didn't have Mürüvvet as a friend or unfortunate Eftalya as a guide. In the places they passed, Mahpeyker could hide not one person, but the whole crowd of people.

Finally, after descending to the lower rooms of the kafes, they reached the hiding place of Ibrahim.

"Ibrahim!" she cried, peering inside. For the first time in years, she didn't lower her voice, calling for her son. "I have come for you."

There was no answer.

"Did you hear what I said? I will get you from here. It's the end of the torment. I'm opening the door. Just don't be scared."

She tucked a huge key into the lock. There was a noise behind the door. Mahpeyker knew what was going on. Ibrahim was hiding his pouch with pearls in panic.

"There are three people with me," Mahpeyker warned. "I will stay outside. They will come inside."

"Hangmen! They are executioners! They can't come in! I don't want to!" His screams were accompanied by terrifying laughter. All three men felt shivers running down their spines.

"No," said Mahpeyker. "They are not executioners. All three are your friends. One of them is Sadrazam Mustafa Pasha. He has news for you."

"Yes, yes, yes!" Ibrahim shouted hysterically. "Murad fooled you! They are executioners. They'll kill me. They'll kill me. Or maybe you are an executioner, too? Will you strangle me?"

"No one will strangle you. Trust me. I'm opening the door. Listen carefully to what the Sadrazam will say."

"I will not, I won't listen. You tell me what they have to say. Don't let the executioners in. They'll kill me... They'll steal my pearls... They are thieves, mother... Thieves of pearls. They will take my pearls and take them to Murad... Murad will decorate his head with my pearls..."

Silent until now, Kemankesh Ali Pasha leaned over Mahpeyker's shoulder and suddenly spoke.

"Murad died. Your brother died, Sultan."

There was silence behind the door.

Mahpeyer turned the key in the lock. She pushed the door carefully. The iron gates opened with a terrible creak.

The first one who saw a pearly glow in the darkness of the room was the Second Vizier.

*A ghost,* he thought with horror. *Dear God. Will we give the empire to a ghost? This man has turned into a ghost!*

Sadrazam showed greater self-control. Without crossing the doorway, he bowed low.

"Your Majesty... Your brother, Sultan Murad Khan died an hour ago. You have become a Padishah. The time has come for enthronement."

"You're lying!" Ibrahim hissed. "You're lying, you thief in a big turban. Will you stuff your hat with the pearls?

The harem aga hastened to help.

"We're telling the truth, sir. From now on you are the Padishah. We have come to take you to the throne, to give a sword to you, to bring subjects to kiss your garments.

"You lie too. Murad will not die... He doesn't die... He does not die... He kills... Murad kills!"

They saw the pearly glow begin to bounce and struggle in the dark. Sadrazam managed to duck at the last moment, noticing an object flying straight at him.

A heavy wooden tambur, which flew over his head, hit the opposite wall and shattered to pieces. If he'd not bent down, his own head would have fallen apart in a similar way.

"Ibrahim Khan!"

That was Mahpeyker.

"He died. Murad died. They are telling the truth. You have become a Padishah, son."

"I don't believe it. They pretend that they want to put me on the throne, but in reality, they will give me away to Murad's hands."

Sadrazam shrugged in resignation.

Mahpeyker didn't want to force her son out of the room. It would take whatever was left of his reason to remove this thought away from his head.

"That's fine," she said with a smile. "What can we do to make you believe it? Will you believe it if you see Murad's corpse?"

The pearly glow ceased to struggle.

"The corpse? I'll believe."

They brought it. They showed it. Sultan Ibrahim Khan saw and believed.

The next morning in the Audience Hall, the sun shone on his head. And it also shone on the head of the older Sultana, the Great Sultana, the Magnificent Mahpeyker Kösem Sultan.

*I did it*, she thought to herself as she looked at her son, with ten strings of pearls on his neck. *I made one more madman a king.*

# Chapter Twenty-Three

## Harem, Kafes
### Night, September 2nd, 1651

She didn't know how she would stand it, waiting so many hours in this dark, stuffy room, but there was no other way. She had two options – to become the head of the state or food for the vultures. There was no turning back. If she fails... Then: 'hello, death! My house is your house. 'This Moscow fox will not let me live!'

Mahpeyker fidgeted restlessly on the wooden bench. Everything hurt her already now. "I just hope Üveys fulfills the task he was entrusted with," she muttered under her breath.

Her own whisper was enough for her to panic. *Did anyone hear*, she thought immediately, staring into the darkness around her. She listened with her breath held – silent, nobody was there.

*And who could it be?* her reason rebelled at once. *Do you think anyone would look into this burrow where you kept Ibrahim for years?*

She didn't think so, but she was worried about it. *Is it my fault?* she murmured in her mind. *Anyone who'd gone through what I have would do the same.*

Who would have thought that the old Great Mother Sultana would wait for Üveys Pasha four floors underground, in a room full of mice, worms, spiders, and who knows what else? Anyone thinking so would have to be crazy.

*You are crazy too*, her reason chuckled. *And what else can the mother of a madman be?*

*I'm not crazy*, Mahpeyker objected. *And even if I'm crazy, it's because my life has made me this way.*

In fact, everything started well. How fitting was the authority of the Sultan for Ibrahim, dressed in a caftan decorated with pearls. The son she had taken out of the dungeons of the kafes and on whose head she had put a sunny crown, was as if reborn.

'Mother,' he'd said on the day of enthronement, 'let me, I'll kiss your hand.'

*The sun was shining on my head, too,* she sighed inside. Everything was great. They both woke up from a nightmare. They were happy.

But then... then suddenly everything went dark.

She nodded. Yes, the life drove her crazy. She was already even afraid of her own shadow. She thought it was safe here, but who knew what kind of threats lurked in these closets?

She left the palace early so that no one would see her go to the kafes. To Ruhsar she said: 'If anyone asks, say that I'm in my chambers. I don't feel well, and I'm lying in bed. Do you understand?'

The girl looked at her with worry in her eyes: 'Where will I find you if necessary, Lady Mother?'

Lady Mother? She was neither a Sultana nor a Mother anymore.

'A Great Sultana,' she'd mumbled. Senior Sultana... Great Sultana... Ah! Everything had gone away and disappeared. Maybe it still survived somewhere, but inside it was empty. The titles, at one time inspiring respect and terrifying, didn't say anything to anyone anymore. She was only an 'Older Sultana.' Or 'Grandmother Sultana.'

"My God," she whispered. "Grandmother Sultana? Me, wonderful Kösem – Grandmother Sultana?"

Now, a blue-eyed Moscow fox called Turhan was a Sultana Mother – a sweet girl she found herself and placed by Ibrahim's nose. This sweet girl now caused her trouble as a fully-grown woman.

She noticed that Ruhsar was still waiting for an answer.

'It won't be necessary,' she'd replied with a bitter smile. 'Let those who feel such need go to the blue-eyed.'

The girl undoubtedly understood that her Lady didn't want anyone to see her there. She didn't know what she was going to do or where she was going to go, but certainly, she too sensed that important things were going to happen. Was there anybody left who didn't feel it, anyway?

It was necessary to go down early. She'd done it for years when she'd been hiding Ibrahim from his brother. If she went to the kafes, and then pretending that she was going to the stable, she would have come up the steep stairs in the evening, after dark. This would be the time when Üveys' coming was approaching, so she'd immediately attract attention. At night, the gates were closed, and nobody could get to the courtyard without permission. It was, therefore, necessary to pass the courtyard at the time when it was crowded so that whoever noticed her, would think, judging from her outfit, that she was one of the kitchen maids that took food to the stable.

It happened exactly as she intended. She didn't attract anyone's attention. And now she was here. The boy, whom she was going to make the Padishah, slept in a cell separated from her by two corridors. He didn't even realize that she would bring him the sun.

"If my plan succeeds... there will be no betrayal... If Üveys manages to carry out my order..." she mumbled.

She was balancing on the edge again. She was used to danger and playing with death, but this time it was different – this time she wasn't trying to get something that did not belong to her. Conversely, she was fighting to avoid losing what she had won, what she had gained, what she had possessed before. She walked along the edge, and a hellish fire burned below.

Thinking about it, it wasn't difficult to go mad. Was it why she had labored and toiled and danced with death for forty-five long years?

She was a woman who'd made the sacrifice of four of her sons for the Empire. Five of them she also put on the throne. She was supposed to put the sixth one on the throne this very morning. What were they thinking? That she would give the crown, reign, and authority, which she had placed with her own hands at her son's feet, into the hands of a clumsy girl?

"No way," Mahpeyker murmured. They will bring her the sun once again.

The crown was about to shine on her head again. Wasn't she the one, every time they said: 'She's dead, it's over, now she's just going to rot in the palace and she'll be gone,' – wasn't she the one who'd come out again from behind the clouds? And now, it was going to happen again. Why? Because that was her destiny. To be a Queen. A beggar in Kumanovo once said to her: 'The Queen.' 'Beautiful Queen!'

She remembered her laughter. 'Can a maid become a queen?'

'You will become the Queen,' he'd replied.

And she did.

And not once, but a thousand times! And she would become one again.

Her heart pounded excitedly.

Will Üveys manage to settle the matter in the barracks?

Will Sadrazam Siyavuş Pasha do what his task was?

She thought about the Georgian Mehmed Pasha. Did he manage to take the steps she had ordered?

*Blond man, you must be careful. You can not rely on him,* she thought and commissioned several tasks also to the blond Tarhuncu Ahmed Pasha. She didn't hear a word of objection. Or maybe it was just a masquerade, make-up? A game?

Hajji Abdürrahim Efendi didn't betray her in the case of Ibrahim – he kept his word. But we will see if Abdülaziz Efendi – as they say, the son of Karachelebi – will issue the desired fatwa?

*If he issues, he issues, if not, that's his business*, she thought, shrugging her shoulders. All he had to do was keep his mouth shut. *This one will go, and we will put Ebu Said Efendi in his place. It's not for nothing he still looks into my eyes.*

Betrayal had become her companion. Didn't she experience enough of betrayals when she was dealing with the enthronement of Ibrahim? But she had to trust somebody. In turn, those who were supposed to take care of it also had to trust her: the success she'd promised to them should have blinded them.

Now, when they would believe that the fox who would become her daughter-in-law would offer them greater prizes, they would have given her away without a second thought – of that, she had no doubt.

*That's the way things are*, she accepted. *The one who pays, orders the music.*

She was forced to rely on others.

She couldn't lead the army herself. The three hundred years old Ottoman customs did not allow the woman to go to fight.

So, she'd persuaded the Pashas that she would satisfy their hunger better than her daughter-in-law Turhan. One way or another, they believed her, for now – or so it appeared that way. There was one more thing – they all knew Mahpeyker Kösem Sultan well.

Each of them knew what she'd done in the past. And, of course, they knew that if she achieved what she'd started, in any cases of betrayal – she would slash their heads.

It was a chain. Each link had to be strong. If even one of them were to break, the whole thing would be ruined. *Me too*, she thought. *I will be ruined, too.*

The mourning selas sung with the morning Ezan, wouldn't announce the death of these two, but her own. She had to occupy herself with something in order not to think. She felt that she'd go mad, otherwise.

*Should I light a candle?* she wondered. She couldn't sit in the darkness like this for hours.

But Ibrahim did. He sat, and her son went crazy. Now, in turn, Suleiman was sitting. Fortunately, he was still young, and since she'd hidden him here, he's not yet got close to madness.

"Damn him," she muttered, rising from the wooden seat. "Ibrahim wasn't any madman – he was a jinn – a jinn who cheated not only Murad but also me."

Even if he had been crazy, after taking over the throne and the whip of power, he suddenly regained his senses. Ibrahim, who had not been touched by a woman's hand, the one who was said to be devoid of desire, before the year passed... Ho, ho...

Mahpeyker laughed under her breath. "Ho, ho and ho, ho" she muttered, remembering the harem adventures of her son Ibrahim.

She took out some tinder from her pocket and rubbed it with the flint for a long time to light a candle. At last a fire shone on the top of the wick from the resulting spark. She got scared that it would go off. Leaning the candle quickly, she waited for the dripping wax to saturate the wick.

Raising the source of light, she looked around.

"Oh my God!"

In the dead, shivering, yellow light, everything was even scarier. The shadows were even more terrifying, the darkness even darker.

Suddenly a voice came in her head. *Hey! One shouldn't be afraid of shadows!* It was the voice of Hodja Hussein Efendi, the healer from Safranbolu.

*To hell,* she ruminated. *Where did that quack come into her head from now?*

Having learned that the healer's breath and amulet could heal any evil, she secretly brought him to the palace. 'Hey! One should not be afraid of shadows!' Those were his words after consulting the jinns.

But she was afraid. Even very much afraid. Just like now.

'Jinns do not like light,' Hodja Efendi had said, putting out all the lights and leaving only one candle; one candle casting light – if you could call it light at all. The flame dancing on the top of the wick didn't illuminate anything except the candle itself. On the contrary, it revived the dead, yellow, menacing shadows all around. The bottomless abyss of the darkness. The reflection of the candle's light on the windows was like the eyes of corpses watching her. Mahpeyker shuddered involuntarily. *In this sinister environment, not just jinns, but literally everything can be brought to life,* she thought.

The face of Hussein Efendi stood before her eyes. He had a big round head of which half of it was his forehead. Under it, the gray scrolls of eyebrows fell over his eyes. She had never met a man with such small eyes before in her entire life.

In the candlelight, they shriveled even more. Hodja Efendi's eyes were small but animated like two jesters. They never stopped moving, even for a moment, running from object to object. He had a nose like a dot and a thin black beard framing his cheeks. In contrast to his nose, were impressive-sized lips, and over them a funny, thin mustache. He didn't have a neck either. It was as if his head had been placed directly on his shoulders.

But this ugly, small, and even funny man, was the master of the terrible powers of the jinns. Mahpeyker had no doubt about it. The hair bristled on her head. It was exactly the moment she lost herself in the shadows, in the darkness lit by a single candle, she understood that she was afraid.

'What are you scared of, madam?' he'd asked.

'Jinns. In such darkness...'

Hussein Efendi wagged his finger, saying: 'Do not be afraid of jinns, My Lady. Saints are like shadows. They are always with us. Either in front of us or behind us. Either on our right or on the left. Shadows are different from the jinns only in that we can see them. Let's just say... I will now summon Salkım Efendi...'

'Salkım Efendi? Who is that?'

'The jinn, who will answer the question you asked me.'

She got scared, causing Hodja Efendi to laugh.

'There is nothing to be afraid of... You won't see Salkım Efendi. What you see will be only a shadow falling on a plate with water. And you shouldn't be afraid of shadows – right? Even if you want it, Salkım will not become visible...'

'Why?'

'Salkım Efendi is very shy.'

Then, despite all her fear, she'd laughed inwardly. She could swear that the healer was an ordinary charlatan, but she needed him. She had to meet this shy Salkım Efendi for the good of the Ottoman family. There was no longer anything she would not do so that Ibrahim would approach a woman and conceive a child – but nothing had worked so far – neither potions nor ointments had helped. Also, Ibrahim slapped the odalisque, who lifted an aphrodisiac potion on a spoon to his lips, which caused her to fall to the ground. 'Do you want to poison me, viper?!' he'd shouted. 'Bring me my pearls right now. It's time to feed the fish.'

In the end, she'd resorted to the help of the praised hodja from Safranbolu, of whom she heard of from girls. 'Look at how many barrens one's, did his spells give twins to,' it was said. 'He sees what nobody else sees, hears, what no one else hears. Hodja Efendi's jinn is powerful.'

Indeed, so it happened. That night, Hodja Efendi tightened the eyelids on his tiny eyes, and tapping the bowl lightly with his fingertips, he murmured softly under his breath.

'Salkıııııım... Salkıııım... Are you on Mount Kaf, on the Moon, on Venus? Where are youuuuu?'

She still couldn't get rid of the darkness, the fear of the jinn, and the horrifying voice of the Hodja from her memory.

'Salkıııım... I see the seaaaa... Cooome... The sea is getting rough before your faaaace...'

Mahpeyker remembered that she was close to fainting. She even felt regret.

"It's good that I chased him away," she murmured. "Otherwise, Salkım Efendi would finish me off."

Could he? He could. The jinn of Hussein Efendi was so powerful. The jinn was obedient to him and did whatever he demanded.

The eyes of Hussein Efendi suddenly opened. The tiny eyes of the man now burned like brushwood engulfed by fire. He looked down at the plate. And then, terrified, Mahpeyker pulled herself together. *God, save my mind!* her thoughts cried out.

Water in the small golden saucer, unmoved by anyone, suddenly stirred like the sea. It was really in waves! It seemed to her that she could still see it foam when hitting the sides. Water splashed around.

'Hello, Salkıııım...' the voice of Hussein Efendi was no longer part of this world. She didn't hear that thick, low, disturbing voice anymore. It seemed as if it was a little boy talking – 'Welcome...'

Then it seemed as if he was listening to someone. Without stopping, he nodded his head in confirmation.

'Is there anyone who is not afraid of your anger? So how could Hussein not be afraid, Salkıııım? But you like to do the goooood...'

He sounded like he was sneaking into the favors of a small child.

'This lady needs your power, your sorcery... Do you recognize her?' he'd said, before he suddenly began to shake as if in a fever.

'No!' A scream escaped from his chest. 'No, it's not like that!'

'What's happening?' she'd asked him in a whisper. 'Did the jinn recognize us? Is he mad?'

Even the hair on Hussein Efendi's beard bristled. Mahpeyker wasn't sure if he'd heard her at all. He nodded his head again as if in a sign of confirmation. His breathing was fast.

'No,' he'd wheezed. 'Of course, I am the guarantor.'

*A guarantor? What guarantor? Who was to be whose guarantor. What was this man babbling? Did jinn Salkım express his objection?* These thoughts had rushed through her mind.

Hodja Efendi, seized by convulsions, uttered some unintelligible words.

'Tarizmay... Budosh gari! Eloy, eloy, eloy!'

Mahpeyker, almost grabbing Hodja's hand, wanted to yell, 'What's going on?!'

And just then, on the darkened face of the Safranbolan healer, something like relaxation appeared.

'Lefayel Salkım Efendi,' he'd whispered. 'Lefayel domaş!'

Whatever it meant.

'Tell him,' he'd said in a whisper, never taking his eyes off the water. 'Speak quickly... Salkım Efendi does not like to wait. Beg him.'

Jinn Salkım liked neither light nor waiting.

'My son,' Mahpeyker began. 'I mean Sultan Ibrahim... He...'

A sudden thought made her afraid – what if the jinns do not like such improper topics... And if the jinn Salkım also doesn't approve of affairs of the heart... If he gets angry, breaks her neck...

'Speak,' ordered the child's voice. 'Tell him... Tell him, but I beg you, be fast!'

'Ibrahim,' she started again.

The sea in the saucer was still waving, but she was powerless. She had to accept the waves.

'How to put it, he can not enter a woman. We've tried everything to no effect. Your power has no limits, Hussein Efendi has said... The Empire needs successors to the throne, mighty jinn... Please, give my Ibrahim power, light a fire in his veins, revive his seed...'

The water in the saucer suddenly became still.

'He left,' said the jinns' Hodja. His face was sweaty. Even his beard was wet. 'Salkım Efendi left.'

He continued to stare at the water.

'So, what will happen now?'

She remembered the words of Hussein Efendi as if it was yesterday: 'It will happen!'

Holy God!

Everything rose in Mahpeyker at that moment. Again, this magical word.

*It will happen.*

The jinns' hodja looked like he'd received a heavy beating. He stooped. He was breathing hard.

Suddenly, a suspicion sneaked into Mahpeyker's head.

'Has something happened, Hodja Efendi? Did the jinn say something you haven't told me?'

'No. He did not.'

'That's it? That's all that Salkım Efendi said?'

'Yes. It will happen.'

'Listen, Hodja Effendi. Let at least one thing happen. Ask for whatever you want now. I will bury you in riches. My word. The word of Mahpeyker Kösem.'

Hussein Hodja was clearly in a hurry. He was ready to leave in an instant and Mahpeyker did not object – she also wanted him to leave as quickly as possible. The courtiers led him unnoticed from the palace.

'The Empire has already given us a thousand names, at least do not let them call us a witch,' she'd said to Ruhsar that night.

The panic in which he left the palace caught her attention, but later she didn't think of it anymore. This one word caused anxiety, but a magic word sowed hope in her tormented heart.

Now the whole trick was to convince Ibrahim that the water on which Salkım jinn had set up the storm was not a poison and urge him to drink it.

If it didn't help either, the Ottoman family would end.

When did the candle burn out? She hadn't noticed. It was only when the fading flame burned her finger that she emerged from the land of her reverie. She threw the candle stump which had given her pain when it died, at her feet. She stepped on it. She drowned in the dark again.

The inscrutable darkness was better than the sinister, deadly brightness.

Not believing, she'd resorted to Salkım's help only out of helplessness, but the power of his jinn showed almost immediately.

It was a miracle. You couldn't call it anything else. Ibrahim, who had never even turn to look at the girls she brought from the harem, each one more beautiful than the last, turned into a lion before a month passed. The screams from his bedroom could be heard even in her rooms.

There were no more odalisques now. For some reason, he didn't want to sleep with the same one again that he'd taken to his bed the night before.

And it was back then, in those days, that they just brought her to the palace.

'A young girl from Russia, taken prisoner by the Crimean Tatars,' the Chamberlain had said. 'Her name is Nastya.'

Nastya?

It was another miracle. She was surprised by such a hand of fate. God, for the extension of the Ottoman family, had sent Nastya another Nastya.

'Where's the girl?' she'd asked.

'At the Novice Courtyard, My Lady.'

'Take me to her immediately, Chamberlain.'

'You, My Lady... But, how come?'

The Chamberlain had the right to be surprised. What would she do in the Novice Courtyard, among the newly arrived slaves, servants, helpers?

'Don't worry,' she'd said in a whisper. 'I know a passage. We'll get through that way. Nobody will see us, but we'll see everything.'

So, she did. Passing through the secret passage that Eftalya had once shown her, they reached the Novices' Courtyard.

The girls in hamam clogs were running around the pavement with the characteristic clattering.

She didn't even have to ask which one of them it was – she was there – like the sun.

'There she is,' the Chamberlain had whispered. 'Nastya. A fair-haired girl who is pouring water from the trough.'

She knew right away. Only that girl could be Nastya. She nodded. She was beautiful. If Ibrahim had not been crazy before, he'd for sure get crazy when he saw her.

'They've changed her name to Hatice.'

Hatice!

For a moment, Mahpeyker thought that such a coincidence must be more than a miracle. Fate didn't stop playing with her. It was his next move.

Hatice! Good, God! What was behind this divine plan?

She went back. She thought and wondered all night. She didn't know what the divine plan was, but God certainly knew what he was doing. She did too.

In the morning she'd called for the girl.

*Come, let's look at you, future daughter-in-law,* she'd murmured in her thoughts, greeting her with a smile. *Give a son for Ibrahim, a descendant for the Empire, a grandson for me.*

Her eyes were like the sea. Golden hair. You couldn't stop looking at her face.

She could be fifteen or even younger.

'Lift your head, let me see it,' she'd said to the girl, whose cheeks got red at those words.

It seemed to Mahpeyker that she was reliving her first days in the palace again. Just as she was once being prepared for Ahmed, so now she was going to polish Nastya for Ibrahim. Hayganoş couldn't manage to thread a needle anymore, so the kalfas trained by her were going to sew a dress for the new fiancée. She was to teach her etiquette and good manners personally. When the time would come, she intended to present her to the Padishah.

'What's your name, my dear?'

'Nadya, My Lady.'

'Did they tell you that our childhood name was also Nastya?'

The girl had been surprised and her cheeks flared.

'They call me Hatice here.'

'We were also called that.' She looked at the girl's hypnotic eyes for a moment. *Ah, Ibrahim*, she thought back then. *Give your mother a grandson from this girl.* 'From now on they will call you Turhan.'

She didn't know where the name came to her from. *Hatice Turhan Sultan, ha,* she chuckled to herself. *It fits. Pretty good. Hatice Turhan Sultan...*

The girl had bowed with a smile.

'Thank you, My Lady.'

'Well, Turhan, do you know who I am?'

She bowed her beautiful head. Her light, silky, waist-long hair waved.

'The mother of the Padishah, they said.'

'That's right. We are called Senior Sultana Mahpeyker Kösem Sultan.'

She gave the girl a scrutinizing look once more; rosy lips and her eyes framed by dark eyelashes were captivating. She had breasts that were big for her age, a narrow waist, round hips, and long legs that would seduce even adult men. Let's just hope she won't make Ibrahim lose his head completely after all those years spent in isolation.

'Would you like me to introduce you to the Padishah?'

The girl had said nothing but her rosy cheeks reddened again.

'That's fine. There is nothing to be ashamed of. But you must be prepared in advance.' The she'd clapped her hands. 'Call the tailors and weavers. We want to see everyone here tomorrow.'

She knew she didn't have much time, so she didn't procrastinate. She'd made sure that twenty days later, Hatice Turhan would be ready to face Ibrahim.

As soon as she'd been presented, Mahpeyker understood that Ibrahim had a passion for the girl.

'His Majesty has expressed the will that Hatice Turhan would be brought to his chambers in the evening,' the Chamberlain said two days later.

For the second time, a Nastya rested in the arms of the Ottoman's descendant.

It happened just as she had thought. The girl charmed Ibrahim. For many days, Padishah did not leave his rooms. People started calling her the favorite Hatice Turhan. Or 'Moscow Rose.'

'Whoever will say that again, I will tear his tongue out,' Mahpeyker snapped one day. She'd had enough. 'Not Moscow or anything, but my daughter-in-law favorite Hatice Turhan. Whoever says something against her, we will treat him as speaking against us and give an appropriate punishment. Let that be clear.'

How nice and polite the girl was. Mahpeyker put her on a pedestal. Before the sound of one, 'Mother Sultana' ended, another one started. When she wanted something, the girl, not giving the courtiers any chance, ran herself and brought it: 'Here you go, Mother Sultana.'

Mahpeyker heard with her own ears how many times she said to the girls: 'My real mother is Valide Sultan. I didn't even know my birth mother well. They sold me into captivity when I was still quite little.'

*Oh, my little turtle dove*, she'd thought, hearing this. *Was I any different? Don't be sad, my little sea-eyed daughter. Where have we come? Who knows what beautiful things God has written in your fate for you. Look, you became the favorite of the Great Sultan Ibrahim. I give you my word, Hatice Turhan – give my son a descendant, and I'll take care of the marriage.*

Turhan seemed to hear her thoughts. Two months later, she confessed to her that she was pregnant. Her cheeks burned like fire.

Mahpeyker was almost flying with joy. That same day, she mobilized all the midwives and doctors. One of the first things she did was to shower Hussein Hodja Efendi with gifts.

'Let him also take Salkım Efendi with him. From now on the respectful Hodja Efendi will live in the palace,' she'd announced.

Ibrahim, upon learning that he would become a father, seemed to calm down even more. At least, he didn't walk around with bags full of pearls. Sadrazam Pasha also no longer ran to her every now and then with a complaint: 'My Lady, our Lord, filled the pond with pearls again. But that's fine. We are collecting them. 'New pearls arrived,' we say, handing them back to him. But now he insists: 'Take us to Sarayburn. The fish in the sea are hungry. Let's feed them well.' Everybody knows what the state of the treasury is. The prices grow out of control. People are starving. What will happen if, in such a state of affairs, news spreads that our Sultan tosses pearls in the sea?'

It would be bad – even very bad. But Ibrahim was getting better. He looked better every day.

*I didn't have to tell him twice anymore*. Mahpeyker stirred on the wooden bench. *If I said, 'Take it,' he did. 'Throw it out,' he threw it out. 'Move it here,' he moved it.* He was the King, but the Empire was ruled by the Queen – that is, by her.

She remembered how one evening he winked at her, saying: 'Mother, if Turhan gives birth to a son, I will be able to cast pearls to fish together with my son, right?'

She was devastated.

Did the relapse start on that day then? Or did he get crazy when he was informed that Turhan gave birth to a son? She didn't know.

The boy born from Turhan was rosy. The Prince was like his mother. He was named Mehmed.

Mahpeyker kept both promises. She gave riches generously to the jinns' Hodja. And she married Turhan to her son.

On the wedding day, her eyes filled with tears. *One more Nastya became a Sultana*, she thought. *Nastya, the slave, was from now on Hatice Turhan Sultan. When the time comes, she will also become Valide Sultan.*

She had everything to be happy about, but she wasn't at all. Everything was going wrong.

Hoping that the birth of Mehmed would heal Ibrahim, she prayed and made vows. Unfortunately, even the amulets prescribed by jinns' Hodja did not help – Jinn Salkım had probably left Hodja Efendi.

But the news that the Padishah had conceived the son thanks to the water that Hussein Hodja Efendi blew on, immediately spread throughout the capital. People seeking healing from the hands of the Hodja and his jinn stormed the palace. The fame of the jinns' Hodja had already reached everyone. Even Mahpeyker. With her permission, he moved to the house she gave him. Hodja Efendi was already as rich as Croesus.

She rose from the wooden bench. Everything hurt her from sitting for so long. She moved her hands and legs. *Fool,* she said in her head. *The jinns' whisperer didn't realize that with the growth of his fame, the number of his enemies was also growing.*

Ibrahim's mind, already the size of a walnut, eventually disappeared completely. He ordered a blanket and cradle decorated with pearls to be made for Prince Mehmed. He also started to sneak out secretly to the headland at night. A rumor spread that the Padishah had begun tossing pearls to the fish. While the situation in the country was discussed at the Divan, Ibrahim, climbing to a window, took off the pearls from his caftan and threw them to passersby in the street. He didn't even realize the value of each tossed bead.

Besides, there were no more slave girls left for Ibrahim any more. After Prince Mehmed, another son was born to him from Saliha Dilaşub. Ibrahim demanded a cradle decorated with pearls for the newborn Prince, too. He ordered two bags of pearls to be taken from the treasury.

'There are no more pearls,' replied the treasurer.

'Then find them,' Ibrahim had yelled.

His eyes were wandering again as during the time he was hidden in the kafes. He didn't listen to her either. Whatever Mahpeyker said, he did the opposite.

She sat down again angrily.

"If you're going to come, come already, Üveys," she muttered. "Otherwise, I'll die here either out of stress or stifled by the burden of the past."

Suddenly, she remembered the day when a deeply embarrassed Sadrazam Ahmed Pasha showed up at her apartments. Blood hit her head again.

'My Lady,' he'd said, bowing his head. 'I am your servant, your subject.'

It was clear that he had bad news. *Come on, tell me, servant, what order have you received?*

'His Majesty, the Padishah, expressed the will that you move to the Old Palace. At once, immediately, today.'

What?!

Was it the same Ibrahim, who on the day of enthronement came to kiss her hand with the words: 'My mother, my blessed guardian,' and fell to her feet, who gave such an order?

'I had to have heard wrong,' she'd said, looking at the Pasha in disbelief. 'What, what did you say?'

No, she hadn't heard wrong. She would rather Ibrahim put a knife in her heart, instead of taking her royal crown. Even Murad did not do it.

And he didn't stop there. A month later he sent her to the palace of Iskender Chelebi in Floria.

One day Ahmed Pasha let it slip.

'In fact, the Padishah wanted to send you to Rhodes. 'Our mother comes from the islands. The air in Rhodes will do her good,' he's decided. But along with Turhan Sultan, who threw herself at his feet, begging: 'My Sultan, My Lord,' we have managed to limit the sentence to the palace of Iskender Chelebi.'

Damn it! They even softened the punishment!

*A punishment.* Mahpeyker laughed bitterly in the darkness. It was a punishment for locking the harem's door to prevent his son from sneaking out to Sarayburn at night and throwing pearls into the sea.

The punishment for Sadrazam turned out to be even more severe. Ibrahim learned that the Pasha had given her the news. He ordered to hang Ahmed Pasha's dead body on one of the plane trees in the Hippodrome. Then he informed her about it.

'This is the fate of those who meddle in our affairs!' he'd said.

In the end, the misfortune she'd expected came. The people and the army, unable to withstand the madness and extravagance of her son, incited by competing pashas and viziers, rebelled.

The day before, the insurgents secretly relayed the message to Mahpeyker.

'Is he with us or against us? If with us, let him find a way out, to not shed the blood. If not, if against us, for God, we will not remember that this is Ahmed's and Murad Khan's blood.'

"There is God," Mahpeyker said with a heavy burden on her heart. "I did not defend. I didn't stand in the way. What was I supposed to defend, how to stand in the way?"

Was she to defend the one who took the royal crown from her head – who'd stolen the sun?

On the day the insurgents moved to the palace, Mahpeyker received Turhan Sultan in the palace of Iskender Chelebi.

'I wanted to see Prince Mehmed,' she'd announced. She was afraid that the child could get hurt. In this way, she secured the safety of Turhan and Mehmed. The success of her plan depended on whether they would survive.

Turhan burst into tears, and Mahpeyker caught her hands. She remembered it like it was yesterday. Without beating around the bush, she'd said, 'Daughter, Ibrahim must leave the throne. If it goes on like this, I'm afraid that he will face a similar fate as young Osman.'

Pearly tears flowed from Turhan's blue eyes onto her pink cheeks.

'What are we going to do, Sultana Mother?'

'Ibrahim will leave, and your son will take his place. It's the only thing we can do.'

How surprised the girl was.

'My son? Mehmed? But he is still very little, Sultana Mother.'

'Don't worry about that.'

How could the girl know that she'd once dealt with a similar issue; that she'd obtained a fatwa, approving the right of the little prince Murad to take over the throne.

'Mehmed will become a Padishah, and you will be Valide Hatice Turhan Sultan.'

'But... but... my son is small... and I'm young...'

She had expected that too.

'I know, daughter, she'd said, smiling sweetly at her. 'You're young too. You still need to mature to rule the state. Until Mehmed grows up and you can deal with these matters, well, I will rule the Empire as an Older Mother.'

"Ah." Mahpeyker hit her knees. *On that day I should have understood that everything was fake in this Moscow fox, that everything was a game.*

By the time she understood, it was too late. And now she was to pay for her mistake.

She felt the deep inner pocket of her dress. Both were in place - the bottles of death.

But Ibrahim didn't want to step aside.

Unfazed, she had a plan ready in her head. She went to the New Palace and bolted the door of her son's room. Then she'd put her then seven-year-old grandson Mehmed on the throne.

Padishah Mehmed, Turhan Valide Sultan. She too was the Queen again. Both were Sultanas. Great Sultana Mother. An Elder Mother. She was the real Queen of the Empire. Mehmed and his mother could play with their toys at will.

If Ibrahim stayed where he was locked away, maybe none of these things would have happened.

"But he didn't stay," she snorted as she continued to relive the past. He'd cried, howled, screamed, called, and moaned: 'My pearls.' He'd shouted at the top of his lungs, 'give me my pearls.'

His wailing turned the court life into torture.

This time Mahpeyker found a different solution. She ordered to put an additional wall around the room where she had imprisoned her son. Now his voice at least, was not so audible.

However, this step failed to bring results, and the capital was shaken by a new wave of rebellion. The insurgents wanted only one thing now – her son's death.

'There can not be two on one throne. Either the father is the Sultan or the son. Let's determine which one. If it's Mehmed, that's fine. But if pearly Ibrahim is the Padishah, we do not agree.'

At the thought of that disastrous day, Mahpeyker shook again. If she could, she would cry. But she couldn't cry anymore. There were no more tears in her eyes. No pain, no unhappiness, put tears in her eyes anymore.

She remembered the moment Sadrazam Sofu Mehmed Pasha and Shaykh al-Islam Abdürrahim Efendi stood before her.

'It's already our duty to bring this matter to an end, My Lady.'

'What does the duty oblige you to do, gentlemen?'

'The executioner Black Ali is with us.'

'Meaning?'

'It means just that, My Lady.'

'What if you do not have our consent?'

'Then Black Ali will have two things to do.'

'Is the Padishah safe?'

'God sees that Mehmed Khan is safe.'

'Sultana Mother?'

'She too.'

'And I?'

'It depends on the said condition.'

She couldn't do anything or say anything. So, what did she do? She turned her back to them. It was an order to kill her own son. *Go, kill my son Ibrahim!*

She couldn't forget her scream in her spirit: *Eh, fate! That's how you played with me. In the end, you made me a murderer of my own child!*

When Sofu Mehmed Pasha and Abdürrahim Efendi left the palace, it turned out that the executioner Black Ali had disappeared somewhere. The inhabitants of the palace, having understood what had happened, hid – not a single servant could be seen. Ibrahim's endless screams, however, continued to come from far away.

'Hey, mother! Mother, the traitor! Give me my pearls! Do you want the fish to starve to death?'

The men caught the hangman and beat him well. Pushing and kicking, they led him straight into the room where Ibrahim was yelling. They demolished the wall, broke the padlock. Later, according to what she was told, Ibrahim greeted Abdürrahim Efendi, who entered his room with the executioner Black Ali, with the Koran in his hands.

'Listen, Abdürrahim!' her son had screamed. 'Yusuf Pasha said that you are 'a godless, unfaithful, cunning scoundrel' for which 'no one should be sorry.' Fearing God, I have not ordered killing you, but I see that you are going to kill me. Here is the Koran. By what right do you want to kill me, you cruel men?'

Nobody cared about any law anymore. His mother had given them the law. When the lifeless body, strangled with greased ropes, had slumped to the ground, they barely managed to open the clenched hand of Sultan Ibrahim. The last portion of fish food fell out of it – two pearls.

"Oh," sighed Mahpeyker. "Oh, and oh! I didn't know that I let out a fox – that I released a viper."

For the first few months, even the whole year, things were fine. Her grandson Mehmed was the Padishah. Her daughter-in-law, the Turhan Valide Sultan. It seemed that everything was as she had calculated. The boy was with his mother all the time, playing together in the inner courtyard. And she was the Queen – the Older Sultana Mother.

But one day she experienced the greatest betrayal of her life. One of Turhan Sultan's courtiers came running to her apartments.

'What is it, girl?' Ruhsar had asked. 'What's that rush? Is this how you enter the chambers of the Older Valide, without permission, without a greeting?'

'That's exactly right,' the girl had said bluntly. 'If Hatice Turhan Valide Sultan says: 'Let the old lady know, let her come as soon as possible. We are waiting,' then this is how you enter.'

*I was crushed*, Mahpeyker recalled. *Let the old lady know, let her come as quickly as possible, huh.*

No betrayal like that had ever occurred to her in her entire life.

'It can not go on like this,' Turhan had said to her, without even offering her a seat – her blue-eyed daughter-in-law with light, silky hair, the mother of the grandson whom she had made a Padishah, the woman whom she even named herself. 'If there can not be two Padishahs sitting on the throne, it is also inappropriate to have two Sultana Mothers in one harem. We order you to move out. Choose the place yourself. Do you prefer the Old Palace or maybe the palace of the Iskender Chelebi again?'

*Light-haired fox*, she gritted her teeth. *The time has come to set the balance straight. Now I've decided to push you out, together with the boy. This time I will put my grandson Suleiman on the throne. Do you know Suleiman? It's the baby of Saliha, whose smell Ibrahim liked better than yours. He's only four years old, but it doesn't matter. There is even a fatwa ready. I will make him a Padishah, and I will become a Queen myself. And who will you be? Don't you know, Turhan? You will die, my daughter. The punishment for treason in the empire is death; haven't you learned?*

# CHAPTER TWENTY-FOUR

*Kafes*
*The Same Evening, After the Last Namaz*

Mahpeyker shuddered. She heard a noise. Something being moved on the ground.

"Üveys," she whispered. "Are you here?"

The sound was coming closer. Someone was coming, carefully shuffling his feet on the ground.

"Üveys, is it you?"

"It's me, My Lady."

Her nerves, tightened to the utmost, loosened at once.

"Where are you? I can't see in the dark."

"Here. On the right."

Something got turned over with a rumble. Mahpeyker's heart jumped to her throat.

"Damn it," murmured the man.

"Ssh! Careful."

A scary outline of a huge silhouette appeared in the darkness.

"Have you looked around well, Üveys? Nobody saw you coming down here?"

"No one. Who would see? Satan himself wouldn't have thought to look here."

"But the foxes will squeeze into every hole. Has everything I said been done, Pasha?"

"Everything to the letter."

"The barracks?"

"There is no reason to worry. The soldiers are devoted to you. And Siyavuş..."

"Shhh... You are too loud."

"Nobody will hear us here. Don't worry."

"I've seen five Padishahs, Pasha! If we're still alive, it's only because we do not trust even the walls. In a place called the palace, the right eye should not trust the left one. Say quietly what you have to say."

"The sailors are divided, but..."

Mahpeyker unexpectedly raised her hand, silencing him. She thought she heard another noise. Outside. As if something moved along the wall behind a barred window. Was someone on the other side? She sniffed the air.

"You are sure that nobody has followed you, right?" she whispered to Üveys Pasha. Without giving him time to answer, she raised a finger to her lips, demanding silence.

They both listened for a while.

There was nothing to be heard.

*Probably a rat*, Mahpeyker thought.

"False alarm," she said to the Pasha. "Go on. You are saying that the sailors are divided?"

"Yes. But we have taken all measures. We moved two troops of Spahis and one of artillery there. Officially, as a part of army exercises. If something happens..."

"I understand."

Removing the deadly pair from her dress pocket, she handed it to Üveys.

"What is it?"

"They'll come in handy for you tonight."

Üveys Pasha examined the bottles, turning them in his hands.

"What's inside?"

"Sorbet!"

"I understand."

Mahpeyker made a gesture toward the bottle in Pasha's right hand.

"That," she hissed, "for the boy's sorbet."

"What if he suspects something?"

"You fool!" Her voice was like a whip. "You think I haven't thought about that?"

"Oh no, how could I... Just..."

"It has no smell or taste. It has a color of tamarind sorbet. You can't notice it..."

There was no one in the palace who didn't know that the little Padishah Mehmed loves tamarind sorbet.

"And the second one, for whom?"

"You are asking me about that?" Mahpeyker hissed after a moment of silence. Her voice sounded as if she was laughing. "It's not good to separate a mother from her son... Into her drink. Don't worry. She won't notice either."

They looked at each other in silence for a moment. The eyes of both burned in the impenetrable darkness.

"First, the child," Mahpeyker said slowly. "Nothing will succeed without it. When that one goes, the other must be ready. Do you understand?"

"Yes."

"Who will accompany Suleiman on his way to Eyüp Sultan for handing over the sword?"

"I will."

"Did you understand everything I said, one by one?" she asked, and without waiting for an answer, she added: "There is no mercy, Pasha. Let everyone have this in mind. Either the head of the state or food for the vultures. Before the morning Ezan everything should be completed."

Unexpectedly, Mahpeyker got up. She heard a sound again. Footsteps, then something like a whistle of breath. "Sshhhh."

They listened. This time Üveys heard the steps, too — as if someone was running. A creeping trot. Suddenly, the sound died away.

"Bloody rats," the Pasha breathed out with relief, "they slipped in through a hole."

Mahpeyker tried to smile to cover up the fear she'd experienced.

"See this through, Üveys. Show what you can do. In the morning, come to me as the Second Vizier. Now go, quickly."

When she turned to look, the darkness had already absorbed him.

The die was cast.

*Death is coming, fox,* she said in spirit. After a moment, Mahpeyker Sultan also disappeared into the darkness. She was about to undersign the biggest assassination in the history of the Empire, the biggest coup. And the sun would once again welcome her as a Queen.

# Chapter Twenty-Five

## The Morning Ezan
### September 3rd, 1651

"My Lady... My Lady... Wake up."

At the voice of her maid, Mahpeyker straightened up in bed. She hadn't slept. How could you sleep on such a night? They were going to bring her the sun in the morning.

She threw aside the quilt.

"Shhh...! Don't shout," she rebuked the watchful girl. "I heard it."

"What time is it?"

"There's not much time left for the Ezan, Mother Sultana. Only a moment left."

Only a moment.

So, it's all over already!

She'd created another Padishah for the Empire. Sultan Suleiman Chan! The youngest Padishah in the history of the Empire!

*Ha*, she thought. *Is it easy to be an Older Valide?* She stood up. She spread her hands so that the courtier could put a caftan on her. She liked this pitch-black outfit very much. The gold embroidery glistened with a clear glow against the impenetrable black of the material. Another courtier ran up to put on her gold-embroidered shoes with curled toes.

The sky outside the window grate was still dark. The day had not started yet. With the coming of the dawn, a stir was to arise, when he'll come out as a descendant of Osman Ghazi of the holy memory, with his sword strapped to his side. The heaven and earth will cry out in unison: 'Long live the Padishah... Long live the Padishah!'

*Only how will they strap a sword to such a small child? But I'm not the one to worry about that. They'll find a way.*

Her eyes brightened. She breathed out. She moistened her face with water from the jug, for which she'd sent one of the girls. She wiped it with the towel passed to her. She walked to the sofa and sat down, resting her back on the pillows.

"Oh," she softly groaned. "This back pain will finish me off."

The thought of death caused a strange feeling in her.

They are both dead now.

Maybe they've even been dead for a long time.

*The Empire should go to bed and get up with a prayer on its lips - for you, Mahpeyker*, she said to herself. *Look, what have you done again? How many Padishahs have you given to the empire?* She counted on her fingers. *Five or six? Osman must be counted, together with her brother-in-law, Mustafa. If we include them, Suleiman is the seventh. Let's say I wasn't the one who crowned Ahmed; in that case, this will be the sixth one whom I helped.*

She smiled. *Oh, this fate,* she thought. *Who would think that after Ibrahim, one more Padishah would come out of the kafes' cellars!*

"Emine," she said to the courtier. "Find out if Saliha Dilaşub came from the Old Palace."

The girl ran out immediately.

The mother of the new Padishah had to be there already. That was the custom. Right after the enthronement of her son, the new Valide Sultan was supposed to move from the Old Palace to the New one.

*Dilaşub will not be like this Moscow fox,* she mused to herself. *One will not have to repeat things twice for her. She will come to kiss our hand even before the Ezan.*

Emine appeared in the doorway. There was a strange expression on her face. She didn't understand what Dilaşub Sultan was supposed to do at this time in the New Palace, but she greeted the old lady with a deep bow. "She has not come, My Lady."

Siyavuş must have arranged everything this way. During the singing of the morning Ezan, Saliha's son was to become a Padishah, and she would become a Sultana Mother. One more sun was rising over Mahpeyker's head. She would become a queen again. This time they would call her the Queen Mother. Saliha too, would certainly not forget showing her the due respect. But why hasn't this girl come to kiss her hand yet?

Apparently, they decided that it would be more appropriate to bring her at the time of the Namaz.

She began to wonder who she would make the Sadrazam this time. *Let's forget Turhuncu and Ahmed the Angel. Üveys is no material for a Sadrazam, either. Siyavuş will be probably the best after all. We'll see. Yes or no... If not, the finger cut off by Sharia... won't hurt.*

Suddenly there was a noise coming from outside. A sound of running steps.

*They're coming*, she listened intently. There are many of them. So, the matter is finished. The new Padishah has been given a sword. They are bringing the Padishah.

The sound of running steps was now even clearer. *Maybe Üveys Pasha decided that it would be safer to take the Padishah to the Sultan Gallery this way*, she thought. In a moment, they would turn into the corridor on the right and move away.

However, contrary to what she thought, the running people did not turn, and instead of moving away, the steps came even closer.

"Allah," she muttered softly. She was confused in her mind because of the excitement. *They are bringing the new Mother Sultana, of course. It is obvious, isn't it?*

"Emine... They are bringing Saliha Dilaşub. The girls need to be ready for orders. Let one of them help me put this hotoz on."

Emine ran to the side door. As the footsteps approached, she heard the nervous whisper of the girls in the neighboring living room. The steps stopped exactly in front of the door to her rooms.

They have come.

She sat in the middle of the sofa. She folded her hands on her knees. She brought to her face the most thoughtful, the most melancholic, and at the same time smiling, reassuring, and encouraging expression. The pain-stricken Elder Sultana was ready to greet the mother of the new Padishah.

She heard the door to her apartments open. She thought she heard a scream. One of the girls probably made a shout of joy to please Dilaşub.

"Emine!" she called to the door. "Let them in, dear. Let's not make our daughter-in-law, Saliha, wait."

Emine didn't answer. She heard numerous steps on the carpet before they stopped in front of her door.

"Come in," she said proudly. "Come in, we are waiting."

The door opened with a bang.


At first, she didn't understand. Who is this black man? She was surprised. He doesn't look like any of the Pashas.

And suddenly she recognized him.

Black Ali. The chief executioner.

His assistants were standing behind him.

The girls were crying loudly.

"Get up, woman," Black Ali rumbled. "You have been sentenced to death. If you do not want to leave as an unbeliever, say the Shahada."

She stood up. While the men were bustling with nodes on greased ropes, she shouted:

"Take the rope from the curtain, reaper! What an audacity, what an arrogance! You want to tie this greasy, bloody, disgusting rope around the neck of the Elder Valide, the Magnificent Sultana, the Great Mother Mahpeyker Kösem Sultan?!"

Among the dumbfounded looks of the executioners, she called to one of the courtiers that were on the verge of collapse.

"Emine!"

The girl staggered over.

"Tear off the cord from this curtain and let the Grim Reaper do his job!"

She approached the executioner.

"Act quickly, Ali! The Moscow fox is waiting for the good news. Take the soul of Kösem, do your duty!"

To be continued in Part III of Sultana Kosem
Mihrimah – Sultan's Daughter
Secrets of the Ottoman Harem III

# GLOSSARY

**Abla**: Big sister; used as a polite expression for women respected by the speaker.

**Ajars**: An ethnic group within the Georgian nation.

**Aga**: The title of officials and commanders in the army and harem, also used as a polite phrase, meaning 'Mister.'

**Akçe**: Silver coin in the Ottoman Empire.

**Akinji**: An irregular light cavalry in the Ottoman Empire. They attacked the lands of enemies on their own, their purpose was to recognize and plunder the enemy; they had the right to detain war spoils for themselves.

**Alim**: A Muslim scholar.

**Azrael**: The angel of death.

**Baksheesh**: A usual tip, alms, given in return for doing some minor activities.

**Bey**: A senior civil servant, as well as a courtesy in the meaning of 'Mister.'

**Beylerbey**: (Turkish: bey of the beys) The governor of the Ottoman province.

**Celali Rebellions**: Rebellions in the 16th and 17th century Ottoman empire.

**Damat:** (Literally son-in-law) A title vested in dignitaries married to Ottoman princesses.

**Dervish**: A Muslim mystic.

**Dirhem**: An old unit of weight corresponding to 1 to 3.25 grams.

**Divan**: Sultan's council, acting as a kind of government.

**Efendi**: A title of nobility, which follows the given name, the equivalent of the English 'sir' but can also mean Lord or Master. The title was usually given to educated people, dignitaries, clerics, and military officers.

**Enderun**: School of elite clerks and military in the Topkapi palace, also the inner part of this palace.

**Ezan** (Turkish): A call for the followers of Islam to a prayer, which is a duty of every Muslim. The prayer is said five times a day.

**Falaka**: A torture instrument, used to administer a punishment in the form of whipping the feet.

**Fatih**: Conqueror, the title of Mehmed II, the Sultan who won Constantinople.

**Fatiha**: Sura (prayer) opening the Qur'an.

**Fatwa**: Official instruction, issued only in writing by the learned theologian, settling a legal or theological controversy.

**Ferace**: Long top coat worn by Muslim women.

**Firman**: An official document; an ordinance issued by the ruler.

**Friday Greetings**: On Fridays, when heading to the mosque for prayer, the Sultan greeted his subjects.

**Ghazal**: A lyrical poetic work.

**Ghazi**: Title granted to Muslims triumphing in the war.

**Giaours**: An abusive description for non-Muslim, especially a Christian.

**Grand Vizier**: The Prime Minister of the Ottoman Sultan, with absolute power of attorney and, in principle, only dismissible by the Sultan himself.

**Grate**: Women could not meet men from outside the harem face-to-face. Conversations took place in a room separated by a latticework screen through which the talks were held.

**Hagia Eirene:** In the Turkish version, the name of the protagonist's family's village is Aya Irini. The Greek variant of this name has been used in this text.

**Hajji**: Honorary title of a Muslim who completed a pilgrimage to Mecca.

**Hanim**: Lady.

**Hamam:** Turkish baths.

**Han**: A caravanserai – a roadside inn with a central courtyard, rooms, shops, and a mosque.

**Haseki**: The preferred concubine of the Sultan, a favorite.

**Hatun**: A woman, lady; title awarded to women in high positions.

**Hodja**: A Muslim schoolmaster. A polite title used for teachers and clerics (including women).

**Hotoz**: A kind of high women headgear in the Ottoman Empire.

**Hüdavendigar**: The nickname of Murad I, successor of Orchan, meaning the ruler. Murad I was the first of the dynasty who used the title of a Sultan.

**Houri**: An eternally beautiful and young virgin of paradise.

**Janissaries**: The elite infantry units that formed the Ottoman Sultan's household troops and bodyguards, from the fifteenth to the nineteenth century.

**Jatagan**: A single-edged Ottoman knife with a double curvature of the blade and a characteristic handle. Also known as Yatagan.

**Kafes**: A designated place for women in the mosque; cage; rooms of Ottoman princes, after eliminating the rule of fratricide.

**Kalfa**: Apprentice; supervisor of white slaves in a harem.

**Kapudan Pasha**: Ottoman counterpart of an Admiral.

**Kavuk**: Turban-like headgear of Ottoman dignitaries. Its size and shape varied depending on rank.

**Kaymakam**: An official who stood in for the grand vizier during the absence of the grand vizier, due to illness, travel, or during the interval between the dismissal of one and the appointment of another.

**Kazasker**: One of the chief military judges of the Ottoman Empire.

**Khan**: The feudal ruler or provincial superior; here: one of the many titles of the Sultan.

**Khutba**: Friday sermon in the mosque, during which the name of the reigning ruler was mentioned.

**Lafa**: (Turkish: Ulufe) Military and civil salary in the Ottoman state, paid every three months.

**Mace**: A blunt weapon with a metal head mounted on the shaft.

**Mahpeyker**: The name Mahpeyker comes from the Persian language, where it literally means: "Beautiful, with a moonlike face." In the harem, girls were usually given names related to some feature of their appearance. The moonlike face in the eastern sense means a face that is light, pale, and full.

**Meleki** (Turkish): Angelic.

**Mihrab**: A niche in mosques indicating the direction where Mecca is located (that is, where to turn when praying).

**Miskal**: A former measure of weight corresponding to 4.5g.

**Muska**: Triangular amulet, usually made of leather, with spells or prayers locked inside.

**Namaz**: Muslim prayer recited five times a day.

**Nemçe**: In Ottoman times, the name used to describe Austria.

**Night of Innocence**: (Turkish: Berat Gecesi) the holiday of remission of sins, celebrated on the night from 14th to the 15th day of the month of the Shaban.

**Night of Destiny**: (Turkish: Kadir Gecesi) a celebration commemorating the revelation of the first verses of the Qur'an, usually falling on the 27th night of Ramadan.

**Odalisque:** A female slave/servant in the harem; sometimes also denotes a concubine.

**Okka**: Measure of weight in the Ottoman Empire equal to 1283g.

**Orchan Gazi**: Son of Osman I, continuator of his work.

**Osman I**: Actual founder of the Ottoman dynasty.

**Padishah**: A Persian term for the Sultan; Emperor.

**Pasha**: High rank in the Ottoman political and military system, typically granted to governors, generals and dignitaries as an honorary title. Similar to a British peerage or knighthood.

**Rumelia**: Area of the former Byzantine empire.

**Sadrazam**: The Great Vizier.

**Sanjak:** A military and administrative unit; the sons of the Sultans were sent to Sanjaks as administrators, which was supposed to prepare them to rule the country in the future.

**Sayyid**: The honorary title granted to the descendants of the Prophet Muhammad.

**Sela**: A prayer accompanying Ezan, often used to remember the dead.

**Selim I**: Warlike ruler, thanks to whom the empire acquired the holy cities of Islam Mecca and Medina, Jerusalem or Egypt.

**Serdar**: The title of commander-in-chief in the Ottoman army.

**Shah**: The title of rulers of Persia and other monarchs of the Muslim East.

**Shahada**: Muslim profession of faith, one of the five pillars of Islam.

**Shahid**: A person who died for faith; it may refer to the person deceased during the plague or in childbirth, or a warrior who died in the fight against unbelievers. It is believed in Islam that Shahids go straight to Paradise.

**Shaikh al-Islam**: In the Ottoman Empire, the title given to the great mufti: a lawyer and theologian issuing official interpretations on private life and national issues related to Islam; he declares his decisions in the form of a fatwa.

**Sherbet**: A refreshing drink of sweetened fruit juice and water.

**Sipahi**: An Ottoman cavalryman.

**Spahis**: The Turkish irregular cavalry. The feudal army troops of the Ottoman Empire; they were vassals of small estates.

**Sublime Porte**: One of the names of the Ottoman state (as well as its court and government), originating from the gate leading to the Grand Vizier's residence.

**Sultan**: A title used before the name by the actual Sultan, or after the name by the son of a Sultan or by the wife, mother, and/or daughter of a Sultan.

**Tambur**: A stringed instrument with a rounded resonance box.

**Tespih**: Muslim prayer string that consists of 33 beads (smaller) or 3 pieces of 33 beads. It helps in pronouncing all the names of Allah.

**Ud**: A stringed instrument with a pear-shaped resonance box.

**Valide-i muazzama**: A great Sultana Mother, a title belonging to the Sultan's grandmother.

**Valide Sultan**: Title held by the 'legal mother' of a ruling Sultan. The most influential woman in the Ottoman Empire.

**Wilayah**: Administrative and territorial unit in the Ottoman Empire.

**Yatagan**: A single-edged white weapon with double curvature of the blade and a characteristic handle. Also known as Jatagan.

**Zittau Agreement**: Signed between the Habsburg monarchy and the Ottoman Sultanate, considered one of the symbols of the fall of the empire.

# About The Author

Demet Altınyeleklioğlu was born in Ankara.

She obtained a degree from Ankara University's Faculty of Political Sciences and Journalism and a master's degree from Haceteppe University in Educational Communications.

From 1980 onwards, she worked as a producer for TRT Turkish Radio and Television Corporation and was a director on various levels. She has translated a few novels and continues to translate. Demet Altınyeleklioğlu lives in Istanbul with her family.

# About The Publisher

Royal Hawaiian Press is a publishing house located in Honolulu Hawaii. It was established in 2005, primarily to promote the works of author and founder, Maria Cowen. Since then, it has expanded to encompass an assortment of other authors from around the world.

Royal Hawaiian Press specializes in providing books in a variety of languages and genres, including translating and publishing existing European-language books into English for the English-speaking market.

To learn more about Royal Hawaiian Press and the books it represents, please visit:

www.royalhawaiianpress.com

To receive an alert when new books are released, subscribe to the Royal Hawaiian Press Mailing List:

http://tiny.cc/rhp

Made in the USA
Columbia, SC
11 September 2020